I0670277

THE DRUMMER

A NIGHT SHIFTS BLACK NOVEL

THE HOLD ME SERIES

ALY STILES

This novel is a work of fiction and intended for mature readers. Events and persons depicted are of a fictional nature and use language, make choices, and face situations inappropriate for younger readers.

Names, characters, places and events are the product of the author's imagination. Any resemblance to actual events, locations, organizations, or people, living or dead, is entirely coincidental and not intended by the author.

THE DRUMMER
Copyright © 2025 Aly Stiles
All Rights Reserved

Cover by Books and Moods
Edited by Michelle Fewer

www.alystiles.com

ISBN: 978-1-961197-07-7

A NOTE (AND INSTRUCTIONS) FROM ALY

Thank you so much for reading *The Drummer*. I hope you enjoy jumping back into the NSB world as much as I did while writing it.

Ten years ago I wrote a book called Night Shifts Black. It was never intended to be what it became, so if you're one of the readers who threw their Kindle at the wall because that story broke all the rules of a rockstar romance, I totally understand. I didn't even know about rockstar romances at the time, so I certainly wasn't aware of "the rules." I was just a lifelong writer and musician battling depression who unknowingly wrote pieces of her story as part of her own healing process.

Maybe it's fitting then that *The Drummer* was just as much of a surprise as the original. I never intended to bring this series back to life after it was completed in 2018, but Casey's story called to me, and I'm so glad it did. One beta reader said it's the missing piece of the story we didn't know we needed, and I wholeheartedly agree.

While I think you can appreciate Casey's book without reading Night Shifts Black, I'm labeling *The Drummer* a companion novel for a reason. It follows the same timeline as the original, just from a different character's perspective. There is plenty of new content, as well as twists on the original, so if you'd like to experience this story the way it was brought into the universe, you may want to consider starting with Night Shifts Black.

And finally, there are a couple moments in the book where you will see an image of musical notes:

These are places where I felt listening to the original song "Greetings from the Inside" would be particularly impactful, whether you listen before or while reading those sections. The song is streaming on all major platforms, so you may want to cue it up and have it ready. We have a unique opportunity to bring a book to life as you listen to the song these artists are creating in real time.

Thank you again for taking this journey with me. I wouldn't even be writing this without all of you. Please know you are important and you are loved.

Love always,
Aly

Content Notice: This book references mental health (on page), suicide (prior event), substance abuse (on page), and childhood abuse (prior event) in a compassionate, realistic manner.

For those who need a spark of hope and a reminder that sometimes the greatest miracles begin with the smallest act of kindness.

PROLOGUE

2015 - ONE YEAR EARLIER

*R*ain pelts my skin. The icy bullets sting with sharp precision before sliding over my body to soak the ground beneath us. I squint over at Luke, who's motionless on his side, facing me. Drops of water slip down the dark strands of his hair and skim over his closed eyelids.

At least, I think that's what I'm looking at. Everything is so blurry, fading. I don't know where my vision ends and the darkness of night begins.

"Luke?" I croak out, and I don't recognize my voice.

The body beside me doesn't respond, just mirrors what I must look like as the steady downpour presses us into matted grass and thick mud. It's probably cold, but I don't feel a damn thing.

The cloying smell of fresh flowers bites my nose as I struggle to pull air into my aching lungs. Vases and bouquets crowd the ornate monument at our heads, a grim wall of decaying beauty.

1

My sister has been dead for almost three months, and still her grave lives and breathes with the constant flow of tributes from people who believe she didn't deserve what she got. They understand she was a good person with a bad husband and a worse illness.

I already know her death will be remembered for all the wrong reasons. And now, the man everyone accuses of "killing her" has seemingly determined to follow.

I've made it my mission not to let him.

Luke Craven is my best friend, my brother. And maybe part of me is selfish enough to know *I* won't survive if I lose him too.

I've followed him into hell to keep him tethered to life. To do for him what I wasn't able to do for my sister. But pain is a sneaky infection, the way it quietly spreads and feeds off itself until it's too late.

Tonight was a mistake. Tonight, we went too far.

"Luke…"

I try to lift my arm, but it's lead at my side. I blink through the curtain of rain and shadows, licking cool drops from my lips.

He's deathly still, and a trickle of fear seeps through me when I realize I'm paralyzed as well.

I can't list all the drugs we've pumped into our bodies tonight. I'm not even sure all were voluntary as we sought distraction in every hedonistic trap we could find. All I know for sure is that after hazy days of clubs, bars, women, fights, and substances, we've ended up sprawled on Elena's grave like two corpses intent on joining her.

I don't want to die, though—not like Luke does—and somewhere beyond the thick barrier of chemicals holding me captive, the fear becomes panic. Is the damage done? Was that last hit the one that will transform me from a loving brother into another tragic story for the Barrett family archives?

"Forgive us," I whisper to my sister. "Please forgive us."

Elena would hate everything about this.

I can almost hear her screams from wherever she is. Pleading. Commanding me not to follow her into death. I'm betraying her with every beat of my heart as that organ pumps more toxins through my veins.

God, she loved us so much. And we loved her. But her sick brain wouldn't let her believe it. It lied to her, poisoned her, tortured her. Until she felt like she only had one choice.

It convinced her an eternity beneath this soggy ground was better than living a few decades above it.

It's not Luke's fault, but his many transgressions have made it his guilt to carry. Tragedy needs a villain, and Luke was branded and sentenced with violent conviction.

No voice screamed the insidious accusations louder than his own. And that will be the voice that kills him.

If it hasn't already.

"Luke…"

My mouth won't even open now. I give up, focusing instead on the cocoon of mud forming around me. The serene calm on Luke's face is the most peaceful I've ever seen him. In a cruel twist, he finally looks like the man I've been fighting so hard to find. Maybe whoever discovers our lifeless bodies tomorrow will believe what I do about him—that he was a good person who'd been dealt a bad hand and wasn't strong enough to overcome his demons.

I'm the only one who's stood by him. The only one who knew him well enough to know the man everyone hated—*including himself*—was the lie. That somewhere locked inside was the person my sister loved so fiercely. The person she thought she lost and couldn't live without.

I want to tell him this now. I want to assure him he's still needed. That it's not his fault in the way everyone is saying. That joining her in the ground solves nothing.

But my mouth won't move. Nothing will. Even my thoughts are becoming a tangled web of incoherent fragments.

In an effort to pull him out of hell, I followed him too far this time. And as my eyes drift closed, so does any chance I have of dragging us out.

CHAPTER 1

2016 - NOW

"We found him."

I go still, my gaze locked on the tile floor of the bathroom. My hand tightens around the phone.

We found him.

I don't even ask who. There's only one name that could follow those three words. One ghost important enough to uproot my entire world.

"Is he okay?" My voice sounds rough, like it's in as much shock as the rest of me.

"He's alive. That's all I know. I'm texting you the address now."

My nod is instinctive. My brain is already somewhere else. "I'll leave tonight."

"Uh, no. You won't. You have two shows this weekend."

I hate that this isn't a video call, so our manager can't see my glare. Or my middle finger.

"Are you kidding me, TJ? We found Luke! Forget the shows. I'm going to see him."

"Casey..." His tone has morphed from friend to manager. "Don't make me regret giving you this information. You have to do the shows. The Label pulled all kinds of strings to get you in. Another screw-up and you guys are done. You know this."

I clench my eyes shut, breathing hard. He's right. I know he's right. Our career has been sputtering into nothing since Luke disappeared. Night Shifts Black without Luke Craven is like pizza without the crust and cheese. For almost a year now, we've been limping from city to city as a glob of decent tomato sauce.

No one wants to see that. Well, no one except the diehard fans still in denial and the delusional dreamers who think this next show might be the one where Luke comes back. They don't know the real story behind the disappearance of their idol. They didn't pass out beside him on a cold gravesite and wake up alone in a hospital.

"We found him."

Three words I prayed for every day, until so much time had passed I forgot to keep praying.

"You still there?" TJ's voice is grating now.

My mind is already packing a bag, jumping on a plane, and flagging a cab to whatever address he's about to send to my phone.

But I can't. I can't do anything except what I'm told now that Luke's absence has made the rest of us irrelevant.

"Fine. But I'm going during the break before the Calisto Festival."

"I understand. Just..." His voice fades, and even through the phone I sense his hesitation. His concern.

I clench my eyes shut at the words he's not saying.

Don't get lost again. Don't you dare abandon us too.

"I won't. Not this time. I promise."

He's quiet for a moment. "Good. Be careful."

I don't respond as I hang up, open the text stream with TJ, and wait.

* * *

My heart hammers as I stare at the numbers on the door of the hotel suite.

4. 0. 3.

Luke knows I'm coming. The manager in the lobby wouldn't let me near the elevator without a call to his room to confirm I'm a welcomed guest.

I got the approval to go up, so I know I'm a guest. Whether or not I'm welcomed, remains to be seen. Maybe that's why I can't bring myself to knock. Time couldn't pass quickly enough when TJ called to say they found Luke, but now that I'm here, I can't move.

No one wants to learn someone they love doesn't love them back.

With a deep breath, I lift my arm and tap my knuckles against the door.

Memories taunt me while I wait. I haven't spoken to Luke since the night we almost overdosed at Elena's burial site. We woke up in separate rooms in the hospital, and by the time I was well enough to visit him, he was gone. Just disappeared, leaving me alone with the fallout and a single handwritten note.

Sixteen words forever burned into my brain.

> Casey:
> I'm sorry. I love you too much to drag you to hell
>   with me.
> Luke

That was it. Our hello, goodbye, and forever.

Until now.

Shuffling at the door has my clammy hands clenching and unclenching at my side. Will he even let me in? Maybe he gave the hotel manager the okay just so he could tell me to fuck off in person.

The door opens...

A silhouette steps into view...

Time stalls.

Luke.

Real.

Alive.

I blink against the burn behind my eyes. Words fail me. Too many years of heartache and joy saturate the thick air between us.

His aqua eyes land on me, red-rimmed and glazed with pain and substances. A brief flash of life gives me hope of something better, but it quickly fades into resignation. He doesn't even speak before stepping back and motioning for me to enter.

I swear I hear a sigh as I move past him.

The door shuts with a clatter that reverberates throughout my limbs. We hover in the foyer of the suite for several long seconds, neither of us sure what to do next. What words can repair two lives ripped apart by tragedy?

"Want a drink or something?" he asks finally.

His voice is different than I remember. Older, but not from time. His hair is longer as well, but short enough to know he's had it cut since our last encounter. Same with the scruff on his face. The tattoos on his arms ripple with defined muscle, which means he's been staying fit at least.

All these things inspire another glimmer of hope, until I see the garden of empty glasses scattered around the large open living space.

He's been taking care of himself as a distraction, nothing more.

"Sure," I say to buy time for my visit. If alcohol is the only thing he cares about, I'll exploit it for all it's worth.

He nods and saunters toward the minibar with an absent gait that makes it clear this is a practiced part of his day. How long has he been at this hotel? *Why* is he here?

When TJ sent me the address, I nearly choked. This city is the last place I expected he'd go. I can't imagine what force would be strong enough to lure him back to this haunted location, but I guess that's partly what I'm here to find out.

He hands me a glass without telling me what's in it, then drops to the end of the L-shaped couch with his own. I don't know what to do other than take a seat on the opposite side.

"How'd you find me?" he asks, his gaze fixed on the floor, like he doesn't know if he can handle the answer to his own question.

"TJ. He didn't tell me how *he* found you, though."

Luke nods and takes a sip of his drink. "How have you been?"

"Great. So, so good. It's been awesome losing my best friend and career in one night."

He flinches and finally gives me his attention. I try to rein in my anger, but fuck if I know how this is supposed to go.

"I'm sorry, Case," he says quietly, looking away again. There's no fight in his words. No emotion. Like everything else, it's just a thin gloss of "human" stretched over a void.

"Yeah, me too. Although, I guess you knew that from the twenty messages I left before your mailbox was full. I'm fine, by the way. No permanent damage from that night. Unless you count the lingering trauma and constant nightmares. What about you?"

His gaze shoots to mine before diverting back to the floor. "I said I was sorry before I disappeared."

"I'm assuming you're referring to 'the note,' because you

haven't *said* a damn thing to me for almost an entire fucking year."

He doesn't respond, doesn't even look at me this time.

I suck back the rest of my tirade. I have months of anger, betrayal, heartache, and love to spew at him. Months' worth of a phantom life he should have been living with me but chose to abandon instead. I could fill the next ten days with the hell I went through after he left, but now that I'm here, none of it seems right.

He's already broken. I see it in the slow movements of his body, the empty look in his eyes. The few words he's said prove there are none that will fix any of this. Handing him my pain will only destroy the little that remains of our relationship.

"Sorry," I mumble.

"No, I get it. You have every right to be angry. How's your family? The band? Jana?"

"Jana?"

"I thought I saw something about you getting back together with her."

I huff a laugh. "Yeah, I bet you did. She loved turning our business into a national headline. No, there's nothing there. Never will be. And the family's good, for the most part. Things with the band suck, but if you're following headlines, you know that too."

His jaw tightens, and I take a calming breath.

"What about you?" I ask. "How's the last year been?"

It wasn't supposed to be a joke, but his haunted look turns it into one. After a second, he directs his gaze back to the wall. The glass turns slowly in his hands as he considers my question. Or, more specifically, how to avoid it.

"Am I the first person you've spoken to since you left?" I try again, forcing a light tone. I even manage a weak smile when he looks up.

His expression doesn't change, but at least he's not kicking me out yet. "Actually, no."

"Right. I guess you have the hotel staff."

"Yeah, but I also made a friend. Sort of."

Intrigued, and slightly jealous, I lean forward on the couch. "Really. Wow. Does this friend have a name?"

"Callie."

Light flickers in his eyes for the first time since my arrival. It's a strange contrast to the heaviness that surrounds him. Just as quickly, it's gone, and he rubs a hand over his face.

"Callie, huh. So this friend is a she?"

"Yeah, but it's not like that. She's..." He shakes his head. "There's no word for it. She just *is*. She's just there. I don't know."

"I see." The bitterness is back in my tone, drawing a sharp look from Luke.

His expression droops again when he realizes what that sounds like to me. She's there, even though he's made no room for me in his life.

"I'm sorry things went down the way they did, Case. Truly. And trust me, the diner situation is not something I asked for or saw coming."

"The diner situation?"

"The thing with Callie. We have breakfast together."

"You have breakfast together," I say dryly. "And what?"

He shrugs. "And nothing. That's it. We have breakfast together. Sometimes we talk. Sometimes we don't."

I nod because I have no other response.

Jealousy simmers inside me again, and I force it away. I could be angry about it. I could be bitter that he let some stranger into his life while rejecting me. But I love him too much to not be grateful to this person for shining even the smallest light into his shadow.

There's something special about this girl. I already know it

11

from the way his eyes change when he talks about her. And I can't shake the feeling that there's more to this story. Something heavy. Something epic I can't begin to understand.

But now isn't the time for that conversation. Luke is struggling just to stay in the moment. I get the sense he'd rather be left alone, and I don't think I could bear that after finding him again.

"You staying over tonight, Case?" he asks, draining his glass.

Surprised, I glance at him to get a read on the offer. Is that sarcasm? There's no humor in his expression. Not much of anything, really, just exhaustion. Yes, that's it. He looks flat-out depleted.

"Sure, if that's okay."

He shrugs. "We can grab breakfast tomorrow before you go."

"With your new girlfriend?"

I regret my joke the second it comes out. His gaze lowers, zero hint of a smile.

"It's not like that, man. I told you."

"I know. Sorry."

"Callie is… special. She sees you, ya know?"

So he's said. Still, seems like a stretch. I get that he's grasping, but some random chick in a diner?

"And the fact that you're Luke Craven of Night Shifts Black has nothing to do with her interest?" Someone has to say it, and even if I'm not the best man for the job, I'm the only one, apparently.

"That's just it. She had no clue."

"Really?" I try to keep my skepticism out of the equation. I've pushed him pretty far already.

"I'm telling you, dude. She's different. Even when she found out who I was, it didn't change anything. I'm still just Luke, and she's just Callie."

"Huh."

Okay, maybe I'm a little more than intrigued. Still not sure I trust this girl, but she's accomplished in a few breakfasts what the rest of us couldn't do in months.

Even more telling, Luke's eyes change when he talks about her. The light flickers on for the briefest of seconds, giving a glimpse of what he could be. It disappears just as quickly, but it's enough to make me think a breakfast to check things out is probably a good idea. Last thing we need is some opportunist taking advantage of his vulnerable state.

"She's a pistol too. You wouldn't guess it at first. She's so sweet and genuine, but then bam, she'll smack you with a one-liner that just rips the rug out."

I smile to myself. Sounds more like my type than his.

"You'll love her, Case. She could definitely handle you."

Is he reading my mind? He always could. A virtual brother thing, and one of the biggest gaps in my life since he left. Funny how much we can miss something right in front of us.

I lean back on the couch with a smirk. "Handle me? I need to be handled?"

"Uh, yeah, dude. If that thing with Jana was any indication."

"Eh, that's over. Again."

"Exactly."

Fair enough. He doesn't know the truth about the situation. No one I care about does.

"So you want me to go to breakfast to hang out with you, or to meet my future girlfriend?" I joke.

He thinks for a moment, a slight smile spreading over his lips. "Casey and Callie. Kind of has a ring to it, no?"

Maybe. And maybe I will stay for breakfast. What could a few eggs and toast hurt? I'll need to eat before hitting the road anyway. Besides, I can count on one finger the number of times Luke has tried to set me up with a woman.

One: Callie, the breakfast club girl.

"I just wanted you to be okay, Case. That's all I've ever wanted." His eyes search mine from across the room, begging me to understand something that can't be explained.

"That's why you left?"

He lowers his eyes. "I had to. I almost killed you too." Stripped raw, his voice sends a shiver through me.

I want to argue, but maybe he's right. Ignoring the truth does neither of us any good. It's what got us here.

"You let me in this time," I say quietly. "What's changed?"

His saturated look has my hands clamping around the glass.

"Not *what*. Who."

I lower my gaze to the amber liquid I haven't touched.

Callie.

"Come with me tomorrow," Luke says, a subtle plea in his voice. "I owe you so much. Let me introduce you."

"You make it sound like you're setting me up with my soulmate or something. How well do you even know this person?"

"You don't have to know a lot of facts about someone to *know* them. Actions are way more honest than words."

My chest is tight with a mix of emotions I can't sort out. "I'm not looking for a relationship."

His mouth lifts in a genuine smile for the first time since I arrived. "Neither was I."

CHAPTER 2

I couldn't tell you the last time I was up at 7am, but I can promise it sucked that day too.

Luke seems tired as well when I shuffle out of the guest room to meet him in the kitchen. And since it's a big part of whatever this breakfast thing is, there isn't even coffee.

Jemma's Café. Some miracle-worker named Callie.

That's the extent of what I know.

"You sure you're fine with me crashing your date?" I ask as I pull open the door.

"I told you, it's not a date. She'll be glad you came."

"How do you know?"

He shrugs and starts down the hall. "Just do."

Great. Well, hopefully this person talks more than Luke or we're in for one hell of an awkward morning.

The elevator attendant, who can't be more than sixteen, grins when we file inside.

"Morning, Mr. Craven," he says as he pushes the lobby button.

"Hey, Aiden. How's your brother doing?"

"Pretty good. He came home from the hospital last night."

"Really? That's great."

Aiden shrugs and makes a face. "Yeah, I guess. Except now he gets to watch TV and play video games all day, while the rest of us have to work."

I hold back a snort, and even Luke's lips twitch at the precocious gripe.

"Well, that part sucks, but it's good he's going to be okay," Luke says.

Aiden nods and glances at me. "You Luke's friend?"

Great question.

"*I* think so. Not sure about him," I say.

Luke shoots me an irritated look. "Casey's my best friend... and drummer."

Aiden's eyes widen. "So you're in the band too?"

"He sort of *is* the band right now," Luke corrects.

Not by choice, I return with my own annoyed glance, but Luke doesn't look at me to receive it.

Another hotel guest joins us at the second floor, ending further conversation.

Once we reach the lobby, we tip Aiden and head to the exit.

We step into the morning sunlight, but instead of climbing into a car, Luke makes a left toward the cross street.

I follow in surprise. "We walking to this place?"

"It's not far. Just a few blocks."

I'd complain if I didn't suspect this might be the only time he sees the light of day. A piece of me is even more grateful for this stranger named Callie who's managed to draw my vampire bandmate out into the sun.

We walk the rest of the way in silence. Had I known the exchange with Aiden the Elevator Attendant was going to be the extent of Luke's interaction during the journey, I would have participated more.

The silence is magnified by everything we're *not* saying. So many unanswered questions and missing pieces to fill, but

Luke's expression makes it clear I won't get them now. He's lost in his head, and all I can do is read him for any clues that could help make sense of everything I've seen and heard since showing up at his door last night.

By the time we arrive at a quaint diner with a vintage sign that says "Jemma's Café," I've reached a frightening conclusion:

Luke might still be alive, but he's stopped living.

* * *

FOR THE SECOND time in two days, I'm intimidated by a door. Yesterday it was Luke's suite. Today it's a glass gateway into a mystery I'm eager—and nervous—to solve.

What is Jemma's?

Who is Callie?

What role do they play in the strange transformation of my friend?

I bury those questions as I follow Luke through the diner. He doesn't stop at the host stand or acknowledge the dozens of eyes tracking us when we breach breakfast routines with our alien presence. The gaping stares make it clear we don't belong here. The scowl from the man in the booth by the door lets me know we're not exactly welcome, either.

Only one person—a young employee at the host stand— looks pleased to see us. Maybe *too* pleased by the way her dreamy gaze fixates on Luke, then me. Luke doesn't give her a second glance, so clearly she's not the guardian angel I'm here to meet.

That person would be…

Holy shit.

I play it cool as we approach a table set deep inside the restaurant. The lone occupant's lips lift in an adoring smile when she sees Luke. Stunning hazel eyes skim my friend, then lock on me with a hint of concern. Even without Luke's description, the genuine aura surrounding this girl draws me in.

Damn. No wonder Luke keeps coming back. I'd love to start my day with that smile as well.

"Callie," Luke says in a flat tone.

"Luke," she replies with similar gravity.

They exchange a small smile that tells me this is some inside joke. Luke still has humor in him. Good to know.

"This is Casey," Luke says, motioning to me.

"Hi. I'm Casey," I echo with a grin of my own.

The young woman is too far away for a handshake, so I settle on a quick wave.

I feel her intense stare as I pull out a chair. She must be evaluating me, wondering the same things I wonder about her. What role do I play in her friend's life? Am I part of the problem, or the solution?

I'm used to being gawked at. Lust, admiration, jealousy, resentment—I can handle them all. But this is different. This woman's potent stare isn't something I'm accustomed to. Questions, but not quite curiosity. Interest, but not quite fascination.

It's alluring, confusing, and completely explains why Luke fell under her spell.

Hell, we've barely said a word to each other and I'm already intrigued. I'm also uncomfortable with the weird silence.

"Do you always get up this early?" I ask to break the tension. Also, I really want to know, because if their start time is negotiable, that'd be awesome.

"If you come later, you don't get to eat. You know how it is once you're spotted," Luke says.

He's got a point, but since when did we care about shit like that? We're always noticed. And ever since Luke disappeared, I've had to endure even more of the spotlight. Maybe he's been hiding so long, privacy is actually an option for him now.

"Welcome to our breakfast club," Callie says with a quick

smile. There's a hesitancy to her tone, like she felt compelled to say something as well.

"Yeah, Luke was telling me about your little breakfast club. Pretty wild story."

Her lips tip up in an adorable grin. "Then I'm sure he also told you about how incredibly witty and smart I am. I'm great company."

Not gonna lie, my stomach does a small flip at the ease with which she settled into my presence. She's nothing like the expertly polished women I'm used to. Maybe that's exactly why she has my attention.

"He's told me some things," I say, not sure where this is supposed to go. Every instinct wants to flirt. Her mischievous glint and the way her stare runs over me again makes me think she might be up for it.

"How about you not be a jerk for twenty seconds," Luke mumbles, shutting that down. I can't help but smile at his defensive reaction. Maybe he wasn't being as honest about his interest in this girl as he pretended to be last night.

"Don't let his puppy dog eyes and sob story fool you," I joke, testing him out. "This man is no boy scout."

"Casey, not now."

"What? I know you, dude. You get lost in your head and shut down."

Luke snaps a glare at me. "Will you stop? It's not your business. Not now!"

I flinch at the outburst. So much for keeping things light.

But the more I study his scowl, the more I wonder if maybe being pushed is exactly what he needs. It's good to see *something* burning in his eyes, even if it's anger. If this woman is the ally he's led me to believe she is, together we might have a chance at getting through to him.

"I'm just looking out for you," I say, more serious this time. "You have to move on. You can't keep doing this to yourself. You screwed up. We all do. That doesn't mean everything that happens from that point on is your fault."

He looks ready to lash out again, and I don't understand why. How can he not see how much I care about him? Even after what happened a year ago, I dropped everything to be here the second I could. Postponed my entire life to have coffee with a stranger because it was important to *him*.

"You agree with me, right?" I ask her, desperate for a break-through. God, anything to bring my friend back to life. "He needs to stop punishing himself. It's been a year. He can't torture himself forever."

"Casey!"

"What? I'm just—"

"She doesn't know," he snaps at me.

My blood goes cold. "What?"

"She doesn't know, okay?"

Shit.

A heavy silence settles over us. She doesn't know? How could the woman who pierced his impenetrable barrier not know the story that locked him there?

My mind spins as I hide behind the menu, wracking my brain for anything that can fix this. Part of me wants to apologize, but I don't even know for what. This dynamic is exactly what landed us here in the first place.

Luke shuts down, and I fucking let him.

I drop the menu on the table. "Hey, man, I'm sorry. I just thought, I don't know, after everything you said about her. I thought you were closer."

His glare makes it clear none of this is helping, and I swallow the rest of my words.

"Um… Okay. I'm gonna shut up now," I mumble.

"That would be a good idea," he returns.

Old anger burns at his hypocrisy. He's blasting *me* for being the asshole when all I'm trying to do is gain an ally in Callie and give him the best chance he's had for support in months. But he's clearly not going to be accepting a lifeline any time soon.

"So, Casey. Are you in Night Shifts Black too?" Callie asks.

I stare at her, not sure if it's the question itself or the fact that she so effortlessly broke up the tension that surprises me more. Once it becomes clear her question was sincere, the shock turns to amusement.

I bite back a laugh when Luke lifts a brow with a *told-you-so* expression.

"What? What did I say?" she asks, scrunching her face in an enchanting mix of innocence and indignation.

Luke shakes his head. "Nothing. You're fine. It's just a funny question."

Her eyes narrow at him. "Why's it funny?"

He returns a quick shrug. "I don't know. It's not, I mean, it's just that we're not used to hearing stuff like that except from old people trying to be nice at charity events."

I snort a laugh at his not-so-random example. "Remember the Morning Star Seniors' Ball?"

"Don't," Luke warns with a threatening look I'm happy to ignore.

Callie's eager smile seals his fate.

"So there's this lady with a... What was that thing again? I don't know, some huge hat and boa thing. Anyway—"

"Case!" But he can't be too mad when he turns to Callie with a smile. "She had good intentions."

Understatement of the century. "She thought he was the one benefiting from the charity because of the 'dreadful condition of his clothing.'"

Exact quote, if I recall.

"I was wearing three-hundred-dollar jeans and a Julian Salitoni jacket."

The entire scene springs to life in my head, and I can't hold in my laughter. The poor woman whining to her friends as if we weren't standing *right* there. Her tiny dog yelping in her arms like it was desperate to explain what her prejudice was too thick to see.

"Oh man, I just about died when that happened. Dude, she was ready to take you home and give you a hot shower and cot in her living room."

Luke rolls his eyes, but he doesn't seem as upset as I would have guessed. He's probably just glad we've moved on to safer topics.

Callie leans back to scan him in an exaggerated appraisal. "I don't know. I kind of see it. I mean, there's the messy hair, and the jeans may be three hundred dollars, but they look like they're one wash away from disintegrating. Your t-shirt could definitely use a bit of mending. I'd slip you a twenty as long as you promised not to buy booze with it."

Luke smiles—actually *grins*. Wow. How the hell did she do that?

"I never would have promised that," he replies.

Callie returns his grin before shifting in her chair to give us each a dry onceover. My heart rate picks up when her inquisitive stare slides over me with more than amused interest. She's supposedly joking as she checks me out, but something tells me she's also... not.

A long-dead shiver of attraction pierces my awareness.

"Okay, fine, so I'm guessing what I'm supposed to take away from this little tale is that it's not often you encounter people under seventy-five who don't know who you are."

"Only because we don't have time to come in contact with those people," I say, then remember where we are and why we're here. "Well, you do, apparently."

I kick myself when Luke returns a dark look.

"Alright, fine, so I get it. You're a super famous rockstar in Night Shifts Black. Then can I ask what you play? Or should I already know that, too?" Callie's smug expression is so stinkin' cute. She's even managed to smooth Luke's sour expression into something more human.

"Now I get why you like her." I direct the comment at Luke, even though it's meant for Callie. "She knows nothing about us, does she?"

"Nope," Luke says with a smile.

Callie tosses her brunette hair over her shoulder and scrunches her face in an adorable pout. "So, what, I'm supposed to grovel at your feet because you're big rock gods? Sorry if I was the only person on this planet who didn't know that."

"No, but now that you know, you should be groveling," I joke.

"Oh boy." Luke cowers with mock concern for my safety.

Maybe it's warranted when she crosses her arms and delivers a challenging look. God, I live for this shit. Luke was right. I'm already in love.

"Really?" she says. "What if I'm an undercover royal princess? Maybe you should be groveling at *my* feet."

"If you're really an undercover royal princess, I will. You'd have to prove it, though."

"Prove you're in Night Shifts Black."

Easy enough. I make a dramatic shift toward Luke. "Am I in Night Shifts Black?"

The traitor holds up his hands in surrender. "I'm not getting involved in this one. You're on your own."

"You're not involved. You're just verifying a fact."

Luke glances at Callie, as if asking her permission. Shit. I guess this won't be as easy as I thought. Their sneaky breakfast club pact means I don't have a chance at winning whatever this is. Then again, if it results in more banter with Callie, I've already won.

"It's okay. He's right," Callie says. "You can answer his question."

Luke exhales in a faux attempt to make it look like he's not enjoying this. "Fine. Yes, Casey plays drums in Night Shifts Black."

Satisfied, I blast her with a smug look. "Okay, there you go. Now, it's your turn, princess."

Unfazed, she lifts a brow and faces Luke. "Am I an undercover royal princess?"

A genuine laugh erupts from Luke, and her stunning grin breaks.

My god. She's magic. I didn't even think he *could* laugh anymore.

"Yes, she is," he confirms.

She shifts toward me, hazel eyes filled with satisfaction. "There you have it."

I squint back and pass a look between them. "Why do I feel like I've been conned?"

"You haven't been conned, just outvoted," she quips.

"Ha, fine. This is all breakfast club politics. I get it."

"There are no politics involved until you order. We only judge based on food selections here."

As if on cue, Luke signals a server hovering nearby.

It's then that I realize how strange it was that no one came until now, almost as if the employees were waiting for something. Like they have a role in this strange script as well.

Apparently, the breakfast club politics extend to the rest of the diner. What exactly is happening here?

After a short, familiar exchange, the server takes off to fulfill our drink order.

"He knows you," I observe.

"He's a breakfast club regular," Callie replies.

Interesting.

"If I'd known about breakfast club, I would have visited sooner." I shoot Callie a smile, loving the way her cheeks flush. Her gaze traces my lips and cuts to my eyes before peeling away.

"Yeah, right. You don't have time to visit," Luke cuts in. "I still

24

can't believe you showed up last night. Don't you have to be in Richmond tonight? I thought you guys were playing the Calisto Festival."

I wince and snap my attention to him. Is he serious?

"I would have stopped by as much as I could if you'd let me. You just didn't want me around. I didn't even know where you were until TJ called a few days ago. I got here the first second I could."

He has no idea how hard it was to wait. What it took just to *get* here. I blew off two commitments, three angry bandmates, and an apprehensive manager to show up at his door, having no idea if he'd let me in or shut it in my face.

Luke doesn't respond, but his bitter expression sinks into resignation. Like he knows I'm right and maybe even regrets taking his anger out on me. I'd feel better if I thought for a second it wouldn't happen again. But I know how pain works. Even Callie's presence isn't going to be enough to solve the massive rift between us over one cup of coffee.

"One of us needs to try the French toast," she blurts out.

Her smile breaks through my clouds, and I suspect that was exactly her intent.

"Why's that?" I ask, taking the bait. Any topic is better than silent sulking.

"We've never ordered it, and I think it's time to diversify breakfast club. What do you think?" she asks Luke.

He barely acknowledges her, but she lets his rudeness roll off her. Clearly, she understands it's not an affront to her but a product of his own demons. I'm surprised again at how well she handles his moodiness. Probably even better than I do.

"So tell me more about being famous rockstars. I want to hear about the groveling," she directs at me.

I reward her attempt with a weak smile, but the mood has shifted. "Well, it hasn't been the same without your friend here, that's for sure. Luke *was* Night Shifts Black. Without him we're basically just a sad cover band."

She leans forward, a spark of interest in her eyes. Maybe they really don't talk about his celebrity life.

"At least you're still touring though, right?"

"Yeah, kind of. But we don't headline much anymore. We can't sell out a stadium without Luke Craven."

"Sweeny does fine," Luke interjects.

I scoff at him, almost angry he'd say that shit to me.

"Yeah, sure," I reply sarcastically. "They're your songs, bro. No one will ever be able to handle them like you do."

Luke lowers his gaze, and I suppress a grunt of frustration. If he's this temperamental and unpredictable at all their encounters, Callie is even more of a saint than I thought.

I feel her intense gaze again, but don't acknowledge it. Maybe she's irritated with me as well. If she doesn't know his story, she certainly doesn't know mine. Heaven knows what Luke has told her... or more likely, *hasn't* told her about me.

The server returns with our drinks, and by his expression, he shares my concern that this meal will be ending before it begins.

"Did you decide on your orders?" His hesitant tone confirms that he's pretty sure the answer is *"Check, please."*

We all focus on Luke, watching him with some tacit understanding that the fate of the next step rests with him. His gaze is fixated on a chair at the neighboring table. I've seen his attention float to that ugly piece of furniture a few times now.

Good to know a chair is more important than we are.

"I'll have the French toast," he says, directing his attention back to us.

Shocked, I look between Callie and him.

"Same," Callie says, casually shutting her menu like the weirdness of the last two minutes didn't happen.

The server still has a skeptical look on his face as he scribbles on his pad. His questioning look lands on me.

"What the hell, why not?" I flip the menu in his direction as well.

He takes it and adds it to the others. "Okay, three French toasts it is. Anything else?"

We shake our heads, and he takes off toward the kitchen.

"Do you think he has to go to counseling now because of us?" Callie asks Luke.

His lips tip up in a smile. "He's at least insisted on a raise."

She grins, and wow…

She brought him back.

I scan the two of them with renewed interest. Maybe I need to ask this woman—someone he's known for days, if not hours—for some lessons on how to handle my best friend I've known half my life.

For now, the safest bet is a subject change.

"So has my boy here told you about his other passion?" I ask Callie.

"You mean, besides music?"

Luke shoots me an annoyed look. "It's not a passion."

I almost laugh. "You have eight of them."

"I like them."

"Exactly. It's a passion."

"And *it* is what?" Callie asks, interrupting our debate.

"Bikes," I say.

"Bikes? Like bike bikes, or motorbikes?"

Her expression triggers a strange warmth inside me. There's an innocence about her that's mesmerizing when juxtaposed against the fearless rock she's been throughout the rest of the conversation.

Everything Luke said about this girl comes racing back in a punch to the heart. I can't resist the urge to tease her and draw more of her sweet fire.

"Motorbikes? I love this girl," I say to Luke. "Where did you find her? She's like my grandma in the body of a cute college chick."

I live for the delightful glare she lasers at me. "I'm sorry, but maybe if you used more adjectives I wouldn't have to ask so many stupid questions."

"Adjectives? Sorry, hon, the writing part was his thing, not mine."

"That's obvious," she mumbles, but the subtle tilt of her mouth, the glint in her eyes... Is she flirting with me?

Damn. A sensation I haven't felt in a long time sizzles through my body.

"Luke is awesome with adjectives," I return.

"He is. One of the best."

Even Luke smiles with an amused headshake.

"Wow, thanks, guys," he says in a dry tone.

"He also sucks at taking compliments," I say.

"How's that possible? Isn't a love of being worshipped part of the superstar thing?" Callie quips. That barb was definitely for me, not Luke, and I can't stop a sly grin.

"It's supposed to be," I return.

"Just let me know if you need me to weigh in on anything about myself," Luke interjects.

He and Callie exchange an affectionate smile that sends a sharp twinge through my chest.

I swallow the strange feeling in irritation. I've lived in Luke's shadow for over a decade. Watched him get everything he wanted, and even the things he didn't. Never once was I jealous.

Until now.

"Actually, I'll make it even easier for you to talk about me and hit the restrooms," Luke says, rising from the table. "I'll be back."

Callie and I watch in silence as he disappears down a hall,

presumably toward the bathrooms. The heaviness is back in his gait, and any lingering resentment fades into familiar fear.

"He's not good, is he?" I muse out loud. I don't even know to whom. The universe maybe. It's already betrayed him so many times, I'm positive it doesn't give a shit.

"No, he's not," Callie answers on its behalf.

My hard gaze remains fixed on the wall as the last few months come flooding back. The urge to unload some of the burden on this stranger is so strong, I have to clench my jaw to keep it in. Luke said she doesn't know his story, and it's impossible to separate mine from his.

Besides, it's not fair to her. She's working so hard to unravel Luke's mess and carry his burden. I can't give her mine too.

A sudden protectiveness settles over me for this girl who probably has no idea what she's gotten herself into. Luke's changed so much, I barely recognize him as the man I knew. That means there's no way this stranger knows the shitstorm she's invited into her life. The way she looks at him—like he's an important part of her life—concerns me. I can't tell if she's falling for him beyond that, but I'm terrified this kind, beautiful woman is going to be an innocent casualty before this is over.

I can't stomach the thought of someone being crushed for their compassion—especially this someone.

"You know, I've barely seen or spoken to him in months," I say quietly. "Last night, today, it's the first time I've really spent time with him in a while. He's not the person I knew. Not even close."

It's kind of a lie, since I haven't spoken to him at *all* in months, but that seems like a truth just for Luke and me. Plus, I don't know. For some reason I don't want her to know how far we've drifted.

"And I can't even imagine him being the person you knew," Callie says.

"We both know two completely different people."

Her gaze skims me in surprise, like she didn't expect my response. Probably thought I was a shallow, self-absorbed rocker. The thought hurts more than it should.

"It appears so," she says.

"He wasn't a good person, Callie. It wasn't all his fault, he had a lot going against him, but he wasn't."

I hate saying that. I hate the way she deflates and how I've chipped off part of her hope, but she deserves the truth. If she's going to stand by him, she needs to know.

Her eyes search mine, and a flicker of hope spreads through me when she softens.

"I think he might be now."

God, I hope so. I need something to cling to.

"I think he might be, too," I say. "I really do... If he recovers."

"If?"

"He's not good, Callie. Luke's been like a brother for over ten years, and I'm telling you, he's not good."

She flinches and looks away, but I don't regret what I said. She needs to hear this.

Fuck. *I* need to hear this.

"People are drawn to him. They always have been. It's hard to stay grounded when you're adored. It was harder for him than most because I don't think he's wired to be adored. He didn't know how to deal with it, and it all happened so fast for us once it hit."

Old images flood my brain.

Clusters of flashing lights. Fake smiles. Scripted lies. Pretenders. Manipulators. Opportunists. Headlines. Lawsuits. Handcuffs.

"I can't do this anymore! Please, Casey. I just need it to stop!"

Callie's gaze shifts to the hallway that swallowed Luke a few minutes ago.

"Is that why he left? He couldn't handle it anymore?"

I pull in a quick breath. That part isn't mine to share.

She seems to understand my hesitation and offers a subtle nod. The strange protectiveness spreads through me again, and I lean forward with an urgency that surprises me.

"You seem like a cool person and it's obvious you care about him. All I'm saying is don't fall for him. Please."

Her big hazel eyes probe mine. "Are you worried about me or him?"

"Both. He can't be worshipped right now. He needs an anchor, not a dreamer."

She shrinks like I hit her.

Dread sinks through me that it's already too late. Of course she's fallen for him. They all do.

A sick feeling curdles in my stomach.

"I understand," she says finally.

Any further response is cut off by Luke's return. His expression is casual as he rounds the corner, still wiping excess water on his jeans.

"So did I miss anything good?" he asks.

His light tone is strained. His eyes hold the suspicion of someone who knows he was the topic of conversation.

"Nope. In fact we learned you know a lot more about yourself than we do, apparently," Callie says.

Luke returns a polite smile that means nothing. "Well, since we're sharing, I learned the third sink in the men's room doesn't work."

An awkward silence falls over us, and we all seem grateful when the server approaches with our food. That exchange was going nowhere good.

Callie's mouth quirks in a smile as she studies her French toast. The sight releases a vise from around my chest. Her light is freaking infectious.

"I like the powdered sugar. Nice touch," I say, half-teasing, half-seeking her attention.

She rewards me with a mischievous smile like she knows. "It's not too much, but just enough to add a hint of sweetness."

"Exactly. With the syrup, it would have been too sweet if they used any more."

"It's incredible, huh, that powdered sugar," Luke cuts in. "They must have invested a lot of hours perfecting this particular application. Do you think they commissioned a full research study or just went with the classic focus group?"

He crosses a knowing look between us, and a wry smile slips out. "You were talking about me, weren't you. Of course you were."

"We care about you," I say.

"What did he tell you?" he asks Callie. It's clear from his expression he thinks I betrayed him.

My stomach grinds with anger and resentment. I love the guy, but I'm not a saint. I have limits too. Feelings. A fucking shattered heart and life god knows I'm still piecing back together.

"C'mon, man. Nothing," I defend.

Callie looks concerned. "Seriously, Luke. Nothing. You have a good friend here."

"Right... You know, just once it would be nice if people stopped treating me like a mental patient," Luke spits out.

"Then maybe you should stop acting like one," I fire back.

Luke shoots me a glare.

"Yeah? Well, I don't remember asking you to stop in and check up on me. I don't want you guys dropping in on me because I don't need a nurse."

He can't be serious.

"*Check up on you?* I'm not checking up on you! You're my best friend, *my brother!* And I thought I was yours. Sorry if I'm supposed to be okay with you just disappearing from my life, but I'm not!"

"You know what? This was obviously a mistake."

"What? Becoming human again for five minutes?"

My fists clench around the napkin in my lap, but it does nothing to temper the simmering anger starting to boil over. I shove it back down with a long breath.

"Look, I get it. You had a rough road," I continue. "But it's time to get back up and move on. You think you're the only one who's suffering? You think yours was the only life ruined? You know that's not fair, and if anyone can understand this, it's me."

My heart is pounding, my blood thick with pain and emotion I can't begin to sort out.

Flashes of cold rain.

Sodden earth.

The horror of watching your best friend die.

The terror of knowing you're about to follow.

"And anyway, what about the other guys, huh? What about your band, your *friends*? What about our dreams and lives that got all messed up when you walked away and left us with a shell of what we could've been? Do you ever think about that? You think we want to be playing nightclubs and opening for singing competition winners when we were booking stadiums a year ago? The Calisto Festival? God, what a joke."

I slam my napkin on the table. "At some point suffering gets old and is just selfish. Call me when you're ready to be friends again."

I launch to my feet and escape before I say something there's no coming back from. The agony on Luke's face while I exploded on him is already choking me with guilt.

He hates himself. I know this.

He sabotages any attempt to get close to him. I know this too.

And still I let my anger get the best of me.

A blast of fresh air when I storm outside immediately cools my temper. I have no idea what to do next as I hover on the sidewalk. My head is spinning with emotions. Remorse. Regret. Fucking *relief.*

I'd been sitting on that poison for so long. For ten seconds, it felt good to let it out. To bring him into *my* pain for one damn second.

But now, standing in the silent aftermath, knowing I just crushed a man who'd already pulverized himself to nothing, only the remorse remains. He may have deserved that, but it didn't fix anything. And now I've done the opposite of what I came to this city to do.

Maybe that's the insight I've been looking for. Maybe my answers are in the questions.

Did I come here for Luke or myself?

What kind of man is Casey Barrett?

What kind of man do I *want* to be?

I run a hand through my hair, paralyzed by regret and the constant fear I've been carrying since the day I learned my childhood "normal" wasn't okay. I've spent the last decade fighting fate. Trying to be better than what the world expects of me, given my hard past and harder present.

Every instinct tells me to book an earlier flight and leave Luke to his misery. No one would blame me for running back to my own mess I've been trying so hard to survive.

But when I reach for my phone, I can't shake the image of bright hazel eyes. A smile that has no business in our disaster, yet plunged head-first for reasons I still don't understand. If her light is strong enough to break through Luke's clouds, maybe there's hope for my own.

Maybe I can be the man I want to be, the man I feared had died with my sister.

So instead of pulling out my phone, I turn right and start walking.

Past the independent bookstore and rusted bike rack. Past

the pawn shop advertising lottery tickets and the bench in desperate need of a paint job.

I walk and keep walking.

Two blocks, then three, toward a luxury hotel with an empty suite on the fourth floor.

I'm not sure if I came here for Luke or myself, but I'm staying for hope—thanks to an angel named Callie.

CHAPTER 3

*L*uke says nothing when he finds me seated on a chair in the hotel lobby. His only reaction is a flash of surprise, then irritation. I don't know if it's at me or himself.

I push up from the leather chair to follow him toward the elevator, and our pact of silence continues on the awkward ride up. Even Aiden must sense the tension, because he's uncharacteristically quiet.

The sound of walking has never been so loud, the distance to Luke's suite so long.

The click of the lock is deafening.

He leaves the door open after entering to let me know I'm welcome to follow.

"I'm sorry," I say once we're inside.

"Don't."

"Luke..."

"*Don't*," he hisses, turning on me. "You of all people will not apologize to me. Ever. For anything. Got it?"

I wince and avert my gaze to the tile floor of the foyer.

His self-hating response only makes me feel more guilty.

I sense his gaze and almost choke when I meet it. It's all there. Raw and messy.

The pain. The love. The regret.

How much he's missed me, needs me, and is so fucking grateful I showed up. But he has no clue how to say it. And I have no clue how to acknowledge it.

So I swallow the words he doesn't want to hear and pack them away with all the other unspoken truths poisoning our relationship.

I love you too, brother.

I miss you.

I wish you'd let me in.

I need you too. So damn much.

He blocks any chance for a heartfelt confession when his addiction to numbing the pain pushes him toward the bar.

I watch with a cracking heart as he fills a glass and kills the moment with an 80-proof bullet.

"You heading out soon?" he asks. I can't tell if there was fear or hope in that question. Does he want me to leave or stay?

"Flight leaves at five. Have to get back for the Calisto Festival."

He nods, but I can't read his expression. "Since I ruined breakfast, order whatever you want from room service."

"French toast?"

He doesn't smile at my joke but I can tell he wants to.

"I'm going to lie down. Room key is on the island if you want to use the gym or pools."

He won't meet my eyes before disappearing down the hall with the crystal-glass best friend that's replaced me.

* * *

I HAVE zero intention of hanging out in a suffocating hotel room alone while Luke drinks himself into a stupor. A workout sounds promising, so after changing into gym clothes, I head to the onsite facilities to blow off steam.

It feels good to strain my body instead of my soul for a while. With each machine and movement, I'm in control again. Only when my muscles are shaky with exertion and my mind is focused, do I let myself leave the gym.

I'm a new man when I head back to the room with a clear head and a few sandwiches.

The main area of the suite is still abandoned, the television droning from some remote corner. It's like I never left it. I could probably leave and come back a hundred times and Luke wouldn't know.

My fingers tighten around the edge of the island countertop. It hurts to think this is what my gifted, once-vibrant friend does all day. If not for his breakfasts with Callie, he probably wouldn't have any break from the isolation.

It makes me wonder what made him go to that café in the first place. Why come to the city that broke you, if all you're going to do is hide from it?

I head to the guest room and strip off my clothes for a shower. For some reason, this room has two of them—a regular shower in the attached bathroom, then some custom deal in the bedroom itself. Lined with a spa's worth of jets, its slate tiles stretch across the entire wall that backs up to the real bathroom. For a guy accustomed to every luxury this world has to offer, I've never seen anything like it. Clearly, someone with too much money and a kink for group bathing arranged for this.

Bet that girl Callie would love to make fun of the absurd contraption. Shit like this is exactly the kind of indulgence she was teasing us about.

The thought brings a smile to my face as I opt for the cozy stall shower in the neighboring bathroom.

I'm still thinking about her when I dry off, wondering what happened with her and Luke after I left. I wasn't waiting at the hotel long before he showed up, so he must have bailed soon after I did.

The thought doesn't sit well with me. We just left her there. Two moody divas stalking off to nurse our wounds while she... what? Waited? Cursed us out? Is she pissed? Sad? Scared?

As I run a towel over my hair and return to the bedroom, I have an overwhelming urge to ask Luke if he has her number. He must if they coordinate meeting for breakfast every day.

Then again, maybe it would freak her out if I messaged her. There were times it seemed like she was flirting with me. Other times, I don't know. She's probably just one of those people who's nice to everyone.

Doesn't matter. I'd only be sending a quick text to make sure she's okay and understands all that bullshit had nothing to do with her. I doubt Luke took the time to reassure her before he skulked away.

I throw on some sweats and make my way down the hall toward Luke's room. His door is closed so I knock and wait. After several long seconds, I hear, "Yeah?"

Well, he's alive at least.

I poke my head in and suppress a cringe. The room reeks of alcohol. Bottles and glasses line every surface of the furniture. He must not allow housekeeping back here very often, because this space is the opposite of the pristine condition of the rest of the suite. Except for the empty glasses, you'd never know someone was living in suite 403.

Until this room.

"What is it?" he asks, impatient. Guess I'm interrupting the "nothing" he's been doing all morning.

"You talk to that girl from the diner since we left?"

His expression pinches into confusion. "Callie? No. Why would I?"

"I don't know, because we acted like assholes?"

His eyes shift like maybe he agrees, but he only shrugs. "Sorry, man. I don't even have her number."

The irritation spreads into frustration, and I step into the room. He returns a cold look.

"So how do you meet her for breakfast every day? How do you know when—*if*—she'll show?"

He shrugs again and turns his attention to the TV like he actually cares about whatever reality garbage is polluting the screen.

"She just does," he says finally.

"So she magically appears each morning, even though she has no idea if you will?"

"I guess."

"And how long has this been going on?"

"I don't know. A couple weeks. Why does it matter?"

His indifference is really pissing me off. I march forward to block his view of the screen.

"What the fuck?" he grunts.

"Exactly what I'm thinking. Don't you see how messed up that whole situation is?"

"What are you talking about? We have breakfast together, so what?"

"That's all it is. Really," I say dryly. "Just two people grabbing some calories to start the day."

His glare is a welcomed reprieve from the apathy.

"Yes, Casey. That's all it is. What's your problem?"

"My *problem*? My *problem* is you. My problem is *this!*" I wave around the room. "I don't have to know a damn thing about that girl to know she deserves better. She cares about you. I have no idea why, but she does. And you shrug her off like she's a coat rack at the café. You want to blow me off and treat me like I don't exist, fine. I'm fucking used to that. But not her. If you can't be a decent human being to that woman, you need to leave her the hell alone. You sure as fuck don't let her fall for you."

He averts his gaze, and I soften when he does.

"I do," he says quietly.

"You do what?"

"Care about her. I mean..." He hesitates, and my heart pounds. "The last thing I want is to hurt her."

My thoughts return to images of her adoring expression when she looked at him. How it stung way more than it should have. She's a stranger. I'll probably never see her again. But *he* will, and that's the problem.

"Then *treat* her like you care. Make sure *she* knows how important she is to you. Don't leave her alone in some random diner every day, waiting like her world should revolve around you. Let her into your life or don't. Make up your damn mind."

I don't wait for a rebuttal, but stalk away, slamming his door behind me.

* * *

I'M a half block from the diner with my carryon backpack when I realize I've walked back to the scene of the breakfast drama. I don't even know why I came. It's not like Callie will be here. Even if our paths did cross for some reason, the more I reflect on our encounter, the clearer it becomes I misread everything.

If what Luke said is true, she must care about him beyond a casual breakfast acquaintance. No one is nice enough to sit around waiting for a chance to be nice.

That can only mean one thing: she's in love with him.

I don't know why that makes me so angry. I'm trying to tell myself it's because she deserves better. Maybe she does, but technically, that's not my problem. Luke's made it clear that nothing in his life is my problem anymore.

"Hey! Excuse me!"

I flinch at the tug on my arm and turn to find an employee

wearing a Jemma's shirt. Her eyes are filled with stars as she gazes up at me.

"You're Casey Barrett, right? Luke's drummer?"

Luke's drummer.

I wince from the sting.

That's me. The Drummer.

"I guess so. How can I help you?"

She grins and holds out what looks like a stack of branded sticky notes.

And a pen.

"I'm Ailee. I saw you this morning but didn't want to interrupt. I was hoping you'd come back. Would you mind?"

"Sure," I mumble.

I scribble my name on the top sheet and hand the packet and pen back to her.

"Thank you!"

She's still staring at me, like she wants to say something else. I've been in this situation enough to know what that thing is. I'm about to let her down preemptively when I realize she might be helpful.

"Hey, um, just out of curiosity, this whole Luke and Callie breakfast thing, how did that start?"

She shrugs, pleased to have my attention. "I don't know, exactly. Kind of just happened. Luke had been coming in to stand around for some reason, but we didn't know who he was. Then one day that other girl showed up and they started talking. Then they started sitting with each other and—"

"Hang on, *he came in to stand around?* What do you mean?"

"Exactly that. He didn't say or do anything. Would just go to a spot in the café and stand there."

I squint at her, replaying the morning in my mind.

"Why, though?" I ask. "What was he doing?"

Ailee shrugs. "No idea. She was the only one who ever talked to him."

"Callie?"

"Yeah. We didn't know he was Luke Craven from Night Shifts Black or we would have been more accommodating."

Of course they would have. I suppress an eye roll.

"What do you know about Callie?" I ask.

She furrows her brows through a flicker of jealousy. "Not much. Never really spoke to her."

No surprise there.

"Okay, thanks."

"Hey, wait!"

I turn back, and cringe at the look on her face. Here it is.

"Do you maybe want to come in for a cup of coffee or pie or something?"

I twist a polite smile. "Thanks, but I have to catch a flight. I appreciate the information. Good luck with everything."

CHAPTER 4

"Yo, what is up with you?" Eli asks, bumping my shoulder with his as he passes. "Why're you acting like someone shit on your kit again?"

I fire a tight grimace at my bass player. "*Again?*"

His smirk triggers all kinds of questions as I return to my absent strum of the guitar in my lap.

I never told the others about Luke. There was no point getting their hopes up until I checked out the situation, and now I'm glad I didn't.

The trip here to Richmond was brutal. No amount of burying myself in my phone and laptop could block out the constant replay of everything that happened since I showed up at Luke's suite the other day. It stings that my presence didn't seem to have any impact on my friend.

But hers has.

She broke through somehow. That girl woke something in Luke. I saw it at breakfast. The spell clearly didn't last, but it was enough to offer hope, even though I have no clue what to do next.

"I'm fine. Just tired," I assure him.

"It's your own fault for cramming your personal shit between shows. Where'd you go anyway?"

Sweeny stops in the doorway of the green room, his gaze landing on me with the same question Eli just asked.

God, I hate lying to the guys, but what else can I say? They're still pissed at Luke for leaving us. Luke is pissed at me for existing. I don't need to close the "pissed" loop.

"I told you. Family stuff. Molly had a thing." I return my attention to the guitar, hoping they won't probe further. "I think we should cut 'Better Get Back' from the set."

"*What?!*" my bandmates cry, the previous topic forgotten.

Mission accomplished.

"That's our biggest track!" Sweeny says.

"Did you see the crowd at sound check?" I return.

"There was no one here at sound check. Doors weren't even open yet."

"Exactly."

I push up from the couch to head backstage. That confusing exchange should keep them busy for a while.

They're still mumbling to each other about whatever's up my ass as I escape down the hall. The fact that this place even *has* a green room was a surprise.

Another surprise? The scratch of new lyrics and melodies that's been haunting me since I boarded the plane yesterday. It's not a full song yet, but it's enough to know I'm in deep shit.

I've spent the last five years surrounded by celebrities and beautiful women, and it's some random girl in a diner who's cemented herself in my brain. A woman I will probably never see again.

What the hell am I supposed to do with that?

Nothing in me wants to entertain this weird compulsion, but I find myself pulling out my phone anyway. I open the notes app and start typing. Maybe just writing things down will purge them from my turbulent head.

For a few minutes, I dump the strange words onto the notepad. It feels good just to be writing again—until I read them back.

A chill runs through me at what I just wrote.

"I can only dream of ending all the waiting
Praying that I'll see you again
Traveling the world, I've seen so many others
But I can't keep from thinking of you
But I still walk alone
Should I just move along
Only time will tell
If I can be the one inside your dreams
Can it be me?"

What the actual hell?!

I scrub at my face and stare at the sappy lyrics that make no sense. My finger hovers over the delete button. Embarrassed and confused, I re-read the lines from the wing of the stage as the dull murmur of the crowd evolves into a cheer when the lights come down.

Delete it. Let it go. There's nothing for you in that damn city.

A smack on the arm startles me, and I glance up to see Marcus with a questioning look on his face.

"You good, dude?" our contract guitarist asks as our intro music blares through the house.

"Fine, why?"

Instinctively, I shut off my phone and shove it in my gig bag beside a crate. I feel Marcus studying me like he caught me with stolen contraband instead of inappropriate lyrics about a woman I've known for five whole minutes.

"Let's do this!" Eli bellows, ending the awkward moment.

He and Sweeny join us to prepare for our entrance, and I plaster a smile on my face.

For the next two hours we pretend all this shit still means something.

* * *

WE'RE thirty-six minutes into an interview at a luxury hotel in L.A., and my brain is exploding. Eli and Sweeny have had to field most of the questions, because I can't get my head out of a different hotel suite on the other side of the country.

It's been four days since I saw Luke. Four days of lying to my bandmates, acting like nothing's changed when my entire universe has been shoved off-axis. Nothing is right anymore. Nothing makes sense, and I—

"Casey, you've been quiet," the journalist says, drawing me back to my present hell. "This next one is for you."

I return a tight smile as dread pools in my stomach. I begged TJ to postpone this interview, but the Label wouldn't have it. Supposedly, this feature in Songset Magazine is going to be the catalyst that propels us back to the top. I would have laughed when he said that if... Wait, no. I did laugh. Which is why he's still pissed at me.

Our manager blasts me with a warning look from where he's leaning against a wall behind the journalist.

I divert my gaze back to the other probing stare locked on me. *Kara Corbin.* This woman has made plenty of careers. Ruined plenty more. Only Mila Taylor did more damage to us after what happened a year ago, and I still don't understand why the Label thought a feature written by the industry's queen of shit-stirring was a good idea.

Redemption arcs only work if all parties are on the same page. Based on the direction of this interview, we're in different libraries.

"Your fall from grace has been well-publicized over this past year." Her tone isn't exactly smug, but it isn't exactly *not*. I lock my glare behind a bored expression. "What are you doing to make yourself relevant again?"

The blow hits hard and fast. Even TJ winces as he turns a pleading look on me.

My fist clenches in my lap. Maybe I'm even more annoyed at her attempt to be delicate. Not sure why the hell they'd start now after ripping me and my life apart for the last twelve months.

"You mean are we planning to relaunch a new brand without Luke or are we going to continue limping along as a pathetic shadow of our former glory?" I fire back.

"Casey..." TJ warns.

My bandmates fidget uncomfortably beside me.

"What? That's what she's really asking, isn't it?"

She returns a casual shrug. "Sure, that's one aspect. Don't you think your fans deserve to know what the future holds? There are rumors you're planning to walk away from Night Shifts Black to pursue other projects."

The room goes still. All eyes lock on me with silent horror and betrayal.

"I never said that. Not once," I hiss. "Who told you that?"

Her eyes bore into me. "So it's not true."

"No. Of course not."

"So you're writing new music for Night Shifts Black?"

"I..." Everyone is looking at me. My heart slams against my ribs. Pressure builds around my eyes, my chest.

Think!

God, I just want to melt into this couch and disappear.

"Casey? Are you writing new music for Night Shifts Black? It's a simple question."

Kara's accusatory gaze slices into me, already flashing with the cruel glint of victory.

"Yes," I lie to a chorus of surprise. "Yes, I'm working on new music."

"But I still walk alone... Should I just move
along..."

Maybe it's not a lie thanks to the mystery breakfast club girl. Technically, I *am* writing again after all this time, even if it's just a few baffling lines that will never see the light of day.

"Really." Her tone is skeptical as she leans back in her chair. Her gaze sifts over me, and my heart beats faster at the challenge pooling in her eyes. "Anything you can tease for your fans? We've been waiting a while."

"Not yet," I say. "But it will be epic."

I hide a cringe at the grave I'm digging. As if I don't have enough of those sprinkled around me.

"Okay, then let me ask you this. I have Jana Furmali on record saying you told her Night Shifts Black was done and she broke off the recent engagement with you after you cheated on her. How do you respond to that?"

By fighting the urge to detonate.

My blood boils as I stare at her in disbelief.

"Casey, how do you respond?" she repeats.

"That you shouldn't be looking to my bitter ex for anything *on-the-record* about me."

"So it's not true?"

"No."

"What about her claims that there's more to the night you and Luke overdosed than people know about? According to her, the two of you were in a violent fight and he assaulted you—"

"Enough!" I jump up from the couch. "This is bullshit," I snap at TJ. "I'm not doing this."

"Casey," TJ warns. "You promised. You have to..." He goes quiet at my hostile look.

"I have to... what? Defend more ridiculous rumors I've already addressed a hundred times? The world knows more about me than I do, apparently! *Everyone* does, so why are we even here?" I wave around the room. "What's this accomplishing?"

Targeted stares burn through me from all sides. Shock and anger from my bandmates. Smug glee from Kara and the producers. Abject fear from my manager who's watching his biggest account slip into oblivion.

And I'm sick of it. I'm sick of being a symbol and a prop and a fucking chess piece for other people to drag over a board while they monetize my trauma.

"So there *was* an assault. Is that really what landed you in the hospital? Is that the real reason for the split? Casey!"

Her questions become shouts as I storm away.

"Are you getting this?" a producer hisses.

"Got it," a camera operator says.

I ignore them and smash through the door.

* * *

TEARS POUND the backs of my eyes as I tear down the hall toward my hotel room. My hands are shaking, my head pounds with old scars and fresh wounds. God, everything hurts, and I can barely function enough to open my door.

As soon as I do, I slam it shut, secure all the locks, and slide to the floor.

Arms trembling, I wrap them around my legs and rest my forehead on my knees. Sobs form in my chest and work their way up my throat. I shake my head and swallow them back down in painful gulps.

I never give in to them. I can't. I have to be the strong one. I'm the one who stayed. The one who survived. The one who was here to bear the brunt of the anger and abuse and frustration and exploitation. Just like I was my entire life.

Casey Barrett, the invincible shield who takes the blows meant for everyone else.

But I'm not invincible. I'm scared and alone and just as broken as the ones I'm protecting.

I pull out my phone with unsteady hands. I don't even know what I'm planning to do with it. Molly is studying abroad in Europe, but I don't dump my pain on my little sister anyway. I don't dump it on anyone, and that's the problem. I only take it. Absorb it and internalize it so other people can survive, even though it never works. All it does is turn me from a victim to an enemy when I'm not enough to save them.

Please. I need you. I can't do this alone anymore. Please don't leave me in this hell alone anymore.

The words blur through my tears. I'm shaking so hard I can barely type them out. In a hazy pocket of agony, I press send before I realize what I did.

When I do, my phone clatters to the floor, my head falls to my knees, and I break down for the first time since that night.

* * *

I WAKE TO AN AGGRESSIVE BANG.

The sound reverberates through me, and I realize it's coming from the door behind me. It's not the first one I've felt since escaping to my room. I ignored the others until they finally stopped and I fell into a fitful sleep.

With the blinds drawn, I can't tell what time it is, but nothing's changed since I left the private lounge on the second floor of the hotel.

"Casey!"

Every inch of my body is cramped and sore as I try to push up from the floor. Another pound on the door is interrupted by a second voice.

"He wants to be alone."

"He needs to fix this!"

"Fuck, dude, cut him a break, will you?"

"It's your career on the line too!"

"Yeah? Well, maybe he's right. Maybe this is over."

"How can you say that?! He's being selfish."

"He's being a fucking human being! You suits keep treating him like some damn commodity! He's a person. His life was ripped apart. Worse than the rest of us. I'm tired of this. You want to keep torturing him, fine, but I'm done."

"Sweeny! Hey! Jeff!"

I clench my eyes shut. There are no tears left, just scratchy pain as I try to soothe the burn inside and out.

I know who's standing on the other side of the door. All he wants is confirmation that I'm not broken. That once I finish pouting, I'll pull myself back together and play my puppet role with a smile on my face like every other time.

But I can't do it right now. I can't take more criticism and anger and disappointment. Even worse would be the pity if anyone saw me like this.

My phone buzzes near my head, and I roll my aching eyes toward the illuminated screen. The surface is covered with notifications. Probably missed texts and phone calls from my bandmates and TJ. Maybe a diatribe or two from the Label when word got back to them about the disastrous interview. I'll pay dearly for that, but it's hard to care when it feels like I have nothing left to lose.

Last night, I broke.

Today...

I don't know yet.

I push up to my elbows, testing my limbs and my blurry vision. My phone flashes again, and I can't help the programmed response of checking the notification.

My heart stutters in my chest.

Can't be.

I scoop up the phone for a closer look and activate the screen.

The name is unmistakable. Not TJ or the Label or a bandmate, but the last person I expect to see.

A new text. A reason to keep going and force myself to confront the reality of what I've done.

I unlock the phone and scroll to my messages. Sure enough, there's an unread stream at the top…

From Luke.

My heart pounds as anxiety erupts in my stomach. The next few words could make or break me, and I don't even know what response would do which. No matter what that message says, everything will change when I open it.

I command my shaking finger to click on it and stop breathing for several long seconds.

Luke: I know dude. Me too. Come back. I need you too.

CHAPTER 5

$\mathcal{M}$ usic blasts, alcohol flows, and the nauseating blend of expensive fragrances streams in and out of my lungs.

The fallout from the botched interview with Kara Corbin was swift, violent, and still mounting. My phone has been blowing up with a constant stream of wrath, which was all the more reason to flee from one hotel to Luke's with nothing but my small carryon and the clothes on my back.

Now that I'm here, I'm regretting it.

His heartfelt text feels more like a joke now that I'm at his suite and see he apparently didn't just need *me*, but all these virtual strangers as well. I'm a little pissed off he called me back here to watch him slip into old habits. Maybe it was one last attempt at proving nothing's changed and I should finally leave him alone once and for all.

If only it were that simple.

Like the unofficial babysitter I've become, I scan the sea of bodies in a recurring ten-minute check to make sure Luke's alive. Ironic, since the band has spent the last eight years teasing me for being the youngest. If I'd known Luke was inviting me to his suite only to recreate the period of our lives I've been desperate to forget, I never would have come.

And yet, I can't bring myself to leave. His pattern of self-destruction may not be new or fair, but it will always be my problem. Tomorrow, once I make sure he survives whatever this spectacle is supposed to be, I'll explain how badly he hurt me—again—and address what's really going on.

Confident he's still alive and functioning for now, I head toward the makeshift bar. It's not an ideal hangout for a guy who's been trying to stay on the straight and narrow, but it's better than being groped on the packed living-room-turned-dancefloor. Being the only sober person at an event like this is almost awful enough to make me not want to be sober.

"Casey! Good to see you, man."

I follow the voice to find Jaxon Anders leaning against the counter beside me. He motions to the bartender to order another round before facing me.

"Hey, Jax. Been a while."

"Too long. It's nice to finally see a familiar face. I was surprised how few people I recognized until I learned this entire guest list got the same call from concierge. Insane and genius, no? But that's Luke for you."

I study the actor's face before squinting through the crowd in the direction I last saw Luke. It's impossible to see him from this vantage point. Not that a visual would help interpret the latest head-scratching behavior of my best friend. Just when I think I've figured shit out, Jaxon Anders says something like that.

"What do you mean you got a call from concierge?"

He tilts his head. "The invitation? Oh right, you're his boy. You must be one of the few who got a direct invite."

"What are you talking about? Weren't you invited? Weren't *all* these people invited?"

"Yeah, by the front desk. I got a call this morning saying

Luke was throwing a party in 403 and to stop by if I wanted. I doubt he even knows most of these people." Jaxon laughs and diverts his attention to the cocktails sliding toward him. "Thanks, man," he says to the bartender while slipping him a bill.

The other man swipes it off the counter and turns to me.

"What can I get you?" he asks.

"I…"

"Hey, good to see you, dude," Jax says, bumping my arm. "Let's catch up later."

He heads toward a woman I recognize from a few B-Movies. She takes a glass as they exchange some words, then shoots me a curious look. I can only imagine what my face looks like right now.

Luke had concierge invite a bunch of strangers to his suite for an impromptu party? Why the hell would he do that?

"Sir? Anything to drink?"

I shake off the trance and settle my gaze back to the bartender. "Yeah. I mean, no."

Shit, why did I come over here again?

I've lost all coherent thought.

"Never mind," I direct at the bartender. "I just… yeah."

I tap the counter and push away. He looks a fraction below annoyed before shifting his attention to an actual customer.

It hasn't even been a week since my initial reunion with Luke. Somehow, he went from reclusive hermit to inviting an entire damn hotel into his life. Not even Callie could be responsible for that kind of transformation. Something is wrong. There's no way this event is about having a good time.

I don't know what it means, but I know it can't be good.

I'm a few steps from the bar when I glimpse another familiar face. My breath catches, followed by a scorching wave of awareness.

Callie's here?

ALY STILES

I don't know why I find it surprising that Luke's only friend would be at his party. Maybe because she's from a different life. She doesn't belong in this glossy, superficial ode to the past. She's hope of a future.

Guess she just came to the same conclusion, because she's heading toward the exit. A strange sense of panic has me chasing after her. I can't let that happen.

She'll never hear me over the noise, so I push through the crowd to grab her arm.

Callie spins around. Her startled expression transforms into recognition, then a hint of disappointment.

Ouch. But I'm not surprised. She came to see Luke and got his drummer instead. I'm used to that, just not the odd sting that's coming with it now.

I put aside the hurt when I realize why I need her here so badly. She's the only other person in this packed crowd who actually gives a shit about the host.

I lean close to her ear and breathe in a quick hit of citrus.

"Breakfast club girl!" I call.

"Rock god!" she returns.

I laugh to ease some of the tension and force away the creeping shadows that have been following me around lately. I need her to stay tonight. I tell myself it's for Luke, but when she turns her big hazel eyes on me, more than gratitude stirs in my chest.

A minute ago, the last thing I wanted to do was get drunk and party. Now, introducing her to our world and making her feel welcome feels like the most important thing I can do for both of us. In a life where I've lost all control, this is finally something I can do.

"Where's Luke?" she asks.

I motion toward the crowd, knowing she won't be able to see him from here. It's petty, but part of me is glad I have to be the center of her universe for a minute.

Because suddenly, she's the center of mine.

I've been so distracted by her presence, I haven't noticed what she's wearing until now. Blood rushes to places it shouldn't as I take in her short silver cocktail dress and sexy heels. Her hair is curled in soft waves, her makeup confident but not overdone. She looks incredible. Completely different from the last time I saw her in that diner.

But I found her just as attractive then. What's changed the vibe in our chemistry is the atmosphere around us. The dim lighting, sensual beat, beautiful people, and heavy ooze of sex throughout the space has my mind disoriented and my body regressing back to a time when nothing was off-limits for a person like me.

Alarms blare in my head. Flashbacks gnaw at the recesses of my brain. I ignore them all. I'm a different person now. A better person. And at some point I have to trust myself.

"Come on! I'll get you a drink," I say, directing her ahead of me.

She returns a quick smile, and I suck in a breath when her ass brushes my hip as she scoots past. The look she shoots back is somewhere between apologetic and intrigued, and I can't stop my gaze from flowing over every curve of her body. Just an innocent peek, but I'm not the only one looking.

A wave of protectiveness floods through me when I catch the predatory stares of other guests. She doesn't belong here. These wolves won't play fair, and since I'm the one who convinced her to stay, I feel responsible for making sure she has a good, safe time.

Her wide eyes broadcast her innocence as she surveys the room, triggering a sudden urge to give her a night filled with excitement and joy. I might be powerless to help Luke, but I can show this undercover princess an actual taste of the royal life.

Not everything about our world is bad—it doesn't have to

be, anyway—and it feels like she'd be the missing piece to give it meaning.

While she takes in the sights and sounds, I return to the bar. The bartender seems almost relieved I'm not as weird as he thought, until I demand a sealed bottle of champagne and two empty glasses.

I hand him a huge tip, scoop up my bounty, and go on the hunt for Callie.

She's balanced on the one-step ledge leading into the living room. Her wide stare scours the writhing bodies on the dance-floor like she doesn't know if she should run in disgust or join in. More guests cross all kinds of lines on the surrounding couches. Others undulate against the walls, leaving little to the imagination.

Her gaze locks on a couple practically sharing a body as they grind against each other to the hypnotic groove of the music. She chews on her lip, sending another spike of heat through me. Her innocent curiosity is a drug, and my body burns with the desire to explore the hedonistic sensations occurring around us. This growing fire inside me is going to be a huge problem.

We need a distraction.

"Here!" I call out from behind her.

She spins around with a small gasp, and I love everything about the relief and excitement in her eyes when she sees me. It's the opposite of her initial greeting. The reservation is gone, the disappointment that I'm not Luke replaced by a glint of heated curiosity. The way her gaze travels over my face, down my button-up shirt, and back to my eyes ignites a fresh current of sparks. Her brain is where I thought it was. Where mine is. Where I hoped, and dreaded, we'd end up.

You're in deep shit, dude. Deep, deep shit.

Before I can do or say something I'll regret, I hold up the bottle with a grin.

"I can tell you're cautious. You don't trust us wild rockers," I tease. A flash of surprise, followed by a small smile moves across her face as I lead her away from the dancers.

After popping the cork and filling the glasses, I pass her one.

"To Luke." I lift my glass in a mock toast.

"To Luke," she replies, taking a sip.

Her eyes go wide, and I snort a laugh at the adorable hypocrite.

"Undercover princess, my ass. You've never even had good champagne before!"

Her cute grin erases this entire week from hell. "A girl could get used to this," she muses.

So could I.

Seriously, Casey. What is wrong with you?

I drain my glass to purge this weird attraction. I can't even remember a time I was the one with a crush, and here I am going all eighth-grade-boy on a woman I spoke to once.

Well, twice now.

When I see her glass is empty as well, I refill it, only to immediately regret it. My days of using substances to cure myself are over.

Her look of confusion when I put the bottle and glasses I just filled on a side table is totally justified. Before she can ask, I grab her hand and lead her toward the dance floor.

"Where are we going?" she shouts.

"To dance!" I toss back.

"What? No way!"

My heart sinks in disappointment, and I'm about to let her go, when I catch her shy grin. She's not resisting, just insecure. My suspicions are confirmed when she turns a fascinated stare on the crowd of moving bodies. It's so obvious she wants to be out there, not observing from a corner.

Challenge. Accepted.

We've almost reached the dance floor when I stop cold.

Oh no. What is *she* doing here?!

61

"Hey, darling!" Jana says, blocking my path.

I lose Callie at the same time Jana's arms fly around my neck. Before I know what's happening, her glossy lips graze my cheek while her aggressive embrace drags me further from Callie. It wasn't an accident. Nothing with her ever is. I could kill Luke for inviting this woman. He knows about our volatile history.

She's clinging to me like we're back at that infamous Oscars after party, not like a bitter ex who just blew up my life on a national scale. Lingering hope that was the final punishment for my betrayal evaporates. She's never going to let me have peace.

"What are you doing here?" I snap, trying to pull away from her.

"Having a good... time! Unlike you, apparently." Her flirtatious grin matches the glassy look in her eyes. She's drunk. Fantastic. "What's wrong, darling? Don't want people thinking we're back together?"

I try to extricate myself from her arms, but she's too far gone in her revenge fantasy for subtle hints.

"I'm with someone," I lie, motioning toward Callie.

Maybe it's not a lie. Technically, I *was* with her when I got abducted.

Callie's confused stare is punctuated with a darker emotion. Is she... jealous? A hot surge of excitement rushes through me.

Huh. Wasn't expecting that.

"*That* girl? What, does she work here?"

I fire a cold look at Jana. Her malicious smile sends a chill over me.

"Wait," she says, eyeing Callie with a devious glint. My pulse pounds in my ears. "She doesn't know, does she? She has no idea who I really am. Who *you* are."

"I have to go," I grumble, ducking out of her arms.

She yanks me back and drags me in for a kiss.

Stunned, I freeze as her fingers lock in my hair and her tongue plunges into my mouth.

What the actual hell?!

I grab her wrists and wrench them off me. Her challenging look when I step out of reach leaves a sick feeling in my stomach, but I have no interest in playing this game with her. The last time was the last time. I made no secret about that, and I thought she finally got the message when she retaliated with those defamatory stories for Kara Corbin.

"Does she kiss you like that?" Jana taunts.

"Have a great night," I reply with a tight smile.

We're not doing this. She's already done enough damage.

I'm having trouble reading Callie's expression as I make my way back to her, but I'm not letting Jana ruin this for my new friend.

"Sorry about that," I say, leaning close. "Ex-girlfriend."

"Ex? Does she know that?"

Her gaze drifts to something behind me, and I can only assume we're still being stalked.

I force a casual smile. There's no way in hell I'm addressing that landmine right now. Hopefully never.

"Sometimes the lines get blurred," I say in a dismissive tone. "Okay, enough stalling. Let's dance!"

I take her hand and drag her into the sea of guests as far from Jana as we can get. I'm not ruining this night with the truth about what Callie just saw. Better she thinks it's exactly what it looked like.

The crowd closes in around us, forcing us together, and I don't hate anything about the feel of Callie's warmth against me. Her arms slip around my neck, while my hands curl on her waist.

It's been a long time since I've been this close to another person. Not since Jana in the latest (and last) "on" of our on-again-off-again cycle.

But this already feels different than anything I've experienced. There's nothing opportunistic in the way Callie's looking at me. Touching me. No expectation or entitlement, just the same innocent wonder she's been wearing since I first made her stay.

A sub bass drop sends her shifting closer as she adjusts to the tempo change. The frenetic house beat is my new favorite rhythm when her body locks into mine. She rubs and grinds in all the right places, and I fight with my dirty mind to keep my hands where they belong.

But hers start to drift...

I suck in a breath when she unhooks her arms, freeing her palms to roam. One smooths over my chest while the other slips into my hair so her fingertips can play. Her touch is sensual and determined and so incredibly dangerous.

Shit, this is brutal.

Any lingering doubt about whether her flirting was intentional or just being nice falls away when her hungry gaze drops to my lips. A flood of anticipation rushes through me. My heart pounds as my body tenses with need. Her grip tightens on the back of my neck. Her hips plaster to mine, scraping over my zipper as if seeking ways to torture me. There's not a chance this person plays games for the fun of it, and when her cheek nuzzles my chin, I know she's wrestling with the desire to kiss me.

Blood pounds through every recess of my body. I'm on fire to taste her and show her how good I could make her feel. Just because my heart has never belonged to anyone else, doesn't mean the rest of me hasn't.

Her gaze creeps to mine with an open invitation. My fingertips dig into her hips as my brain fights my dick.

This isn't her world. She's drunk on an experience she will regret tomorrow.

The thought of her ever feeling regret when it comes to me is enough to break the spell.

With incredible fortitude—and against the protest of my body—I step back with a weak smile.

"I'm thirsty. Let's go get a drink," I explain.

Her expression sags with frustration I feel in my bloodstream, but it's the right thing to do.

I didn't come to this city to fix one person and break another.

At the bar, I ask for two waters and find an empty stool for Callie to sit.

Her gaze is saturated with questions, confusion, and maybe a touch of hurt.

I have no idea how to explain what just happened, especially while shouting over the music. So instead, I press the glass of ice water to my head as if to cool down.

"Whew. It's hot in here, huh?"

When her expression doesn't change, I brace for what's bound to be an awkward exchange.

"Is everything okay? Is it your ex-girlfriend?" she asks, cutting a quick look at the dancefloor.

I flinch in surprise and release a dry laugh. "Jana? No."

I hadn't even thought about her since Callie reclaimed every brain—and body—cell I have.

Her face scrunches in an adorable pout. "Oh, I see. So it's me. I'm just a terrible dancer."

I can't stop another grin. "Yes, that's it."

She lifts a brow, and I sigh. Guess I'm not getting out of this. Might as well go all in.

I lean closer and catch her gaze.

"You don't want to sleep with me, Callie."

She coughs through a swallow of water. "What?"

I search her face with a challenging look of my own. "Am I wrong? Is that where you wanted that to go?"

It's too dark to tell if she's blushing, but her nervous fluster doesn't require light.

"We can't dance without sleeping together?" she counters, but there's no conviction in her voice.

"You tell me. Would you have let me kiss you out there?"

I know the answer. And I know she does too when she lowers her gaze.

"Probably," she mumbles.

"You would have. And you would have loved it," I tease to lighten the mood. I didn't sacrifice the kiss I so desperately wanted just to scare her away with the explanation.

Her eyes find mine again, and that strange protectiveness returns. In some ways, she's so mature beyond her years. In others, her naivete is as alluring as it is terrifying. She's walking a path she can't begin to understand, and her guide is the last person on this planet she should be following. I haven't seen Luke in a while, but I know him well enough to know he didn't invite all these people here to prove how great he's doing.

He's also my best friend, so I'm not eager to rip him down in front of the only true friend he seems to have left besides me.

"Anyway, this isn't your scene. I'm trying to remember that. The normal rules don't apply."

Her gaze locks on something behind me and goes dark. I twist back, positive I'll find Jana, but what I see is even worse.

Shit.

Anger spikes through me. Resentment. Maybe it's not fair, but I'm human too.

Haunting flashbacks mix with the present scene as I watch my intoxicated friend hide his pain in chemicals and women. One of the models who's attached herself to him like an appendage is a dancer from our "Better Get Back" video. She's always had a crush on him. The other two I've never seen before. Probably friends or friends of friends.

Or guests in Room 216 or whatever.

This is exactly the shit that ruined our lives. I get that addiction is an illness, but understanding something and living with the realities of it are two very different things. A year ago, I let his addiction almost end my life. He clearly hasn't changed like I hoped, and maybe that's the part that hurts the most. All I've ever wanted for him was to be okay.

He said he needed me. I came back for him. Maybe he does, but he doesn't *want* me. At least, not as much as he wants his pain and self-destruction.

While I'm still wrestling with whether I can invite this chaos back into my life, Callie filters into view.

Fuck. I can't imagine what's going through her head right now. I tried to warn her, but there's no preparing someone for the demons of Luke Craven when they come out to play.

"He doesn't care about them," I say, attempting to read her fears. "I doubt he even knows them."

It's not entirely a lie. In the state he's in, he probably wouldn't recognize anyone, let alone some dancer he saw for all of three seconds.

"He's completely wasted. He can barely stand," Callie says. The horror in her expression tugs at me, but I have no idea how to explain what's actually happening right now.

"Yeah. Believe me, they wouldn't have a shot otherwise. He doesn't fool around like that anymore."

Her wide eyes tell me we're not even close to being on the same page about this.

"Wait, what are you saying?" she asks in alarm.

I squint back, confused. "I'm not saying anything."

"Shouldn't we do something?" she cries.

"Do what?"

What exactly does she expect me to do? If she knows how to reverse a decade of spiraling, by all means, have at it.

"Casey! This isn't him! We can't just let him do this!"

"Do what? What are you so upset about?"

"That! They're taking him back to his room!"

She's right. The party is moving to somewhere more private —like every other time we've been in situations like this.

"*Taking him?* You act like he doesn't want to be alone with three models. He's a big boy, Callie. He can handle himself."

I bury painful images of the countless times I've watched this scene play out. The only difference is, I'm not being dragged into it this time.

Except I am. In the worst way possible.

Once again, I'm watching my life derailed by his bad choices.

You're not being fair.

No. None of this is fucking fair.

I snag another bottle of champagne from the bar without even waiting for the bartender this time. She needs a new distraction, because the one she's chosen is only going to chew her up and spit her out.

"Here, have another drink," I offer before she does something she can't undo.

Dread seeps through me at her determined expression. Even worse, she now seems mad at *me.*

She shakes her head with a glare. "No, this isn't like him. Something's wrong!"

I bark a bitter laugh at the irony.

"This is exactly like him. That's what I tried to tell you at breakfast. You don't actually know him. The guy you know is very different than the real Luke Craven."

My words come out harsher than I intended, but I didn't expect all the old trauma to come rushing back.

The time his reckless behavior got us jumped in an alley.

The time I woke up in some random person's hotel room with no memory of the night before.

The time over and over and over again I paid the price for his choices.

All the times I picked up his broken pieces while the gravel and mud swallowed up my own.

But this is our damage, not hers.

"Look, you're a very sweet girl," I say as gently as possible. The demons are shrieking around me. I ignore them. "I totally understand why Luke wants you in his life, and I'm sure you're really good for him, but he's not good for you."

"What's that supposed to mean?" she snaps back.

Maybe I'm losing patience as well. I don't even understand why we're fighting about this. What does she know about him other than what he orders off a damn breakfast menu?

"Luke is a force," I say as evenly as possible. "He's my brother and I love him, but you're lying to yourself if you think you're going to fix him before he destroys you."

Her startled look morphs into resentment. "You really think so little of your *brother?*"

Her words cut deep. She has no idea how precisely she drove the knife into my heart, but what does it matter anymore? This is pointless. This argument, this uphill battle to escape Luke's shadow, this entire attempt to come back and save him from himself.

If she wants to push the boulder up the mountain for a while, fine.

"Whatever. Good luck with that." I grip the bottle and take off toward the other side of the room. I have nowhere to go, but I can't be here anymore.

Guilt creeps in the further I get from the bar. I see her take off toward the hall leading to the bedrooms. Maybe I should be concerned. And maybe part of me is even relieved that someone is going to intervene in his mess. The part of my soul that will always love him hates what I just did. It still worries about him. Still thinks about what could be happening in that back bedroom. So yeah, *that* part of me is glad someone is willing to take on his demons.

Because Luke still needs help, and right now that person can't be me.

I'm too tired. Too angry. Too hurt to be anything but an enemy and an obstacle. If Callie wants to tag in, she's more than welcome.

For a minute or two, I'm fine with that. I'm not even bitter that Luke's drama stole another relationship from me. I expect that now. I knew the moment he mentioned Callie with that little smirk, he'd unintentionally ruin any chance I had with her or anyone else who drifts into our orbit.

You can't survive Luke, and as I watch our old pattern play out in real-time, reality crashes in.

My heart breaks.

Everything goes dark and muddled around me.

Luke knows all of this as well. He knew he couldn't prevent himself from destroying everything in his path, so he had to divert his path away from the only person he still cared about.

Me.

How does a deadly hurricane show love? By leaving a sixteen-word note and fleeing as far from his next victim as possible. I read his note all wrong. It wasn't an apology. It was a goodbye.

My blood goes cold. I can't breathe as the truth constricts around my lungs, lodging in my heart.

There's only one place he can go that's far enough to protect me from himself, and it isn't a luxury suite in a distant city.

> Casey:
> I'm sorry. I love you too much to drag you to hell
>   with me.
> Luke

He didn't come here to hide. He came here to stop existing. This party? It's the cover. And these strangers have no idea they're not guests. They're witnesses.

Oh god.
What if I'm too late?

CHAPTER 6

*M*y heart slamming against my ribs, I push through the crowd toward the hallway.

The women who were with Luke a minute ago are now grumbling in the opposite direction to return to the party. There's still no sign of Callie or Luke, and I'm terrified of what I'll find at the end of the hall. Whatever it is, Callie shouldn't have to deal with it alone.

I run the rest of the way, breathing prayers I haven't uttered in a long time. Not since that night at Elena's grave.

I knock on the closed door out of habit but don't wait for a response. When I push through it, Callie is perched beside him on the bed, a devastated and helpless look on her face. My heart breaks for her. Both of them.

I knew we'd end up here the second I learned about Callie The Breakfast Club Girl. I just hoped it wouldn't be like this.

"Is he okay?" I ask, urgently scanning Luke's still form.

The rise and fall of his bare chest relieves some of my tension.

She studies him for a second as if she's not sure how to answer that. Of course she's not. There is no answer. But for now, I have to translate our past into the present for those who don't speak our twisted language.

"I don't know. What are the different stages of substance abuse unconsciousness?" she says.

That's all the invitation I need.

I charge into the room and drop to the floor beside Luke. Nausea swirls in my stomach at the sensory memory of this familiar situation. So many panicked evaluations, desperate pleas, and jarring movements to wake him up. But I can't think about that now.

All that matters is this latest time.

I test his pulse and his breathing. Both are strong. A scan of his room doesn't reveal any paraphernalia other than alcohol. It doesn't mean he hasn't taken anything else, but it's unlikely. We need to clean out his system just to be safe.

"He'll be okay," I say with more confidence than I feel. Callie doesn't need to carry the full reality of this situation. For now, we just have to deal with the present. "We need to try to wake him up in a bit and get some water in him. Has he thrown up, yet?"

She shakes her head, and my stomach drops.

"Not that I've seen."

It was a longshot anyway.

"Okay. We'll have to do that, too. Let me get some water. Hang on."

I push to my feet and head to Luke's bathroom. Hopefully, there's a spa kit. If not, a garbage bin will work. I'm relieved to see a basin filled with personal care amenities.

After dumping them out, I return to Callie and hold it out to her.

I cringe at her confused look. Yeah, this is definitely not how I was hoping our night would go when it started. Should have just kissed her.

"It's for soaking feet, but in case you need this before I get back," I explain. "I'll be right back with the water as soon as I can."

I take off with a new sense of urgency.

After gathering some supplies from the party and ducking out of several conversations, I return to Luke's room for the well-rehearsed marathon. I hate how quickly it all comes flooding back.

Callie's gaze darts to me from where she's seated beside Luke on the bed. With my hands full, I kick the door closed behind me and lean over him.

"Gonna be a long night," I explain as I motion for her to take the plate of snacks and bottle of water balancing on my left arm. "Sorry, they didn't have French toast."

The worry lines ease on her face when she laughs. It's amazing how much that sound affects me. It's like a high I want to keep chasing.

She scoots closer to Luke on the bed, leaving room for me on her other side. I place the rest of the snacks on the night-stand and join her. We'll need to get the poison out of Luke soon, but first I have to build my strength for that behemoth task.

I align myself beside Callie and free a heavy sigh. I hadn't even realized how much tension I was holding onto until I let myself take a breath.

Our eyes meet in the mirror on the wall across from us. It could be awkward. Maybe it is, I don't know, but after a few seconds, it feels like I need to say something.

I even know what that thing should be.

"I'm sorry about how I acted out there," I begin quietly. "It hurts, you know? Seeing him like this. Sometimes I'm not strong enough to deal with it the way I should. I try to pretend he's the same person now that he was then, but he's not."

Her brows knit. "Messing around with supermodels?"

The true weight of this situation presses down on me. "That

wouldn't have been a cause for concern a year ago. But you were right to be worried. It doesn't mean now what it meant then. It's just..."

God. I don't even know what I'm trying to say. I study the ceiling, unable to look at her or myself in the mirror. I still haven't sorted all of this out, so I'm not sure how I'm supposed to explain it to someone else. All I know for sure is that I love this man beyond logic, and it's the hardest thing I've ever faced.

"I want to help him, I do, I just don't know how. At some point..." I turn my head to meet her eyes directly this time. "How can I help him if he won't even let me? You remember what happened at breakfast. He doesn't want to be helped. I'd be here every day if he let me."

Warmth spreads through my hand, and I glance down to see her palm tucked against mine.

I don't know what to do at first. Instinct warns me to pull away. I've been touched plenty of times, too many times, but this feels different. There's no lust or expectation, just gentle compassion to remind me she's here.

Who *is* this person?

My gaze flickers to Luke with a silent apology.

I get it now, dude. I really do.

This girl just creeps into your life and starts exploding shit with her light.

A peace I haven't felt in a long time settles over me, and I find my thumb moving in lazy arcs over hers, as if seeking more of it.

"What about you?" she asks, breaking the long silence.

"What about me?"

Her smile warms me from the inside out.

"What's your story?" she says.

I can't help but laugh. "You're not some undercover inves- tigative reporter or something, are you?"

It's almost easier for me to believe that than the fact there's a person like Callie on this hellhole of a planet.

She lifts a brow and shrugs. "Would that change your answer?"

Another unexpected grin leaks out of me. "I guess not."

I settle back against the headboard and find her in the mirror again. It's weird how I feel so exposed and so comfortable at the same time. Her question wasn't meant to be hard, but there's nothing about me that's easy.

There used to be, though. I was always joking around, the life of the party. I used humor to protect myself from a lot of things that could have broken me. And none of them did. Not until this one thing.

That's the real tragedy of tragedy. It doesn't just change the present, it skews the future and rewrites the past.

"I was one of ten," I blurt out. Might as well just go for it. Everything else about this night is freaking weird.

Her face erupts in shock. "Ten? As in ten siblings?"

I smile back. "Yes. Lucky number seven actually."

She huffs in disbelief and drops back against the headboard.

"Wow. I'm surprised you ended up with Luke and Night Shifts Black then. Shouldn't you be committed to some cheesy family band? Geez, with ten of you, you could have the whole road crew too."

I snort a laugh at the irony. "Oh, believe me, my parents tried. Three of my siblings actually still play together."

"Really?"

"Yep. They've even put some albums out. I could never get into the country thing, though. The black sheep, I guess."

Her amused gaze cuts to mine in the mirror. "Seriously. When you made a left, you made a hard left, huh. Well, it seemed to work out for you anyway."

She has no idea how hard I veered. Very few people do.

"What about you?" I ask before she can go too far into that minefield.

Her quick smile tugs at me. Why would that standard question make her uncomfortable?

"No bands. Not even country ones."

"You know what I mean. Luke said you're a writer."

Her deflective shrug is just plain annoying. If we're going to do this, let's fucking *do* this.

"I guess," she says in a noncommittal tone.

"You guess? What does that mean?"

I don't believe her smile any more than the last one she tried to throw at me. "It means that saying 'I'm a writer' implies I'm actually making a living at it."

I wince, irritation building again. I don't like anyone minimizing her, including herself. "Really? I thought it meant you spend lots of time writing things."

She shifts uncomfortably, and my fingers tighten around hers in a silent warning not to squirm out of this conversation. "I guess it can mean that, too. Would you still consider yourself a musician if no one paid you to play?"

"Of course. Let's hope that doesn't happen for a long time, though."

Her chuckle draws a smile from me as well.

"How much do you make for a show anyway?" she asks.

I almost choke at the random question, and she cringes in the mirror. "I'm sorry! I don't know where that came from. Don't answer that."

I shake my head with a grin. Too cute.

"Not as much as you'd think," I say. "Well not anymore, anyway. We used to get three to four hundred in guarantees. Now, it's more like one or two. Less when we're not headlining."

I can't help but smirk at her skeptical look. Not sure what she was expecting. "Two hundred? Like two hundred dollars? That's it?"

Ha!

"Oh my god, I love you. No. Two hundred thousand."

Her bewildered expression is even more amusing. How is she making this boring conversation so entertaining?

"Wait, *per show?* And that's not much?"

I tilt my head, trying to read her. "I mean, it's fine, I guess, but it's not where the real money is. We make most of it through writing and performance royalties." I nod toward Luke. "This guy here hasn't touched a guitar in a year and is still making a fortune passed out on his ass, believe it or not."

"Okay, Luke I get, but I thought you didn't write. You said at breakfast Luke was the writer. You weren't good with adjectives."

I shake my head in disbelief. "Seriously? Do you remember everything?"

"Am I wrong?"

I can't help another chuckle at her smug expression. Her attempt at "smug" is everyone else's "first sip of morning coffee" face.

"I guess not. I did say that. But to answer your question, I was just messing around. My name's in the credits too. It's true, Luke tends to bring the magic to the lyrics, but I'm the music guy. That hook in 'Better Get Back' that they use for all those hockey ads? All me."

"The hockey song is from one of your songs?"

Right. I keep forgetting she isn't obsessed with us. Maybe that's why I'm enjoying this so much.

"Yeah. It's not one of our bigger ones. Well, it wasn't when they negotiated the rights to it."

"I'd say it is now," she mumbles.

She hums the melody, and I *might* free an eye-roll.

Great, now I'm The Hockey Song Guy.

"Yep, that's it."

"Wow, I had no idea. I actually really like that song."

"You sound so shocked," I say dryly.

She returns a sheepish grin. "Sorry. I guess... I don't know. I try not to think too much about Luke the Superstar, so I haven't made much of a connection between him and his music. You know, staying out of the whole pop culture bubble thing so I can see him for who he really is. I guess I did the same for you by association."

Wow.

Now I really get why he gravitated toward this person.

"I like that," I say, thinking out loud. "He needs someone in his life who's real, but you should still pick up our stuff sometime. If you truly want to understand your new friend here, you need to listen to his music. I think it might surprise you."

I hesitate when my focus lands on Luke, heaviness settling over me again. "Or maybe it won't."

"'*Step back, fast, I'm coming for you. Step back, you can't handle what I've got.*'"

Callie's voice carries through the silence as if she's visualizing the hockey opener.

"That's it," I say with a quick smile before the humor drains away again. There's nothing soft or funny about that bitter anthem. "People think it's an aggressive song. A challenge to someone, and the hockey link certainly doesn't help."

Her gaze shoots to me. "It's not?"

"No. That's not what Luke's saying at all. It's actually saturated with self-loathing."

"Saturated with self-loathing?" she echoes in a dry tone. "What do you mean you're not good with adjectives?"

I fire a smirk in her direction. "I've been known to string a few together. Anyway, the part you know is just the hook. The chorus is, '*I'm the anchor drowning you. I'm your infection, better get back. I'm the hurricane, angel, shred those wings. Step back, better get back.*'"

The lyrics swirl around us like they're caught in that deadly hurricane.

She shudders. "And that was even before Elena's suicide?"

I flinch and go numb.

My chest tightens until it feels like my heart is being stung by a thousand needles. Guess she's learned more of the story.

"Yes. Elena was..."

Words flood in, jumbled and raw. They press on my throat with a strange urgency.

I don't get to talk about Elena anymore. Not in a way that matters, the way I *need* to. The media wants superficial sound-bites. My therapist wants breakthroughs for my file. Even my family deals with her loss like she was a beloved miniseries they watched a while ago and remember fondly. Everything sugar-coated and "glossified" into a completely different reality that doesn't help anyone.

Luke was the only one who understood my pain the way I felt it. Who was willing to face it head-on and let it bleed him dry like it was doing to me. It hurt like hell but it felt good at the same time. Necessary. Elena was still real when we were together. Her death happened and meant something. She was a three-dimensional part of our story, beautiful and flawed and angry and sad and strong.

When Luke left, he removed the only true connection I had to my sister and my grief.

"She was a beautiful person, inside and out," I explain, desperate for her to understand. "Deep down, he never thought he deserved her."

I study Luke's sleeping face. He looks like a completely different person than he is. He looks like the person he could be. "I think that's why he did the things he did."

"What things?"

I flinch again, kicking myself for going down this road. I

should have just left it at that. I avert my gaze, but end up with a direct hit in the mirror.

"You know, things," I hedge. "There are a lot of temptations out there. On the road. For us."

"He cheated on her?"

"A lot," I confess in a hesitant tone. "He never should have married her and he knew it. For her sake. He couldn't be the person she deserved. Not with the way things were for us. He couldn't forgive himself before, but especially after. God, you want to see a person who hates himself?"

She follows my stare back to Luke. A knife twists through my heart like it's happening all over again.

"And what am I supposed to do?" Now that the words are flowing, I don't know how to stop them. "What do you say to a monster you love who's finally figured out what he is?"

Fuck.

The unintentional mic drop sucks any remaining light from the room.

But I can't take it back. I shouldn't and I won't.

I also can't sit here and do this anymore. I've stalled enough anyway.

Time for the real nightmare to begin.

"I should go check on the party and see if I can wind it down," I say. "When I get back we'll try to get some alcohol out and water in."

My hand feels warm and relaxed in hers. I don't want to let go, but I have to. It's best for both of us if we keep whatever this was confined to a moment of shared sympathy.

With a quick squeeze, I force myself to let go.

Then get the hell out of there before I screw things up... again.

CHAPTER 7

$\mathcal{M}$y intentions of shutting the party down are derailed by Lou Clempson and his posse.

"I'm not doing this with you," I growl at the bitter songwriter as he blocks my path to the DJ. "It's late. We need to shut this down."

"Oh, right. Because you're *so* responsible now. How's that arrest record going?"

"Better than your Oscars shelf."

His mouth opens. Eyes bulging, he steps toward me, violence practically vibrating in his stance.

Yep. Should have kept my mouth shut, but this dude begs to be provoked.

"You have no right to that award!" he roars.

"An entire Academy disagreed with you. It's been three years since the snub, dude. Let it go."

"You would think it's that easy, wouldn't you?! You don't even understand what it means to win an award like that because you're not a real artist! You're a populist hack with a pretty face and nice abs!"

Hmm… maybe I got this situation all wrong.

ALY STILES

"Aww. Sounds like someone has a crush on me."

Hyped up on whatever he's got flowing through his veins, he lunges forward.

I step aside with a curse and keep moving toward the DJ. This guy isn't worth a lawsuit.

A hard shove from behind sends me crashing into a table.

"What the hell?" I shout, twisting back.

I duck as a fist comes flying at me, avoiding the hit, but not the mental strain of this bullshit.

This isn't even my party.

Furious, I fire a lethal look and reverse course back to the hallway. I don't have time for this shit. Not with the other— literal—mess I have to clean up.

I'll have to try again later.

I use the journey back to Luke's room to pull in soothing breaths. My ribs ache from the collision with the table, but it's nothing compared to the storm inside. I won't survive the night if I don't get a handle on the chaos in my head.

Luke is stirring when I return to the bedroom, which means it's time for the real pain. Callie hangs back as I drag him from the bed and heave his naked drunk ass to the bathroom.

"Get... the fuck... off me!" he slurs, swinging his arm.

I pivot my head just enough to avoid a direct strike for the second time in five minutes.

"No. Now shut up and move your damn legs. Less punching, more walking."

"You're a-a..." He can't finish the insult, so he twists out of my arms instead.

He almost goes down, and it takes every bit of strength I have to haul him back up.

At least he's conscious. That's a good sign.

We finally make it to the bathroom, and I slip into autopilot for the rest. It's the only way I can deal with this shit.

"I hate you," he growls as I wrestle him to the floor by the toilet, positioning myself on the cold tile directly behind him to keep him upright.

"Yeah, I know."

"No, really. You—"

I turn my head for the retching. God, I despise this part so much. My own stomach is thick with nausea, but we've just begun.

Luke slumps back, weak and covered in sweat. I lock him against me so he doesn't fall to the floor. His labored breaths quiver against my chest.

"I'm... a dick," he mumbles.

"Not now, Luke."

"No! I am. I-I love you. You... you're my brother. I don't deserve you."

I clench my eyes shut as emotion builds in my throat.

Fuck, I can't do this.

"Case? You know I love you, right?"

I can't I can't I can't...

"Tell me you know that!"

"Yeah, man. I know."

You love me enough to cut yourself out of my life. To make me wonder if a stupid party was an excuse to cut yourself out of living entirely.

Apparently it wasn't, but that's a question I'm going to have to carry at every pass.

In the doorway, Callie chews on one of her nails. I can only imagine what she's thinking through all of this. I hate that she has to see it, but maybe it's for the best. You want to love Luke Craven? This is what it means.

He lurches forward again, and I lean back to give him space.

When he finishes, I catch him once more.

I don't know how long this goes on. It feels like hours. Maybe it is. In some ways, it's a lifetime.

When we finally reach the point where the first round of

purging seems complete, I ask Callie for a wet cloth to clean him up. Then, we combine forces to get the patient back to bed.

I grab a water bottle and hold it to his lips.

"Here, drink this."

Luke swats at the bottle. "I don't want it."

"Drink it, you idiot." I tip the bottle as I prop his head up with my other arm.

His curses roll off me, along with the water dribbling from his mouth to his chest.

"Can you find a pair of boxers or something in his drawer?" I call to Callie.

She seems relieved to have something to do, and I know that feeling well. There's nothing more helpless than watching someone you love destroy themself.

After she hands me the shorts, she heads to the bathroom to see what she can do with that mess. As if I needed more evidence she's an angel in disguise.

Once we're alone, I peel back the bedsheet and do my best to slide the shorts on Luke. He's stopped fighting me now, and even lifts his hips to help. When I finish, I see he's holding the water bottle on his own, studying me with glazed eyes.

"You shouldn't have… come back."

I freeze. My grip tightens on the edge of the sheet.

His face is a mask of pain and confusion, and I swallow the riot of responses in my throat.

"Not now, Luke," I say instead.

"Yes now. You… You're better than this."

I snap a glare at him. "Better than what? You don't even know what you're saying right now. So just stop, okay? We'll talk about it later."

"Casey…"

"No! I'm serious, dude. I'm not having this conversation with you. Just get some rest and we'll deal with it in the morning."

He opens his mouth to respond but must think better of it.

Slumping back to the pillow, he's the picture of defeat. His haunted stare follows my every movement like I'm the freaking sun, moon, and stars. And the part I really hate? It makes *me* feel like the dick. Yes, suddenly I'm the villain in my own story.

But I can't bring myself to apologize. There's nothing to apologize for. That's the travesty of this situation. We're all just sorry about everything and nothing. Just shaking and disgusted and so fucking sad.

I press the heels of my palms to my eyes and try to catch my breath.

Get it together, man. You knew this is what it would be if you came back.

I can't break now. I have to—

Footsteps clap behind me, and I quickly drop my arms. With a ragged breath, I shove the pain back down. I've stored it there for twenty-five years. What's a few more hours?

Callie wears a concerned look when she comes into view, and I'm terrified it's for me, not Luke this time. She can't know what this is really costing me.

"He'll be okay," I say with as much confidence as I can muster. He's already drifting off again. "We'll get more water in him a little later."

"Casey."

I direct my gaze to her and grit my teeth. Whatever she's about to say, I can't hear it right now. Maybe she senses as much when she clamps her mouth shut. After a short pause, she seems to change course.

"Um... you can go enjoy your friends if you'd like. I'll stay with him."

And just like that, she punctures the cloud.

A slow grin escapes. I can't help it. The absurdity of it all...

"Are you kicking me out and telling me to go play with my friends?" I push to my feet with a smirk.

My shoulders feel like they're caught in a trash compactor. I roll my strained muscles, trying to relieve some of the pressure. People acknowledge the mental and emotional workout of these incidents, but you don't hear much about the physical toll. I'll be sore tomorrow.

"No, that's not what I meant, I just..." Pink splotches bloom on her cheeks, and it's almost as cute as her attempt to mother me. "If you want to... I like your company."

A trickle of warmth seeps in for the first time since she stormed away from me hours ago.

"Well, they're not my friends, anyway," I say. "I don't even know most of them. I'm not sure Luke does either."

I get a rancid whiff of my shirt and shudder at the thought of how I must look and smell. "I could use a shower, though. You never really get used to puke."

Her small laugh makes me feel lighter as well. "Not a bad idea. There's a nice one in the extra room, but what about all the guests?"

Right. Still have to deal with that. Based on the time, I might have more success than the previous attempt.

"I think it's late enough that we can wind this down without damaging Luke's reputation. Be back in a minute."

* * *

MAYBE IT'S the puke on my shirt. Maybe it's the later hour. Or maybe it's the fact that Lou Clempson reportedly took off in a huff after our altercation. Whatever the reason, my second try at shutting things down is much more successful.

Once I quiet the DJ and close the open bar, the exodus organically begins. When I'm confident things are moving in the right direction (i.e. out), I empty the guest room of partiers and strip down to test out the weird bedroom shower.

I've bathed countless times in my life, sometimes in amenities more absurd than this one, but this is by far the cleansing I needed most.

With the door locked and the thunder of water drowning out my thoughts, I close my eyes and let the powerful jets soothe the ache gripping my entire being. Inside and out, I feel the tension swell and melt away.

And with it, the last remaining tether on my turbulent emotions.

My eyes burn from more than shower water as I drop my forehead against the cold glass wall. Memories rush in. Some fresh and raw. Others ancient and crusted into fossilized pain.

Scene after scene mirrors tonight's horror. Blurred faces, fuzzy timelines.

Many in vivid detail I will never escape.

Each one gets a screen in my head, blaring and crowding in until it feels like I can't breathe.

The weight in my chest grows with each stifled trauma, until I have no choice but to let it out.

Tears blur my eyes. The sound of my choked sobs echo around me in a surround sound of buried grief.

God, I'm trying so hard. Giving every damn breath I have to survive and keep the people I love alive. And it's still not enough. It's never enough. I couldn't save Elena, and now I'm watching Luke slip away right in front of me. *Again!*

I'm not enough for the band.

For the Label.

For the fans and the masses who expect me to be Luke, and hate that I'm not.

That's what it all comes down to, doesn't it? Trying to hold the world together while being punished over and over for the choices of someone else.

And still, I love him. *Still,* I come back.

I scrub a hand over my hair, gripping the wet strands as I

drive my head into the wall with slow, weak hits. A sickening beat forming the steady rhythm of my failures.

Salty drops mix with the streams of water down my cheeks. My quiet frustration mercifully drowned out.

I gasp in air, fighting to pull myself together. I don't have a choice. I have to get back to Luke. There's never time to worry about myself. I have to make sure...

Except, this time Callie's there. She has him for now.

I pull in a lungful of air. Water pelts me from all sides, and I spend the next few minutes focusing on the physical sensation so my brain can relax.

The storm quiets.

The dizzying trauma reels fade.

I'm finally able to straighten from the wall and turn my face into the stream to let it cleanse me back to the man I want to be.

* * *

I REMEMBER an entire shower too late that I didn't bring a clean change of clothes. I came right from my previous hotel, so all I have is the small carryon I packed that was supposed to be for a quick overnight trip.

Good thing Luke and I are about the same size.

After wrapping a towel around my waist, I head to his room to raid his wardrobe. In the opposite direction, I hear the clatter of the main suite door, which means more people are leaving. The riotous atmosphere has faded into the din of murmured conversation. Hopefully, by the time I'm dressed, I'll only have a few stragglers to deal with.

Callie looks up when I enter the room, and I manage a bright smile. I do feel a lot better than I did a few minutes ago.

"Man, you weren't kidding!" I say, running a hand through my wet hair.

Her gaze locks on me, but she doesn't speak. In complete

silence, her eyes roam over my body in slow perusal like she's mad at me again. Or confused. I don't know, but it's awkward as hell.

I break the weird staring contest by turning my attention to Luke's dresser.

"Have you tried it? The wall one?" I call back in an effort to make conversation. "Completely ridiculous."

"This morning, actually," she says finally. "Well, I guess, technically, it was yesterday at this point."

I find a pair of jeans that should fit and tug them on beneath the towel. Callie's back to her silent treatment, and I face her again while using the towel on my hair. Her expression is still a mix of reactions I can't interpret as she watches.

Intense hazel eyes scour my chest, down my stomach to my waist and...

Oh.

Hell.

Yes.

I suppress a grin and decide to torture her instead. Just for fun, I adjust to a more relaxed position against the edge of the dresser, leaning back in an open invitation to look. On cue, her gaze drops to the newly exposed skin along my hips. It might be the first time in my life I'm grateful Luke is slightly bigger than I am, because these jeans are the perfect amount of loose right now.

"Who the hell needs a wall shower? What's that about?" I say casually, as if I haven't noticed the energy shift in the room.

She shrugs. I don't even think she heard me.

This. Is. Amazing.

When she randomly climbs off the bed to leave, I can barely keep a straight face.

"Where are you going?" I ask innocently as she's forced to stop where I'm standing.

Her gaze darts to every point in the room except me.

"Nowhere. Just thought I'd take a break from this room for a while. Luke is doing fine. He woke up a second ago and mumbled some stuff that made no sense, but at least proves he's starting to work his way back to our world. Is it safe yet?" I swear she said all that in one breath.

So freaking funny.

"Out there?" I point toward the door. You better believe I'll drag this out as long as I can.

"Yeah, is everyone gone?"

I shrug and clench the edge of the dresser on either side of me. Her gaze lingers on the flex of my bicep. Down to my forearm. *And* back to some speck of invisible dirt in the ceiling.

"Got me," I say. "Probably. I cut off bar service, so I doubt anyone will stick around much longer."

"I'll go check."

Of course she will. But I can't let her off the hook that easily.

I school my expression into concern. "You got weird all of a sudden. You okay?"

She blinks back a panicked response before forcing the worst fake smile I've ever seen.

"Fine, yeah, just need a change of scenery for a bit, that's all."

I return a grave nod, because that makes so much sense. "Okay, sure. Let me finish up here and I'll meet you out front."

She pauses for a moment, waiting for me to move out of her way.

I could.

But I don't.

Her tiny dress means it's easy for me to see her chest move in a sharp inhale when she has to squeeze past me.

Also, she one hundred percent just sniffed me with that quick inhale.

I'm still grinning as I turn back to the dresser to find a shirt.

* * *

BRIGHT LIGHT STREAMS into the hall from the main living space when I head back to check on things. The murmur of indistinct whining and muttered curses drifts through the air, making it pretty obvious what's happening.

My grin becomes a straight up chuckle when I reach the end of the hall to see the blaring recessed lights igniting the room, and our girl manhandling a gathering of entitled A-Listers.

"Does anyone need a cab?" she calls in the perfect mix of sardonic sincerity.

No one bites, but she earns plenty of scowls as the irritated guests file past. For the record, from the look of it, she gives zero fucks. If writing doesn't work out for her, she'd be great at concert security.

I could watch this all day.

"Thanks, everyone," she hums. She even does the genteel courtesy wave she's probably seen on TV. I hold back a snort. "Thanks for coming. Actually, if you ask for Mara Jacobson in the lobby, I'm sure she'll be happy to book a room for you. Thank you."

Her suggestion is even funnier considering almost all of these people are here because they already have rooms.

"Oops, your purse..." the ever-alert hostess points out when a guest drops something. "Yes, there... Thank you... Thank you... Thanks..."

She snaps a look in my direction and goes still when she sees me. Her expression is somewhere between relieved and annoyed, and I love that I have no idea if it's because of me or her thankless task of crowd control.

I perform a slight bow, urging her to continue.

Her eye-roll is priceless, but she must want to clear this room more than banter with me, because she quickly regroups.

Thing is, she already kicked ass at kicking ass, and the place is empty.

Almost.

"You missed one," I joke as I come up beside her.

We stare down at the passed-out media mogul on the couch. The last time I saw this man, I was a starving artist and he was an opportunistic asshole shaking my hand with a toothy grin. It was a disturbing look for a man who'd just demanded a shady photoshoot at his personal residence in exchange for a feature in something. I don't even remember what.

I passed on the shoot.

"What do we do?" Callie asks, tilting her head like he's a problem she can't solve.

"That's Orin Cantea."

"Who?"

"Orin Cantea? Rhinehearst Media?"

Her irritated look stays glued to the snoring CEO. "Does that mean he freeloads on other people's couches?"

"Freeloads?" I laugh. "The guy is a gazillionaire."

She shrugs and turns back to him. "Good. So he has people that can come get him."

I blink at her in awe before shaking my head. Unbelievable. "Nothing fazes you, does it? Or is it, no *one*?"

"Probably both," she replies in a flippant tone. "I'm beat, but not ready to sleep. Want to watch a movie or are you ready to crash?"

That's an easy question. Only one answer involves spending more time with her.

Just one problem.

"What about him?" I say, staring back at Orin.

With an annoyed huff, she waves toward the loveseat against the far wall.

"Think we can move him over there so we can have the good couch?" she suggests.

I bite back another smile and nod. "Probably. You get his feet. I'll get the top half."

CHAPTER 8

*C*allie picks a horror movie. Of course she does.

I couldn't care less what's on the screen when she drops down directly beside me. There's enough room on this couch for ten people, which means this growing attraction isn't one sided.

A smile plays on my lips as I remember her reaction to my accidental strip tease earlier.

"What's so funny?" she asks.

"Nothing."

I school my features and squint at the TV.

"Casey!"

"Shh. I'm trying to watch... what are we watching again?"

She shoves me, and my smile spreads into a grin. Especially when she eases against the backrest, tilted even closer to me. Our thighs are touching, and with her short dress, that's no easy thing to ignore.

It's easier than it should be, though, since it's her scowl when she's yelling at me I love the most. Luke warned me this would happen. He knows me too well.

I dismiss thoughts of Luke for now. I have to give my head

and heart a break if I have any hope of surviving Phase Two of his spiral.

Giving my tortured brain a rest is much easier than usual now that I have the world's biggest distraction cuddled up against me. I lean down to say something and clamp my mouth shut.

With her eyes closed and lips slightly parted, my pit-bull princess is out cold. I shake my head with a smile. The opening credits are still rolling on this stupid movie.

Now what?

I'm afraid to get up and wake her, but I also can't sit here without moving for the rest of the night.

I brush some stray hair from her face, hoping she stirs enough that I can shift her to a more comfortable position. When she doesn't budge, I try a slight skim of her cheek.

Damn, she's beautiful.

So beautiful it's making my innocent gestures feel creepy. I shouldn't be touching her when I'm this attracted to her.

I do my best to shimmy out from under her and gently lower her to the cushions. I grab a decorative blanket flung over the back of the couch and secure it around her.

Curled up and tucked in the fuzzy cocoon, she's back to being the wide-eyed girl from the diner. It's nearly impossible not to return to the couch and draw her into my arms. I just want to hold onto her forever. Ensure all the terrible shit that's happened to me never happens to her.

Case-in-point: the jerk on the other couch.

There's no way in hell I'm leaving her alone with that predator, so I make another attempt to wake him. When words don't work, I shake his shoulder. He swats my hand away, and I do it again.

"You need to go now, Orin."

He mumbles something and sinks right back into a deep sleep. I grunt in frustration as I scan his giant body. Callie and I barely dragged him five feet from the couch. There's no way I'm getting him to the door on my own.

With no other choice, I plop down at the end of Callie's couch on the side closest to Orin. If he wakes up, he won't be able to get near her without waking me. But I'll do my best not to fall asleep. I'm not taking any chances.

I reach for the remote and let the marathon begin.

* * *

LIGHT STREAMS in from the floor-length windows. Disoriented, I squint into the glare for a clue about my surroundings. I'm... somewhere. On a couch.

In Luke's hotel room.

I drop my head back to the armrest. Something soft tickles my skin, and I glance down to see the world's fuzziest blanket tucked around me. It still smells like Callie's citrus body wash, or whatever it is she uses.

Man, that's a dream to wake up to.

I don't move for a second, enjoying the thought of her transferring the blanket to me. Then I remember the reason I gave myself a neck cramp on the couch instead of taking the huge guest bed.

The blanket dislodges from my chest when I push up to check the other couch. Thank god it's empty. Orin must have taken off sometime during the night. Good riddance. I still don't understand why Luke would invite that pig.

Oh wait. He didn't. His *concierge* did.

Yeah, we're going to be discussing that one later.

I order my aching body to stand. As feared, every muscle feels like it's been beaten with a hammer. If I never have to drag another body across a room, I'll be grateful. Guess that means serial killing is out.

Callie is nowhere to be seen, and a wave of panic runs

through me when I squint toward the door and find her bag missing. What if everything that happened last night freaked her out? Luke's illness. My flirting. Did I come on too strong? I barely came on at all by my normal standards, but she's not the kind of woman I'm used to.

Oh god. What if Luke still doesn't have her number and I'll never see her again?

Shit. Luke.

I move toward the hall to check on my friend and freeze when I hear water running behind the guest room door.

Relief floods through me. That's either Orin or Callie, and there's no way Orin would stoop so low as to use a spare bedroom shower.

It's frightening how happy I am to hear running water, so I force myself to continue down the hall before this gets any weirder. When I reach Luke's door, I brace for the worst.

The shades are drawn, but there's still enough light for me to make out the lump on the bed. When it rolls toward me, I let my hand drop from the door.

"Hey," the lump croaks. "I'm good."

I swallow a rush of sickening nostalgia at the familiar scene. "Five or six?"

"Five."

Five out of ten on a scale of "passed out by a gravestone" and "rocking a stadium." Not bad for the mess he was last night. He's never above a six. Anything below a five would have been a "not good."

I stare at the floor, not sure what to do next. I don't know this script anymore.

"Okay. Well, let me know if you need anything. I'll order coffee and food. Also, I'm going to steal some of these complimentary toiletries, if that's okay."

"Of course. You can also charge whatever you need to my room."

"Thanks."

I start toward the bathroom.

"Hey, Case?"

I stop and pull in a quick breath.

"Yeah?" I turn to face him again.

Luke is sitting up now. I can't see details of his face, but I can tell he's looking at me.

"I *do* remember some of last night. And I'm still a dick and I still love you."

My chest goes tight. My fingers clench around the door frame.

"And I still believe you," I force out. "Take a shower and let's get some food in you."

He doesn't stop me when I duck into his bathroom and raid the pile of hygiene products.

The water is still running in the guest room on my way back to the living room. After ordering room service, I clean myself up in the half bath attached to the great room, brush my teeth, then settle in to brave my phone for the first time in... well... almost a day. I don't think I've checked it once since I arrived at Luke's suite. There wouldn't have been anything on there I wanted to see, but I don't have an excuse anymore.

I stare at the long list of notifications with a sigh. Who knew becoming a twenty-five-year-old rockstar meant you'd have a hundred overbearing parents constantly on your case.

TJ: CALL ME. Why is everyone talking about a party in Luke's room?? You better be working on those tracks.

I ignore that one for now. Our manager is just going to yell at me, and it's too early for that many expletives.

Sweeny and Eli must have heard the rumors as well because they want to know what's up and why they weren't invited. That could get messy, so I assure them the rumors are overstated and they didn't miss anything. They probably won't see my response for a few more hours anyway. It's only ten in the morning here which means it's... bedtime for them there.

The next one sends a chill through me, so I ignore it completely.

My email inbox is even worse. The Label is still pissed about Kara Corbin and demanding something. I don't open the message to see what. The preview was enough. There's an attachment though, and that's never good.

The weekly reminder about my "contract obligations" is a separate email.

Below that is another request from a publisher about a book deal. I can't help but wonder if people would be so interested in cashing in on my life if it *hadn't* gone to shit in such spectacular fashion. Funny how The Rise is a fleeting news article and The Fall is a blockbuster bestseller.

I'm more than relieved when the food arrives. Not only am I in need of an interruption, I'm starving. Other than the few snacks last night with Callie, I haven't eaten a full meal in... I don't even know how long.

I didn't really have a plan when I jumped on a plane. I still don't. Everything feels contorted right now. Like I'm running down a path and just realized there is no path and I have no clue where I am.

Thank the heavens for pancakes, eggs, and coffee.

And Callie.

I hear her before I see her. Her hair is wet and she's back to casual street clothes.

And I still can't take my eyes off her.

I forget to chew the eggs in my mouth and almost choke as she approaches. I swallow them down and fight not to cough like an idiot.

I'm afraid I didn't pull it off when she frowns and scans me with an expression I can't interpret. Hopefully, she's just hungry and in desperate need of coffee. I can't take two grumpy suitem-ates at once, and I don't see Luke taking on the role of resident bundle of sunshine.

"Morning. I had some food sent up if you're hungry," I say with a wave toward the dishes on the island. I had to scrub away substances I don't even want to think about to accommodate the family-style dishes I ordered. I never know what, or if, Luke will eat, so we go with a mini buffet on days like this.

After one peek at the mess when they delivered room service, the hotel employee assured me housekeeping would be up shortly. Hopefully, they're sending an entire crew. I'll be raiding Luke's wallet for the tip on that one.

Callie plops down on a stool, staring at my hair like it's offending her.

To be fair, other than the quick check during my cleanup, I haven't looked at myself today. It's possible I'm kind of a mess. I run my fingers through it, trying to determine by feel if my appearance is scowl-worthy.

But when her gaze catches mine, it darts away like it did last night in Luke's room when she… oh shit. She's checking me out again.

Well, damn.

I shove a forkful of eggs in my mouth to stay cool.

"You sleep okay?" I ask.

After another short silence, she seems to warm up to the idea of post-party breakfast. I have to remember this isn't her normal.

She lifts the lid on the first dish to inspect its offerings. "I think so. You?"

I wash down the bite with coffee. "I guess. What'd you think of the movie?"

Her sardonic look and eye-roll is worth the price of admission.

But the amusement fades too quickly.

"Have you checked on Luke yet?" She shoots an anxious glance toward the hall.

Ah. Right. The real reason she's here.

"Yeah. He's fine. He's awake, actually. Working up the energy for a shower."

"Good. Thanks. I should have done that before my own. Sorry."

Her words grate on me, and I focus on my plate to temper the rising irritation. Not at her, just... I can't stand the thought of her going down the same road I have to travel. She deserves so much better than that.

"You're not his mother or his nurse," I say. "Your life doesn't have to revolve around taking care of him."

"Says the guy who literally had to wash his puke off last night."

I cringe inwardly and manage a wry smirk. "You know what I mean. I think it's great that you're looking out for him, but you can't be consumed by it. You can't let it define you or you'll start to internalize his issues and judge yourself for things you can't control."

Please don't become the villain of your own story too.

She's way too special for that.

"You've been there," she says quietly.

I snap a look at her, annoyed I revealed so much. "There's only so much you can do, Callie. You can't force someone to heal no matter how much you care about them. Not if they don't want to."

She averts her eyes, and I'm afraid I screwed up again.

For all my years with Luke and celebrity life, I still don't know how to navigate this. I feel just as lost as the first time I returned to our room to find my best friend unconscious from going too far in his attempt to silence his demons.

Years later, we've only gone backward, it seems.

Something about this time feels different, though. From the

moment I saw Luke last week, I felt it in the air. There's a finality that wasn't there before. A resignation that makes my stomach churn and keeps a constant chill running through my veins.

Something is very wrong, but that's not the only difference.

There's also a chance I won't have to be alone in my quest to drag him back to the shore this time.

I don't want to scare her, but the thought of Callie leaving scared *me* this morning. I can't do this on my own, and neither can she. We don't have the luxury of taking things slow.

"Hey, so hear me out," I say, watching her closely. "We wrapped up our tour last week and I was thinking of crashing here for a while and seeing what we can do about Luke. Maybe between the two of us we can make some progress?"

Her expression fans through varying states of shock, and I pray I didn't just blow things up before they even began. It's not just my life on the line for this one.

After a long pause, she shifts on her stool. I hold my breath, waiting for the verdict.

Her eyes brush mine before returning to the counter. "Yeah, I mean, if he's up for it. I guess it would be fine to have you around more."

Relieved—and amused by the glowing vote of confidence—I can't help a short laugh.

"Thanks?" I say in a wry tone.

Her blush tells me all I need to know about her true feelings regarding the arrangement. Thank god.

"Sorry, I didn't mean... I meant..." Her brows furrow as she picks at an imaginary scratch on the island. She makes this too easy.

"You meant, 'Why Casey Barrett, I am simply tickled at the thought of seeing your sunshine-lemonade face every day!'" I tease in my best southern belle voice.

"Hey!" she counters in faux offense. "I do *not* talk like that!"

"True. Except when we're on our motorbikes."

I'm rewarded with a light smack on the arm. She even had to reach hard for that.

I hold up my hands in mock surrender. "Okay, okay. Sorry."

"And anyway, so what if every other thing out of my mouth isn't about 'effing the establishment,'" she quips.

I almost choke on another sip of coffee. "*Effing the establishment?* Oh my god, you can't even curse in your mock quotes!"

Her eyes narrow in the most adorable glare. "What? So that's a thing? Making fun of someone for their lack of cursing?"

I can't believe we're even arguing about this. I haven't had this much fun in forever. "Please, please do me one favor, though. Call it 'foul language,' not cursing. I just need to hear it once."

She smacks me again, and I pretend cower while stifling another snort.

"And also," she continues in a miffed voice that would make Ms. Pierson, my violin teacher, proud. "I like that you were more concerned that I didn't use the word 'fuck' than the fact that I basically called you a stereotypical anarchist rocker."

The snort escapes. "You just said it."

"Said what?"

"Fuck."

Her look of vexation is pure art. "Seriously? What are you, eight years old all of a sudden?"

If this is stressing her out, she would absolutely hate it on the road with us. "I'm just pointing out that the universe didn't explode. I doubt any old ladies even died from it." With the exception of Ms. Pierson, maybe.

I get another eye-roll and the cutest smug expression I've ever seen. "So that's twice now," she says, crossing her arms.

"Twice what?"

"Twice that you've skipped over the part about raging against 'The Man.' Is that your thing or what?"

God, I love this girl—and hate how much I'm reading her to see if she *wants* that to be my thing. It's hard to judge her thoughts when none of the rules I'm used to apply.

"I don't know. Maybe it is. Maybe not." Deflection always works. "How much will it bug you if I don't respond?"

"Alright, that's it," she snaps, sliding off the chair.

Shit. Maybe I took this too far.

"What are you doing?" I ask as she reaches for her phone.

A cold sweat runs over me at the thought that my oasis is coming to an end. Is this the part where she wants a photo op to post on her socials? The inevitable point where I become a namedrop instead of a person?

"I want to hear your music," she says.

My panic doesn't know what to do with that one.

"What? Like, right now?" My voice sounds strained.

"Yes, right now." She grabs her phone and starts typing. My heart is thumping, and I don't even know why. "What should I start with?" she muses as she scrolls. "Oh wait, I know. I remember one of them from Luke."

Why the hell am I so nervous? Well, besides the fact that it's every musician's worst nightmare for their art to be heard through a crappy cellphone speaker.

I make a living from sharing my music. I've played freaking sold-out stadiums, and I'm chewing the inside of my cheek like I've just submitted my first demo.

Who cares what she thinks?

I do.

A lot, apparently.

I lean across the bar to try to see her phone. "What are you looking for?"

She tilts the screen away, and her playful smile eases some of my tension.

Then she plays the song she was looking for.

All humor drains out of me when the violent intro to "Argyle" scratches through her phone.

How the hell is this the one song Luke mentioned? The panic returns full throttle. What did he tell her about me?

"That's the one song Luke talked about?" I ask, probing as casually as possible.

Please don't know everything. Please.

Her nose scrunches as she studies me. She must be able to tell I'm rattled. "In passing. It wasn't in reference to the song itself, but something about guitars and tuning? It just happened to be the only title I remembered."

Oh thank god.

A huge weight lifts. "Yeah, the guys like to tune down half a step so they can play it open."

Did I write the song in D-flat to be a dick? Absolutely. That was the whole point of the song.

"Who wrote this one?" she asks, triggering another spike of anxiety.

"All of us, like everything," I answer, but I must look as shady as I sound.

She seems to have no intention of dropping the issue. "Okay, then who had the original idea for it?"

I wince, caught in an impossible trap. This is an easy question with an easy answer. *She's* the one who's making it hard because she doesn't ask questions the way most people do. She looks for more. For the secrets behind the question, and that's a place I'm not ready to take her. I like her too much to lose her to my shadows.

"What do you think of it?" I ask instead.

She scans me for a second, like she knows I'm deflecting.

Please let this go.

"Honestly, it kind of sucks," she says in a serious tone. "I'm more of a country girl."

My stomach sinks, but she can only hold the straight face for a split second.

I breathe a sigh of relief when she grins.

"Liar," I say with a smirk.

Her chuckle removes the rest of the tension. "Yeah. I'm kidding. Actually, I like it a lot. Not what I was expecting."

"Really? What were you expecting?"

"I don't know, the way you guys talk, I thought it would just be lots of incoherent screaming and banging."

Screaming and banging? I shake my head with another laugh. "There's some of that."

"Yeah, but it's beautiful too, in a way. I love the strings in the chorus. Right there! That part you can hear under Luke's voice."

Her pensive expression tugs at me as she leans closer to the phone. She's really *hearing* it, despite the grating scratch of the music from the awful speaker. The fact that she specifically noticed the violin solo I did for that song means a lot too. Inserting my classic violin background into one of our songs for the first time was another F-U to my father.

For the record, listening to music without proper equipment should be outlawed.

"Wow. He's really good," she muses in quiet awe. "Like, really, really good."

I almost laugh again. "Shocking, huh? Bands generally prefer frontmen who can sing."

I get another eye-roll before she goes serious again. "That's not what I mean. I just never heard him doing his thing before, that's all. Well, that I recognized anyway. I never truly listened. It's like learning something new about him."

I swallow another uncomfortable feeling rising in my chest. "Yeah, this is a pretty old one, too. That's why I was surprised Luke brought it up."

I watch her face for any more clues.

"He was talking about the time your gear got stolen from the motel parking lot."

A burst of old anger shoots through me. I don't think I'll ever get over that one. "Oh yeah. That sucked big time. We were all broke to begin with, and of course, those bastards took off with most of my stuff."

"Luke said they took the stuff they recognized."

"Yes, and apparently drums and cymbals are pretty obvious, even in their cases."

"Well, thankfully you've recovered."

Not really. All the money in the world can't buy my very first kit. Something that symbolized my journey out of the ashes. It meant everything to me.

"Interesting choice," another voice says from behind.

We twist back to find Luke moving toward us. He gives me a curious glance, and I motion with my eyes toward Callie. He knows what this song really is—and that there's no way I'd choose it for any situation, let alone this one.

"You couldn't at least play our good stuff for her?" he says, deflecting.

I shoot him a grateful look.

"She picked it," I point out in the same light tone.

"I like it," she argues. "Besides, we were actually reminiscing about your gear getting stolen."

"Please tell me your reminiscing includes coffee," Luke grunts, scanning the counter.

"Here, dude." I slide the carafe toward him. "There's food too."

He cringes as he fills a mug. "Let's go with coffee first."

Stillness settles over us as the song continues. My nerves return, while Luke's expression takes on a careful consideration I haven't seen in years. It's like he's hearing this song for the first time. I don't know what to make of it, and stare down at my plate.

The music cuts out, leaving an awkward silence in its wake. None of us seem to know what's supposed to happen next. Least of all me with the riotous state of my head.

"You know, Casey wrote most of that one," Luke says finally.

Callie and I snap our gazes to him for different reasons. I fight the increase of my heart rate with a casual shrug.

"Black sheep, right?" I curl a weak smile.

Callie searches my face, and I pretend to be interested in my cold eggs again. She clearly suspects more than she's saying. Fuck. Can she tell this song is about my dad beating the shit out of me?

"It's basically what got us signed," Luke continues.

"Well, that and our devastating good looks," I joke before this goes any further.

Her gaze runs over me again, stirring a new kind of heat.

"She thinks it's pretty," I continue. A reassuring smile cuts across Luke's face like he knows exactly what I'm doing.

"Pretty? 'Argyle?' She would," he mumbles in a conspiratorial tone.

"I would? What's that supposed to mean?" Callie returns.

Luke shrugs and takes a sip of his coffee. "Nothing, I'm just not surprised, that's all."

I feel badly about turning this conversation on her, but it's better than where it was headed.

"Well, excuse me if I'm not dark and depressing enough for you edgy rockers," she quips.

Luke's amused gaze blasts me with a silent *"See? What did I say?"*

When Callie crosses her arms with a scowl, I'm officially hooked. "What? What did I do now?"

"Nothing," Luke says in a soothing tone.

But Callie isn't buying it and looks to me. I have no clue what's happening right now but it's funny as hell.

Her ire seems directed equally at both of us. "Fine. I should probably get going anyway," she fires back as she slides off the stool.

Hang on. Is she seriously upset? Now I feel like a dick.

"Callie…" I reach for her as she brushes past. "We didn't…"

She rips her arm away and stalks toward the hall.

"Callie!"

I stare after her, still not sure what's going on. We've been bantering since the moment we met. How did it turn into this?

"Let her go," Luke says, probably sensing I'm about to run after her.

"What just happened?" I ask in bewilderment.

"Stress. Fear. The sudden realization that she's totally out of her element and has no idea how to process all this shit?"

I blow out a breath and run my hand over my head. "Right. Yeah. This whole thing can't be easy on her. Last night was… a lot. It rocked me. I can't imagine what she must be feeling right now."

He lowers his gaze. Guilt washes over his face, but we have bigger problems at the moment.

"I'll go talk to her," I say. "Make sure she understands we're the assholes in this equation."

Brows furrowed, he glares into his mug. "Pretty sure I get the crown on that one. I should talk to her."

"No, seriously. It's fine. She and I have been going at it all morning. I thought it was in good fun, but maybe I've been misreading the situation." My stomach grinds at the thought that all of this was in my head.

"No, man. Trust me. She's into you."

I shoot him a look. "How do you know that?"

"It's pretty damn obvious. She's never looked at me the way she looks at you. The chemistry you two have is off the charts, but dude, you know what that means, right?"

I roll my eyes. "You're not seriously going to give me the protective big brother speech, are you?"

"Do I have to?"

Nothing squeezes my heart more than the thought of hurting that woman. "No. I understand that, man, believe me. She's different. She's special. And we need to make sure she knows that."

I push away from the counter, but he grabs my arm.

"Please, Case. Let me talk to her. After last night… I have to explain and try to make things right."

My insides twist with mixed emotion at his plea. "You *can't* make things right. You get that, don't you?"

His shoulders drop as he releases me, his gaze drifting to the empty hallway. "Yeah. Of course. Doesn't mean I shouldn't try."

I search his expression and find the pain and sincerity I'm looking for. After a brief silence, I sigh and rub at my face. "Fine. Just… don't lie to her, okay? You can jerk me around all day, but not her. Don't make promises you know you can't keep."

He flinches, but I don't regret it. The time for being gentle has passed, and if we're going to fix this, we're going to have to break some shit.

I hold my breath until he nods. "I'll be straight with her. I promise."

"Good."

He smacks my shoulder with a "wish me luck" expression before following after Callie.

To say I'm jealous, and still nervous about what's about to happen, is an understatement. This feels like one of those crossroads moments—Callie will have to decide if she's going to stay on this convoluted path with us to heaven knows where, or run back to the security of her own world.

I know I shouldn't, but there's no way I'll be able to sit here pretending to eat congealed eggs while a life-changing conversation is happening a few feet away.

Once I hear a knock, followed by voices, I creep down the

hall to hide just out of view. The door is still open a crack, leaving me relieved and terrified I can hear everything.

"You know we fought over who would come in here," Luke says.

"You lost, I guess?" she mumbles.

I shake my head in frustration. She really has no idea how special she is.

"No, I won!" he laughs in the same disbelief I'm feeling. "God, Callie, don't you get it? We don't *want* you to be like us! We want you to think our music is pretty and tell us when we're being assholes. You have to stop thinking that the gap that separates us is because of a shortcoming on your part. Did you ever think that it might be on ours?"

Damn. No wonder he's the wordsmith of the band.

"I can be a major pain-in-the-ass," he continues. "I know that. Last night…"

I see clear images of his struggle to explain when he pauses. I've seen it so many times.

And I need this time to be different. For so many reasons. If it is, it will be because of the girl in that room.

"Anyway, my point is, I'm sorry," he says in a sincere tone. "I'm sorry for last night. I'm sorry for this morning. I have a ton of issues, but I never want you to think you're one of them, okay?"

Another long silence follows, and it's everything I can do not to burst through the door. I hear movement, and a twinge of jealousy runs through me when I guess why. Callie's muffled voice when she speaks confirms my theory that they're hugging. I fight the ugly feeling spreading through me. This moment isn't about sex, but once again I'm reminded that I'm the third wheel in this relationship.

"I was so scared last night," she says quietly. "I didn't know… I mean, you… I hated seeing you like that."

More silence. I clench my fists. I really need to leave before I hear something I can't unhear. They're not doing anything wrong. *I'm* the piece that doesn't belong.

"That used to be normal," Luke says.

"I know."

"Casey told you."

I cringe at the accusation in his tone.

"Casey loves you and is probably the best friend you have." Her voice is firm and almost threatening. "No. You need to listen to me, Luke. Last night it was *Casey* who took care of you, not me. It was Casey who wiped the puke off your face and nursed you back to health."

She stops. "You need to let him back into your life."

A sharp breath expels from my lungs. I scrub at my face as every part of me wants to run from his response, but I can't move. I have to know. After all this time, I need the honest truth.

Does he want me in his life?

"I can't," he says.

My heart cracks open.

Years of memories burn behind my eyes, peeling away any lingering scraps of hope.

He doesn't want you.

You're not enough. You failed him. Like you failed Elena. Like you failed the rest of the band, your siblings, and probably Callie too.

I slump against the wall, crushed beneath an unbearable weight.

"You have to," Callie says.

"You don't understand."

"Okay, then explain it to me," she challenges. "We're past the 'no personal stuff'… He's a good person, Luke," she says when he doesn't respond. "And after what I saw last night, I'd venture to say, better than both of us."

I lift my head in surprise. Does she really believe that?

"What?" Callie persists when Luke *still* doesn't respond. "I don't know if maybe you've had a falling out in the past, but he wants to make it right again. He wants to be a part of your life."

"He can't be part of my life," Luke spits finally. "I'm not doing that to him again."

Luke bursts into the hall before I can react.

Time stops when his startled gaze locks on me. A flurry of emotions streams across his face, but I can't read them. Without a word, he takes off toward his room.

I can't move, stuck between wanting to go after him and run like hell.

All I know for sure is that I can't let Callie find me spying as well. I fight to remove all evidence of my fractured heart from my face as I rush back to the kitchen.

I pick up my phone as a cover, but don't even unlock it. My brain is in a tailspin.

She can't see me like this. She can't know I'm breaking apart inside. I'll have plenty of time to shatter after she leaves, because there's no way she's sticking around with what I just heard. I never should have trusted Luke to handle that delicate situation, and the fact that it fell apart over *me* stings that much more.

As usual, I'm going to pay the price for his choices. And based on the way my heart leaps and aches when Callie comes into view, the cost might be more than I bargained for.

Her devastated expression says it all. I'm about to lose the only remaining things I care about...

Again.

CHAPTER 9

*D*amage control. That's all I have left. If she's going to leave, I have to make sure it's without a lawsuit or headline that will blow up our lives even more.

The way she stalks toward me with determination is a bad sign.

"You're still mad," I rush out. "I'm sorry, we didn't—"

Her arms shoot around my waist, her head drops to my chest, and she squeezes tight.

Stunned, I inhale sharply and pull her close.

My eyes slip closed as I let the strange warmth spread through me. I don't even know the last time I've been hugged by someone without an ulterior motive.

"What is it? What's wrong?" I ask gently.

It doesn't even matter what her answer is. She's still here.

She burrows closer. "I want you to stay," she says faintly. "No matter what happens, what he says or does, you need to stay. Please?"

She leans back to lift sad hazel eyes to me. Our gazes lock, and something shifts between us. I don't know what any of it means, but all I can do is nod.

I'd do anything for her in this moment. The fact that what she's asking is a desperate plea on behalf of all three of us is a testament to the person she is. Another small bud of hope curls up from the depths of my soul.

I can't save Luke. Neither can she. But we can save each other from the abyss that will threaten us when we try.

She drags her gaze away and settles close again.

"I can't help him alone, Casey. I know that now. He needs you. I need you too."

I rest my cheek on her damp hair. She feels so small in my arms, yet strong at the same time.

"I'm not going anywhere."

My tone may be soft, but my oath is not. I understand what I'm committing to better than she does.

"Promise?" She tilts her head toward me again.

I return a confident nod. "Promise."

Her weak smile breaks my heart. It's her compassion leaking out. Her genuine love for Luke and her sudden awareness of how close she is to losing him.

She turns trusting eyes to me, her hope and her rock. For me to be either, we have to lay it all out.

"He told you he wanted me gone, didn't he," I say on an exhale.

Her slight cringe doesn't surprise me. Those words hurt even more the second time around.

"Yes, but not for the reasons you'd think. I actually think it's because he believes he's bad for you. I think he's afraid he'll drag you down with him." She takes a quick breath. "He said 'again.' What does that mean?"

My stomach drops. Old trauma rallies with fresh fears. I don't even know how to begin answering that question, but I'll have to start if we want any chance at fixing this.

"Please, Casey, I'm tired of being involved in your lives and yet not knowing anything. I don't know how to help, how to even act, when I'm around you two."

She's right. We'll get nowhere if we keep avoiding the fundamental reason we're here.

Like a good hypocrite, I check the hall to make sure Luke isn't eavesdropping, then lead her to the couch. This beast of a story is a "sitting down" conversation.

I pull her to the cushion beside me, and we shift to face each other. But once her wide, expectant eyes are trained on me, my courage drains away.

I don't even know where to start. What's the beginning of this story? The middle? The end? It's all just a mass of pain folding in on itself.

All I can do is pull at a thread and see where it goes.

"If you think things are bad now, you should have seen what happened after Elena," I begin. A sharp twinge moves through my chest at the mention of my sister.

"Luke completely imploded," I continue, fighting a swarm of memories threatening to surface. "I doubt he even remembers the first month. The band took a hiatus, everyone understood, and the publicity actually helped us. You know how tragedy goes... Well, as long as it's not your fault."

I study the weave pattern in the area rug as the words build into an avalanche. "And it wasn't, and the media had a field day with it. Our Label didn't help matters and sucked every last dollar and headline they could out of Luke's devastation."

Bitterness is creeping into my voice. I swallow it back down and turn off my heart as much as possible. It's the only way I'll be able to tell this story.

"The problem is, it kind of was his fault. Not in an obvious way, a criminal way. But the kind of way that tears you apart inside and turns compassion into poison."

ALY STILES

"Stop asking how I am! Don't you get it? I should be asking you! I'm the only person in this entire situation who doesn't deserve that question. You want to ask something? Ask why the fuck you're still here."

I shiver through the vivid memory. The scent of soggy earth and cut flowers. The sting of ice cold pellets of rain. The fear that I'm going to die because *he* wanted to die.

"Everyone said he just needed time... and space," I recall quietly. "Even the other guys let him go. They wouldn't have known what to do with him anyway, but I couldn't. I stuck by him."

I dare another look at her and wince from the concern echoing on her face. I still don't understand how she can care so much, but it feels good to finally let some of this poison seep out. I spent plenty of time in therapy trying to sort through it, but no therapist ever looked at me the way she is now. They're paid to keep walls between you, not tear them down.

I didn't realize how much I needed someone to share my pain—*live* it with me—until this moment.

Luke's was the hardest kind to carry. The kind you had to fight for.

"Leave me alone."
"No."
"Casey! Get the hell out."
"So you can fuck yourself up? No."
Doors slamming. Fists flying.
Insincere words carving honest wounds.

I was never going to let go. He knew that better than I did.

I release a harsh laugh at the memory. "Oh, he hated me for it, believe me, and made nothing easy, but he was my brother,

118

and I couldn't just abandon him and take advantage of his pain like everyone else."

I sink back against the cushion, lost in another flashback. They're flooding in now. Mila Taylor's scathing public attacks. Lawyers. Threats. Flaming pitchforks and violent condemnation.

All the brutal screens are back to light up my skull.

"You know, at one point the Label almost cut me because I refused to be part of some major cable 'special' about the whole thing. I don't know why Sweeny and Eli did it, but they did. I guess the Label realized Night Shifts Black couldn't afford to lose both Luke and me, so they agreed to let me sit out the interview, if I agreed to participate in another tour. We had canceled the rest of the current one after what happened."

I feel her probing stare, but can't meet it this time.

"And Luke blames himself for almost getting you kicked out of the band?" she asks.

Two paralyzed bodies sinking into the mud.

"No, Luke blames himself for almost getting me killed."

She flinches, and I divert my gaze to the carpet again. It's a lot safer than her compassionate patience.

"I'm not an expert at grief, and I certainly wasn't then. I didn't know what to do with Luke, how to take care of him. I was full of my own pain too. All I knew was that I wasn't going to abandon him like everyone else. But I'll admit, in the beginning, I made the mistake of thinking 'being there for him' meant 'joining him.'"

The shadows are closing in again. Cold sensory memories creep through my limbs and freeze around my heart.

I flinch when warmth floods into my hand.

It happens so fast, so seamlessly. Her fingers lace with mine, and I hold on as the memories claw at my soul in a desperate attempt to drag me back.

"I tried to be the responsible one, but failed more times than not. One night..." The hazy nightmare gets caught on my tongue, and I swallow it back down. That moment will always belong to Luke and me alone.

"Anyway, we both ended up in the hospital, along with a ton of headlines the Label was not happy about. Unfortunately, since I'm not Luke Craven, I didn't get the grace Luke did. They basically gave me a choice at that point—distance myself from Luke and rejoin the band, or they'd drop me. So I had to make a choice. Career or friend."

"And you chose career."

I bark a laugh. "No, of course not. I chose Luke, but he wouldn't let me. We fought about it for days, and then suddenly, he just disappeared. Abandoned his house, his accounts, every-thing, and stopped answering his phone. No one knew where he went, including me."

That's not entirely a lie. Only the timeline. She doesn't need to know the arguments during "those days" led to the spiral that landed us in the hospital. In fact, the more I talk, the more I realize a lot of this story will have to be edited for public consumption.

And they want me to write an entire book?

"To this day, I don't know if he ran for my sake or his..." Okay, that one's a blatant lie. "But the result was the same. I had no other choice at that point. If I couldn't help him, I had to go back. So I did. Cleaned myself up, got back on track, and was thrilled when our manager called to say he'd finally heard from Luke. That he was here. I came as soon as I could, which was during our quick break before the Calisto Festival."

"The day you came to breakfast club." Light returns to her eyes. It's frightening and freeing how much I want to keep it there. What would it be like to chase the sun instead of where I've been for the last year?

"Believe me, I was in shock he not only let me in when I

showed up, but let me stay the night. It was a short honeymoon, as you saw, but at least we started talking again."

I smirk when I think about his text.

Come back. I need you too.

I still can't sort out what that meant, given what I found when I got here.

"He invited me to his party, right?" I manage to keep the irony out of my tone.

"He loves you." She squeezes my hand as if trying to convince me. "He does, he just hates himself too much to let anyone love him back."

I wince and look away again. It's amazing how she figured out in a day something that took me over a year.

"I know. I mean, most of the time I know. It's hard to believe that sometimes, but I try to keep hoping he'll let me back in at some point. I don't know how to help him if he doesn't."

A buzz erupts in my pocket, vibrating the space between us. We let go of each other as I reach in for my phone.

TJ. Of course it is.

In any other situation, I'd let the call go to voicemail, but I'll take a conference room full of angry record execs over continuing this conversation. While I don't regret anything I said, I've had about enough of what I can handle in one dose.

Might as well take the beating while I'm already down.

"I should take this. Give me a minute?" I say with an apologetic smile.

She returns it, and maybe she seems relieved for the interruption as well. That had to be a lot for her take also.

I push to my feet and accept the call.

"Casey, finally! I've been texting you all night. I even tried Luke."

"Yeah... Wait, what? Why would you do that?!"

"You weren't responding, and I knew you were with him last night. You're the band now, Casey. You have to answer your phone."

I scrub at my face and take deep breaths to calm my nerves. "No, I know. I just—"

"So you saw Luke yesterday?"

"Yeah."

"What about today? Do you know where he is?"

"Yes, I know where he is. I'm with him now."

"Great! Get him on the phone too. We can finally sort this out."

"No, it's not—"

"Casey! You're not understanding the position you're in. The Label is done waiting. That's what I've been trying to tell you. I had a call with Alberto last evening about the Kara Corbin situation. They are *pissed* and out for blood. You have until Friday to deliver a demo or everything's off and you're getting sued for breach of contract. You getting this? I don't care if it's fourteen seconds of Luke sneezing, I just need him on a damn track. Why can't you just get me that?"

"Because he's not ready!"

"Well, when will he be ready?!"

"I don't know. I'll figure something out."

"We don't have time for that! How are you still not getting this? We need that demo *now*."

"Dammit, TJ, I told you I know! I'm working on it!"

"I sure hope so. You better deliver this time. No more excuses."

"Okay yeah—"

"Look, you know how much I love you, but I can't cover for you anymore, Casey. You have less than a week to decide if you're in or out."

"Okay, just don't—"

"I can't go back to them and ask for anything else. They already conceded as much as they're going to."

"No, I know. Just don't call him again, okay? Call me if you need anything. *Me,* not him."

"Then answer your damn phone!"

"Okay—"

"I'm trying to help you, Casey. I'm on your side."

I take a deep breath. This conversation is going nowhere.

"Yeah, okay."

"Good. Take care of yourself, all right?"

"You too."

I can't hang up fast enough.

"What an idiot," I grumble to the phone gods.

Do all managers like to hear themselves talk so much? And he wonders why I never pick up the phone.

Then I remember Callie.

Shit.

"Sorry about that," I mutter. "You know, sometimes I wish my life was more shallow, but then I talk to TJ. He always snaps me out of it."

"TJ?"

"Our manager."

"Oh."

"Yeah… He's awesome at what he does, it's just unfortunately *all* he does. He tried to call Luke."

Her eyes go wide. "Oh…"

"Yeah."

Only TJ would think that was a good idea. Let's call the guy who blew up the band to harass him with mandates to put it back together. I'm surprised we didn't hear a phone hitting the wall in Luke's room.

My gaze crosses to the hallway as the gravity of my conversation with TJ sinks in. As irritating as his animated delivery can be, he's not an alarmist. If he's worried, I should be too.

Do I talk to Luke? Try to smooth things over? Maybe TJ's right. Maybe now's the time to finally have a heart to heart about the future of the band. It's not just my career on the line. Sweeny, Eli, the entire army of staff and crew who are already making arrangements to follow us around the country in the fall...

No. I can't bring it up yet. I'm still trying to convince him not to kick me out of his suite.

I have no idea how I'm going to pull off the impossible.

With a long exhale, I focus back on Callie. "We have four months before our next tour and they want at least three new tracks. We should be releasing an entire album and building the tour around that, but they know that's not going to happen. They're okay releasing the album next year if we can have some new material now."

Her expression sags with understanding. She read the part I'm not saying.

"But without Luke..." she finishes quietly.

I press the heels of my palms to my eyes and shake my head. "I don't know, Callie. I honestly don't. I mean, I've got some ideas, but..."

"Maybe I can help."

I drop my hands and stare at her. "What?"

She returns a shy shrug. "I mean, I've never written a song before, but I write a ton of poetry. Is it a lot different?"

Is it a lot different... jotting down some pretty words in a journal versus navigating the cannibalistic vortex that is the music industry?

Yeah. It's a lot different.

But I'm not about to take any chances with teasing her after what happened earlier. It's sweet that she wants to help. Of course she does. She probably would have made the same offer if I needed a kidney. It's just who she is.

I pass a quick look around the disaster of a living room.

Honestly, it could be fun to explore our creative sides together. Heaven knows we need something to fill the hours in this suite waiting for The Emperor of Brood to emerge from his cave.

My career-saving demo probably isn't the best project for our first collaboration, though.

I try to keep my tone as sincere and humor-free as possible. "Well, it's not that I don't appreciate the offer, it's just, I mean, it's not that easy. There's a lot of politics to songwriting. The band, the Label, legal stuff..."

"Okay, so we don't write for Night Shifts Black. We just write to have something to do while we hang out, and try to find you some inspiration."

Damn. Did she read my mind? A shiver runs through me at how in sync we are.

I search her face when a hint of doubt creeps into my head. People don't just give their time and talent without expecting something in return. I've been burned more times than I can count, in ways I never saw coming. By reaching the top, I've achieved the status of being the connected ladder rung people step on to reach their own summit.

"Really? You'd do that?" I try not to sound as skeptical as I feel.

But her casual shrug shows no sign of exploitation. She looks like it makes no difference to her if I say yes or no. This really is about me, not her.

"Of course. I mean, it's not like I do anything else with my writing. No one's ever even read it."

I study her in disbelief. "Wait, what? You've never shared your stuff?"

She chews on her lip with another shrug. "I never really thought about it. I write because it's part of me, but I could never actually be a real writer."

Huh? That doesn't make any sense.

"Why?" I ask in genuine confusion.

"Why?" she scoffs. "I don't know, because that's not realistic. You don't just get to 'be a writer' because you like to write."

My skepticism must be all over my face when her eyes narrow.

"Don't get mad," I say, holding up my hands. "I'm just not understanding what you're saying. You like to write, so write. Why do you have to put labels and expectations on it?"

Her brows knit, and suddenly it feels like we've landed at another crossroads. Maybe this is my chance to drag someone in the *right* direction for once.

"Show me something," I say before she can shut this down.

"What?"

"I want to see something you've written. I saw you come with a bag yesterday. You have to have something in there."

"Oh, you know writers so well?"

Is she serious?

"I *am* a writer," I remind her.

If she wants to play this game, fine, but she better brace herself. I may be easygoing on the outside, but I grew up sandwiched in the middle of nine siblings. I'm as competitive as they come.

She looks genuinely confused as I leave her on the couch to head down the hall. After retrieving my carryon from the office beside the second bedroom, I make my way back to the living room. She hasn't moved from the couch and looks just as bewildered as when I left.

"I kept my stuff in the office," I say as I comb through the contents of my bag. I may not have brought clean clothes or toiletries, but I never go anywhere without the most important things.

I find the beat-up notebook and tug it from the space beside my laptop.

"I do all my serious stuff on the computer, but carry this for any spurts of unexpected inspiration."

Her eyes fill with understanding, like she knows exactly what I mean.

I flip it toward her and she stares at it. Her gaze scans the cover, then my face, like this is a joke. I motion for her to take it, and she tentatively reaches for it.

I get it. These journals are sacred. There are times I'm even hesitant to show Luke my unfiltered thoughts. But I really need her to see it. I need her to understand the only thing that separates my art from hers is my willingness to put it on display.

She finally seems to accept what's happening and flips through the pages with slow reverence. She stops on a maze of scribbles for a new song that's been haunting me for a while.

I'm relieved the words I wrote about her are safely on my phone.

"I know. It's kind of a mess," I say, explaining all the weird notations. "I hear the music in my head but it's hard to get it down exactly right without a guitar or piano, so I just make notes to myself for later."

"I thought you played drums."

I snort a laugh. She's too cute.

"I do. I also play guitar, keyboard, and violin. Well, with any skill, anyway. I dabble in a bunch of others, but those are my main ones."

"Then you probably sing, too." She says it like having another talent would be downright offensive.

I can't help but smile. "Yeah, a little. We back Luke up at the live shows."

"What's this one?" She holds up the notebook.

A wave of nostalgia washes through me.

"Oh, that's actually the rough outline for 'Fourth Chair.'"

While I remember where I was when inspiration struck for most of our songs, that one was special.

We were on a flight to Australia when someone recognized us. Well, recognized *Luke,* like usual. The person gushed and gushed and gushed, while I sat right next to him. It wasn't until the very end that they turned to me hesitantly and asked if I was in the band too. The way they clutched the paper they had him sign made it clear they only asked to check if they needed my signature too.

I said no. I was just going to visit my chiropractor in Sydney.

Luke and I laughed about it the rest of the trip, but somewhere along the line, in the sleep-deprived haze of an endless flight, the stereotypical interaction hit harder than it ever had before. I've lived in other people's shadows my entire life.

"Wait, I think I know that one!" Callie says with way too much excitement. It's hilarious how hard she tries to stroke our egos to make up for not knowing who we were in the beginning. "It's about an orchestra or something."

An orchestra. My god. So funny.

I shake my head. "It's about realizing your dreams don't always match reality and accepting what is. That the world owes you nothing and will kick you in the face if you live like you think it does."

Her expression clouds with an emotion I can't read before she turns back to the pages. I watch her finger drift over the words and notations. Chills run over my skin as if she's touching me instead.

"*You're nothing but a fourth chair, baby,*" she reads quietly. "*Forget the lights, your day ain't coming. Roses are red but they're not for you, just remember they die for the first chair too.*"

Her smile when she looks up warms me from the inside out. I'm not used to seeing admiration like that when Luke is within reach.

"I thought Luke was the lyric king," she teases.

I shift on the cushion, not sure where this is supposed to go. I've never been here before. "He is. I just happen to have the orchestra background," I deflect.

"I guess. But apparently, you weren't very good," she teases back, and all tension lifts.

Another grin seeps out. For her. For memories that should be painful, but are now just important. That's what art does. Transforms the scars into something beautiful.

"At organized accompaniment? No. Not at all. My parents withdrew me from orchestra after a couple years, but I'm pretty sure the conductor didn't give them a choice. No matter how good you are, you eventually have to fall in line. I guess I just didn't always agree with the musical decisions of Strauss and Mozart."

She has a first-chair laugh. We should record *that* and send it to the Label on Friday.

"So you switched to drums and became a rocker," she concludes.

"Well, it wasn't that easy of a transition, believe me, but ultimately, yes. My parents were not on board, I can assure you of that." Understatement. "I was kid number seven, so according to the plan I was supposed to be a concert violinist."

Her brows lift in supportive indignation. "Really? Then who was supposed to be the drummer in a disgustingly successful rock band?"

I smile back with a quick shrug. According to my father...

Yeah, never mind. That asshole doesn't deserve even a passing thought in this special moment.

"Okay, your turn," I say, bringing the conversation back to where it belongs.

She sucks in a breath. Her teeth sink into her lip.

Is she seriously going to back out?

"What? I showed you mine."

"I know but..."

"Callie." I blast her with a challenging look, making it clear I'm not backing down.

After a short standoff, she huffs in resignation. "Fine. Give me a minute."

I'll give her an hour if she finally opens up and admits to herself the truth about what she is.

"I'm not a writer."

No, what she meant is *I don't have the accolades and validation of other people.*

Guess what. It's all bullshit. Sure it feels good for a split second, but it doesn't last. No amount of awards and charts can drown out the screams of self-doubt when they take over. If anything, the higher you climb, the harder it is. How do you top the last success? How do you please people who thrive on finding the flaws in others? It's a lot easier to surpass expectations when there are none. Once the bar is set, it's impossible to jump over it.

I twist back at the sound of shuffling, but it's not Callie returning with her notebook.

Luke hesitates as if he's not sure if he should keep moving forward or scurry back into hiding. I swear, he's become the world's prettiest, most talented cockroach.

"You can stay, you know," I say dryly. "I promise not to make you cuddle or talk about your feelings."

His lips twitch in the slightest arc. "Damn. That's the whole reason I came out here."

I smirk, relieved when he circles the couch to drop a few feet from me.

"What are you doing anyway?" he asks.

"Actually—"

"Okay, but you have to promise not to laugh…" Callie shouts from the hallway.

Luke's eyes widen, and I bite back a snort at what he must think is about to happen.

"Promise not to laugh at what?" he calls back when she steps into view.

She freezes. A terrified look spreads over her face.

Uh-oh.

"Um, nothing…" she mumbles before retreating back down the hall.

I ignore Luke's utter confusion. We can deal with that in a minute.

"Callie!" I yell after her. "Where are you going? It's fine! Come back!"

Nope. Nothing.

Well, shit.

"What the hell is going on," Luke asks, passing a look from the empty space behind us to the well-worn notebook on the table.

"She was going to show me some of her stuff," I say, more than a little disappointed. I'm dying to know what's in her head when all the barriers are down.

"Yeah, she writes poetry." His gaze locks on my journal. "I see you got the bible out. You let her see it?"

I nod and fall back to the cushion with a sigh. "I was hoping if I showed her, she'd open up."

"I bet it's good."

"I bet it is too."

He snickers. "Guess I'm not her favorite anymore. She never wanted to show me anything."

My stomach twists with a torrent of mixed emotions. Somehow that makes this situation better and worse at the same time.

Footsteps draw our attention, and Callie reemerges with a terribly executed fake smile plastered to her face.

"Sorry, guys! Just realized I had grabbed the wrong book. Got it now." She holds up her notebook, and we pretend that wasn't a flat-out lie. I'm just relieved she's changed her mind about sharing with us.

"You're back," she says to Luke as she joins us on the couch.

His easy smile jars me for a second. No one gets those anymore. "You know me. Just have to pout for a while, then I'm good."

He waves toward the notebook she's clutching to her chest.

"So Casey says you're finally going to let us see some of this mysterious poetry. Gotta say I'm jealous that I couldn't get a look after a month, and this loser got in after a day, but whatever. Let's see it."

She passes another deer-in-the-headlights look between us before staring down at her journal.

With tentative fingers, she pages through it slowly. Her other hand has the cover in a vise grip. For several seconds, I'm afraid she's going to change her mind and flee again.

"I told Casey this is my private book. Ideas mainly. I clean them up and do the actual writing on my computer." It comes out like an apology, which only annoys me. No one should ever apologize for their private art.

Besides, it's not like Luke and I don't understand the creative process. Does she think we poop out chart-topping hits? No. Every masterpiece was once a brain fart.

But I try to be sympathetic at how hard this must be for her. If you've never shared your work before, handing it over to be critiqued by Luke Craven and Casey Barrett of Night Shifts Black is probably not your first choice for a debut.

The thing is, we're not what she thinks. We're people too. Artists who worked our asses off to get where we are and who have the ability to meet other artists where they're at. In some ways it's easier for us because we've been there.

She stops on a specific page. Her jaw clenches as she skims the words, and I can almost see the moment she decides to let us in.

She looks up and scans us in another quick evaluation. I'm more than a little surprised when she chooses to hand the notebook to me instead of Luke. I thought for sure now that he was back in the picture, I'd be taking my place as Fourth Chair again.

I take the journal and reverently stare down at the words.

My breath catches. No fucking way.

Fractured images crash in again.

"This isn't you, Luke!"

"You don't think I know the monster I see in the mirror every damn day?!"

"Exactly! That 'monster' you're seeing isn't you! *It's a distortion! A lie your brain is telling you. Just like Elena—"*

"Don't," he growled. "Don't you dare go there. Not now. Not ever."

I smother the rest of the memory when my throat closes up. The more I read, the more my heart twists into my stomach.

Every word. Every image. God, it's exactly what I was trying to explain to Luke that day, but couldn't. I couldn't find the words in that moment, but this woman—this virtual stranger— found them hundreds of miles away.

"Holy shit," I breathe out.

I skim her face in amazement before landing my focus on Luke. Maybe he'll finally hear what I've been trying to say if it comes from her. If it comes like *this.*

"Listen to this," I say.

> "Mirror mirror, what do you see, when you look
>   at me
> Mirror mirror, what are you thinking, I see those
>   eyes staring
> Mirror mirror, what are you saying, it's always
>   something I believe
> Mirror mirror, you're a liar, so why do you
>   own me

Hello hello greetings from the inside
Hello hello framed in all your lies
Hello hello how you love to see me cry
Hello hello always so unkind

Mirror mirror, why the tears, you made me
Mirror mirror, who do you think you are
I made you!

Hello hello greetings from the inside
Hello hello framed in all your lies
Hello hello how you love to see me cry
Hello hello it's time to say goodbye"

She had to have been where Luke is to write this, but she's clearly not there anymore. She fought the mirror and won, which means there's hope. It also means she speaks his language in a way I never could.

This is why art is so important. It speaks in emotion. In connection. It reveals pieces of ourselves to each other in ways conversation can't.

"What else do you have?" I ask as I review the next page. And the next. There's a sense of desperation leaking in. If she's been there, then maybe...

"What? Nothing," she says.

No, that can't be true. I turn to another page.

"What else? I want to see the rest."

I'm crushed when she plucks the notebook from my hands.

"There is no more," she says definitively. "I mean, not here, not finished."

I shake my head and lean toward her, almost pleading. "It doesn't have to be finished. Please, Callie?"

I need to see it. I have to know more about that side of her.

The distorted mirror. I have to know if there's a roadmap to drag Luke back to the light.

"What's the last thing you wrote?" I ask.

A shadow passes over her face. She averts her gaze. "I don't really write much anymore."

"Why not?"

She shrugs, still not looking at me. "I don't know. I guess… Maybe there's no point? Like I said, I'm not really a writer. Well, not a real one."

No! I'm so sick of this.

"Will you stop with that?" I snap. "That's bull."

I feel Luke's surprised warning look. But he doesn't get it. Of course he doesn't because he has the luxury of not caring about anything anymore. I do. And so does Callie.

"It's not!" she fires back. Her defensive reaction fades back into the insecurity that's becoming a theme with her. "I just… I don't know."

I curb the urgency and try to be as understanding as I can. "Look, I don't want to pressure you, I just really want to see it."

"But it's not even finished!"

"So what? I know how the process works."

"Dude, she says she doesn't want to show you. Let it go." Luke cuts a hard look at me.

I flinch and sink back as the budding hope wilts around me. I just want them to see. I need someone on this journey with me. I'm so tired and alone and—

"No, it's fine. Sorry. Here," Callie says suddenly, handing me the book. "But like I said, don't expect too much."

Her gaze brushes mine, and I see the apology there. As usual, somehow she knows this is about more than poetry to me. Somehow she understands the secrets I may never be able to share.

I turn back to the notebook and voraciously skim the words.

"I think he likes it," Luke jokes.

"Hell yeah, I like it."

I read through a few more poems before circling back to the mirror one.

Melodies are already forming with urgent clarity I haven't had in a long time. I need to get them out. I have to.

"Dude, where's your guitar?" I shoot at Luke. His scowl returns, but I don't have time for that. "Come on, man, not now."

He gives me a hard look. "You know I don't play anymore."

"Yeah, and I also know you don't go anywhere without that piece of junk. Just get it for me and then you can sulk all you want."

Even the Sultan of Sulk cracks a smile. "It needs new strings. I haven't touched it in forever."

"You think I care about that right now? I'm not gonna play a show in the lobby, I just want to try something. Come on! Don't be a dick for once. *Please.*"

He hesitates for a fraction of a second before accepting the inevitable. He knows what's happening right now and doesn't have the energy to fight me on it. The infection has taken hold. Better he just gets me the damn guitar and leaves me to my illness.

While Luke heads back to his room, I return to the poem.

It's the chorus that's gnawing at my head. It will continue to torture me until I can form it into something tangible. A verse melody worms its way in. Another line of the chorus.

Where's Luke? What's taking him so long?

He finally returns with Percy, his guitar, and I grab it from him as soon as he's within range.

I already know it will have to be tuned, so I impatiently take care of that beneath Luke's silent humor. He's seen this a thousand times. He knows the manic artist I become when the music strikes.

Luke is mumbling something as he shuffles back out of the room, but I'm not listening.

Once I get the tuning as good as it can be under the circumstances, I work out the tempo in my head. I try a few keys with single strum progressions, humming the tentative melody until it finally feels right. Focusing back on the notebook beside me, I test out some melodies to solidify the line.

After a few more experiments, I finally feel ready to make a real pass at a full chorus. I have no idea what's going to happen, but it's been a long time since I've felt this kind of excitement. The buzz that comes with being on the verge of something. It's almost more addictive than when you find it.

I play and sing for a while. Stopping, starting, testing and adjusting. The chorus, especially, is turning into something worth pursuing. The verse, not quite yet, but I get completely lost in the adventure.

Movement in my periphery grabs my attention, and I remember Callie.

Right.

Callie.

I scratch at my cheek as embarrassment chips at the previous enthusiasm. Unlike Luke, she'd have no idea what's happening. There's a vulnerability to the challenge of transforming an idea into something tangible. It's hard enough on your own, let alone in front of a virtual stranger who doesn't understand the metamorphosis.

I feel almost nervous as I grip the neck of the guitar and build the courage to face her. What if she just lost all faith in me? I'm used to facing criticism and disdain, but I don't think I could handle it now. Not from her. For *this*.

She shifts on the couch, as if trying to get my attention, and I finally find the strength to meet her gaze.

A look of gentle wonder blasts away the fear. "That was amazing," she says, her gaze running over my face, the guitar, back to my face like she can't believe what she just saw. "I never thought my words could sound like that," she whispers.

The rest of the wall crumbles. There's nothing she could have said that would've brought greater joy. That's exactly what music is supposed to do and exactly what a moment like this is supposed to be.

A smile breaks on my lips as I return my focus to the guitar. Reassured, I let the music consume me fully and completely. If she wants her words to transcend, then lets shoot them into the fucking stars.

CHAPTER 10

I sent Callie back to wherever she goes when she's not in our mess to retrieve her laptop. It's funny how I hadn't really thought about the fact that she has another life somewhere else. She's become so embedded in my world, I forgot she wasn't a part of it until two days ago.

She has a story too. Dreams, trauma. Family? I don't even know. She learned more about me in one conversation than I've learned in the entire time I've known her. I need to do a better job focusing on her and not getting so wrapped up in my own drama.

I've just finished putting in a lunch order when Luke makes his way down the hall.

"I heard the door. She leave?" he asks.

There's a hint of panic in his tone I know well.

"Just to get her laptop. She'll be back. Hey, what do you know about her, anyway?"

"What do you mean?"

"What's her story? She just drops her life and moves into ours? Who does that?"

He frowns. "You say that like you don't trust her. She's not after anything, if that's what you're worried about."

"I'm not. It's just everything since she's been here is about us. Don't you want to know her story as well?"

He shrugs and leans on the counter. "She's shared some stuff. My honest opinion? I think she's just as lost as we are. Helping us with our shit is giving her meaning. You see how she is. She needs someone to fix as much as we need to be fixed."

I stare at my phone as if it's a sudden link to her. So she was searching for broken souls at the same time we needed an angel. Serendipitous or a cosmic joke? Guess it depends which side of the disaster you're on.

"You ordering food?" Luke asks, nodding toward my phone.

"Already did. I got you green curry. That okay?"

He lifts a shoulder in agreement.

"What about for Callie?" he asks.

"I got a few things. Figured we could share."

He nods and moves to the fridge for a sports drink. I feel his gaze on me as he twists off the cap, but pretend to watch my screen. I'm not sure I'm ready for whatever he's thinking.

"Case?" There's a crack in his voice that sends a chill through me.

"Yeah?" I say as casually as possible.

I look up and squirm at the way he scans my face, like he's struggling to say something, and my fingers tighten around the phone.

"You know it's not your fault, right? If anything ever happened to me... there's nothing you could have done to stop it."

I go ice cold.

His haunted eyes slice into me, stripping all words from my head.

He rips his gaze away. "Anyway, I just need you to know that," he mumbles on his way to the hall.

"Hang on," I call after him. "Dude, you can't just say something like that and walk away."

He turns back, regret all over his face. I hate that it's probably for opening up to me, not any of the million other things it should be about.

"I know. Forget I said anything."

Anger rises in me. "Not gonna happen. That's not something you can take back."

God, I can't breathe.

"Luke. Look at me."

He doesn't. Only the floor gets his attention.

Rage like I've never felt burns through me. "No! You're gonna listen for once. I don't know what asinine plan you have in your head, but after all we've been through, don't you dare do that to me," I seethe. "Don't you dare leave me alone with that kind of loss! *Luke!*"

His gaze lifts for a fleeting brush of mine before landing back on the laminate tiles.

"Say something!" My voice cracks.

He just shakes his head.

Because he doesn't want to lie to me again.

Because he knows he can't promise his mind isn't where I'm terrified it is.

Tears pound the backs of my eyes. My throat closes as my thoughts spiral into chaos. I don't know what to do, what to say. He needs help, but I don't know *how* to help. All I know is that he won't open himself up to the people who would.

A bang on our door interrupts the suffocating tension.

Relief flashes across Luke's face when housekeeping calls out, and he flees down the hall, back into hiding.

I remain motionless in the kitchen, staring into the shadows, shaking and lost.

"Housekeeping!" the hotel employee shouts again.

I hear the whir of the lock when the person assumes the

place is empty. The door opens, and the woman gasps when she sees me.

"Apologies, sir! I'll come back."

"No, it's fine. Perfect timing," I mumble.

She gives me a curious look, then scans the mess of the room.

"Yeah, um, sorry about this," I say.

Her weak smile is somehow the exact response I needed. "It's okay. My supervisor warned me. She said there was an... event... last night."

"Ha. Yeah. It was definitely that. Hey, I'm Casey. What's your name?"

Her surprise transforms into another smile. "Cameron."

I nod. "Nice to meet you, Cameron. Mind if I help?"

"Oh no! You don't have to do that. It's literally my job."

"This disaster?" I wave over the mess with a smirk. "This is no one's job. This is a hazardous waste site."

She chuckles and rolls her cart into the room.

"Seriously. You'd be doing me a favor. I need something to do."

She casts a nervous look at the door. "I..."

"If your supervisor sees us, I'll tell them I'm making the mess while you're following me around cleaning it up."

Her laugh eases some of the weight from my shoulders.

She shakes her head and sighs. "Okay, if you're sure."

I gather an armload of empty bottles off the counter by the fridge. "Where do you want these?"

She points to the bag, and I go back for another load.

For the next hour, I help Cameron erase last night and give us a fresh start.

* * *

LUNCH ARRIVES SHORTLY after Cameron leaves. I'm still opening the takeout containers when Luke ventures out.

I know better than to approach the volatile subject from earlier. Instead of words, I pass him a plate.

He takes a seat at the table and reaches for one of the boxes.

"Food's good," I say through a bite of drunken noodles.

He looks almost guilty as he scoops rice onto his plate.

"The room looks clean," he says, glancing around. "Guess housekeeping was here?"

"Yeah. Cameron. Did you know her daughter plays cello?"

"No. Is she the one with the long brown hair?"

"No, she had short red hair."

"Oh. Yeah. I know who you mean. Hold on, she has a daughter old enough to play the cello?"

"Right? I thought she was about sixteen when she came in. But no, she's twenty-nine."

"Dang."

I don't know how much longer we can drag this conversation out, but we're certainly going to try.

We're halfway through the roll call of every employee on site, when the door lock hisses with another visitor. Who just walks into his room without knocking?

We shoot our attention to the entrance, and Luke seems relieved when Callie tentatively pokes her head in. I'm glad to see her too, just... confused.

She shuts the door, and Luke waves toward the table.

"Thai," he says by way of a greeting.

She squints at his plate. "With your hangover?"

"Burns away the alcohol?" His grin is so out of place. It makes no sense with the rest of the morning. He's a completely different person when Callie's around. It's bizarre and...

She has a key.

He gave her a fucking *key*!

A cold sick feeling sinks through me.

God, I'm such an idiot.

"What, so she has a key now?" I blurt out.

Their intimate smiles for each other fade as they direct their attention to me.

"She's here all the time anyway. I gave her the guest room," Luke says in a casual tone that makes me want to throw things.

She's *living* here now?!

I can't believe how stupid I've been! All this time, he's pushing me toward her and she's flirting back and...

Was it all in my head? Some twisted game? What exactly is happening right now?

She lowers her bag to the floor and takes a seat across from me. Her gaze brushes mine before scanning the containers. So glad I was able to provide a lunch date for the two of them.

"It's more convenient, that's all," she explains in a further gut-punch.

Convenient? Convenient for *what?* There are very few things that require immediate access to a hotel room. None of them are things that aren't tearing at my stomach.

But it's not them I'm mad at. It's myself. For being so naïve and ridiculous. I barely know Callie. Just because I warned her about falling for Luke at breakfast a week ago, doesn't mean I own the playbook to their lives.

They're adults. Free to make their own choices.

And mistakes.

I've been watching Luke steal every person in the room since we first started playing together, including my own sister. Just because I finally convinced myself this time would be different doesn't mean it is.

She loves him. Of course she does. That's her choice.

But this changes everything.

My feelings for Callie aside, I don't think I can stick around to watch Luke destroy another sweet, trusting, beautiful person.

I just... can't.

I'll get what I need to keep working on the song, then leave them to their nightmare fairytale.

"Did you bring your laptop?" I ask Callie. My tone is colder than I intended but I don't know how to fake this.

She shoots a look at me but quickly averts her gaze. Guess she knows I'm onto them.

"Got it," she says.

"Okay, good."

"Heard you working on something. Sounded pretty good," Luke says in an attempt to lighten the mood. I almost bark a bitter laugh at the irony. So he's going to keep the peace now?

Whatever. I'm over it.

"Yeah. Got a call from TJ today…"

Luke's expression fills with understanding, and I'm just glad I don't have to explain more, because I don't feel like discussing anything right now.

"I'm surprised they weren't on your case sooner."

I grind my teeth. He has no clue what this last year has been like for me. Hit after hit after hit meant for him, but I was the one present to take the blows.

"They've been bugging me, but this was the first 'do or die' call."

"What do they want?"

Great question. I stare at him, not sure how to answer it. Part of me wants to flip him off and leave. The other part is in disbelief he even gives a shit enough to ask that question. Even if it's because he's trying to make conversation, it's more than I ever thought I'd get.

"New tour in four months with at least three new tracks."

His smirk grates on me. "Got tired of waiting, I guess."

"I'd love your help, man."

It's only in the tense silence that follows that I realize my words were part plea and part punishment.

I'm not remotely surprised when he won't look at me. "Yeah, well, that's not my thing anymore."

Of course it's not. Nothing is *his thing* except drinking and accidentally seducing the only woman who genuinely cares about him.

I have nothing to lose, so might as well go out with a bang.

"I know, but maybe if—"

Luke shoves back from the table. "Alright, well, I know I'm full. What about you guys?"

His dismissive tone hurts more than his abrupt retreat.

While he stalks away, I slide my chair back as well, fists clenched. I watch him go, forcing away the twinge of guilt clawing its way up my chest. We can't keep tiptoeing around him. Catering to him. Walking on eggshells because he's the king of the universe and the rest of us—

"You okay?" Callie asks.

Am I okay? No, I'm not fucking okay!

I don't even try to hide my frustration when I face her. She's just as guilty in this. Maybe more because she broke a promise. At least he never pretends to be better than what he is.

"You're living with him?" I spit out. "Why didn't you tell me you two hooked up? Don't you think you should have led with that?"

She winces, but those doe-eyes won't work on me anymore. I still believe she's genuine. None of it's an act with her. It's *me* who read everything all wrong. This is my issue, not hers, but I still need the truth.

"What? Whoa, wait a second. We didn't hook up."

I release a harsh laugh. "No? But you moved in?"

"It's not like that! I mean, I know what it sounds like, but it's not."

My anger falters at the urgency in her delivery.

"I didn't move in, I just keep some stuff here in case it gets late," she continues, eyes pleading.

My stomach sinks. I want to believe that. So much. It's just... history. Every bit of evidence in front of me.

"Come on, you know he's not ready for a real relationship," she says, searching my eyes. "I know you know that better than anyone!"

Yeah. I'm the one who warned her. And she...

Ah!

I scrub at my face. Evaluate hers. There's nothing but sincerity there. And something else. Fear. Why would she be afraid right now unless...

My pulse picks up. Her hazel eyes are screaming for me to believe her. There's no reason for her to fight so hard for a lie.

I release a breath, struggling to sort the mess in my head. Just because everyone else lies to me, doesn't mean she's not the one person who isn't.

"He's not, you know," I think out loud. I scratch at an imperfection in the table. "I'm not sure if he'll ever be. I warned you about that from the beginning."

She scoots closer, drawing my attention. "I know that, trust me. I'll admit in the beginning I had thoughts, but now I just care about him. I want to help him. Just like you."

Her eyes.

I consider everything I've seen. Everything she's saying. Would I even be questioning her story if jealousy wasn't a factor?

No. And the reality of the situation streams into sharp focus.

I'm falling for her.

I want her to look at me the way everyone else looks at Luke, and it crushed me just now when it seemed like that would never happen.

I exhale a heavy breath, mad at myself more than anyone.

"God, I'm sorry, Callie. It's just..." I don't know how to explain what just happened. The past, present, and future collided in an atom bomb in my head.

147

"They all fall for him," I explain in a fractured voice. "Every single one. How can they not? I'm not saying he does it on purpose. Maybe sometimes, but mostly he just doesn't realize the effect he has. But I know where he's at right now, and you will get hurt. I know you will."

"Where is he?! Tell me!" Elena sobs.
"I... Don't make me do this."
"Then tell me where he is! He's with someone else, isn't he?!"
I clench my eyes shut, shaking my head, even though she can't see me. Neither can he. They definitely can't see each other because they stopped doing that months ago.

Callie's earnest nod contains a touch of something else. Desperation. That's it. A deep need for me to understand because... it's not in my head. It's not just me.

"I know," she says, her gaze scouring mine. "Seriously, Casey, I know, okay? It's not like that. I don't have those kinds of feelings for him anymore."

Her eyes finish the sentence. Those feelings are for someone else.

My heart pounds. My blood runs hot.

I'm stunned when she gets up and moves toward me. Suddenly, the bitter shove of rejection that sent me away from the table is an opening for the opposite as she hovers in front of me.

She takes my hands and laces our fingers. Closing the distance between us, she straddles me on the chair, still standing. For a few confusing seconds we stay like that. Me staring up at her, wondering, hoping... I don't even know for what.

We went off script a long time ago.

I pull her down at the same time she leans in, drawing her lips to mine.

Her soft gasp when we connect echoes relief and longing.

She tugs her hands free to frame my head, still kissing me as she lowers herself to my lap. I slide my palms down her back and let them rest just above the waist of her jeans.

Her lips are soft and warm, testing instead of demanding. She uses her grip on my cheeks to guide and explore, like she's just as surprised this is happening. Like she wants it to last, instead of the urgent lust I'm used to in first kisses.

It feels so... real.

Personal and focused.

She's kissing me because she wants *me*. Not because I'm Casey Barrett of Night Shifts Black.

For these few precious seconds, I'm not The Drummer anymore.

I'm just Casey.

CHAPTER 11

"*H*ey, what do you think of this for the chorus?"

I play through the progression I've been working on, while singing the lyrics. The flow is perfect, until the last line.

"Always so..."

I palm the strings to quiet them. "We break here, and *'unkind'* moves to the first bar of the turn.... Hey, you listening?"

She's just staring at me.

"No? Yes?" I say, trying to read the confusing expression on her face. "Uh, okay. So I was also thinking we need to tweak the lyrics for verse two. I like what you wrote, but it doesn't fit the melody we just worked out."

Still just eye-stalking me.

I lower the guitar and study her strange demeanor. "Okay. You're freaking me out. What's wrong?"

"Nothing." A silly smile plays on her lips, and I raise a brow.

We've been working for a couple hours now, and this song is actually turning into something legit. I'm already thinking it might be good enough to get TJ his demo if we bust our asses for the next few days. I'll have to track down a midi controller and interface but—

"Seriously, Callie. Why are you looking at me like that?"

I grip the strings and give her a playful warning stare.

Her smile becomes a grin as she leans back and pulls her knees to her chest. She wraps her arms around them and rests her chin on top. Her weird behavior is starting to unravel me.

"If you don't like the melodies, we can do something else."

"I love the melodies."

She scours my face, my hands, the guitar.

"So…?"

"Can't a girl just enjoy a moment?"

"Not when that moment involves staring at me with an evil villain smirk."

Her mouth drops open. "You think I look like an evil villain?!"

"No, I said your *smirk* is very 'I'm secretly building a pint-sized clone army and you're about to be my minion.'"

A pillow comes flying at my head, and I swat it away with a laugh.

"And the nefarious campaign begins," I tease.

Her mock glare might be the cutest thing I've ever seen.

"Why can't I just enjoy the fact that an incredibly talented, hot guy is sitting a few feet away?" She draws a circle through the air around me. "You have no idea the toll you take on a girl's lady parts."

I snort a laugh. Oh my god. "You did not just say that."

Her smile widens, and she returns an exaggerated shrug.

I shake my head, still grinning. I have no clue what to do with that, but I can't say I hate it.

"Come here," I say, putting the guitar to the side. "Bring that throw pillow." She squints in suspicion. "Just do it," I encourage, motioning toward me.

She reluctantly grabs the pillow and takes a tentative step. When I reach for the pillow, she clamps it to her chest.

I give her an accusatory look. "You're the one who uses these as projectiles, not me."

Her stern face cracks with another laugh. This time when I pull, she comes with it.

Of course I have to steal another kiss.

She freezes when our lips meet, but quickly relaxes into the kiss and straddles me.

She breaks apart to speak, still just a breath away.

"I'm serious," she whispers against my lips. "I have the biggest crush on you."

My grin is cut off by another kiss, this one urgent and messy.

Her hands slide into my hair, gripping hard as our mouths wrestle and explore. She slides against me in a slow steady pulse I feel in my bloodstream.

This wasn't even close to my plan for that pillow, but I'll take it.

I'm on fire when she finally pulls back. Her eyes are shining, and a mischievous smirk that looks eerily similar to her evil villain face returns.

"That's what I think of the chorus," she says smugly.

She leans in for another quick peck before climbing off my lap.

"Now, where were we?" she says tapping her chin. "Oh, right. The turn bar or whatever."

I'm still frozen in stunned silence as she retrieves the pillow and holds it out to me.

I exhale another laugh, taking the pillow.

"Sit." I point at the coffee table in front of me.

Her look of suspicion might be more justified this time, but she slowly lowers herself to the edge.

"Balance that pillow on your lap. Yeah, just like that."

I jump up from the couch and jog to the kitchen. With

sloppy urgency, I comb through the drawers like the world's worst cat burglar. I eventually find two wooden spoons and return to my now very confused co-writer.

I drop back to the couch in front of her and twirl the spoons in my hands like drumsticks. With a tap on the cushions to my left and right, I test my impromptu kit.

"Toms," I explain. I tap the pillow on her lap. "Snare."

Her eyes widen, and I'm pretty sure I'm about to get attacked by my snare drum.

"You did not just turn me into a drum set!" she cries.

"Of course not. You're just the snare. That coffee table is too low to pull it off."

She laughs, jaw hanging open in mock offense. "Fine, but I better get some kind of album credit for this."

"Absolutely. First ever credited 'pillow drum holder.' Hey, that means you'd probably be a lock for the Grammy in that category."

And there it is.

The pillow comes flying at my face.

* * *

AFTER HOURS OF WORK—AND plenty of flirting—we're both hungry, so I offer to get us dinner.

With Callie's key in my wallet, I take off in search of sustenance.

We could have ordered in. But honestly? I needed a break. As much as I love spending time with Callie, I'm feeling a little claustrophobic in that suite. After experiencing the walls closing in for just a couple days, it makes me even more worried for Luke. He's spent weeks, maybe months, like this.

The brisk air feels good as I stroll down the street. It's amazing what a little fresh air and sunlight can do for the spirit. While it's great Luke let Callie into his life more literally, maybe we need to convince him to resume breakfast club so he gets at least a few minutes of daylight.

Speaking of breakfast club...

I go numb when I realize what I did. Somehow I ended up in front of that diner. It wasn't on purpose, but now that I'm here, I have a driving need to see inside.

I peer through the clear glass windows, searching for anything that makes this place more than a casual urban restaurant. Something brought Luke here. Of all the locations in the world, this is the destination he chose to fracture apart and expose his pain to the world.

I think back to what that employee Ailee said.

"Luke had been coming in to stand around..."

If I squint hard enough, I can picture his ghost, hovering between two tables as it stares at... what? What was he searching for?

I shake off the disturbing image and keep walking before I become the next hovering weirdo.

Maybe Callie knows. I'll have to ask her later.

Once I'm a safe distance from the diner, I pull out my phone to check the map for Adaline's. I saw the pin on an earlier search so I know it's close. They have the best burgers. Now that Callie's been exposed to good champagne, she has to have a good burger.

According to the notifications, I have two missed calls. Weird. They must have come in while Callie and I were working.

When I see the name, I return it immediately.

My sister Molly answers on the second ring. "Casey, hey! I've been trying to reach you."

"I know. That's why I'm calling you back."

Molly chuckles. "Right, yeah."

"What's going on? Is everything okay? Wait, aren't you supposed to be in Europe?"

"Yes. And I am, but..." She goes quiet, and my stomach drops. "Did you talk to Mom recently?"

"Mom? No. You know I don't really talk to her."

"Yeah, it's just..." She takes a deep breath. "Nate called me to catch up tonight. Well, the afternoon for you. He mentioned Luke was back. Multiple people saw him around."

"Really? That's odd, because Luke is with me on the other side of the country."

"Hang on. Are you serious? He's back?"

"Sort of. Still trying to figure that out."

"Oh."

I intentionally don't tell her in which city. It's bad enough I had to come back to this haunted place. I'm not putting that on Molly. Especially not until I figure out what's going on.

"Is that really why you called me from *Europe*? To tell me someone thinks they saw Luke. I mean, you know I love hearing from you, Mol, but shouldn't you be drooling over castles and shit?"

She laughs, and I can hear the eye-roll in it. God, she and Callie are so much alike. They're going to love each other.

The strange thought plummets through my heart. Did I really just think about introducing Callie to my favorite sister? I'm not sure I even know Callie's last name.

"The castles are amazing," Molly says. "You should use your trillions to buy one."

"I've told you a hundred times. It's billions not trillions."

She snorts again. That's not true either, but my millions could probably scoop up a decent estate somewhere.

I resist the urge to convince Callie to move into a castle with me.

"Seriously, though. I'm telling you, Luke was home. Maybe he was just visiting and is now wherever you are, but

Jill saw him. You're going to tell me Jill wouldn't recognize Luke?"

Yeah, okay. She has me.

"When was this?"

"Um... I don't know. Nate didn't say. He thought he texted you. How has no one told you?"

Because very few of them even talk to me anymore.

"Did Nate say what Luke was doing?"

"Jill wasn't sure. He was super shady when she tried to talk to him, but apparently Mr. Tomlinson told her he was leaving the office of a law firm."

My skin feels like ice.

"A law firm? Which law firm?"

"Does it matter?"

"Yeah, actually. A lot."

Law firms tend to specialize in very different things. If this is true, it could be a huge clue into what's happening here.

"Well, sorry. I'm not sure. You can see if Nate knows. Or get a hold of Jill."

I almost drop my phone when a horrific thought seeps in.

No.

There's no way it's that.

"Casey?"

I rub at my scalp as I try to pull myself together.

"You okay?"

"What? Yeah." I clear my throat when my voice comes out hoarse.

"Because you're sounding kind of... off. You sure everything's good with you? If you're with Luke, that's great news, right? I would have expected you to be more... you."

More me. I don't even know what that is anymore.

"Everything's good. Just a lot of pressure from the Label." I inject more brightness into my tone. "Hey, thanks for the information. I'll ask him about it, but I have to run."

157

"Sure, yeah. It's great to hear your voice. I miss you, big bro."

"Miss you too. We'll catch up when you're back in the states."

"Or you're in Europe."

"Fair. Talk soon."

"Love ya."

I hang up and stare at my phone, shaking. Right there on the side of a busy street, I'm frozen in time.

Eyes clenched shut, I drag air into my dry lungs. A heavy ache sinks through my chest and lands in my stomach.

Molly may not know why Luke would fly home to meet with lawyers, but I can think of a few reasons.

If it's the one I fear most, Callie didn't just butt into his life. She may have saved it.

CHAPTER 12

J've pulled myself together by the time I pick up takeout from Adaline's and make my way back to the hotel. The wait and walk gave me a lot of time to think.

While Molly's news supports my growing fears, it doesn't necessarily prove anything. And it certainly doesn't change the reality of our current situation. I already knew Luke was teetering on the edge of the cliff. It was just a gut-punch to have it so vividly spelled out.

If he already went as far as to settle his affairs, Callie and I are on borrowed time.

I pick up my pace, suddenly desperate to see them both.

I also remind myself Molly's call, while concerning, is also outdated information.

For one, Luke seems to be turning a corner. It's subtle and definitely not enough to let our guard down, but I've seen glimpses of light returning to his demeanor. Mostly when Callie's around. The difference between when I first saw him a week ago and today is so stark, it's hard to argue something isn't shifting inside him. It could be an act, but he has no reason to put on a show.

I'll keep an eye on him and talk to Callie about it.

For now, we'll love him and stay close.

When I get back to the suite, the main living area is empty. I think I hear voices down the hall, so Callie and Luke must be talking in her room.

I use the time to unpack the food from the bag, and by the time I've pulled everything out, I hear a door open.

I look down the hall to see Callie exit a room and start toward me.

Any lingering darkness immediately falls away when our eyes lock. This world is just a better place when she's around.

But the look on her face quickly drains any optimism.

"You okay?" I ask when she approaches. "Wait, did you just come out of the office?"

I squint down the hall again, wondering if Luke's about to come out as well. Other than storage, I didn't think that room was used.

"Long story," Callie says. "What'd you find?"

I shake off the gloom to allow ourselves a brief oasis into Burgerland. I need a mental escape for a few minutes, and based on her heavy expression, she could use one too.

"Burgers. But not just any burger. Here, try this."

Her expression transforms into a hilarious shade of suspicion when I hand her a box.

She studies the packaging way longer than anyone should ever look at a piece of recycled cardboard.

"You're not going to laugh at me again because I've never tasted a burger that costs more than a pair of socks, are you?"

Ah. Here we go.

"A bit sensitive, I see."

"Well, sorry, but you seem to take pleasure in exposing me to all the forbidden fruit of rockstar living."

I huff a laugh at her latest weird expression. I still chuckle when I think about what she said on the couch earlier. She really shouldn't be mentioning her lady parts to me. My brain is already way too intrigued by that topic.

"Now you're just being dramatic," I say.

"Am I? First the champagne, now the fancy burgers."

Fancy burgers. There's nothing fancy about me.

"I'm from a family of twelve. Trust me, I do not need to eat like this to survive." I hesitate, suddenly feeling self-conscious. "I don't know. I just thought..."

I'm not even sure what I was thinking. I wanted to make her smile and give her new experiences. It was never my intention to point out the differences between us. In fact, the guys are always making fun of me for still living like I'm kid number seven in a lower-middle class family. We got by growing up, but I certainly wasn't eating burgers from Adaline's.

None of that means Callie feels the same way.

"I wanted you to try something you otherwise wouldn't. I thought you'd like it," I finish, trying to read her.

My stomach sinks when she places the burger on the counter. But there's nothing negative about her expression as she stalks toward me.

Before I know what's happening, her arms are around me and her cheek is pressing against my shoulder. The tension in my back melts away, and I instinctively brush my lips against her hair.

"What's this?" I say with a soft laugh.

"Nothing," she mumbles against me.

I pull her closer when I feel her grip on the back of my shirt. This must be about whatever happened in that office. I have no idea how to tackle a subject like that.

"Will Luke be joining us?" My tone also contains the answer to that question.

"I'm not sure. Maybe." Still holding on, she leans back to study my face. Her look is pensive instead of layered with the typical angst we've come to expect from encounters with Luke.

"Something happened while you were out," she says quietly. "I don't know what yet, but something. It may be what we've been waiting for."

Her eyes fill with liquid hope, and she's never been more beautiful. I don't think anything has. I tip her face up with my thumbs and brush away a few strands of hair obscuring perfection.

"Thank you," she whispers in a tone that says much more.

For the burgers.

For being here.

For being you.

When her gaze heats with anticipation, I lean in for another kiss. This one drives for more, intentional and demanding. She adjusts to pull me into her, returning my kiss with an urgency that tells me she needed it too.

I taste a hint of berries from her lip balm and breathe in the scent of clean muted citrus. She tastes amazing. Feels just as good. Her body is always so soft and warm when she presses into me, and it doesn't take long for my starved libido to make calls for further action.

But that's not what this moment is about, so against every instinct that wants more, I gently pull away to rest my forehead on hers.

We catch our breath for a moment, absorbing what just happened.

"Wow," I say, straightening. "Now, that's a proper thank you. You could have just gotten me a beer."

Her eyes widen in disbelief before... yep. A playful smack.

God, I live for those.

"Yeah, well, these burgers better be worth it."

* * *

WE'RE HALFWAY into our meal when I spot a shadow moving down the hall. I still don't know what happened in that office, but I can guess whatever it is needs a burger break more than a tense grilling… no pun intended.

I nod to Luke with a quick smile and place the food I got him in front of an empty stool.

Luke scans the box and twists a small smile. "Adaline's?"

"Thought we could all use a dose of heaven after our night of hell."

Luke stares back at his box, and I wonder if he's thinking about the last time we had Adaline's. Not all of our memories are nightmares. Some are the reason I will never give up on this person.

"Callie, here, is a convert already," I say before this gets awkward.

"How can I not be?" she mumbles through a mouthful of food. I was wrong about my initial impression. She'd fit in perfectly on a tour bus.

"We should take her to 49th & Finch," Luke says.

The thought excites me for so many reasons.

The main one—it means including Callie in another facet of our lives.

"We totally should. Oh man, they have the best bar food," I tell her.

I could survive for a month on their jalapeño poppers. Also, I use the term "survive" loosely.

"Bar food?" she asks, eyeing us with her signature skepticism. "So basically you guys just upgraded the same stuff you ate when you first started out as a garage band ten years ago."

She's not wrong.

"Basically. Although to be fair, we still eat that stuff, too."

Her laugh makes it pretty clear she's not buying that. "And you still look like that, how? Because I'm pretty sure I wouldn't."

I lift a shoulder. "I don't know, good question. Stress?"

She shakes her head in motherly disapproval. "Okay, first of all, if you're going to hang with me, you're going to learn to eat a vegetable."

"What about fruit cups?" Luke quips. There must be some story there when they exchange an amused look.

"Yes, that's a start," she replies.

"Fruit cups?" I ask.

"Part of my standard balanced breakfast order at Jemma's," Callie says.

"She doesn't drink coffee either," Luke announces with the appropriate level of distaste for that sin.

"I noticed that this morning!" I say, mostly to watch her face do what it's doing now.

"I like tea. So what?" she fires back. Even crosses her arms in an adorable tantrum. "You know what? I'm so sick of your holier-than-thou attitudes. You think I'm the one who baffles the mind? What about the two of you?"

I have no idea where this is going, but I'm so here for it.

"Yeah, what about us?" I ask in a casual tone I know will drive her crazy.

She squares her shoulders like she's about to mount an epic courtroom cross-examination for the ages. I wish I could bottle this shit. We'd make a fortune.

"Okay, well, first of all. Explain to me why two guys with more money than they probably know what to do with, two guys who have an entire mall's-worth of clothing options just a personal shopper away, point to the plain, ratty t-shirt and say, 'Yes. That's it. That's what I want.'"

I snort a laugh, and even Luke makes a humored sound I haven't heard in a long, long time.

Based on his expression, this is another storied point of contention.

Let's call it Exhibit A.

"Again with the t-shirts," he says, confirming my suspicion. "You really have a vendetta, don't you?"

Her brows lift in a challenge as she gives each of us a thorough onceover that feels way more self-serving than she's going for. Not gonna lie. She will win every argument with me if it involves visually undressing me like that.

She waves over us in a mock critique. "Am I wrong? You two look identical right now."

I brace myself on the edge of the island, loving how her gaze scales my arms like she's powerless to stop it. "Well, first of all, if you recall, I'm actually wearing his clothes, so…"

"And, second of all, I thought we already established pink polo shirts weren't my thing," Luke adds.

Her shoulders droop in defeat, but I don't even get to celebrate my win before she's back to lawyer mode.

"I didn't say you had to dress like an investment banker. I'm just saying, would a little color or design kill you? I mean, really. It's appalling."

Appalling! She's going to make an amazing great-aunt one day.

I will never grow tired of pushing her buttons.

"She just wants us to take our shirts off," I say to Luke in a casual tone without looking away from Callie. For another direct hit, I lean back on my elbows with the sole intention of tormenting her. I even add the grin I know she loves. When her gaze scans the thin tee stretched over my chest, then drops to the newly exposed cut of my lower abs, my brain begins an internal victory parade.

I cannot wait to see how she gets out of this one. Luke is snickering as if he knows where I'm headed.

"Whatever," she huffs in the most unconvincing deflection of all time. "You're just mad because I don't drool over you all the time like you're used to."

Ha!

Luke shoots me an obligatory warning look, but there's no conviction in it. He's enjoying the show too much.

"No? Really." My tone oozes skepticism as I come around the island to face her.

She sucks in a breath when I tug my shirt over my head. As her eyes flare hot, I step into her, crowding her against the counter.

I fix my gaze on hers, more than a little turned on when the fight in her stance drains into anticipation. Lust flares in her hazel irises before she tears them away to trace the lines of my chest and abs.

"Not even a little interested?" I tease in a husky voice.

Her fingers clench and unclench in her lap. Her teeth sink into her lip.

I reach for her hand, and when she instinctively squeezes my fingers, I know she's all in on whatever is happening right now. We've kissed, but never skin to skin or in front of anyone. The way her mesmerized gaze travels over my tattoos is downright addictive.

I guide her hand to my chest, and as soon as her fingers brush my skin, she takes over. I let her explore, loving how her hungry touch triggers all kinds of delicious heat.

Yeah, I'm going to say we both won this round.

Luke is practically laughing at this point, drawing us back to the present debate turned seduction. Her expression becomes almost resentful, as if it's my fault she's so attracted to me.

I mean, maybe it is?

"Geez. Put your clothes on. Luke's trying to eat," she snaps.

"I'm good," Luke replies, and her scowl for him is almost as fun.

Her blush is the perfect ending to this dispute as she rips her hand away from me with a playful glare. She scoops my shirt off the ground and flings it at my chest with an indignant pout. My grin stretches across my face.

"And also," she continues in a smug tone. "I don't believe for a second that you can look like that sitting around watching TV and eating bar food, so that makes you a liar on top of everything else."

I snort a laugh as I pull my shirt back on.

"Of course not," I say, dropping the act. "I was kidding about the junk food and stress. Trust me, they keep us on a pretty tight leash." Although, it's been way too long since my last workout. My anxious mind is in need of the exertion as much as my body.

I turn to Luke. "Speaking of which, I was gonna ask if I could borrow your key and go hit the gym later."

Luke casts a quick look at Callie before nodding to me. "Actually, if you want, I'll just call down and have Mara get you one of your own."

I freeze. Luke's hesitant gaze finds mine. A decade passes between us, and I swallow the thickening mass in my throat. The last thing I want to do is turn this monumental shift into another setback.

"Thanks, man," I return as evenly as possible.

He returns a quick nod, and I'm glad I played it correctly when he relaxes.

"Sure. Thanks for the burger."

CHAPTER 13

"Guess you're staying?" Callie says once we're alone.

I'm still having trouble processing what just happened.

"Guess so."

Luke appeared exhausted when he retreated back to his room to make the call to the front desk. This must have been a taxing day for him. Now I'm really curious about what happened in that office.

"What about your life?" Callie asks suddenly. "I mean, don't you have somewhere else you're supposed to be?"

I toss a smile at her. "Trying to get rid of me?"

She returns a sardonic look. "You know I want you here. I just... I don't know. You must have a whole other life. Obligations."

"Obligations," I scoff. She has no idea. "Yeah. But nothing I can't do from here. Don't worry, Mom, I'll be where I need to be when I need to be there."

She returns a weak smile, and I soften the teasing. She's just trying to be considerate, and I realize for all we've been through in this short time, we really don't know much about each other. She probably doesn't know any more about what my life is outside this suite than I know of hers.

"Anyway, I do have my own place," I explain. "But it's nothing worth missing. I'm on the road so much I never thought there was any point in setting up roots." I scan her as the mood shifts. "I could say the same to you."

Her dry laugh cuts through the humor. "Please. My life is literally nothing. Talk about a pointless existence."

I wince, staring at her with a mix of confusion and irritation.

"Sorry, that didn't come out right," she backpedals, reading my reaction.

Liar.

"I don't know. Maybe it did," I challenge. "What does that mean? Who are you? I don't even know your last name."

She averts her gaze, and now I'm getting annoyed. A minute ago, she was taking me on at every pass. Now all of a sudden she's going to cower in the face of basic questions?

"No one worth your time, believe me," she mumbles.

Is she fucking serious right now? I can't believe what I'm hearing.

"You do understand you're insulting me, too, when you do that?" I counter in an accusatory tone.

She withdraws into herself even more. "I didn't mean it like that. I just... I don't know. I just meant I'm no one."

I run a hand over my hair and shake my head in frustration. "What the hell does that even mean? You're no one? So am I just an idiot then to be wasting entire days and nights with 'no one'?"

She winces, and part of me feels badly, but she needs to hear this. Maybe we're not just here for Luke. Maybe we all have scattered pieces that need to be assembled.

"No. That's not what I meant. Of course not."

Her placating response just pisses me off more. I think back over the course of our time together. All the jokes, all the debates. They were all in good fun, but clearly there was an undertone I didn't truly pick up on until now.

This woman actually has no clue how incredible she is.

"No, I know what you meant," I say in a firm voice. "I know exactly what you meant. Your face isn't slapped all over the internet and some stupid magazine so therefore you don't count as a person in my life just because mine is."

I scrub at my face. "God, Callie, we basically met two days ago and I can't even imagine not having you in my life at this point. Luke didn't know you existed a month ago and now you're his best chance at survival. You're doing what no one else could! You write poetry that cut into me, and have made me laugh so much these last couple days it's actually starting to get painful."

I take a breath as the words sink in. I'm hearing them for the first time as well. The magnitude of what's happening in this suite. Three broken souls coming together to fill the cracks in each other.

And right at the center? This person who thinks she doesn't even belong here.

"So stop with the 'I'm a nobody' bullshit and tell me who you really are!"

I quiet and stare her down. My heart beats wildly as I wait to see what she does with this ultimatum. I could lose her, but I've already lost her if I can't get this message through.

She bites her lip and squirms in her seat. Seconds tick by. Quiet looks and awkward stillness.

She pivots away from me.

It hurts like hell when she hides her face, but maybe this is the hard truth she needed to hear. I command myself to stand strong. To wait for her to sort through her own demons instead of taking them on myself like I always do. I didn't allow Luke to fight his battles and look where it got us. I'm not about to make the same mistake with Callie.

After a torturous pause, she finally straightens, still facing the wall.

"I'm Callie Roland, twenty-three, born and raised in Shelteron, Pennsylvania."

She swivels slowly on her stool, as if afraid of my reaction.

All I feel is colossal relief.

I drop to the seat beside her and hold out my hand.

"Casey Barrett, twenty-five, born and raised in Houston, Texas."

She takes my hand with a weak smile.

Then stops cold.

Her eyes go wide.

"Houston?" Her voice is barely above a whisper.

Her strange reaction shatters the air around us.

She didn't know I was from Houston, but she must know the significance based on her shock. And if she didn't know that, then she probably doesn't know the rest. How would she unless Luke told her. There's zero chance of that.

I force a nod and offer a stiff smile to soften the blow. "Elena Barrett Craven was my sister."

Her stunned expression confirms my theory.

"I'm sorry to just dump that on you," I continue, breaking the heavy silence. "I thought you should know. Maybe that matters, maybe it doesn't."

"Of course it matters!" She looks rattled, and I wonder what's going through her head. Knowing her, it's more than the average person.

I study the windows in the distance. "More pieces of the puzzle, huh?"

"More insight into you."

Warm pressure spreads through my hand, and I shift my focus to our fingers locking together.

"I'm so sorry, Casey," she says with a mix of pain and bewilderment. "And yet you stood by him? Cared for him?"

She's not the only one who has trouble understanding the contradiction. This sordid story is full of them, but I suspect she's had enough surprises for one conversation.

"We were both hurting," I say, tracing the floor tiles with my eyes. "Maybe I thought we were standing by each other in the beginning. But I wasn't the reason for her downfall, he was. I was able to forgive myself and continue to love her after she was gone. Luke's pain was different."

With a sharp exhale, she tackles me with a vigorous hug. I close my eyes as her arms constrict around me.

"You're a special person, Casey Barrett," she murmurs against my neck.

I release a sad laugh. "You've only known me a few days. I'll get on your nerves soon enough."

Her arms tighten as if rebelling against the thought. It feels so good to be close to her. To connect with someone who truly gets it. Gets *me*. It gives me strength I haven't felt in years. Hope I haven't felt in... ever.

It's incredible, surreal, and so freaking exhausting.

My soul needs a break.

We part just enough to see each other. A spark catches in her eyes when they search mine with a quiet plea. My body reacts, screaming for the same thing.

But we're both rocked by what just happened. I'm afraid this kiss wouldn't be about us, but about my trauma, and that's the slippery slope that got me into trouble in the first place.

With incredible effort, I withdraw from her arms and force the brightest smile I can muster.

"So does that mean I've won enough points to continue our *Dead Head* marathon?" I ask.

There are some things only zombies can fix.

Her melodramatic groan drops us right back into our easy banter.

"Do we have to? Right before bed?" she whines.

I give her my best puppy dog eyes.

She sighs with plenty of self-asserted martyrdom. "Fine. But I maintain the Power of the Mute Button."

CHAPTER 14

 $\mathcal{M}$ ovement wakes me the following morning. My neck feels like it's in a trash compactor from two nights on this couch, but I've slept on way worse for a lot longer. Those early years of touring put us in some questionable sleep situations, not to mention the hard decade before that.

I struggle to a sitting position and squint toward the presence hovering over me.

"Morning sunshine," Callie greets, way too chipper for this time of day.

She motions for me to move so she can join me on the couch.

But instead of settling in, she slides her open laptop onto my chest.

Confused, I remain still as she drops a quick kiss on my forehead and says she's going to shower.

I blink after her, wondering what the hell just happened.

Once she's gone, I glance at the screen a few inches from my face and inhale a sharp breath. *No way.*

I shoot a stunned look in the direction she just left, but it appears she really did just drop this bombshell and run.

My gaze settles back on the screen, and I adjust to a better position to read the poem.

Then read it again.

And again.

It's clearly meant for me, and each pass lands deeper, igniting vague melodies in my head. For not being a songwriter, she naturally writes in lyrics.

> "How was I supposed to know your smile was only
> a distraction?
> How am I supposed to feel, stuck in veiled
> conversation?
> Because you never let me in, now I have to watch
> you drowning.
> Quiet suffering, speak!
>
> I'll stay here, don't look down.
> There's nothing waiting for you on the ground.
> You're stronger than you're feeling now.
> I'll stay here.
> I'll stay."

I pick up the guitar to play with some of the melodies tickling my brain. A few stick, but my mind keeps going back to the mirror song Callie and I were working on yesterday. That one is going to be something special. I feel it.

I'm so engrossed in the music, I don't even notice Luke until he's practically in front of me.

Dampening the strings, I watch his gaze cut to the kitchen, the hall, and back to me, like he can't decide what to do next. I know the choice he would have made the first time I visited a couple weeks ago, and it's a testament to how much things have changed that I honestly don't know what he'll do now.

When he moves forward and drops beside me, I keep my shock and inner middle-school squeal locked down.

"Is that the song you've been working on with Callie?" he asks.

"Nah. Something else. She, uh, wrote me something last night."

He snaps a look at me, and I shrug.

"That it?" He nods toward the coffee table.

"Yeah. It's got a natural chorus. I've been playing around with some progressions."

I return to absent strumming as he leans forward to scan the screen. After a few seconds, he sinks into the couch and tips his head back to stare at the ceiling.

"Did you know Elena asked me out first?"

My fingers stall on the strings. I glance at him, but he's still focused on the ceiling.

"I thought you asked *her*," I say. "Wasn't your first date that weird lawn party at your aunt's house?"

To my amazement, a smile cracks his severe expression.

"Aunt Gina was trying for a Kentucky Derby vibe."

"Yeah, well, without horses, it was just Uncle Nestor in a green tux that never should have been invented and whatever the hell your aunt was wearing on her head."

He snorts a laugh. "I'm convinced that entire thing was just to give her an excuse to wear the hat she found at the estate sale."

"I guess social events have been conceived around less. So that *wasn't* your first date?"

"It was."

I squint over at him, and he rotates his head to give me a quick smile before returning to his staring match with the ceiling.

"But we all watched *you* ask her. In the most obnoxious, melodramatic display of all time, if I recall."

"I did ask her."

"Dude. You lost me."

Another smile skims his lips at a memory. "It started the day we were rehearsing for that open mic night at the farmer's market. Remember that?"

"Six people, lots of baked goods, and way too many questionable wood carvings. Go on."

"Yeah, well, during our break, when I went to the kitchen to grab a drink, Elena pretty much tackled me in the hallway and dragged me into the laundry room. I thought I was in trouble or something, but instead she told me I was going to invite her to my aunt's party. Oh, and I'd be doing it at the family barbeque that night."

"What?!"

He laughs and shakes his head. "Yep. She specifically said I had to be the one to ask, because she was afraid your dad wouldn't accept the reverse. For good measure, she wanted it done as publicly as possible."

I straighten on the couch. "Hang on. So *that's* what all the flowers and bended knee bullshit was about?"

"Yep." He chuckles and rubs at his knees. "She said she knew I was into her but was too 'chicken shit' to act on it. Her words, and she was right."

He goes quiet, lost in a memory, and I return to plucking on the guitar. My mind drifts back to that time ten years ago. Back when two teenagers had already lived through hell, but still had dreams of something better.

Realizing there *is* nothing better is what nearly breaks you.

Shuffling behind us ends the spell, and Callie comes into view.

I can't guess where Luke's head is after that random confession, so I'm surprised when he tosses a smile in her direction.

"Wow, Callie, I'm a little jealous that he gets a poem and I don't," he jokes.

She hesitates, then comes to a decision about something.

With deliberate movements, she stalks toward us and swipes the laptop off the table.

"Hey! I wasn't done with that!" I whine, and she returns a mock glare.

"I'll give it back in a second." She pivots to Luke. "I did one for you as well, but you weren't awake."

Luke seems startled, and maybe I am too.

"Really? You wrote two last night?" he asks.

"Couldn't sleep," she says as she searches for something on her computer. She must find it and tries to hand the laptop to Luke.

He shakes his head.

"No, you read it."

She shrinks back. "What?"

"I want you to read it. I want to hear it how you intend it to be heard."

So do I. I'm already jealous at the thought that Luke will get her words in her voice, while I had to read mine on a heartless screen.

She takes a deep breath, debating. "I…"

"Read it," I say before she goes down the self-doubt spiral. "I want to hear it, too."

She passes a look between us and finally gives in.

Damn, she seems nervous, and as she starts to read, I feel bad for pressuring her. She's clearly uncomfortable with this, and it's my fault for pushing her. There's a fine line between encouragement and bullying, and I'm afraid I've crossed it.

She stops suddenly.

"No. That's not it. I'm starting over."

Standing a little straighter, she transforms into a different woman right before our eyes. This is the woman brave enough to approach a complete stranger in a diner to save his life.

She glances at me, and I offer the most supportive look I can.

After a quick evaluation of Luke as well, she launches into the poem again.

This time with the confidence and grace of someone who believes in their art.

"I could have told you everything would be alright.
I could have told you it gets easier the harder
    you try.
But I couldn't lie to you, even though I'd die
    for you.
And I could have told you instead of just holding
    you.

But what could I say that my eyes haven't already
    said?
And what words could heal the wounds that bleed
    like this?
How many tears will it take to drown away the
    pain?
I don't know, but I can hold you.

And I could have taken you far away from here.
But where would that leave you? It'd be the same
    even there.
I won't hide you, even though I'd like to.
And I could have spoken instead of just loving you.

But what could I say that my eyes haven't already
    said?
And what words can heal the wounds that
    break us?
How many tears will it take to drown away the
    pain?

I don't know, but I can hold you. I can love you.
I can hold you."

Fuck.

A loud silence replaces her voice. The haunting words echo around us. Callie looks terrified as she watches Luke. He looks like he's been punched in the stomach.

This must be related to what happened in the office yesterday, and whatever it is has cut fast and deep.

"Can I see that?" Luke asks quietly, surprising all of us.

Callie hands him the computer with trembling hands. I want to pull her into my lap to comfort her, protect her, but this is between them. When her gaze creeps toward me, I sense the wonder and empathy bubbling up inside me pour out to her.

"That was beautiful, Callie," I say softly.

She returns a weak smile.

"Thanks, Callie," Luke echoes faintly.

He hands the laptop back to her, then pushes to his feet.

Without a word, he disappears into the hall, probably stopping at the office based on the sound of the door closing. That damn office again.

Callie looks stunned as she stares after him.

"He loved it, but it was a lot for him," I say to reassure her.

"I know." She gives up on the empty corridor and joins me on the couch. "He's with The Chair."

Um...

"The chair?"

She nods like that's a thing people do all the time. "He stole it from the café. I think it has something to do with Elena."

Stunned, all I can do is blink at her for a long second. "I'm sorry, what?"

She returns a casual shrug. "The Chair is how we met. I was sitting at my table one day at Jemma's, and he came in and asked me to move. Apparently, I was in his chair, *that* chair. He'd go into the café every day and stare at the same one for several minutes. Freaked out the servers and café regulars, but no one asked questions or stopped him."

She takes a breath, but I can't. What the hell is she talking about?

"Finally, the day of the party this past weekend he just lost it and basically marched down to the café and stole the chair in broad daylight, right in front of the patrons and staff. I'm surprised there hasn't been more about it in the news."

I open my mouth to respond but nothing comes out. Words and images are streaming through my head, but none are fitting together.

"Luke... stole a chair. A cheap café chair?"

It doesn't make any more sense out loud.

I rest my elbows on my knees, my eyes locked in a perplexed stare on the coffee table.

More images are rushing in. Memories. Nightmares.

And the biggest of all I still can't answer: Why *here?* Why a chair in *this* city?

"Yep. Just a chair. He was obsessed with it before he stole it."

My head moves in absent arcs. "And now what? What does he do with it? I don't remember seeing it."

"He keeps it in his office and sits in it."

"And does *what?*" I return, frustration mounting.

Just when I thought we were finally putting the pieces together...

There's a stolen diner chair in the office.

She seems unfazed by any of this. In fact, she seems more upset that *I'm* upset than the fact that our friend has traded iconic musician for furniture thief.

"Nothing. He just sits there. That's where I found him yesterday when he finally broke down."

More pieces snap into place, but the result is even more

baffling. More infuriating, because the most important parts are still missing. We have everything except the key to unlocking this entire situation. I don't know how we're supposed to do anything without that key.

I need to get it. It's time to have it out with him once and for all. No lies, no games, no coddling. Just brother-to-brother, soul-to-soul.

"What are you doing?" Callie asks when I push to my feet.

"Going to find out what the hell is going on."

She grabs my arm with an urgency that stops me cold.

"No, you can't." Her eyes are pleading.

"I *can't*? You're telling me my unstable friend has some kind of obsessive relationship with a piece of furniture, and I shouldn't go try to find out why?"

She nods and tugs my arm. "Yes, that's exactly what I'm telling you. It's not just a chair. It's something else, and he's not ready. If you barge in there now and attack him, you're going to undo everything we've done!"

I rip my arm away, feeling completely lost. Fingers laced above my head, I pace along the length of the couch, breathing hard.

I respect her. I trust her. But this is… How can leaving him alone with a chair be the best thing for him?

He went home to meet with fucking lawyers!

Callie grasps my arm and drags me toward the couch.

"Please, Casey. I'm asking you to let it go," she begs. "Not forever, just for now, okay? Let him have this. I'm telling you, he needs this."

She frames my face and digs her gaze into mine until she's the only thing I comprehend.

"Can you just trust me?"

The longer I get lost in the hazel pools of compassion, the more the storm settles.

A tortured exhale expels from my lungs.

"This is crazy. I mean, he's always been odd, but a chair?"

"I don't know what the chair means, but I know it's significant. He'll let us in when he's ready."

"And until then?"

"Until then, we keep fighting for the small stuff."

Fighting for the small stuff...

A smile cracks my heavy cloud.

"What?" she asks, furrowing her brow.

I bite back the humor as it tries to poke through. "Nothing. Just you."

"Me? What about me?" She crosses her arms with a stern look.

"You're like a cross between a motivational poster and a shrink. And my mom."

Her eyes widen as she coughs out a laugh. "Your mom? Really? You made out with me—twice—and I remind you of your mom?"

Three times, but there's no way I'm pointing that out when she's already taking swings at me.

Literally.

I duck as an arm comes flying at my chest and hold up my hands. "I don't know! You're always yelling at me!"

"Ha! I do not!"

"I don't eat enough vegetables. You don't like my clothes. I'm too mean to Luke..."

But instead of snapping back, she loops her arm through mine and rests her head on my shoulder. Our hands intertwine and we sit in silence while she traces the tattoos on my fingers.

I don't know what to make of the vibe, but I like it. Not heavy and draining, but not fluffy and light either. It's somewhere in between.

Somewhere pretty near perfect.

"You're thinking about my mom now, aren't you?" I ask when I see the pensive expression on her face.

"Maybe. What's she like?"

Well, that's a complicated question, but I think I'm ready to explore the hard ones with her.

Over the next hour, we plunge into the difficult topics of our lives.

I tell her about my dysfunctional family. A perfect façade on the outside, but rotted on the inside. My father didn't like a lot of his children's choices, but he hated mine the most and made sure everyone knew it. Especially me.

Her parents were no better. I learn about her absent mom and opportunistic dad. Her short description makes me want to march to Shelteron and introduce that man to my fist, but even he gets bumped down my hit list when she tells me about her asshole former employer. I've never wanted to destroy someone as much as I want to annihilate the sick bastard who hurt her.

She tries to laugh it off, but I see through it. I do the same with my own trauma. Wrap it up with a neat little joke or two until I can share it in a way that makes it more comfortable for others.

"So that's pretty much it," she says with a shrug. "I came here, not to make a name for myself in lights, but to disappear. I wasn't running to anything, just running *from*, and have basically been trying to figure things out ever since."

She goes quiet, and I sense there's more to this. Maybe it's the key to *her* story.

"When I say 'I'm no one' it's not even about self-esteem," she continues quietly. "I just don't know who I am, what I am. I don't know where I'm going or what I want from life. I just knew I didn't want to be the slut from the grocery store. Or Kyle and Nora's daughter. I wanted to be no one, so I could start fresh and hopefully be someone else one day."

Her words hit hard. I think back to what Luke said about Callie being as lost as we are. Needing purpose and direction.

He was right on with that analysis, and probably didn't even know how close he was to the truth.

"What happened to you isn't right and I'm glad you got some retribution, even though I wish that bastard would have gotten jail time instead," I say, still working through my thoughts.

"*But...*" she drags out.

I shoot her a look. "How do you know there's a but?"

"It's all over your face."

Great, so she even understands the things I'm *not* saying.

"No, not so much a 'but' as a caution about the ending of your story."

She lifts a brow. "Oh, you don't like the ending."

"No. I don't. You make it sound like your value is in your identity, and your identity is something that doesn't exist unless it's concrete."

"Concrete?"

"Definable. I don't like you defining yourself by what you're not, and therefore concluding you're no one. What about what you are?"

"What I am?"

It feels like we're on the precipice of something.

"Your identity shouldn't be an occupation or a status. Hell, it's not even dreams and aspirations. Those things will flow out of who you are once you embrace it. You have to stop looking at what's missing and focus on what's here."

She returns a sly smile. "Now who's a walking motivational poster."

She's not wrong, but we're also not as different as she thinks. In some ways, at some basic level, we're all the same. We all need to believe that we matter.

"Well, you need to hear it, that's all," I say. "You know why I'm here? Because when I was sixteen, Elena Barrett told me that our dad was a liar. That I wasn't a worthless piece-of-shit just because I didn't meet his expectations. That I was smart, and caring, and a talented musician. And even though I was just a kid fooling around with drums in a stupid band with my friend Luke, it was important because I loved it."

"You found something you love, Casey. Do you have any idea how incredible that is? No matter what happens, promise me you will never give it up. I don't care if you're playing in a basement for yourself or on a stage for millions. I just need you to play and stay passionate."

Ten years later, I'm still playing. Against the odds. Against all the forces that tried to stand in my way, Elena's words drove me against the tide. Maybe Callie never had an Elena to push her in the right direction, but she does now.

"That's why I'm here, Callie," I say in an earnest voice. I search her eyes, fighting for her the way my sister fought for me. "Because she told me what I was when everyone else in my life was telling me what I wasn't. Once I started focusing on what I was instead, that's where my identity came from, my dreams, the drive."

"It all starts with believing in yourself," she recites in a droll tone.

I squint in frustration. Not at her. Just at our world that is so quick to define and lock people in boxes until they trap themselves.

"No, that's a lie. It starts with accepting yourself. You can't believe in what you don't understand. And if you're still telling people you're no one, then you don't understand yet."

She goes quiet, but I see her mind working. All I can do is hope that some of this is getting through. Because it would be a terrible tragedy if her beautiful light flickered out because she never understood how brightly it shines.

"Can we work on our song again?" she asks in a tentative voice.

My heart soars. No other response would mean more to me.

"Which one?" I ask.

She sucks in a breath. "What do you mean?"

Time to show her what a beacon she is.

"Fire up that laptop."

CHAPTER 15

$\mathcal{I}$ let Callie pick our next meal and immediately regret it when she chooses salads. Not because I don't like salads—we practically live on this stuff—but I've never felt more like a museum exhibit as I do right now.

"What?" I ask as her weird smug stare follows yet another bite of lettuce from the container to my mouth. My fork dangles in the air like it's not sure if it's about to get an award or written up by the principal.

"Nothing. Just enjoying the moment." She even leans back in her chair like she's settling in for a show.

I narrow my gaze at her. "And what moment is that? Enjoying a meal with a super hot rockstar, or watching me eat vegetables?"

Her sly grin could go either way. "It can't be both?"

"You're acting like my mom again." That threat worked before, but she's unfazed this time.

"Good. You need it. Vitamins, Casey. You need vitamins."

"There are vitamins in fries."

"What would TJ say?"

My fork nearly falls from my hand. She really does

remember everything. I'm in deep trouble if this romance becomes a thing.

"TJ... Don't remind me. Please."

Her arms cross in an attempt to level up on the mom-stare. "What? You know I'm right."

"Right about what?" another voice says from behind.

I swear Luke has an alarm that goes off when food enters this suite.

He grabs the unopened container and drops to a chair at the table.

"TJ would want you to consume a well-balanced meal," Callie explains in her apparent quest to turn salad into my next fight with Luke.

"TJ Barringer?" Luke directs at me.

Guess we're going there since.... We're already there.

To my surprise, Luke huffs a laugh as he opens his lunch. "How does she know TJ?"

"I don't," Callie says, way too late to turn this train around. "Only by reputation."

"Oh, really? Interesting," Luke muses.

I try to read his face, but he's not giving anything away.

"She was with me when TJ called about the new tracks," I explain, studying his every movement.

He hesitates for just a moment before digging into his salad.

Still can't get a read.

"Not to mention you guys talk about him. I remember stuff," Callie chimes in.

"Don't we know it," I grunt.

Callie's glare is inversely correlated to Luke's smirk.

At least I'm not the only victim of her otherworldly recall.

"Heard you kids working again," Luke says when the conversation dies.

I glance at him in shock. I don't know which rocks me more,

the fact that he spoke when he didn't have to or the fact that it was about music.

I stay casual, not wanting to break the spell. "Yeah, Callie has a lot of good ideas."

"Oh, please," she huffs in a dismissive tone. "I sit there and offer moral support while you work your magic."

I return a playful warning look that's also kind of... not.

"Those aren't my lyrics," I point out.

"They're not lyrics, they're verses," she quips. "It's a poem."

"Not anymore," Luke cuts in.

She stiffens and lasers a look at him. "Wait, whose side are you on anyway?"

Luke lifts the corner of his mouth. "Sorry, hon, but poetry set to music is called a 'song.'"

She tries to play it off, but a late smile betrays her. "Fine, whatever."

"Accept it, Callie. You're a songwriter now," I say.

I don't know why this is so hard for her to grasp.

"No, I'm not. Wait. Really? But..."

I shrug and offer a quick smile before facing Luke. "I'm having trouble with the hook into the chorus, though."

I wince at my stumble into our old routine. The words came out before I could stop them. It's Callie's fault. She's swept away so many of the eggshells, my brain forgot they were there.

I wait for Luke to seize up and run. Instead, he says, "Let's hear it."

I go still, like my head and limbs don't know what to do with that.

He lifts a brow, and I haul my brain back into gear.

"Okay, yeah, sure," I stutter as I get up from the table.

I grab the guitar from the living room, certain when I turn around he'll be gone. Or I'll find myself on the couch sleeping because this is a dream.

But there's no corporeal body on the couch and Luke is still at his seat when I return. His eyes track me with casual interest, like we're backstage or on the bus, messing around with new ideas.

I'm not sure I've ever been as nervous as I am when I pluck a few test chords. My hands are shaking as I clear my throat and launch into the verse and chorus of what we have of the mirror song. My fingers struggle with the pick, my voice strained like I'm back in kindergarten at my first violin recital.

Except it's not a strict violin instructor and overbearing father sitting in the audience judging me. It's my entire past, present, and future on the line. Everything I am and want to be.

If Luke hates it, I'll be heartbroken.

If he runs away again, I'll be crushed.

Either way, this ends with me in pieces.

I almost play through the song a second time, just to avoid the moment when the music stops and I have to face the pain of the inevitable. I can't even look at Luke while I wind down the final chorus. I know it will rattle me, and I'm not going to let nerves ruin this chance to have him back into the music with me, as brief as it might be.

Too soon, the song comes to an end. It has to. It's not formed enough to be the barrier I need. That's the whole point.

When the final chord rings out, I dampen the strings to cut it off in a silent confession that I know it's not finished. I still can't look at him. It will be even harder to see his disapproval or hasty retreat.

So instead, I find an invisible scratch in the table to examine, while he examines me.

The silence that follows is brutal, but I expected nothing less. It's the next part I don't know what to do with.

When I hear his inhale like he's going to speak, my own breath freezes in my lungs.

"It's good, Case. Really good. I see what you mean about the hook, though. Try throwing the F-sharp minor in after the A and add an extra two beats to the break."

...

What?

It takes a moment for the words to register. When they do, a burst of warm excitement floods through me.

"You mean, bring the chorus back in late on the offbeat?" I say.

I finally dare to check his face.

For the first time since Elena's death, he looks like my co-writer. My best friend and brother.

Emotion burns behind my eyes, and I blink it back.

"Exactly," he says. "Plus, the minor at the end of the bridge will give it a bigger cut. Hanging on the four was fine, but I think the two will give you more depth."

His eyes lock on mine to speak the real conversation. Our mouths are talking about music, but our hearts are somewhere far beyond that.

"Case, the chorus is killer." His eyes flash like he knows the magnitude of what those words mean to me, and loves me enough to give me this gift. "Really, really good."

I can't speak. I never in a million years expected this. I was just hoping he wouldn't run away. Instead, he's done the opposite.

He's taken a step back to me.

Still speechless, I'm relieved when he offers a small smile like he understands. He turns to Callie to give me time to process and recover.

"You, too, Callie. I know those are your words," he says in a gentle voice.

"Mostly. Casey changed them around a bit and added some."

Although less flustered than I am, she seems affected as well. Of course she would pick up on the significance of what's happening. She might not know music jargon, but she reads people better than anyone.

"Yeah, but you understand that's not because there was anything wrong with the original," Luke continues, sounding more and more like the confident icon I remember. "They just have to flow with the music. It's all a give and take in the process."

Her smile finishes the unspoken part of their exchange. "Of course. He made it better, there's no question."

I'm still trying to wrap my brain around what's happening when Luke turns to me.

He motions toward the guitar. "Can I see that?"

I stare at him. At the guitar. My brain short circuits.

I want to give it to him, but it's like I can't figure out how.

How do you hand a king his scepter?

I cradle the guitar in both hands and lift it toward him. Even then, part of me thinks he'll refuse it. That this is all some cruel joke. A punishment for disrupting his despair with my hope.

But Luke pulls it into his arms.

I don't move, barely breathing as he traces the strings like he's forgotten what they feel like. As if he's just recovered a lost limb he never thought he'd get back.

It's almost easier to believe he'd regrow an arm than what I'm seeing now.

Slowly, his touch transforms from exploratory to determined. There's purpose in him again as he positions the guitar into the place it's had in his life for as long as I can remember.

His left hand loops around the frets. His right rests on the strings.

He draws in a deep breath as he braces himself.

We all do. And when the first note comes out, I almost choke on a swallow.

That note leads to another, and a third, and a fourth. Soon, his fingers are dancing on the strings with a confidence that transports us back to a basement, a tour bus, a stage. I can see the lights, the crowd. Luke at the mic, owning that stage like it's the only thing that matters. Sweeny beside him, his guitar wailing the melody that's drifting toward me now.

"Sweeny's lick," I breathe out.

Luke's gaze flickers to mine. A flash of convoluted emotion skims his blue-green irises. Joy, pain, relief, confusion. He doesn't know what to do with what's happening any more than I do.

But he's still here.

He's still fucking trying.

"For the bridge. I think we just layer rhythm for the chorus. Maybe some killer reverb on the 'hello' vocal?" His casual tone betrays the monumental shift that's happening inside him, inside all of us.

I swallow the rush of emotion exploding through me. "Definitely. I was thinking even a tight band-pass filter on the second line."

A stuttered breath betrays the internal storm Luke is wrestling with. "Yeah, that could work too. I'm hearing it."

I feel Callie's shock and excitement beside me. She remains silent through the entire exchange, as if sensing the words we're saying isn't the conversation we're having.

Luke and I continue to discuss production ideas as a weak translation of the real work of art being formed in our hearts. Somewhere along the line, our cover becomes real. The song we're pretend writing takes a turn into viable ideas I'm itching to explore.

"How easy do you think it would be to get into Jackson Street tomorrow?" I blurt out. "I know we haven't used them in a while, but Julian's a pro."

Luke's expression doesn't change. "I don't know. TJ might be able to get you in. You want to lay some of this down?"

I try to read him. Could I dare to hope he's feeling any of the excitement that comes with new ideas as well? We used to get high off that rush.

"Thinking about it," I say. "I mean, why not? It's out there now. Might as well see what it sounds like. Wish we were home and could just use our own stuff, but Jackson Street is cool. Julian has gear we can use, right?"

Luke still isn't giving me any clue about where his head is. "Probably. He's got his studio guys, too, if you want to mess around. You might need to give him a heads up though so he can get them in. Send TJ a work tape. He'll lose his mind."

Another question is pounding at my skull. A week ago I wouldn't have dreamed of asking. I'm still terrified, but I will never forgive myself if there was a chance to bring him all the way back and I didn't take it.

His eyes broadcast the rejection before I can even ask, and my heart drains into my stomach.

His apologetic look stings more than the resentful ones I've grown accustomed to, because this look tells me how much it's hurting him to hurt me. How much he wants to give this to me but can't.

He tears his gaze away. "I can't, man. You know that. I just… You've got my support on this."

A consolation prize that does the opposite.

"Yeah, no, of course," I grit out. "It would have been…"

Impossible. Fucking impossible.

"No, yeah," I say through a harsh laugh, mostly at myself for the absurd hope.

I don't know what the hell I was thinking.

"Good luck, though. I think you have something," Luke says in another unintentional dagger through the heart. He's trying to soften the blow, and when he rests his hand on my shoulder as he passes, it feels like a third-degree burn.

I want to reassure him, but I can't. My heart is too broken. My hope too shattered to pretend otherwise.

Once he's gone, I have this overwhelming need to disappear as well.

"I should go call TJ and see if he can set something up," I mutter.

I can't look at Callie. She'll make me stay and drag the poison out, but I'm not ready to hand it over. I need it to hurt. I need it to sink in and make its mark.

"Casey..."

I get up from the table. "It's fine. Not a big deal. I'll be back in a few minutes."

Pulling out my phone, I head toward the office to make the call.

It's only when I lock myself inside with the chair that I realize what I've done.

CHAPTER 16

*A*m I surprised we can't get into the studio until Friday? No. That's just the way things are going to roll for this it seems. I'm sure if it was Luke Craven asking, they would've found a way to make it work, despite the history there.

I'm also not surprised Callie gets tired of dealing with my transformation into a moody artist. Even the most compassionate, patient woman on the planet has limits, so it's not exactly breaking news when she decides she needs to go back to her place to catch up on "stuff."

I agree some space might be good for all of us, until she's gone and I feel like a massive dick.

A bored, lonely one.

It's not a great combination, and after working off some frustration in the gym, then the pool, I'm feeling less like a brooding artist and more like a repentant boyfriend.

I take a quick shower and grab a snack before staring at my phone, fighting the temptation to message Callie. She probably gave me her number "for logistics," not so I would bother her while she's trying to get a break from us.

Maybe just an apology?

My finger hovers over her name.

When did you become a needy teenager?

With a sigh, I shove my phone back in my pocket and decide to check on Luke. I'm a few steps into the hallway when I notice the office door is open a crack. My heart beats faster and a cold sweat breaks over my skin. I've never encountered a ghost, but if I did, this is what it'd feel like.

Part of me wants to turn around and go back to the living room. Actually, no. Most of me votes for scrolling streaming menus and pretending I didn't see anything. But the piece of my soul Callie owns is screaming at me not to let this go. If she was willing to step into a complete stranger's weirdness, what level of strange should I be willing to tolerate from my best friend?

I don't bother knocking. He'll tell me to go away or say nothing at all, so I just push through the door.

Light streams into the room. My gaze shoots to the corner where I expect to find him on a chair like a horror movie jump scare. Instead, he's seated on the edge of the desk, staring blankly. He turns his head in surprise when I enter, and I offer a weak smile before tracking his line of sight to the opposite corner of the room.

Ah. So the creepy chair *is* there. He's just not sitting on it.

This might actually be worse.

"Sorry about earlier," he says.

"It's fine. I get it."

I don't know how to ask the obvious question, so I let my wandering gaze do it for me. Luke rests his stare back on the chair and studies it in silence for a long time, so I park myself next to him and get a good look as well. I don't know why I'm surprised it looks exactly the same as all the other chairs I saw at Jemma's. Maybe I expected this one to be the gilded version caked in diamonds or something.

But no. It's... a chair.

"Do you believe in ghosts?" he asks in a conversational tone.

A shiver runs through me.

I scratch at my temple, not sure I'm equipped to do this. "I don't know. I believe we don't know as much as we think we do. Every generation thinks they've figured it all out, and the next one proves how little they knew."

He nods without looking at me. "Like The Enlightenment and shit?"

"Yeah. I mean, if you asked a dude in the Middle Ages how the brain worked, he'd tell you with one hundred percent confidence it was because a million tiny elves were running around inside your skull banging on shit. Doesn't mean he was right about it. How do we know the stuff *we're* so sure about won't be laughable in a hundred years?"

"So you don't believe in ghosts but you don't *don't* believe in ghosts," he muses. A smile cracks his severe expression.

I can't help but laugh. "Yeah. I guess. I believe if you want to believe in ghosts you have as much basis for that as someone who *doesn't* want to believe it."

He nods again and squints back at the chair. "Am I still a bad person, Casey?"

I go numb.

His gaze slowly tears away from the chair to find me. All humor is gone from his face. His eyes search mine, open and waiting for the truth.

But what *is* the truth? That was my point earlier. It's all about perspective. What he's really asking is if his framework for being a bad person has changed.

"I'll answer that after you answer a question for me."

He sucks in a breath. The nervous glance he shoots at the chair makes me think he's afraid I'm going to ask about it. I will. One hundred percent. But not right now. Callie was right. We'll know when it's time.

"What's the question?" he says when I hesitate.

"What would have happened if Callie had stumbled upon the

old Luke in Jemma's instead of who you are now? Would you have made room for her in your life?"

He flinches and tightens his grip around the edge of the desk on either side of him.

After a long silence, he releases a heavy exhale.

"No. I wouldn't even have noticed her. I would have been too distracted, too full of myself to give her another thought. She would have hated me."

"Yeah, probably," I say through a chuckle. "She would have hated me too."

His lips tip up but quickly flatten.

I sigh and follow his gaze back to the chair. "I don't think I *can* answer your original question. I don't think anyone can. But I can tell you this—darkness can't tolerate light and evil can't tolerate good. So if Callie has wedged into your life, there must be something worth saving."

His eyes slip closed.

My own feel hot and sore.

I rest my hand on his for a second, then slide off the desk to leave him alone. I don't know if I believe in ghosts, but I believe *he* has one he needs to deal with.

As soon as I'm back in the hall, I pull out my phone.

Me: Hey, sorry for being an ass. You were right to choose dirty socks over us.

I add a silly emoji and shoot the text off to Callie.

If the universe is going to give me a supernova like Callie Roland, I'm damn well going to hang onto it as long and as hard as possible.

* * *

"You hungry?" Luke asks as he saunters into the living room.

I look up from the couch and adjust the guitar in my lap.

"A little, yeah. Want me to order something?"

"I got it," he says with a weak smile. "Indian food okay? There's a great place two blocks down. I can order in."

"Sure."

While he places the order, I return to the guitar. I recorded a rough worktape of the mirror song earlier for myself. It was my intention to improve on it and iron out some of the kinks before sending it off to TJ, but without Callie, it's just not happening. Every take seems to be worse than the last. Everything feels... off.

Our short text exchange earlier became a phone call when she said she wasn't coming back until tomorrow. Things got a little tense when I couldn't shut down the privileged asshole in me as much as I should have, but after *another* apology, we got back on track. By the end, she didn't seem upset, so I believe her when she says it's not personal, just logistics.

I still miss her like hell.

Come to think of it, maybe that's why I can't get the music to flow. My head is stuck in another apartment somewhere in this city.

"Food will be here in forty-five minutes," Luke says, taking the seat perpendicular to me. "Working on something?"

"I was trying to, but it's not happening."

My fingers launch into an absent strum like they always do when a guitar's in my hands.

"That sucks. You seemed to be on a roll."

"Yeah, I was. I don't know what happened."

A smile slips over his lips.

"What?"

"You lost your muse," he says in a smug tone.

I narrow my eyes at him. "No, I just..." I sigh. "Yeah." I shake my head. "I don't know, man. It's just different with her, you know? She drives me crazy, but when I'm with her, I'm just Casey."

Whoa.

Luke must have heard the same thing I did when he snorts a laugh.

"Here we go," he mumbles.

I ignore him and straighten on the couch to reposition the guitar. I switch the tempo of the progression I'd been playing to something more fun. Soon, I have a groove that has Luke shaking his head with a knowing smile while he scrolls through his phone.

I jot down some lyrics and iron them out.

"What rhymes with 'made me'?" I ask Luke.

"Save me?"

"Too angsty for this one. Amaze me?"

"Too cliché." A thought runs through his head and he smirks. "I know. Grammy," he jokes.

I laugh. Then stare at my notes app.

Hang on.

> "They say I'm a rockstar, baby
> But that's just what they made me
> Ignore my wall of Grammys, right now I'm only
>   yours."

I chuckle to myself. This is so freaking cheesy. Callie is gonna hate it. And love it. Not that I'll ever play it for her. But hey, at least I'm writing again.

"That's actually not terrible," Luke calls over without looking up from his phone.

He's right. It's not, and I fight a grin at where this is going.

> "I'm a superstar or pathetic cover, it's all in your
>   power, lover

You're everything I need to know, let me be yours"

"I'm no titan, babe, a…"

"Shit. Any ideas?" I ask.
He finally looks up. "Play it again?"
I play through what I have, and he cocks his head.
"Liar, maybe," he says with a sly smile.

I'm no titan, babe, a liar, maybe.

"Heh. Yeah. I like that."

"I'm no titan, babe, a liar, maybe
I'm no one else you need to know
You unravel my maze, the light in my…"

"Haze," Luke offers.
"Perfect." I type that into the lyrics.

"You're everything I need to know
You may drive me crazy
But when I'm with you I'm just Casey,
and that's how I know,
that's all I need to know,
I'm yours"

A grin cuts across my face as I lean back on the couch.
Luke crosses a look to me, shaking his head. "Dude, that's…"
He huffs a laugh I've known him long enough to interpret.
It's ridiculous, silly, and amazing at the same time.
There's a knock on the door.
Food's here.
He pushes up from the couch and circles around me.

"You've got it bad, bro," he says with a smirk as he passes. "You're damn lucky she does too."

I bite my lip and stare back at the phone screen, just as it lights up with a text. From Callie.

My heart jumps, and I'm just glad Luke doesn't have X-Ray vision.

I open the message and grin.

Callie: Listening to your stuff now.

Me: Yeah? What do you think?

Callie: That I can't believe you even spent two seconds on my stupid poems.

We spend the rest of the night chatting like she never left. Until it all goes to shit again.

CHAPTER 17

*I*t feels like I've just fallen asleep when a buzzing sound jerks me awake.

With a groan, I squint toward the noise and grunt at the flashing display. The lamp on the end table casts an eerie glow over the large space while my eyes continue to adjust. I hide my face in my arm, trying to orient myself.

My decision to ignore the call changes when it occurs to me it might be Callie. Maybe she needs help. Or misses me. Either scenario is an auto answer.

I swat at the coffee table in an attempt to retrieve my phone. When I finally grasp it, the call is missed, but immediately jumps to life again.

TJ? At six in the morning?

Movement in my periphery grabs my attention, and I see Luke stirring on the other side of the couch. Guess he crashed here too. I'm tempted to silence the call, but if our manager is on a mission, there will be no escaping him.

"Yeah?" I croak into the receiver.

"Casey! Thank god. Were you sleeping?"

"It's six AM, dude. What's up?"

"So you haven't seen it, then."

"Seen what?"

His urgent tone has me picturing him pacing his office in rapid streaks. The guy does "stress" at a whole other level.

I push myself up to a sitting position and adjust the phone.

"It's all over the place," he continues. "Video and everything. Something about Luke and a chair and some new girlfriend? What's going on over there?!"

Shit.

I rub a hand over my face and cast another quick look at Luke. He seems to be waking up as well.

"It's nothing," I assure TJ. "I don't know what they're saying, but I'm sure it's bullshit."

"It's not bullshit! They're saying he's erratic and violent! Stealing property? Threatening people? Sky high on who knows what substances? And who's this girl? You didn't think we'd maybe want to control the narrative on Luke's first partner since the Elena thing?"

The Elena thing? Man, I hate this guy sometimes.

He goes quiet, and I actually feel his cringe through the phone.

"My bad, Casey. I could have phrased that better."

"Yeah. You could've," I say dryly.

The Elena thing... as if the worst day of my life is a tab on a spreadsheet.

"Anyway, my point is this is bad. It's blowing up and the Label isn't happy. I just spent hours trying to convince Alberto not to drop you over the Kara Corbin disaster, and then you pull this shit five minutes later? How could you let this happen?!"

Anger surges through me, burning away any lingering drowsiness. "First of all, I didn't *let* anything happen. I wasn't even here when all this went down. But even if I was, I'm not responsible for Luke's behavior."

Luke shifts on the couch, and I sense his intense stare from across the room.

"And second of all, the *event* you're talking about is clearly being blown out of proportion."

Hopefully. I don't actually know. Luke still hasn't told me anything about that damn chair and why it was worth blowing up our lives again.

"So he didn't steal a chair?" TJ returns, hopeful.

"I mean… yeah. But—"

"Shit. What about the girl? Is there a girl?"

"Yes, but it's not—"

"Dammit! Okay, listen, I'm getting Alberto on the phone. Expect a call in a couple hours. I'll let you know who will be on it when I find out. And Casey, keep Luke on a leash. No more drama."

I don't even get to tell him off when he hangs up without a goodbye.

"Fuck," I hiss, shoving my phone back on the table.

I dig the heels of my palms into my scratchy eyes.

"It's out there, isn't it," Luke states in a flat tone.

I sigh and drop my hands. "Yeah, man. TJ is going to set up a call for damage control."

"What are they saying?"

Luke's expression is still unreadable as he watches me from several yards away.

"TJ didn't give many details, but dude, Callie's involved."

He winces and sinks back against the couch. "Fuck."

"Yeah. They're saying you two are together."

His gaze locks on mine. He knows the magnitude of what that means. And it means a whole lot more to him than a spreadsheet called "The Elena Thing."

He runs a hand over his head as he thinks. "I should be on the call."

"I don't think that's a good idea. I'll take it."

He shakes his head. "You can't keep fighting my battles for me. You weren't even part of this."

"No, but I am now."

"Casey…"

"I'm serious, man. It's gonna be brutal, and I have a layer of insulation from it you won't. They won't expect you to be involved. Let me handle it."

He deflates with a heavy exhale. "What about Callie? We need to warn her. Should we call her?"

The thought of waking her this early to blow up her life ignites a dull ache behind my eyes.

"No. I'll break the news when she comes over. Which should be in just a few hours anyway. Plus, I'll know more after the conference call."

He lowers his gaze, pain flashing across his face. After a long silence, his eyes find mine again.

"I'm sorry for dragging you into this," he says quietly.

"It's not a big deal. It'll blow over. You know how it goes."

He shakes his head. "No, I mean all of it."

I flinch and go quiet as his words sink in. I don't even know how to respond to that. Anything I say will be a lie and he knows it.

"I'm gonna shower and crash," he says, laboring to his feet. An invisible curtain is sinking down on him, crushing him, veiling him right in front of my eyes. "Let me know if you change your mind about the call. I'll take the hit."

I believe him. Worse than that, I believe he *wants* to take the hit because the pain will feed that sick part of his brain that insists on torturing itself.

I also know that call would undo all the progress we've made over the last couple of weeks, and there's not a chance in hell I'm letting that happen.

My phone buzzes again, and I glance at the screen to see a text from TJ.

Everyone will be there. Bring your A Game.

* * *

THE CALL GOES ABOUT AS BADLY as it could. Maybe worse. At one point, the Label even says they're done with us and activating their "Morality Clause" to officially sever ties.

TJ and our PR team manage to quell the fire enough to give us a chance to fix things. We have twenty-four hours to come up with an alternate narrative. It's also hammered home that the demo on Friday *will* be delivered and it *will* be good.

The harsher the vibe gets, the more grateful I am that Luke isn't participating. It would've been so much worse for all parties involved, and we likely wouldn't have gotten the brief reprieve. I take the repeated beatings and concede to all their demands, even though I know I probably can't deliver any of them. At least I've gained a day to *damage control* my own life before it implodes on a public platform.

After we hang up, I stare at the wall for a long time. My head is spinning with the threats, warnings, and tirades meant for someone else. My chest aches. My stomach is in knots. The only thing keeping me remotely grounded is the thought of seeing Callie soon.

It's almost eight, so I'm hoping to hear the door at any second.

Luke hasn't emerged from his room.

I haven't sought him out.

It's better this way. I don't trust my ability to tame the riot inside me if I face him right now. The last thing I want is to explode on him and defeat the entire purpose of me taking the punishment on his behalf.

I didn't go through that hell for no reason.

By the time the door lock triggers around nine, I've shifted my zombie state from the couch to the kitchen. It was my intention to make coffee, but I never got past leaning on the island, staring into space.

Callie pokes her head around the door, and the heavy weight crushing my chest melts away.

Her expression is almost shy when she approaches with a paper bag in one hand and a small suitcase in the other. I can't imagine why she'd be nervous, until I remember our rampant text flirting the night before. God, that seems like forever ago.

"You came back," I say with a smile.

"And brought food as commanded."

"Good, I'm starving."

She drops the bag on the island, and I join her at the end.

"I got a few kinds of cream cheese. I wasn't sure what you liked." Her voice is still hesitant, like she's not sure how this encounter is supposed to go. I try to remain bright and positive for her sake, but her day is about to get ugly.

"Plain."

"Got that."

She fishes a container from the bag and passes it to me, along with a plastic knife.

I grab a bagel and dig into the cream cheese.

"How's Luke?" she asks.

The air drains from the room. I can't hold the act through the surprise hit, but maybe it's better this way. There's no point dragging this out.

"Uh-oh," she says in an ominous tone.

"Yeah. It wasn't a good night. I didn't want you to worry so I didn't say anything, but remember that thing you told me about with the chair?"

Her shoulders sag as she nods.

"Well, it hit last night. Freaking blew up. I've been on the phone since six this morning with TJ, the lawyers, the Label PR people. What a mess."

Her expression grows pensive. "I was afraid of this. What are they saying?"

Nothing and everything. Lies that become truth. The great juxtaposition of our media obsessed world.

"All bullshit. You know how it goes. No one actually knows anything so they all put their own 'hypothetical' spin on it, which then becomes fact. You should hear some of the stuff they're saying. Totally crazy."

She frowns and watches her finger make absent stabs at her bagel. "What kinds of things?"

Every instinct in me wants to protect her from exactly that, but she has a right to know. She's going to find out anyway.

"Stupid stuff," I mumble. "That he was high. That he got in a dispute over a bill. Oh, and you'll love this. You're in the story now, too."

Her head darts up. "I am?"

Anxious hazel eyes search my face with a hint of fear. Being forced to watch her go through this fallout might be harder for me than for her.

"Yeah, pretty much the main story, actually. Just a heads up. Anyone you've ever known—like, ever—is going to be trying to contact you within the week. Better turn your phone off and plan to stay hidden."

I spend the next few minutes relaying the bad news about what it means to be under the celebrity microscope. Then, the really bad news that she'll be the focal point of the drama.

She seems rocked by the whole thing, but in typical Callie fashion, after absorbing the shock, she settles into determination.

"So what do I do? How can I help?" she asks, taking a stool. Literally, getting down to business.

A smile plays at my lips. "We're working on that. I explained the whole situation, everything, to our people, and they're going to put together a response."

Her knee bounces as her brows knit with concern. Knowing her, she's probably more worried about us than herself.

I take her hand to reassure her. "Hey, it's going to be okay. I promise."

When she shifts to fall against me, I pull her close and instinctively brush my lips on her hair. I will do everything in my power to protect her from this.

"It would be so much better if they just thought I was your girlfriend instead," she mumbles, and I go rigid. She pulls back with wide, urgent eyes. "I'm sorry! I didn't... I meant... for Luke's sake."

We both know that's a lie.

My body goes hot, then cold. Instead of the joy I expect, it's fear coursing through my veins. I've been waiting weeks to hear those words, and now I'm paralyzed by them.

Maybe it's this small dose of reality, or maybe I've just been in denial, but suddenly, the thought of officially dating Callie, permanently dragging her into our world, seems impossible. Worse than that. Cruel and pointless.

She hides her face in her hands as she gathers herself together. My brain is screaming for me to say something. To put her mind at ease and tell her I feel the same, but I can't speak. There are no words in my vocabulary for this situation because I've never let myself be in it before.

There's a reason I've never had a serious girlfriend. A lifetime of reasons my starved heart conveniently forgot until this moment.

"I should go check on Luke," she stutters out, sliding off the stool.

I have to stop her, make her understand, but I don't know how. All I can think to do is grab her arm and pull her around, even if it means telling a small lie or two.

But I miscalculate the strength of my tug and end up with an irresistible temptation just a breath away. Her gaze locks on mine, and for a brief moment, neither of us knows what to do.

Except I'm the one who invited this. It's on me to fix it.

"You don't actually want that, do you?" I say. The words just pour out. "I mean, do you have any idea how hard it would be to date someone like me?"

Her broken heart is all over her face, and I can't look at it anymore. I stare at the wall instead. My brain isn't processing things fast enough. The truth keeps changing faster than I can keep up with it. What I want, what is, what should be—all questions I just realized I can't sort out.

"I'm sorry, Callie. I know you didn't mean it like that. I just wanted to make sure... I mean, even if I really liked you, and I do... I wouldn't be able to live with myself if I hurt you, and I'm afraid I would."

Her weak nod does nothing to soften the blow. The irony that I'm crushing her in my effort not to crush her is not lost on me, but I've been so stupid to think this could ever work. Not to mention a total asshole for leading her on. Of course she'd think we were headed toward something. I thought so too until twelve seconds ago.

Until reality slapped me in the face this morning.

Look what's happened because she was caught having breakfast with one of us. Imagine what it will be when the real shit hits the fan. It's better for both of us if we face the truth now before it goes too far. Before I can't do the right thing and end up breaking her like every single relationship I've witnessed since I was a kid.

Love destroys people. I've seen it over and over and over again. Hell, the tragedy that brought us together is the ultimate testament to what it means to put your faith in another human being.

"Yeah, of course," she says in an even tone, but I hear the

waver in her voice. See the glossy film settling over her eyes. God, it hurts like hell.

"Um... Yeah, I should go. I..."

She yanks her arm away and stalks toward the hall, probably to flee to Luke's room.

You know you fucked up when someone turns to Luke for comfort over you.

"Shit," I mutter, running a hand over my face.

Now what?

*a*lone in the kitchen, I have no idea what to do next.

I can't go after her. Feeling like shit about what just happened doesn't change any of the realities that made it happen in the first place.

I also can't imagine stewing on the couch for the rest of the day. Plus, I'm feeling claustrophobic again. After the compounding stressors of this morning from hell, I need something physical. I learned a long time ago, if I make my body hurt, it can ease the pressure on my mind.

The gym is busy but not packed. Would it have mattered if it was? In my current state, I would have picked up the last remaining free weight and lifted it in endless reps until my arm gave out.

After a warm-up mile on the treadmill, I start working on my shoulders. Ten minutes into my reps, a disturbing sensation of being watched chills my sweaty skin. I make a discreet scan of my surroundings, and my stomach rolls when I spot him.

What the fuck is he doing here?

Our eyes graze each other long enough for Orin Cantea to assume it's an invitation to approach. He occupies the empty machine next to me, and I grit my teeth as I go back to my workout. This is the last thing I need right now.

"Hey, Casey. Good to see you again."

I toss a curt nod in his direction and pretend to be engrossed in my workout. Not that narcissists like him give a shit if their desires are inconvenient to other people.

His invasive stare makes the vibe flat-out creepy as I work out beneath his intense scrutiny. I'm not particularly interested in giving him a show.

A few minutes in, I let the bar drop and sit up on the bench. Grabbing a towel, I wipe the sweat from my neck and face as I twist toward him.

"How can I help you, Orin?"

His sly grin makes it clear he didn't catch my irritation—or doesn't care.

"Actually, it's the other way around. It seems I may be in a position to help *you*."

Something twists in my gut at the way his gaze travels over me.

"Yeah? How's that?" I take the bait, mostly because I need to know what sick plan he has cooking and if it's another threat we'll have to prepare for.

"Your boy had a busy night in the news cycle. Things are looking pretty bleak for him and the future of your band."

"And?"

"And I can help spin it for you."

I return a tight smile. "Thanks for the offer, but we already have our people on it."

He smirks. "You know your people are owned by my people, right?"

My fingers clench around the towel. "Right, well, it's not really my call anyway. The Label is handling the PR for now. You'll have to contact them for a statement."

"Word is *the Label* isn't so happy with you either. How long is that going to last? What happens to you and Luke when they decide it's not their problem anymore?"

My gaze darts to his before I can stop it. His smile grows until it's downright chilling.

"What are you talking about?" I hedge. I know, obviously, but I want to see what he knows, and have no intention of giving more away than I already have.

"Come on. You're smarter than that. You've been in the game long enough to know how this works."

"Apparently not, because I have no idea where you're going with this."

He shifts on his bench, and I swivel to face him on a more even level.

"I think you do."

"I'm not gonna fuck you, Orin."

His eyes go wide. His face flushes. "How dare you! Why would you even—"

"Save it," I spit out, impatient. "Just tell me what you want."

He looks like he's about to continue his pointless denial when he decides better of it. Good. I'm already sick of this conversation.

"I want an exclusive."

"From whom?"

"Luke."

I hurl a bitter laugh. "Never gonna happen."

"Fine, then you."

I grit my teeth. "Which publication?"

"All of them."

"Yeah right," I scoff.

"What's the difference? If I own you, I own you. What does it matter where?"

I free all my resentment and anger into my scowl.

After a short standoff, he sighs. "Look, I'll make it look good, I promise. I'll even let you submit the questions as long as they're substantial. I don't care what the story is, I just want it juicy and I want it first."

For the hundredth time today, I scrub at my face. I hate everything about this. It doesn't mean everything he's saying isn't true.

Luke's latest stunt put us over the edge, and right now, I have no hope of getting a workable demo by Friday. Our entire legacy crashes in four days if I don't do something.

Orin and his media empire have the clout to turn this thing around for us. If he keeps his promise, we'd be back on top like none of it even happened. The Label would be thrilled and forgive anything. More importantly, the pressure would ease off Luke and Callie. For now.

"Let me think about it," I say finally.

His face lights up with surprise and excitement. Clearly, he wasn't expecting that answer.

"If it happens, I want everything you just said in writing, got it?" I warn with a cold stare.

He holds up his hands. "Of course. Whatever you want. But remember, I want substance. I'm not making this offer for some disclosure about your strawberry allergy as a kid."

"Yeah, I got it," I mumble, dropping to my back on the bench again.

This time he takes the hint and rises from his machine. I feel his hungry gaze as he walks away but ignore it.

Sleazeballs like him always end up on top. It's easy when you're willing to step on and exploit every other person in your path. As much as I can't stand the guy, he's just a photocopy of most of the other industry movers and shakers I've encountered over the years. And for some reason, this one has always taken a special interest in me.

The irony is, because he's an egotistical, self-indulgent opportunist, I actually take him at his word. I *do* believe he'll make us look good and do what he can—not because he wants to help, but because it would serve his needs. He gains nothing from adding his voice to the existing cloud of criticism. Bucking the trend is where the attention is. Plus, I doubt he'll want to betray his promise and alienate me after finally trapping me in his web.

Maybe it wouldn't be the end of the world if I used that to my advantage. Would it be so bad to turn the tables and exploit *him* for once?

I just need a story worth sharing.

* * *

MY HEAD IS STILL GRINDING when I return from the gym. Already on edge from the repeated blows this morning, my unsettling encounter with Orin pushed me off the ledge. It took a very long time to work off the demons crawling in and around me. I could barely walk by the time I made myself quit. No point adding physical trauma to my long list of mental ones.

Callie is in the kitchen, and just seeing her ignites a spark in the shadows crowding my soul. I hesitate to approach for her sake. She understandably wanted space, but I have nowhere else to go, and honestly, after what just happened with Orin, I'm in desperate need of a brush with the opposite end of the humanity spectrum.

She glances up from the bagel she's preparing and offers a tight smile.

"Hit the gym?" she asks in a forced casual tone.

I nervously play with the edge of the towel slung over my shoulder.

"Had to work off some steam." I manage a diplomatic smile as well.

She shifts on her feet, and for a brief moment looks like she's going to say something. I'm disappointed when she shakes it off and picks up the plate on the counter.

"Okay. Well, we're watching spy movies in the back."

She moves toward the hall and it physically hurts to have her light ripped away. I know it's my fault. I know it's not fair. But after everything… God, I feel so alone again. So scared and helpless and I just can't handle being on bad terms with her as well.

"Callie, wait. Please."

She pauses, and I hold my breath.

When she turns, her expression is unreadable.

I swallow the pang in my chest. "I'm sorry about earlier. I just need you to understand that it's not you. Please know that."

"Yeah. It's not you, it's me. Got it." She spins on her heel back toward the hall.

"Stop! Will you just stop?" I reach for her arm, and pull her too close again.

Gorgeous hazel eyes peer up at me, glistening in the sunlight like they're reflecting the depths of her inner radiance. I'm a moth to a flame. A vampire who's been staked and drained over and over. My gaze drops to her lips, and she rips her arm away.

Her gaze narrows with justifiable resentment.

"What is your problem, Casey? What do you want from me? You want to fool around for a bit before you head back on tour with your real model girlfriends? I'm not interested in that, okay? I was pretty sure you were smart enough to pick up on that."

I reel from the blow, not because of her words, but because she's right. None of this is fair to her. She's the only blameless one in this entire nightmare and we keep jerking her around to suit our needs.

Somehow I need her to know this. To understand *we're* the damaged ones, not her. Images of the last few days crash into me. All the laughter and smiles. The admiration in her eyes when she looks at me. I know she's not using me like others do, but it doesn't mean she hasn't idealized me into a fantasy I can never live up to.

She wants me to be her rock, Luke's savior, and right now I feel just as weak and broken as anyone.

"It's not like that, Callie. I don't know how to explain it. I just don't want to hurt you. I'm afraid I'm not what you think. I'm afraid I can't live up to your expectations. I mean, I'm not..."

The prince you think I am.

I'm not... enough.

"At the end of the day, I'm just a guy," I say instead.

I wince at her harsh laugh.

"My *expectations?*" she fires back. "I didn't even have any! I wasn't interested in Casey Barrett, the rockstar. I don't know him! I was interested in Casey Barrett, the seventh son of Mr. and Mrs. Barrett of Houston, Texas. The guy who would stand beside his friend when no one else saw any reason why he should. The guy who didn't shy away from someone else's puke, or late nights, or fights with a powerful label because they were hurting someone he loved. The guy whose smile literally got me through the last few days of emotional hell, and who's been nothing but a rock for all of us."

Angry tears cloud her eyes and she wipes them away with rough movements. I feel like shit. Worse than shit. All I wanted to do was fix a mess, and instead I made a bigger one.

"I was interested in the guy who was finally starting to make me believe in myself," she continues, burning a hole through my heart. "So if you're not actually that guy, then I guess you're right. We can just end this, whatever it is, now with a clean break."

She doesn't wait for a response when she spins around and escapes into the shadows.

Once again I watch her walk away because I'm too selfish to live with the consequences of my own choice.

But with all the painful challenges on my plate and more

brimming on the horizon, none seem worse than the prospect of facing them without Callie.

After a quick shower, I've re-centered myself and decide to try again. I still don't know how to fix this, but I can't stop trying until I do. If not for myself, for her and Luke.

I trace her earlier steps to Luke's room and knock briefly before peeking into the room. I need a change of clothes anyway.

Callie's gaze sweeps over mine before returning with determination to the screen.

Ouch. And completely deserved.

Luke scans my half-naked body in a towel and shakes his head.

"Dude, you really need to send for your stuff or go shopping," he says as I fish through his drawers. I shoot him a wry look, and his lips tip up with a secret only he knows.

"What are you watching?" I ask to break the tense atmosphere.

"*Absolute Descent*," Callie says in a curt tone.

I cross a look to her, but she's avoiding me, so I return to my task.

"Any good?" I ask.

"So far it's fine," is her dismissive reply. "Just started fifteen minutes ago."

Guess she's going to make me work for this.

"Can I sit?" I ask after pulling on shorts and a t-shirt.

Callie looks about to say no, but Luke has other plans.

"Sure, man. We can go out to the living room if you want."

Relocating solves nothing. I need forced proximity.

"No, this is fine. There's room."

Famous last words.

It takes exactly three minutes and a few heated exchanges before she's fleeing from me yet again. This time back the way she came.

224

Luke turns a warning look on me as she stomps away, presumably "to get a drink."

"I don't know what you did, but you need to go fix this," he grunts.

He's not wrong. If he has any grand ideas how, that would be great, because right now I can't seem to do anything right.

I release a heavy exhale and slide off the bed. My original plan was to play it civil for a while, let her get used to my presence, like acclimating to the heat. *Then* I'd make another attempt at smoothing things over.

But I miscalculated. I underestimated what this woman does to me, and once we were pressed against each other, my brilliant plan dissolved in a rush of need to be close to her.

Now she's further than ever.

And it's all my fault. Everything is my fault these days. I'm trying so hard to keep all these ships afloat, but it's getting impossible to breathe, let alone carry the catastrophic weight crushing me.

I'm so fucking lost. And scared. And paying for crimes I don't even know I'm committing anymore.

She squares up when I approach, and I brace for another blow.

But the longer she searches my face, the softer her stance becomes.

"I'm sorry, Callie... I..."

Emotion creeps into my voice, and I choke it back. I don't have words. I have nothing. I'm going to lose her and I don't know how to stop it.

I lock my fingers above my head as stray thoughts assault me from all sides. Memories, fears, past and present, they dive-bomb me in one massive attack. All I can do is close my eyes until they swirl into a single message.

And when they do, I only have one choice—complete honesty.

"I don't date, Callie."

"Not ever?" she asks in surprise, because she knows that's not true.

"Not seriously."

I drop to the end of the couch, as if the mental weight has finally trampled me. I can't even stand anymore. She pauses, then tentatively takes a seat a few cushions away.

I pull in a breath and compel myself to continue. "My whole life has been spent witnessing one endless string of bad relationships. I grew up watching my dad beat my mom, older siblings getting dumped, older siblings wrecking others by dumping them." I shiver at the next image. "Then the finale of Luke and Elena."

I tip my head back and dissolve into the cushions. Just that small moment of peace is enough to keep going.

"Luke was my best friend, Elena my closest sibling. When they started dating, I wasn't surprised, but I was terrified. I knew Luke. I knew he couldn't be what Elena needed. And I knew Elena couldn't handle what he was. I tried to warn them. I…"

Shit. I can't crack. Not now. I've held it together for so long. I'm not going to break.

I rub my palms on my face, fighting the emotion. The memories.

"Tell him I hate him! Tell him I never want to hear from him again!"

"Elena, please, just—"

"No! Don't even try to defend him. You're my brother! You're supposed to be on my side!"

"It's not that simple. There's the band—"

"Ah! Then I hate you too!"

Click.

I clear away the memory. There are so many. A constant looping vortex that eventually sucked them both into the abyss.

"Anyway, they wouldn't listen to me. They were both so in love with each other, it didn't matter what anyone said. There was nothing I could do but brace myself and watch the disaster unfold."

My eyelids slip closed again. Heat burns behind them, and I know I'm losing the battle.

It's too much pain, too much loss to carry. I pull in a fractured breath, trying to clear my lungs, but it's no use.

I know when I speak again the words are going to come out as broken as I feel, but there's no other way to tell this story.

"And that's what I did," I scratch out. "Watched for three years as the two people I loved most in this world absolutely destroyed each other and themselves."

I find her again, needing her to understand. She might be the only person who can.

"Do you know what that's like?" I blink back threatening tears. "It killed Elena, and now it's killing Luke, and I swore I'd never do that to someone else. I would never, ever, hurt someone I loved the way they hurt each other. The way my dad hurt my mom. I don't know how else to do that except to stay away from them."

I lean forward, elbows on my knees, and hide my face in my hands.

I'm not surprised when I hear movement. She's probably running away from the disaster in front of her. I don't blame her. In some ways it's what I want. In all ways it's what I expect.

I flinch when warm pressure infuses into my arm. She squeezes until I look at her, then takes my hand.

"You're not Luke. I'm not Elena." Her tone is gentle but firm. Her eyes bore into mine, reinforcing the message.

Hot liquid drains down my cheeks. I hate it, but I can't stop it. It's been trapped inside me for too long. I shake my head, trying to clear it.

"You don't know that." My voice is barely above a whisper. "What if I am?"

Isn't it already happening? This time it's *my* mess forcing this strong woman to steel herself in preparation to fight for someone else's soul.

"You know what? Maybe you are," she says in a determined voice. "But you're worth the risk to me. You just need to decide if I am. You've told me many times I have to start trusting myself. Trust who I am. So do you."

Trust in who you are.

The man who stood in for Molly when our father lost his temper.

The man who stood by Luke when even he punished me for it.

The man who stood up for the band and took blow after blow to protect a future I'm not even sure I still believe in.

Callie's words soothe and sting as they echo through my head. I want them to be true. So much. But wanting something does nothing to change reality. We're not even addressing the other obstacle standing in our way.

I shake my head. "We can't, though! Don't you get it? I've got maybe three to four months, then I'm gone again. I'm on the road all the time, and even when I'm not, I've got obligations and expectations that take me everywhere and—"

"Casey, stop." She tugs my hand with an incredulous look, bordering on amused.

"I'm not asking for a ring, here," she says with a short laugh. "I'm talking about just letting whatever this is develop while it can. We can decide later what to do with it."

She softens and squeezes my hand. "You can't force yourself to be alone forever just because other people made some poor decisions. What happened to Luke and Elena... I can't even imagine what that was like for you, but that's not going to happen with us."

"But..."

She cuts me off with a stern look. "Casey, even if you break my heart, you will not break me. You won't."

She pulls me toward her.

The second our lips meet, the pressure around my heart releases. The pain, the fear, the loneliness, it all melts away. It will still be waiting for me somewhere in the shadows, but for now, I'm encased in light.

Our kiss deepens with a desperation I haven't felt before. Hunger and need for more than carnal pleasure. I want substance and time. Trust and hope.

We adjust on the couch until I'm stretched over her, our mouths still fighting to possess and own. Her hands claw at my shirt, scaling my body and spreading hot streaks wherever she touches. If a single kiss could tell a complex story, this is it.

"Casey?" she whispers.

"Yeah?" I breathe out.

"We're going to be okay."

I lift my head to find her eyes. When I do, joy like I've never felt seeps from my soul onto my lips in the form of a soft smile.

"You think?" I say.

"Yeah."

Her grin is everything as she traces my jaw and searches my eyes.

It's impossible not to kiss her again, and I indulge the craving.

She slides her hand up the back of my neck, tangling her fingers in my hair. It feels so amazing to be owned by this person. And she does. I'm hers, in whatever broken, messy way she wants me. There's no point fighting it anymore. She's right. This could all end in catastrophe like everything else, but that doesn't mean we shouldn't try.

We separate slowly, exchanging a tender, intimate smile.

I climb off her and reach out a hand to tug her to her feet.

As soon as she's standing, she's in my arms again. She settles against me, and I guard her close, daring anything in this big ugly universe to try to hurt her.

And suddenly, I know what I have to do. I would do anything for this woman. *Anything.*

Including sell my soul to Orin Cantea.

"Would you be upset if I tell them to fix the PR mess by reporting that you're my girlfriend instead of Luke's?" I ask. "No one would care then and they'll leave you both alone."

It's not even a lie. That's exactly what I plan to do, it's just not my label's PR company that will get the story.

She tips her head back with a look of surprise. "I don't know. It depends. Is it true?"

Is it true...

Twenty-five years of history beat down on me.

Mountains of trauma.

Volumes of reasons not to do this...

But it's all silenced by the look in her eyes.

"Um... I don't know. Do you want it to be?" I still can't believe she would want that after everything.

"You're kidding, right?" she scoffs.

I return a weak smile. "Well, I didn't want to assume... I mean after being such an ass the last couple days..."

"You were," she jokes before growing serious again. "You have my permission to call it whatever you want, but *you're* my choice, Casey, not Luke. Any rumors floating around about me should revolve around you."

I pull in a sharp breath. It's almost like she phrased it that way on purpose. Like she knew what it would mean to me to be chosen after a lifetime being the fourth chair. And there's not a single thing I'd want more than this.

She reaches for my hand, and I love the possessive way she holds onto it. It's hers. For as long as she'll accept it.

"Should we get back to the movie?" she asks, already dragging me toward the hall.

I'm about to agree until my gaze snags on the guitar. Maybe I *do* have something I can offer her after all.

"Not yet. I have something for you."

I grin as I guide us back to the couch. Picking up the guitar, I prepare to show her what she means to me with the best evidence I have.

"They say I'm a rockstar, baby
But that's just what they made me
Ignore my wall of Grammys, right now I'm only
　　yours.

I'm a superstar or pathetic cover, it's all in your
　　power, lover
You're everything I need to know, let me be yours

I'm no titan, babe, a liar, maybe
I'm no one else you need to know
You unravel my maze, the light in my haze
You're everything I need to know

You may drive me crazy
But when I'm with you I'm just Casey,
and that's how I know,
that's all I need to know,
I'm yours"

CHAPTER 19

$\mathcal{I}$ hate lying to the two people I care about most, but they can't know about my deal with the devil. While Callie and Luke watch a movie in the living room, I tell them I'm going to get some air.

There's nothing I like about heading two floors down to suite 208 instead.

I take the stairs to avoid being seen. I'd like to encounter as few people as possible. The door to the suite opens the moment my knuckles make contact, as if he was waiting for me.

"Come in. Didn't expect to hear from you so soon." Orin's oily smile triggers a twinge in my stomach.

I enter the suite, but stop just inside the foyer. The door shuts behind me with an ominous click.

"If I do this, I want all the pressure off Callie and Luke. Spin whatever the hell you want to make this go away, but I want it gone."

"Callie?" he asks with a predatory edge. "The new girlfriend?"

"Swear it. I'm not saying shit until you do."

He searches my face in the light of a crystal chandelier. No matter how hard he looks, he won't find a single flinch or sign of weakness. I've never been so sure about anything in my life. He already sent the documents confirming what we agreed on, but I want to hear him say it with my stare cutting into his.

His shoulders sag slightly before he squares into battle mode. "Fine. But whatever you have better be good. What can I get you to drink?"

Somehow I manage not to laugh when he heads toward the main area of the suite. As if I'd ever accept a drink from this person.

"We can do this right here," I say, holding my ground.

He spins back in surprise. "You're not serious."

"I'm not going further into your room, Orin."

His gaze turns dark, but at least he doesn't insult me with weak protests and pretend confusion.

"Fine," he snaps. "This better be good."

I wouldn't be here if it wasn't.

After a long pause, I force the words out. "I will give you three exclusives. Also, as soon as we're done here, I'm calling my manager and the Label to let them know I spoke with you. If you fuck with me, you'll have them to deal with as well, got it?"

He holds up his hands. "Of course. Damn. When did you get so paranoid?"

I ignore the ridiculous question. "The first is about my on-again-off-again relationship with Jana Furmali."

"The actress you've been dating?"

"Yes." I take a deep breath. "It was never real. Well, it wasn't supposed to be. It started as a PR move. The engagement she keeps talking about was part of the original plan. We would have called it off, eventually, but she needed a boost and the Label wanted to inject fuel into NSB's sputtering PR engine. We were becoming irrelevant, and I was the only band member left with a high enough profile to matter."

His brow furrows as he considers my story. I don't have to

tell him I went along with it because I didn't have a choice. He already knows that. He knows how this game is played even better than I do. Hell, he's the instrument paid to drive these rumors.

"If what you're saying is true, her people aren't going to be happy you outed the scheme. Yours as well."

"I'll deal with that."

She's become insufferable anyway. And now that Callie's in the picture, everything's changed. This has to stop once and for all. I'd told Jana I was done with the façade weeks ago, before I even knew Callie existed. Jana was pissed and fought it, as I knew she would. I thought she got her payback with the Kara Corbin retribution, but I was wrong.

Learning at Luke's party that she wasn't done with me was a gut-punch. She might never get over it, continuing to punish me for the rest of our lives if I don't do something.

I'll tell Callie before the article comes out. I have to for us to have a real future together, but things were too unstable and raw for that bombshell before now. Callie doesn't know our world. She wouldn't have understood. And there were already so many other obstacles standing in our way. I never expected our relationship to go so far so fast, but now that it has, I'll have to come clean.

I deserve the hit that will come with the truth.

"Okay. That's something, but not exactly a major headline," he says dryly. "Publicly, the narrative is you two split anyway."

"Yes, which brings us to story number two. You asked about Callie. The woman seen with Luke."

A glimmer of anticipation flashes in his eyes. "You know who she is?"

"Yes. She's my girlfriend. My *real* girlfriend."

He goes still. His shocked gaze locks on me, and I know I've got him. This alone should make him happy, and I haven't even dropped the biggest story yet.

"Wait, so she was seen with Luke because...?"

"They're friends. They hang out. So what? I've been on the road finishing the tour, so I wasn't around the day of the diner thing. But the three of us are back together now."

"The *three* of you? Are you saying there's a—"

"No," I interrupt with a glare. "Not even close. It's just Callie and me. Luke is a friend, nothing more. And if you say anything different, you will never get a conversation with me or anyone else in the band ever. Understood?"

"Yeah, yeah. Fine. Okay, so you're dating this girl. Is it serious?"

I swallow hard. That question shouldn't be as easy to answer as it is.

"Yes, it's serious, and of the three scoops, I want this one leaked first. We need to shut down the rumors that she and Luke are together. You can even tie it to the Jana thing later on. Say she's why I'm finally coming clean about that. I don't care."

In some twisted way, that's true.

He's a second away from rubbing his hands together in maniacal glee. "And the third thing?"

I take a deep breath. "You know that new artist blowing up the charts right now? Penchant for Red?"

He returns a suspicious look. "Yeah. First album just went platinum. We've been trying to get to them for months, but they're behind a freaking wall. No one knows anything. It's like the music came out of thin air. The mystery is part of what's driving the buzz. You know something about them?"

"Yes. A lot."

He's practically salivating. The publication that finally breaks the story and solves the mystery will have the industry headline of the month.

"Can you get me an interview?" he asks, eyes wide.

"You already got one."

He squints in confusion, and I take a deep breath.

"It's me, Orin. Penchant for Red is my side project. I had to keep that information locked down for obvious reasons. I couldn't have people knowing I was working on something else while everything was so up in the air with Night Shifts Black. Honestly, I wasn't ever planning to tell anyone because I don't want the publicity, but shutting down all this other bullshit is worth it to me."

His head moves in a numb arc as he stares at me. "I don't... No... How?!"

I shrug. "Easy. I have lots of time on my hands, if you haven't noticed. I needed an outlet to escape all the dark shit that fell on me after Luke disappeared."

"But now that he's back, does that mean Night Shifts Black is—"

"Dude." I hold up my hand to stop him. "I just gave you three big stories. That's all you're getting."

His shoulders droop, but his expression quickly recovers. I just handed him a goldmine, and he knows it.

"I have to run," I say. "Remember, the Callie story first. Give me at least two weeks on the Jana and Penchant stories. I have personal shit to take care of before that breaks. Can you just give me that? No one else will get the scoop, I promise."

His eyes bore into mine, scouring for deceit. Liars always expect lies, but I'm not a liar. Well, not a malicious one.

"Deal, but I want an in-depth on-site interview about the Penchant story so we can do a major feature. Cameras and a full spread. The whole deal."

I grit my teeth. "Fine. We done?"

His greedy stare scans my face. A sly grin slices into me. "It was a pleasure doing business with you, Casey."

I give his outstretched hand a quick shake before exiting his suite.

Once I'm safely in the hall, I take a deep breath and brace

myself for the real storm that's about to come. My afternoon from hell is just getting started.

* * *

TJ and the Label aren't thrilled I went rogue with Orin Cantea and do their due diligence in making sure I understand how much I screwed up and should never, ever, *ever* do something like that again. I wait patiently through the hours of getting yelled at, lectured, and berated, knowing once they had their fill, they'd come around.

Beneath the righteous indignation, they're just pissed I acted without looping them in. They know what I did was best case scenario. I don't tell them about the Penchant secret or that I leaked the Jana setup. I'll let the dust settle from this brush fire before igniting another one. Still haven't exactly figured out how I'm going to do it yet.

When the last call finally ends, I feel like I just ran back to back marathons while stabbing myself in the eye.

I toss my phone on the table where Callie and Luke are eating takeout. I'm really starting to hate that annoying little device.

Pulling my hands through my hair, I try to shake off the previous five hours. When I look up, they're both staring at me with entirely inappropriate amusement on their faces.

"Oh, I'm glad you guys think this is funny," I grunt.

Callie waves toward a chair and an unopened container. "Eat something. It's bar food. Not a single vegetable."

My tired brain actively fights the smile creeping from my soul, but Callie's expression is just...

"I'll get you a beer," she jokes, ending any chance of avoiding it. Should have known she'd remember my previous reference about the proper way to say "thank you."

The funniest part is, I'm not even the biggest fan of beer, or much of a drinker at all anymore.

"What'd they say?" Luke asks.

I lean back in my chair, trying to organize an answer to that question.

"Alright, so here's the deal. Lawyers are pretty sure there isn't much legal risk. The leaked footage clearly shows the restaurant manager giving you permission to take the chair. The only person endangered was Callie when you took a swipe at her, and I'm going to assume she doesn't intend to press charges." I laser an accusatory glare at Luke. "Really, man? You swung at Callie?"

His eyes broadcast his guilt before he lowers them to the table.

I'm still pissed about that, but what's done is done and there's no point blowing it up further since he clearly knows he fucked up.

"Anyway, legally we're good," I continue. "Publicity-wise, they actually think we're good, too, as long as nothing else comes out and we lay low. While the blow up part with the chair isn't great, we can spin it as a painful outburst of a hurting icon on the mend. With no laws broken, the public is going to like that Luke is back out of hiding and clearly reconnecting with people again, even if it is with his best friend's girlfriend."

I direct my attention to Callie. Not only did the Label ultimately sign off on Rhinehearst leaking the truth about Callie and me, they added their own demands to commandeer the narrative.

"Which, for the record, now means you have to be seen with me at at least two high profile events in the next month. Sorry, but it was non-negotiable. We need to prove that you and Luke were just hanging out as friends, and you and I are madly in love. If they see the three of us together, even better."

Her expression looks about as concerned as it does when I

eat greasy food. Does she really not care that we've just changed her life forever?

"Any questions?" I ask, pretty sure I'm missing something.

My fears are confirmed when she raises her hand with a "first grader having to pee" face.

"Yes, Callie," I say, playing along.

She points at the container of appetizers. "Are you going to finish those mozzarella sticks?"

She yelps and takes cover when I launch one at her.

CHAPTER 20

"hat about kids?" Callie asks, staring at the ceiling with her head in my lap.

We're cuddled on the couch, enjoying each other's company in a rare moment of light-hearted peace. My left hand plays with her right in random caresses as we talk about everything and nothing.

For hours.

I have no idea what time it is, because I turned my phone off. After spending the entire day being tortured by that possessed device, I've earned a break and don't even want to look at the thing until tomorrow.

Right now, every brain cell I have goes to Callie. We've shared basically every bit of information two people can share with each other. I've told her things I've never told anyone. Even a few I never *should* have told anyone. It's amazing how it all just pours out with her. I've learned to be guarded. To always assume anything you say or do will come back to hurt you. But with her, it's the opposite. I want her to know everything I am. And the trust I feel with her is something I haven't experienced with anyone except my sister Elena.

"Casey. Kids? Any thoughts?"

"Do I believe they exist? I didn't used to, but my uncle said he saw one in the woods once—ow!"

She smacks my chest, and I grin down at her.

"You know what I mean. You come from a huge family. Is that something you want as well?"

I huff a dry laugh. "No. Not even close."

Huh. Interesting. My response came out so effortlessly. Without dating a serious partner, this is a question I never officially thought about. But I guess I have my answer.

"That doesn't mean I'm totally against the idea of having kids, just not... ten of them."

She shudders. "I still can't wrap my brain around that. I'm not sure I'd be able to handle the standard two-point-five."

"Which half would you want?"

"Of the point five?" she laughs out. "Top half."

"Really? I feel like that would be more work than the bottom half."

"Why are we assuming a horizontal split? Doesn't vertical make more sense?"

I squint at the wall. "Hmm. Yeah, probably. We're gonna need the right side, though, because that kid will be an artist like his dad."

Her lips tip up, and our fingers slide together until our palms meet. With a soft sigh, her eyelids flutter in an effort to keep them open.

"You can go to bed, you know," I say gently.

She yawns and turns on her side, her head still resting on my thighs. "Not... tired..."

She tugs our joined hands down and pulls them to her chest. Within seconds, she's asleep.

I shake my head with a smile and brush the hair from her face with my free hand. It feels like I could spend hours staring down at the ray of sunlight in my lap and I'd never get bored.

But I'm exhausted as well. This day has drained everything I have mentally and physically. Tomorrow could be even harder.

For a brief moment, I wonder if I should wake her and move her to her room, but the thought of not being close to her for an entire night seems painful. We're on a massive ottoman jutting from the couch, so there's plenty of room for both of us.

I maneuver as gently as I can until I'm lying on my side and tuck her against me. With a careful stretch, I grab the throw blanket and drape it over us. She stirs at the disruption, but quickly falls back to sleep once I'm settled behind her again.

I breathe in a hint of something floral, and a second later I'm out as well.

* * *

I'M startled awake by the most obnoxious sound. It takes me a second to realize it's a phone, but not my phone. Or any phone made since the year I was born.

With a groan, I push up on my elbows to track the culprit, and find the hotel phone on the end table blaring. No wonder people don't use those things anymore.

Callie is gone, and since she's not in the kitchen, she's probably in the guest room showering.

I swat for the phone and yank it off the receiver.

"Yeah?" I croak.

"Mr. Craven? It's Mara from the front desk."

There's no way I'm waking Luke up to talk to Mara.

"Hi, Mara." My voice is still so scratchy, I can easily pull off Luke's monosyllables.

"Sincerest apologies for disturbing you, sir, but we have an *Eli Blake* and a *Jeff Sweeny* in the lobby who say they're friends of yours?"

I burst up from the couch.

"Excuse me?"

243

"Should I tell them to leave?"

"Oh, um, no. They're fine. Just wasn't expecting them..." *At all.* "...so early."

"Of course. I can have them wait or come back later," she suggests.

"No, it's fine. Send them up. Thanks."

"Of course, sir."

I hang up and stare at the wall in disbelief. Eli and Sweeny are here? How?! Why?! And why didn't anyone tell me they... oh.

Well, shit.

I stagger to my feet and retrieve my phone from the island. Sure enough, the screen floods with missed calls and texts when I turn it on.

Guess what. Eli and Sweeny are coming.

They tried to contact me multiple times. There's even a heads up from TJ letting me know he gave them our location since we need to get working on the demo. A trailer with our gear is on its way as well.

The demo!

I never made a better recording, so I'd sent TJ the original one. I told him it was rough and unfinished but thought it had potential.

I scroll through the text stream to find a missed voice message.

I press play and hold the phone six inches away at his shouting.

"Casey! Holy shit! What the hell, man?! Why didn't you tell me you had this?! I'm calling Alberto right now to say we're in business! I'll reach out to Eli and Sweeny too! We need to get you guys in the studio A. S. A. P. Jackson Street is close to you! I'm calling Julian next! Wait, after Alberto. Shit shit shit!"

Guess he likes it.

The second message is similar to the first, except with more expletives and an update that the Label is just as excited and sending a trailer with our gear that should get here Friday.

I've barely started processing the whirlwind when a knock rings out at the same moment Luke comes shuffling down the hall.

"What's going on? Why does it sound like TJ is in the living room?" he asks.

"Because he was," I grunt. "Also, Eli and Sweeny are at the door."

"Huh?"

I wave him off because the guys are now pounding like they're the freaking fire department.

"We're coming! Chill," I call out.

"Quit making out with your girlfriend and open it!" Eli calls back.

"Shit," I mumble as Luke snorts a laugh.

"Guess they heard about Callie," he says.

"I swear, TJ would give out our pin numbers if he knew them."

I yank open the door and immediately get tackled by a world-class bass player and lead guitarist.

"Baby Casey! We missed you!" Eli cries in the most dramatic greeting of all time.

"It's been four days since Richmond. Relax."

I can tell by his smirk when he pulls away he's just being an ass. Their greeting for Luke, though...

The mood changes into something more somber when the three former bandmates stare face-to-face for the first time in a year.

I bite the inside of my cheek as I wait to see what happens.

After a few seconds of stunned silence, Luke gets tackled as well.

"Little Luke! We missed you!" Eli cries in the same obnoxious voice he used for me.

It's hard to see Luke's face with two dudes crowding him in a suffocating bear hug, but when I finally get a glimpse, a slight smile lifts the corner of his mouth.

True to form, Eli and Sweeny release him and launch into conversation like nothing's happened.

While the three of them catch up, I go in search of Callie. There's no way I'm letting her walk into an Eli-Sweeny ambush without a heads up.

She doesn't answer my first knock, so I peek into the room and see light coming from under the bathroom door.

I close the main door behind me and call to her. A moment later, I'm staring into the sun, wrapped in nothing but a towel.

Damn. This is not great timing.

She slides past me with an irresistible smile somewhere between shy and smug, like she's fully aware of what's happening to my bloodstream right now.

"Wow." It's all I can get out.

Her smile tips further into a smirk. "Don't get too excited. It sounds like we have guests."

"Yeah, but... Wow."

She's saying something else, but all I comprehend is her bare skin, still wet with lingering drops, and that inadequately fastened towel.

"You came in here for a reason?" she reminds me with amusement.

Right.

After filling her in about our visitors and the plan for the song, I deal with her shock, horror, back to shock, insecurity, and finally, the inevitable playful swat when I push the teasing too far.

She's still laughing when I dodge her smack and tug her toward me.

Her smile fades as her eyes lock on mine. A flare of heat sears her gaze, and she presses closer. Her body is still damp, but warm, her hair wet and saturated with that floral citrus blend I love so much.

There's no way not to kiss her. We reach for each other at the same time.

The collision is harder and more frantic than the last few. My lips chase hers while she tangles her fingers in my hair and drags me to her. My mind races toward the bed just a few feet away. My body is on fire at the feel of her barely covered form rubbing against me.

I scour her lips, her chin, her neck, sampling rogue drops of water and the tart hint of soap. She tastes so good, feels even better. There's no way in hell we should be doing this right now, but I can't stop. When she gasps out my name in a reluctant reminder of reality, I briefly resent the guests on the other side of the door.

"I know," I concede through a stuttered exhale. "I know."

But instead of pushing me away, her hands find the button of my jeans.

Shit. Blood rushes in hot pulses as she runs her hand over me, then drives her hips into mine at a torturous angle. Nothing but a towel and thin layer of cotton separate us now, and our kiss intensifies into something dangerously close to the limits of control.

We have to stop. We just…

I wrench back abruptly, breathing hard as I drop my forehead to hers. Several long seconds pass, lust and scorching replays saturating the misted air.

It's nearly impossible to let her go, but I have to. There's no way this can go where I want it to. Where *she* wants it, based on how she's still looking at me. Still touching me.

I'm incinerating, aching for her. She has to see the torture all over my face because I feel it radiating from me.

My fears are confirmed when her lips curve in a knowing smile.

Wait...

"You did that on purpose," I accuse in a strained voice, still hoarse with lust.

"Did what?" There's nothing innocent in her return grin.

Now she's seducing *me?*

I let out a breath and shake my head with a smile. This girl never ceases to surprise me.

"Come out when you're ready, you vixen."

I press a quick kiss on her forehead and escape while it's still possible.

* * *

I TRY to play it cool when I return to the guys. Based on the sheer delight on their faces when they see me, there's zero chance they're going to go easy on me.

"That was quick," Eli quips. "Poor girl."

"Shut up," I grunt. "I was just warning her you guys were here."

"With your dick?" Eli returns, motioning toward my jeans.

"Shit." I zip my pants and secure the button.

Sweeny bursts out laughing. Even Luke has an amused smile on his face.

"Whatever," I mumble. "You'd understand if you saw that woman in a towel."

Luke lifts a brow, and I cringe. "Wait. No, that's not what I meant."

Eli and Sweeny are now straight up cackling.

Assholes.

I fire warning glares at both of them. "If you even *think* about her, I'm ending both of you, got it?"

They lift their hands in mock surrender, still chuckling, and I shake my head.

"I'm ordering food," I snap, moving toward the island.

I take as long as possible to order lunch for all of us, mostly so the conversation veers away from Callie. At any moment, she'll walk out of that room, and I don't want this to be any weirder for her than it already will be.

As hoped, the redirect sends Eli and Sweeny to the half bath across the room to freshen up after traveling all morning. Luke joins me at the counter.

"This look good to you?" I hand him my phone to review the takeout order before submitting it.

He scans it for a few seconds before his expression changes.

His gaze shoots to mine with alarm, then something close to anger.

I furrow my brows at his weird reaction to my lunch order. "We can change it if—"

"Why the fuck is Orin Cantea texting you?" he hisses, shoving the screen at me.

Shit.

Orin must have messaged me while Luke was looking at the menu.

His gaze shoots to the other side of the living room to make sure we're still alone.

"I had to fix the Callie-Chair thing," I whisper back. "It's fine. I've got it handled."

"Nothing is fine when it comes to that predator! You've been fighting him off for years and you sell your soul to him *now?*"

I snatch my phone back with a hard look. "I said, it's handled. I gave him some scoops in exchange for fixing the narrative about you and Callie, so what?"

"So what?! He does nothing for free and you know it."

"He didn't do it for free," I fire back. "I told you, I traded information."

"Like what?"

It's my turn to check for spies. "I told him about Penchant."

Even *he* doesn't know about Jana, since he was already gone when that whole thing went down. Hell, his abandonment and the pressure it brought was what *made* it go down.

His eyes widen. "Casey..."

"What? What else was I supposed to do?"

"Let our own PR manage the situation!"

"You don't even know what the situation *is*, so don't lecture me on how to 'manage' it!" I retort before I can stop it.

He flinches and sinks back. Guilt creeps in for my harsh response, but I don't have the energy or patience to fight this battle on three fronts.

After a long silence, I fear he's going to lash out again when he moves closer. I'm surprised when he rests his hand on my shoulder. His eyes search mine, and I see the remorse and pain hiding in their depth.

"You're right," he says quietly. "I *don't* know, and I've left you alone to handle the fallout of my choices for a long time. I'm sorry, Case. I'm sorry that my actions forced you into this position."

He squeezes before dropping his arm, and I stare at him, speechless. I have no idea how to respond to the unexpected apology, but it doesn't matter when the rest of the band makes their way back.

Their animated conversation dies when they reach us.

"Whoa. Vibe shift," Sweeny observes. "What's going on?"

I shoot Luke a pleading look. No one else can know about Orin. *He* wasn't even supposed to know.

"Nothing," Luke says with a quick smile. "Casey's ordering Mexican food, but we just did that last night, so I wanted something else," he lies.

I breathe a sigh of relief. "This place is fast and close," I say.

"Fast and close sounds good to me," Eli chimes in.

Of course it does. The dude can put away calories like I've never seen. We always joked that we should have two riders in our contracts—one for Eli and one for the rest of us.

We catch up for another twenty minutes until movement in the hall draws everyone's attention. All gazes shoot to Callie as she emerges. My breath catches when I see why it took her so long.

Damn. She looks amazing.

The guys toss me a discreet glance of appreciation, and I whisper a prayer they'll contain their inner asshole for the foreseeable future.

"There she is," I say before they get a chance to screw this up.

I can tell she's nervous as I introduce her to the band, so I lean in for a quick encouragement kiss on the cheek. It was supposed to be innocuous, but once I get a whiff of her shampoo, all kinds of inconvenient memories of what just happened in her room come racing back.

Her heated glance tells me she's feeling it too. We're going to have to figure this out at some point. Soon.

We exchange more small talk, until Eli turns to me with a change in expression.

"Oh hey, it's still downstairs, but we brought some of your stuff, Case. TJ said you were looking for a few things to prepare for Friday."

A rush of excitement shoots through me. "My gear?" I ask. I thought I was going to have to wait until Friday to do any serious production on the song.

Eli grins like he knows he just made my day.

He says they couldn't bring all of it, but what he lists is plenty to get started.

I don't even realize I'm bouncing like I have to piss until Luke scans me with amusement.

"Just go, Case," he says, knowing I don't want to wait for the porter.

That's all the encouragement I need.

CHAPTER 21

*M*ara is not happy that I try to tip the bellhop supervisor *not* to deliver the luggage for 403. She assures me someone will get to our belongings soon, but the crate and guitar case resting on a cart five feet away call to me like mythological luggage sirens.

"I need the workout," I explain, grabbing the cart beneath her scowl.

She would have to physically stop me at this point, and I'm pretty sure an altercation with a guest over the transport of their own belongings isn't a hill she wants to die on.

"Peter, take this one next!" she calls to a porter. The man releases his grip on a cart with the most button-up shirts I've ever seen and joins us.

"Thank you, Mara. You're the best," I say in a sweet tone.

She returns a stiff smile and spins on her heels to stomp toward the next crisis.

Aiden is more enthusiastic when we enter his elevator domain.

"That looks like a guitar," he says as he helps us pull the cart onto the elevator.

"It is. Along with a midi controller and some other production equipment."

His eyes go wide as he scans the items, then looks to me. "Are you and Luke and those other guys gonna record something here?"

"Not *here*, but we're going to write and rehearse."

"Wow," he says under his breath, but I sense it's not the thought of rockstars in his hotel that's got his attention. He'd be used to weird shit like that.

"Yeah, should be fun," I say, subtly probing.

His gaze shoots to mine before landing on the porter beside us. The other man does a good job pretending not to be listening to our conversation.

We reach the fourth floor, and Aiden helps the porter get the cart over the hump. As I hand the younger man a bill, he hesitates and glances at the porter again.

I check the guy's name tag and offer a sincere smile. "Thanks, Peter. I'll meet you at the suite in a second."

The man glances between Aiden and me before nodding. "Of course, sir. Take your time."

Once the cart is squeaking down the hall, I turn back to Aiden, who has the elevator on hold.

"What's up?" I ask the teenager. His typically sunny smile has sagged into a worried frown.

"I probably shouldn't say this, Mr. Barrett, but... I'm glad you're here. You and Callie both. I was worried about Luke. Right before you showed up, he completely stopped leaving the room. After a few days of that, I knocked on his door to check on him. He was in a bad state and said some really scary stuff. I didn't want to tell my supervisor because I'm not supposed to approach the guests, but I was worried about him. People shouldn't be alone like that for so long. They get in their heads and start thinking things that aren't real. I've seen it before. I was afraid that was happening to Luke."

Aiden flinches when the elevator buzzes from being open too long.

Knowing he's on borrowed work time, he takes the bill and shoves it in his pocket. "Anyway, thanks. Luke seems like a good guy. I don't believe all the stuff people say about him. Or at least, I don't believe that stuff is true anymore."

Stunned, I return a tight smile. "Thanks for saying that. I'm glad we're here too."

He nods, and I clear the elevator so he can leave.

As the doors close, he waves with a smile, but I can't move. My thoughts are taking off in all directions again. Nothing he said about Luke's state surprises me. It's the fact that a teenage elevator attendant picked up on it and cared enough to look out for him that's left me stunned. While Luke hid in his room, lying to himself about how much everyone hated him, a virtual stranger was willing to put her life on hold to help him, while another was willing to risk his job.

I stare at the door of 403 in the distance, now blocked by a luggage cart and impatient porter. Even when Luke sought complete isolation, there were people in his orbit who saw him. Aiden, Callie… He never would have noticed from the prison of his head, but there are always people willing to help if we can reach just a fraction of a hand above the surface for them to grasp.

Just because you don't see someone, doesn't mean they don't see you.

By the time I join the porter, I've bottled the angst and packed it safely away.

After tipping the man (very) well, Luke unpacks the crate while I handle my guitar. Man, I missed this thing.

I pull it out and strap it on like a favorite hoodie. The familiar smell of the wood and feel of the curve against me takes me back to so many vivid moments over the years.

Writing with Luke in the basement, on the bus, backstage…

Hours of shoving my pain, grief, and frustrations at the strings until they transformed it into something else…

I do a quick tune, grab a pick from the case, and launch into the progressions I'd only heard on Luke's beater until now.

My excitement is already exploding into joy at how that small change is turning this song into something special. Once I get some real production going, it will be epic.

"So do we get to hear this new masterpiece or what?" Eli asks.

I flinch at the interruption.

Right. Forgot about them.

And the food that's coming.

More importantly is the fact that no one has heard this song the way I hear it in my head, and I don't want their first experience to be less than the masterpiece it could be.

I feel like a diva when I say no and tell them I'm moving to the office, but doing it right is worth their merciless teasing.

Gathering an armful of equipment to relocate, I almost run into Callie standing beside the table.

"Can I help?" she asks, motioning toward the remaining gear. Her intrigued expression brings a smile to my lips. I have no doubt once we introduce her to our world, she'll fit right in.

I tell her to grab the interfaces and cables, while I handle my laptop and the controller. It's only a 49-key, non-weighted keyboard so it's not heavy.

By the time she joins me in the office, I already have a makeshift workstation set up on the desk. While she unloads, I fire up the DAW on my laptop and open a new project. Still not sure what to call this thing, I type "Mirror Song."

"Can you pass me the USB cable?" I ask.

I point it out and connect the controller to my laptop, then hook up the sustain pedal.

"You've been calling it a controller more than a keyboard. Why?" she asks.

Warmth spreads through me at her question. I love that she cares and is so invested in what I'm doing. As much as I'd like to lock myself away for hours and get lost in production like I usually do when the muse hits, I want to bring her along with me this time.

So instead of building tracks, I spend the next few minutes demonstrating the basics of music production. Everything I show her elicits more questions and wonder. It's addictive, being immersed in something you love *with* someone you love, and soon I'm bursting with the same infection I have while creating.

While she runs to her room to grab her headphones, I pop in my own in-ears and record some quick sample tracks for her to listen to. If she thinks this shit is cool, wait until she sees what we do with it for real.

Once she returns, I spend several minutes guiding her further into the world of music production by explaining the DAW, plugins, and even showing her basic sounds.

"Tell me an instrument you want to hear," I say, loving how seriously she takes this when her face scrunches in thought.

"Violin." Her answer and corresponding smile feel like a bear hug for my heart. I love that she remembered my background and wants to tie it to the present.

I load my Stradivarius virtual instrument into a new track and copy the midi notes into the grid.

"Okay, now listen," I say.

Her eyes go wide when I press the space bar.

"I can even hear the vibrato," she whispers.

Blowing her mind might be my new favorite activity. I nearly forget about the song as I take her on another in-depth tour through my digital universe.

"This is wild," she says, still in awe.

The best part is, we've only scratched the surface. If she's truly interested in this stuff, we'd have days, weeks, *months* of lessons and material to play with and still not cover all there is to know. The technology and trends are always changing, so there's always something new to discover.

"I know. It's awesome," I say. "And see all these buttons and faders? I can program all of these to control anything I want to. It's especially valuable when playing live because it allows me to change sounds and trigger what I need right from here instead of messing with my computer."

Her face scrunches in adorable confusion. "But I thought you're a drummer."

"Yeah, I don't do this for NSB. Just on my own projects."

I cringe inwardly at the unintended confession. As usual in her easy presence, the words just slipped out on their own. Only Luke knows about Penchant—and now Orin.

She absorbs the comment with a shake of her head.

Thankfully, the interaction slips into flirting instead of more questions, and when she climbs into my lap to straddle me, all previous topics evaporate. Her coy expression triggers an explosion of sparks throughout my body. Guess her smile has become my own personal midi controller.

She leans in slowly, so the kiss isn't entirely unexpected, but the quick escalation into desperation is. She clutches the collar of my shirt to lock me against her as she pulses on my lap to the rhythm of our tongues. I knew she was a natural musician.

My hands slide down her back to curve over her ass, which only seems to drive her intensity. Our tongues sweep over each other, our hands roaming and claiming whatever they can find.

My muscles tense with need and frustration. Once again, our terrible timing is going to end in unsatisfied lust.

We both know this can't go where we want it to, and can't seem to decide if that means we should stop or chase as much as possible before reality intervenes.

With incredible effort, we finally separate, breathing hard.

My lips sting in the best possible way from the spontaneous

attack. My lungs take a moment to fill with air. Her smile, her eyes, her sweet spirit... she's layers of human tracks forming the most perfect song.

And she's mine.

"Wow, computers really turn you on, don't they," I tease, because what else is there to say?

Totally worth it when I get a smack.

And another wild, messy kiss.

* * *

CALLIE MAKES me break for lunch, but as soon as I've shoveled down a few tacos, I'm back in my makeshift studio.

The diner chair in the corner provides an eerie audience while I work. There's a weird chill in the room that's turning that haunted object into a silent collaborator. My gaze keeps crossing to it like it knows something I don't. I can't help but wonder how many hours Luke has spent in here staring at it like he was when I found him the other day.

I've just finished setting up the framework for the song and doing one full take on keys when Luke pokes his head in. When he sees I'm not recording, he enters with Callie behind him.

"How's it going?" he asks.

Any irritation at being interrupted yet again fades with his sincere interest. As usual, I try to play it cool so I don't break the spell.

"Well, it's been all of ten minutes, so not much to show so far. Basically got the tempo set and first midi track lined up. I did one pass with keys but I think I'm going to run it on guitar, too, and see what that sounds like. I could use some input. Do you have your ears?"

My tone is casual, but there's nothing trivial about that question.

I hold my breath.

He hesitates.

Please, Luke.

I can't even look at Callie.

His nod feels monumental. "Yeah, in my room. Just a sec."

I release the air in my lungs as he takes off, still in disbelief this is happening. Maybe he'll change his mind once he gets to his room and has more courage to break my heart.

Callie rounds the desk to hover beside me.

"So, Penchant for Red, huh?" she says nonchalantly while squinting at the DAW like *that's* her main concern.

My initial shock transforms into humor at my sneaky spy.

"Luke told you."

She turns and leans against the desk to face me.

"Is there anything about you that isn't going to make me swoon? What else is there? You also have a PhD in physics and founded a franchise of orphanages?"

I snort a laugh. "Swoon! There's my old lady. Love it."

What I don't love? How distracted I am whenever she's close.

Once again, I find myself flirting and sharing an urgent kiss with a goddess before I even realize what's happening. This song is never going to get made with Callie hanging around.

Luke returns too soon and not soon enough. His smile when he sees our scramble to separate eases the tension at being caught. This has to be weird for him.

"I can come back," he jokes.

"No, it's fine," Callie says.

They continue chatting, but my mind is already embedded in quantizing the keys track I just recorded. I put my left IEM in to listen back to the opening intro. I don't like the strict timing. I think I want the first notes of the chords slightly ahead of the beat to sound more natural.

"You cool with that, Case?" Luke cuts in.

"Fine with me," I reply, having no idea what I just agreed to. "Hey, so here's the first take at the keys. Before I clean it up, I just wanted to see what you thought of the general direction."

Luke puts his ears in and hands me the cable to plug into my laptop.

My heart races while he listens, my knee bouncing below the desk like I'm next up at the DMV. I'm always anxious about feedback, all artists are. But this is different. This is the past, present, and future converging into one rough layer of keys.

Relief plunges through me when an approving smile lifts his lips. He pulls his IEM out and glances at me.

"It's good, Case. Maybe a little aggressive on the verses. I love the intro, though. I can totally hear the piano riff followed by the band coming in with the crash of the drums and guitars."

Somehow I knew he'd say that. He always thinks my keys are too aggressive. This time he's right, but it's only because I'm using it as a base for the scratch track. Most, if not all of it, will come out in production.

"That's what I was thinking," I say. "One pass of piano for that first progression, and then all-in hard on the second."

Luke's brows arch like they do when he's on board. "Yeah, I like that."

It feels so damn good to slip back into our instinctive collaborative mode. Too good when it leaves an awkward silence after the easy exchange.

My head and heart belt the ugly truth I've been trying to ignore since this song started forming. I thought I'd be okay doing it on our own. That we could find a way to fill the gaping hole of Luke's vocal. But this song is too good to hand to anyone else. Too special.

Too fucking important.

I squirm from the twisting in my stomach. "I'd love if you could help me with the vocal. You'd kill this one. You know you would."

He winces at the surprise ambush, and so do I. He's probably just as shocked as I am that I asked again after the disaster of the last time. I sense Callie's concern as well.

God, I'm such an idiot. Why do I do this to myself?

I divert my gaze back to the safety of the screen. My chest feels tight as I pretend it hasn't just been ripped open and gutted.

"Yeah, sorry," I say quietly before this gets worse.

I don't want an explanation or apology. I just want to kill this torturous hope once and for all. It hurts too much, and I just—

"Casey..."

I can't look at him. I hear it in his voice.

"No, I know," I grit out. My jaw aches. My eyes. My throat. I don't even know why. "Sorry, it's fine. I shouldn't have asked."

It's fine.

Such a bald-faced lie.

My heart feels like it's been crushed and doused in gasoline.

"No, it's not fine, Casey. It's not fine."

Luke's firm voice echoes through the room as he covers the distance between us. I look up to see a storm of emotions on his face. I can't begin to sort through them, and I'm not surprised when he closes his eyes. I feel like doing the same. No one wants to witness chaos like the internal mess we just threw at each other in that single glance.

After a long, painful pause, he opens his eyes to deliver the crushing blow.

The apology.

The rejection that will somehow make *me* feel like the villain for having hope in something better.

"Can you run through it with me a few times first?" His voice is almost a whisper.

I go numb.

There's no way...

"I only heard it that once, and I know you changed some of the melody anyway," he explains.

I can't speak. Can't move. I just stare at the screen until tears obscure my view. I blink them away, my ribs aching beneath the weight of what's happening.

"Um, yeah, of course. Just..."

Fuck, I can't even get words out.

This can't be real. I have to be dreaming, and I'm going to be heartbroken when I wake up and realize I'm alone on a plane with my laptop and a lifetime of charred memories.

But the sudden pressure squeezing my shoulder feels so damn real, and when I dare to look up, so does the man standing beside me.

My best friend.

My brother.

My lead singer.

His eyes scream everything I'm feeling as he pulls me in for a tight embrace. His arms constrict around me, suffocating the darkness. I hear everything he wants to say in the way he holds on, and my cheeks are wet with tears I've been needing to cry for so damn long.

"I'm sorry," he whispers in a choked voice. "I'm so fucking sorry."

"I know," I return softly.

And for the first time, it's the truth.

CHAPTER 22

"Hello, hello. Greetings from the inside. Hello, hello framed in all your lies..."

I pivot my chair further from Luke, grateful he's staring at the lyrics on his phone. He can't see my face right now. The way my soul is spilling out in barely tempered emotion as his familiar voice cuts through every part of me.

"Hello, hello. How you love to see me cry..."

More tears slip down my cheeks, and I discreetly wipe them away.

I never thought I'd hear him sing again. I never thought my melodies and his words would twist together in the magical formula that shot us to the top. I thought we lost the future of our music, but here it is, pouring out and filling a crowded room that's much too small to contain it.

His voice needs to be heard. The raw emotion only he can bring to a song takes me back to the basement of his aunt's house, where two troubled teens found healing and purpose. Bonds were formed that seemed impossible to break.

Until they did.

Until the night they tore apart and were left hanging as severed shards of what they should have been.

"Always so... Hang on, stop it for a sec?"

I clear my throat and press the space bar to pause the track.

"I'm not getting the timing on that part. Is it..."

He quiets, and I rub at my eyes.

"You okay? What's wrong?"

I make the mistake of glancing at him, but seeing him there, in-ears hanging around his neck like we're backstage again, it's too much.

"Nothing, man. It sounds great," I say in a strained voice.

"Seriously, Case. If this isn't working you can—"

"No!" I rush out, swiveling to face him. "No. It's amazing. It's..."

I don't have words for what this is. Hell, I don't even *know* what this is yet, and his expression softens with understanding.

"Yeah, man," he says quietly. "I get it. I feel it too."

"You do?"

My gaze lifts to his and he returns a weak smile. "I'm not ready to make promises or put labels on it, but yeah, I feel it." Moisture fills his eyes when he directs an absent stare at the desk. "And for someone who stopped feeling anything months ago, it's..."

His voice fades out. He scrubs at his eyes before directing them to me. "Do you know how good it is to feel something again? *Anything?* Shit." More tears cloud his gaze. He shakes his head, looking lost.

I push up from the desk chair, and he pulls me in for a hug. For a long time neither of us moves. We just stand there and let the music heal us like it did all those years ago. Like it will the next time we need it to do what nothing else can.

"I don't want to do this without you anymore, dude," I whisper, breaking the silence. "I don't think I can."

His arms tighten around me, and I'm praying he feels how much I need him.

After a long silence, we separate with an awkward smile and turn back to the laptop in unison.

"Can we change the lyrics in verse two?" he asks. His voice is as raspy and damaged from emotion as mine.

"Of course. What are you thinking?" I pull up the notepad app with the lyrics.

When I glance back at him, he's staring at the diner chair again. His gaze is distant, like he's somewhere else.

"The mirror needs to break," he says faintly. "No... It needs to shatter."

I swallow a mass in my throat. "Yeah, man." I try for casual, but my hoarse tone gives me away. "How about, 'mirror mirror you're shattering, there's more than meets the eye with me'?"

His gaze cuts back to me. He searches my face.

"Let's try it," he says. "You want to run it again? I think I'm ready to record this time."

* * *

I'M EXHAUSTED by the time we wrap our session. Mentally, physically, emotionally... but I wouldn't trade a single second for the world. This is the shit we live for, and being back in the studio with Luke—even if it's a hotel room—is everything.

I'm not surprised when he heads back to his bedroom to recover. I feel drained as well when I find Callie in the living room. Based on how depleted I am, I can't even imagine what that session did to him. But it's different this time. I'm not scared when we part ways. I know he'll be back. And it's the first time since he left me alone in a hospital room a year ago that I can say that with any certainty.

"Want a beer?" I ask Callie on my way to the kitchen.

She's alone, so Eli and Sweeny must have gone to their rooms… or somewhere else to cause trouble. Secretly, I'm glad. Luke isn't the only one who needs time to recover from what just happened.

"Sure," Callie says. "Sounds like it's going well."

She takes the bottle I hand her as I join her on the couch.

"We're both pretty happy with the direction. It's going to sound awesome with our actual gear in the studio."

"I can't wait to see you play drums."

I go still at the thought. "That's right. I guess you haven't even seen me play yet."

"Just violin and that weird string-choir-air sounding thing."

I bite back a grin. "Pads."

"Huh?"

"That sound. It's called a pad."

"Oh." She settles against me, and I tuck my arm around her. "How's Luke?" she asks softly.

"Good. Better than I've seen him in a long time. It was like…"

I don't even know how to finish that sentence. It wasn't like anything. It wasn't even like before. Nothing can ever be like the past once the present gets in the way.

Her fingers lace with mine, and I breathe a sigh.

"It's going to be slow, but it's going, Casey. I think it's finally going," she says, reading my mind like always.

I turn my head and rest my lips on her hair. "You're amazing, Callie. I don't know how you got through to him, but you did."

She's quiet as she considers everything.

"All I did was force myself into his life and refuse to let him hurt me."

I almost laugh at her ridiculous attempt to downplay the impossible. "Yeah, well, no one else managed to do that."

"How many people really tried besides you?" she returns.

I cringe and study the bottle in my other hand.

"It was timing, too, Casey," she continues. "It was a lot of things. Sometimes it takes a stranger. Friends know too much."

"True. You hold on too tight with friends."

"Although, let's be honest. I'm the one who got the best deal out of all this."

A smile threatens my lips. "Oh yeah?"

"No question."

She twists toward me and blasts beautiful hazel eyes at me.

I don't move, desperate to take in as much as I can. We exchange a smile, and she lifts up enough for a soft kiss. It's the perfect explanation. No words necessary.

"Promise me one thing though, Callie," I say when we pull back. Her brow furrows as she meets my gaze. "No matter what happens with the two of us, we will always be there for him." Emotion is pressing on my chest again. "I can't lose him, too. I *can't*."

Her grip tightens on my hand. "Neither can I."

Even though I know as much, it feels better to hear her say it. Maybe there's finally a reason to hope. Maybe I can start thinking about promises and a future again.

"Want to hear what we've got so far?" I ask.

It's her art as much as ours, and I'm giddy at the thought of showing her what we've done with her words.

"Are you kidding? Since the second I left the room."

CALLIE LOVES THE EARLY PREVIEW, but I knew she would. She always looks to the heart behind everything she sees, and there is nothing more beautiful and pure than the soul of this song.

The real viability test will be Eli and Sweeny. They haven't lived our experience and will be coming at it from an outside artistic perspective much closer to what the average listener will hear.

Part of me is nervous when we gather later that evening for the reveal. This isn't the average first listen—this is freaking everything. Luke's relaxed confidence as he lounges on the couch goes a long way in soothing my nerves. If he's confident, I know we have something good.

Eli and Sweeny scale back their energy to a rare pensive state while I cue up the song. As soon as I press play, I watch for clues, but their uncharacteristic somber expressions make it hard to judge their thoughts. Even when the outro rings out, I don't have a solid read on where they're at.

"Play it again?" Sweeny says with a furrowed brow.

I run it again, my jaw tight with nerves.

Eli's fingers are moving in imaginary basslines, giving me some encouragement. Sweeny is—

"There! Right there! Stop it!" he bellows, making us jump.

I pause the song, my heart racing. I don't know what I'll do if they're not on board with this after everything it took to get here.

Luke shoots me an encouraging smile, as if he knows what's going through my head. Of course he does.

"You're going to hit the kick hard on that build, right Case?"

My gaze darts back to Sweeny with a hint of confusion. "On the bridge into the chorus? Yeah. Definitely a fill too at the end. I was thinking Eli would come in hard with some killer run too."

Sweeny leans back. "Okay. Yeah. That lead guitar riff is sick. Wanted to make sure we were supporting it."

He's in! I finally take a full breath.

"Absolutely. You can thank Luke for the riff."

Luke smirks. "It's nothing. Casey did everything else."

"And Callie," I add.

"And Callie," Luke echoes.

Callie looks ready to shrink into the cushion, but I love that she's part of this. I especially love that the guys have welcomed her into the band without hesitation.

"Love it, Case. Really," Sweeny says. "You know, I like that for an album title, too. *Greetings from the Inside*."

"*Greetings from the Inside*," I muse out loud. Has a ring to it. "Yeah. I like that."

"Luke, you slayed the vocal," Eli says.

Luke returns a casual shrug, but I see the smile fighting to come out.

"You sound like a rockstar or something," I tease, just to draw it to the surface. It feels like more than a victory when he aims it at me.

Eli pulls out his phone, and I shoot my gaze to him. "What are you doing?"

"Calling TJ."

I wince. "TJ? Why?"

"To see if he can get our trailer here by tomorrow instead. I want my bass."

CHAPTER 23

"*S*hit." I catch the familiar silhouette of my fake ex-girlfriend turned stalker laughing with her friends on the other side of the restaurant.

Tonight was supposed to be about celebration and relaxation. The staff at 49th & Finch have been beyond accommodating since we arrived—until they seated Jana and friends in my direct line of sight.

"Oh, man. Sorry, Case. You want to leave?" Luke says, following my gaze.

Yes.

But we've been promising Callie a visit to our favorite hangout in this city for a while, and I'm not letting Jana ruin yet another experience for her.

"Nah, it's fine. Maybe she won't see us."

Luke's snort echoes the doubt in my head. "Jana Furmali? That woman has a freaking radar for you."

I shoot him a hard look. "Yeah. And thanks for inviting her to your little get-together, by the way. She practically tackled me."

His eyes narrow on me in irritation. "Of course I didn't invite her. She must have come with Davis and Kane."

Davis and Kane... Those social leeches aren't exactly besties of ours either, but there's no point having this argument now.

I pick at the stitching in the cloth napkin, forcing away thoughts of our last few volatile encounters. Things are only going to get worse once Orin goes public with the truth about our highly publicized "romance."

A soft hand plucks mine from the napkin, and some of the tension falls away. I can't guess how Callie is going to take the news about my fake romance, but the longer I go without saying something, the harder it will be. Maybe tonight. Or...

She tugs gently to draw my attention. I twist a quick smile. I can't come clean to Callie here. Not in front of the guys with the object of my torment within visual range.

"Sorry," I mumble. "She's just..."

Bitter. Vindictive.

"Persistent," Eli interjects.

It's the perfect out.

"Yeah, persistent," I confirm. "We went out a couple times a few months ago and she will not let go. I told her it wasn't going to happen."

It's not really a lie. Neither is anything I've said about the woman. What it became is exactly what it looks like. It's just how it started that hasn't been entirely transparent.

"I picked up on that at the party," Callie says, and a cold feeling washes through me. When my gaze jumps to her, her expression softens with understanding. "I'm not worried," she says, squeezing my hand.

I don't know what to do with her understanding response. In our scheming world of jealousy and exploitation, we're not used to being given the benefit of the doubt. I can't help but brush my lips on hers.

"Dude, she just saw you," Sweeny hisses.

I breathe a curse when Jana's gaze locks on me. To my horror, she pushes up from her chair and starts in our direction.

Callie must read my panic, because when I ask her to let me kiss her again, she seems more than happy to play along. And based on her vigorous acting, I'm guessing she's enjoying staking her claim as well. Maybe if Jana sees I'm serious about someone else, she'll finally move on.

"Hey, guys! So good to see you!" Jana says, forcing Callie and me apart.

I can tell by the bite in her tone this is not going to go well for me.

"Jana, how's it going?" Sweeny says blandly.

"Great! Good." Her sharp stare cuts into me. "Casey, how have you been?"

Somehow I manage a twist of the lips. "Fine."

Callie grips my fingers, and I hold up our joined hands for Jana to see. "Hey, did you get a chance to meet my girlfriend Callie at Luke's place last week?"

Her eyes go dark with warning. She knows what I'm doing and I don't think it's having the effect I was going for. Shit, maybe the opposite.

"Um... no, I don't think so. Hi," she tosses dismissively in Callie's direction.

"Hi," Callie returns in an overly bright tone. "I love your dress."

The guys suppress a laugh as I swallow a wave of dread. Yeah, this is not going to end well.

"Thanks. It's a Bella Amberosi," Jana replies in a smug tone.

Callie doesn't look impressed. Or remotely interested.

Jana scans her with a derogatory look. "I like your..."

"Boyfriend?" Callie finishes, lifting a brow. Oh boy. Here we go. "Yeah, I know. He's amazing. I don't blame you."

Jana looks ready to combust, and I hold my breath. Part of me is high-fiving my girlfriend so hard right now. The other part knows this night will be ending in blood. Whose? We'll probably find out soon.

My fake ex's gaze sears into me with warning, but to my surprise, rather than snap back, she pivots and stalks back to her table.

Whoa. Once again, Callie accomplishes the impossible.

While the guys celebrate the win, she gives me another dose of encouragement.

"Thanks, Callie," I say softly. That simple word can't begin to capture the complex mass of gratitude moving through my chest.

As usual, she seems to understand anyway. After a quick nod, she tilts her head with a pensive expression. I brace myself for whatever she's got loaded up to fire.

"What exactly is a Bella Amberosi?" she asks with a severe expression.

The guys burst into laughter as I draw her in with a smirk.

* * *

DESPITE THE ROUGH start to the evening, the rest goes well. Luke and I order everything we think Callie would like so she has a chance to try it. They've even added some items to the menu since the last time we were here that *we* want to try.

Through it all, I can't stop smiling and studying my girl with relaxed fascination. A rush moves through me every time I take in her infectious excitement. Watching her experience new things has reinvigorated my own appreciation for life. We've become so jaded, our journey so punctuated with pain, that I'd forgotten about all the moments of joy in our story as well.

Callie brings it all back, and not just for me. Life is blooming in Luke's demeanor for the first time since Elena's death as well. And if I'm honest, the decay goes back long before that. What happened that night wasn't a fluke, but the result of a long, ugly slide into the darkness.

Even Eli and Sweeny are quickly under Callie's spell. They've always embraced "the rockstar life" more than I have, especially after our fall from the top. Everything is a party, everyone a guest in their narrative, but not with Callie. They treat her with a gentleness and respect I didn't even know they had in them. Within hours, she's one of us. It's like she's been here since the beginning.

I'm so caught up in the wonder of it all, I nearly forget about Jana.

That is, until I hit the restroom late into the night.

After washing my hands, I push through the door into the hall, only to be ambushed by a livid movie star.

Jana's hostile glare erases every ounce of peace I had in me.

"What the fuck is wrong with you?!" she hisses, backing me toward an alcove.

"Not now," I return with a cold look.

"No? Then when? You won't take my calls. Every time I approach, you treat me like I'm some jealous ex and not—"

"Because you're *acting* like a jealous ex," I fire back. "This! What's happening right now is exactly why I called it off! You never played by the rules."

"We had an agreement!"

"Exactly! To *pretend*, Jana. It was fake, and you kept trying to make it real!"

"What?! No, I—"

"The Oscars after party?" I charge with a glare. "Where was that in the *agreement*?"

She tenses, squirming beneath my accusatory stare. I still feel her hands on me, the dread in my stomach the entire night as she used every opportunity she could to take advantage of our situation and shred every clause of our verbal contract.

After that, I was done. No publicity was worth that kind of

humiliation, so I "broke up" with her the next day as dramatically and publicly as possible. I needed it to stick that time.

"Oh please," she scoffs, resecuring her anger. "What did you think was going to happen that night? How exactly were you planning to show the world we were together without actually being together."

I shoot daggers back, but I'm done with this. I'm so tired of having this conversation.

"Whatever. Just leave me alone, okay? It's over. Done. Go find someone else to boost your numbers."

I push past her, stunned when she grabs my arm and shoves me back into the wall.

"No. What it *is* is breach of contract, sweetheart," she sneers. "We agreed to six months and an engagement. You barely made it three."

"No, *you* broke our contract. We said limited physical contact *for appearances only.*"

"Ha! You're such a hypocrite, you know that?"

I shake my head at the irony. The fact that I'm not a hypocrite is the very reason I couldn't make this work, and I'm more angry with myself than anyone for the misjudgment. This mess is my fault as much as hers. I was vulnerable and weak from my world breaking apart when PR came at me with a "brilliant" plan. I knew these fake relationships were a thing, but I'd never done it before. I had no clue what I was getting into, and it only took a few public appearances to make it clear I'm not built for these games. I couldn't do it, and the after party from hell was the final straw.

"I just don't understand! What did I do wrong?" she asks, changing tactics. Her tone is less angry and more desperate now.

"You didn't do anything wrong!" *I* did by agreeing to the asinine plan in the first place.

"But we had such a good time," she argues, and I almost bark a laugh.

She clearly has a very different narrative in her head than I do. But I knew that from our first "date." What I didn't know was how things would escalate. Or that my life would collide with a ray of sunshine like Callie.

Yes, Callie, the woman who makes me feel the *opposite* of how I'm feeling right now.

"Yeah, and that's all it was," I say flippantly. "Look, I don't want to be a dick, but I have to get back. To my friends. To my *girlfriend.*"

I try to move again, and she blocks my path.

"Just give me one more chance! I'll get you that meeting with Reese Aster!"

This time I can't stop the harsh laugh. Six months ago, I would have done anything for a sit-down with the editor in chief of The Daily Star. I *begged* her to set up an interview with her contact so I could tell my story and set the record straight after everything went to shit.

She refused. Wasn't part of *the contract.*

Of course she makes the offer hours after I sold my soul to Orin Cantea.

Now I can't wait until she sees those headlines.

"Are you actually bribing me to go out with you?" I taunt. "Come on, Jana. Don't. You don't need that. For the hundredth time, I'm seeing someone. You need to let go."

Even if our arrangement hadn't been a total disaster from the beginning, the fact that I'm in a real relationship now changes everything.

"No, I don't believe that!" she hisses. "There's no way you're seriously dating that little country slut."

Blood drains through me, cold, then hot. I'm so livid I have to clench my fist to keep from breaking something. "Don't ever talk about her like that!" I seethe. "You don't know anything about her."

This is bullshit. I'm done.

"Get out of my way," I snap, moving past her again.

"Casey!"

Her fingers cut into my arm, and I wrench it away. "Let go of me! It's not happening, Jana. Ever!"

I storm back toward the restaurant and stop cold.

Callie.

Oh god.

Shock turns to panic at the look on my girlfriend's face. How much of that did she hear? All I want is peace to be with her and start over, and now...

"Callie..." Her name is all I can get out. I don't even know what else to say.

Her gaze scans me briefly before settling on something to my right.

"I think he's made himself pretty clear," she says to Jana. "Even a 'country slut' like me can understand his message."

My tension eases. The fear melts away. She's coming to my defense! She should be pissed, and instead—

I don't even see the hand before it's colliding with my face. Pain spreads over my cheek as I stare after Jana in disbelief. She's already several yards away by the time I process what just happened.

Fire rips through me, every muscle rigid as I watch her go.

Callie is immediately in front of me, but I barely notice until her soft touch fans over the sharp sting.

"Hey, are you okay?" Her voice is gentle, even though she must be furious. Probably because she knows I need compassion more than rage right now.

And god, I want so much to be the person she believes I am.

My eyes slip closed as I try to control my labored breaths. "Fine."

But I don't sound fine.

I sound like the broken teenager who wrote "Argyle." The bloody and shattered kid who hid in Luke's room for a week after the beating of a lifetime. The boy who had no idea what to do with the pain so he started turning it into music with the help of a best friend who was desperate to do the same.

"Casey..."

She drags my conflicted gaze to hers.

I swallow the memories. My cheek burns, but not as much as the seared edges of my soul.

My head, my heart... I don't even know. All I know is things feel manageable with Callie's hand in mine.

"It's definitely not you... it's her," she says with a straight face.

A smile breaks through the pain. The air lifts. "Yeah, I know. I saw that coming after our third date. That's why there were only three."

Her laugh soothes the burn in my soul as much as her touch soothes my skin.

"Well, I'm sorry if part of that was my fault. Ironically, I came to find you to give you this."

Confused, I search her gaze until she leans in to wrap her arms around me. She holds on for several long seconds, and I feel my blood pressure easing.

"Thanks, Callie. I needed that," I breathe out.

"Me, too," she says softly.

My heart is still pounding but at least I can breathe again.

CHAPTER 24

*T*he limo ride back to the hotel is quiet but not
awkward. Eli and Sweeny had already left in pursuit
of other entertainment by the time Callie and I returned to the
table, so it's only the three of us now. A pensive aura hangs over
the inside of the car, as if we have a mutual understanding that
we each have our separate internal demons to sort through.

My cheek still smarts from its collision with Jana's palm, but
not nearly as much as my heart.

There's no point in waiting any longer.

"I have to tell you something," I blurt out. "It's about Jana."

Callie stiffens against me and sits up straight.

Luke shoots a concerned look from the seat across from us.
We don't do the pretentious limo thing very often, but thought
Callie would find it fun. She did, of course.

Well, until this moment, I guess.

Luke's gaze practically pleads with me not to ruin our new-
found serenity with drama from the past, but we can't have true
peace until those ghosts are cleared from the present. We definitely can't have a future. He should understand that better than
anyone.

Callie's pained stare scours my face, and I can't meet it. I'll just have to plow through to the end, or I'll get derailed and make a bigger mess than I already have.

I check the privacy window to make sure it's secure, then lower my gaze to the leather seat below it.

"Another story is going to break in a couple of weeks," I say in an even tone. "In order to fix the narrative about you two, I had to trade something."

"I thought you gave him the Penchant reveal," Luke says in confusion.

"I did. But it wouldn't have been enough. I had to give them something else, so I told them the truth about me and Jana."

The air turns stale as I try to pull in a deep breath. I feel their stares burning into me, but I still can't meet them.

"What truth?" Callie asks, an edge in her voice.

My lungs constrict as my fingers curve around the edge of the seat. "The truth that the whole thing was fake. It was a setup by our PR teams."

Before I lose my nerve, I launch into the rest of the story. I tell them about the agreement, the terms, and how she broke them almost immediately. I explain how everything they saw and thought was real *was*, even though it was based on a lie.

I can't guess what they're thinking as the truth pours out, but it feels good to finally come clean. Luke probably won't care except for the fact that I told Orin before him, but Callie...

She's impossible to predict. Her ability to read people and scrape at the core of their actions is frighteningly strong. Her compassion, her grace for mistakes when accompanied by sincere regret—it's part of what makes her so special.

But she also doesn't know our world, and has shown unfiltered disdain for the ugly aspects of fame and fortune. There's no question this story falls into that category.

Then again, so does my sincere remorse for doing something stupid.

When I finish, I dare a look.

Neither of them said a word the entire time I was talking. I thought it was better that way, until now.

Luke releases a breath. "Damn, dude. Let me guess, this was Vince's idea?"

"Barry's, but Vince made it happen."

He huffs a dry laugh and shakes his head.

I have no choice anymore. I've put it off long enough and force myself to confront Callie.

Brows knit in thought, her hazel eyes glisten with a mix of emotions I can't read.

"So let me get this straight," she says finally.

I squirm in the seat beside her and brace for the bombshell. The only question is, will we be able to salvage the pieces?

"You pretend-dated Jana, but she wanted to turn it into real dating?"

I chew on the inside of my cheek as I think. "Yeah, I guess that sums it up pretty well."

"And then because she was acting like you were 'real' dating, you broke off the pretend dating with a real breakup."

I nod.

"And now there's going to be a huge blowup about the fact that your pretend relationship was fake but your real breakup was real, and the guy who's going to do all of this is the dude we caught snoring on the couch after Luke's party?"

"Um... yeah. Right."

She shakes her head and leans back to face front with a baffled expression. "Wow."

"I know. Cal, I feel terrible about it all. I just... God, I don't..."

I have no idea how to finish that sentence. Luke's silent warning urges me not to. Callie's going to need time with this. How long, I don't know. Hours, days, weeks? Whatever it is, I'll wait. She's worth a lifetime if it comes to it.

After a long silence, she crosses her arms and blows out a breath. "Well, this is almost as confusing as the time in ninth grade when Abby Hennox and I pretended to be best friends so Josh Sherman would date Amanda Thompson. But it turned out Amanda didn't even *like* Josh, we just thought she did because Abby saw them kissing at the football game." She turns a grave look on me. "Turns out, she was only kissing Josh to make Marlon Torres jealous because *he* was the guy she liked."

I stare at her.

"Crazy, right?" She lifts a brow. "You don't even want to know what happened at Homecoming when all of this came out." She shudders at the memory. "So many balloons. *So* many."

Luke snorts a laugh.

Her grin breaks.

Color explodes back into my world.

* * *

I'M exhausted and ready for bed by the time we return to the suite. Callie and Luke appear beat as well, but when the three of us converge on the couch, there's revelation in the air. Maybe my limo confession opened a vault in all of us, because the way Luke keeps looking at me, I know there's something he wants to say.

And I will pump my veins with caffeine until he does.

Callie curls up beside me on the couch, her warmth infusing into my tired body and soul. Luke stares into a glass from the couch across from us.

"I told her some things," he says, casting a fleeting glance at me.

I tense, more surprised at the speed of the unsolicited confession than the words themselves.

"Yeah?" I say to confirm he's got my attention.

He nods and focuses back on the drink in his hands. "About how we got started, about that time with your father and Molly. Just thought you should know."

My insides constrict from an involuntary chill. Memories surge back, my teeth clenching at the sting of old pain.

"Fun story," I manage beneath their probing stares.

Callie slips her hand into mine and entwines our fingers.

"I want to know all the stories," she says quietly. "Fun or not."

A hungry silence pulses around us, demanding more information.

I squint at the coffee table. "I don't talk to him anymore."

The voice sounds like mine, but I don't really hear it. All I hear is my sister's sobs. The sickening thud of flesh on flesh.

Physical assaults aren't like the movies. There are no dramatic sound effects announcing each blow. They just come, rapid and random, landing in scattered chaos. You can't even see much when it happens. It's just swatches of moving color through the gaps of your arms. Gasps of air leaving your lungs. Even the full extent of the pain comes later.

That moment is for fear and fear alone.

"I'm the only one who doesn't," I continue in a distant tone. "But he always hated me more than the others. I wasn't as afraid of him as he wanted."

Not until that night anyway.

That night changed everything. So many things broke— literally and figuratively—but that wasn't the lasting legacy of those few horrific hours. In a sick, twisted way, the very monster my father was trying to beat out of me was born into reality by his actions.

"He hates that he was wrong about you, Case," Luke says gently. "He hates your success. I saw him when I went home a few weeks ago. He's a bitter, miserable man."

The reminder of Luke's mysterious trip triggers a sudden

shift in my attention. Luke's right about my father, but it's the casual confession about going home that's twisting everything inside me. I don't want him to know I was already aware of his trip. I want to hear *his* version of his story, not get sidetracked by the gossip.

"You went home?" I ask. "Why? Why didn't you tell me?"

When he winces from the answer in his head, my world goes dark.

My heart races as he studies the carpet.

Please tell me. Please let me in.

"I was... putting things in order. Preparing for..."

Oh god.

He stops speaking, like the words are burning his throat the way they're scorching my ears.

I thought I wanted to hear him say it, but it's so much worse out loud. My lungs feel frozen. His eyes drift to mine, and just that brief flash of pain is unbearable. He quickly diverts his gaze back to the floor.

Callie is rigid in my arms. If this is how I feel with the benefit of a warning, I can't imagine what she's experiencing right now.

A glossy sheen obscures Luke's eyes as they stare blankly toward the floor.

"A month ago I was ready. I was done."

His words form a toxic mist in the air. I breathe it in, paralyzed by its painful truth.

But that's exactly why he needs to release it. Tear open the wound and let it seep out. Or that poison will pump through your veins until you can't live with it anymore.

"That's why I started visiting Jemma's. The chair," he continues in a fractured voice. "To say goodbye with one final punishment for what I was. What I'd done. To force myself to confront my failure..." He swats at his eyes. "A month ago was supposed to be the end."

Callie chokes on a sob and bursts up from the couch. She rushes toward him and throws her arms around him. His tighten in return, like she's the only thing tethering him here. A few weeks ago, she was.

It was supposed to be the end.

Supposed to be...

Fuck, I can't breathe.

I rub my chest, blinking through a veil of stifled tears.

I need to see. I need to witness the magic of watching two virtual strangers break apart and heal right before my eyes. With her unflinching compassion and her courage to confront someone else's pain, Callie did what no one else could.

She thinks she's nothing? She's a fucking miracle.

When they finally separate, Luke has the haunted look on his face I got so used to seeing before he decided to hide it from me permanently.

But there's something else there now. I can't label it, but it eases some of the pressure behind my ribs.

Callie still has his hand clutched in hers when he closes his eyes and starts to speak.

> "It's a perfect day for candlelight, let it cast its
> shadow.
> It's a perfect day for apathy.
> It's a perfect day for tragedy, eclipsed by a moment
> in time.
> It's a perfect day, why not today?
>
> It's a perfect day, don't wait up for a tearful
> goodbye.
> It's a perfect day for illusion.
> It's a perfect day for solace, I'll make this easy
> on you.
> Don't you worry, it's a perfect day, why not today?

Can you hear me, screaming some lie, disguising
    the truth
Can you see me, bleeding, I'm unraveling
Shattering

Do you remember what you told me, 'Everything
    has its place and time?

Well, that's fine, you can look away, you're just
    proving it's the perfect day."

No one moves. My heart is cracking apart inside.

I see him in that diner chair, breathing those words into an empty void that echoes them back at him. Elena screaming the same as the poison took control of her until she couldn't fight it anymore. All the people crying out for help without making a sound, until one split second explodes into a cry that reverberates for eternity.

Tears stream from my eyes as Callie crawls back to me. I pull her back to my chest, burying my face in her hair. I can't sort the mess inside me. It's just a knot of sadness and incredible gratitude.

I couldn't help Elena. In some ways, we can't help Luke, either—only he can take the journey toward healing. But we can stand in the void and stop the echo. We can shatter the mirror and destroy the lying reflection that tortures him.

"What's The Chair, Luke?" Callie's words splinter the silence. "What's its power?"

I direct my watery gaze back at Luke and blink away the film. I have to see. I have to understand.

Luke rubs at his eyes and fixes his gaze on the table. "Things were really bad with Elena," he says in a haunted tone. "They had been for a long time, but… I loved her… God, I loved her so much… I just couldn't stop hurting her."

He clenches a fist in his hair, and I wince at the hostility in his tone, the self-loathing. It hurts like hell, but the poison has to come out. The mirror has to break.

"We'd talked that day," he continues, releasing his hold to swat at his cheeks. "She couldn't take it anymore, the way things were. She wanted to try to work things out. I agreed to meet her that night at a little café called Jemma's. One last shot to fix things."

He chokes on a memory and scrubs at his eyes. My chest feels like it's caving in.

"I didn't show," he continues in a tortured voice. His gaze goes dark. "No, worse than that. I ended up in a hotel room getting wasted with two girls I didn't even know. I just... I just left her there! Fucking abandoned her!"

He's trembling when he reaches for his phone, and so am I.

My own confession is heavy on my tongue.

Tragedy needs a villain. Sometimes more than one.

The phone shakes in his hand as he holds it out. Callie takes it, and over her shoulder I see a photo in a text stream.

From Elena.

My heart stops. I can't breathe.

We know that chair. It's a dozen yards away in its office vault.

I go completely numb at the text below it.

Guess I'm talking to a ghost tonight? Fuck you, Luke. I hate you.

"I left her there to die." His splintered voice cuts through the air, but I can't look at him. I can't face the rest of the truth I already know. "She killed herself shortly after she gave up and left.

"No, sorry, wait," he spits out. "*I* killed her that night. I was supposed to be there! I should have been in that chair. But I'm not, am I? I'm not there! If I had, if I'd just..."

He implodes before us, and I can't take it anymore.

Callie must understand when she shifts so I can get up. I move toward him and pull him into me without a word. His arms latch around my back, and his tears burn through my shirt.

"I need you to forgive me. Forgive me for killing her. *Please.*"

His desperate plea slices into me and tears up any remaining resistance to the truth.

"I do," I say quietly. "You know I do. Just come back to us, okay?"

His grief releases in a gut-wrenching torrent. I clench my eyes shut, my own demons circling now, screaming at the other villain in the story. The one I didn't even recognize I blamed until this moment.

My heart has been pumping toxins through my veins as well. Truths I've been holding onto because I thought I was protecting him. I thought it would only hurt him more to know the rest, but now I see how badly I messed up.

I wasn't protecting him. I was protecting myself.

All this time, I insisted it wasn't his fault, when the truth was I needed a villain just as much as everyone else. I needed a reason, and better that it was Luke than myself.

If he's going to be brave enough to confront his monster, I need to stand up to mine.

"She called me too that night," I force out.

I feel his flinch before we let go. I back away, unable to look at him.

"Obviously, I didn't know what she was planning to do. I thought it was weird that she called just to say she loved me and was proud of me. But I didn't ask. I didn't understand until after... until they called and said..." I shake my head, but it won't clear the memory. "And then..."

*"You're a great musician, but an even better man. I'm so damn
proud of you, Casey. Never forget that."*
"Thanks, El. That means a lot."
"I love you so much. You know that, right?"
"Of course. Love you too. Shit, my ride's here."
"Okay, but—"
"Gotta go. Text you later!"

And I did. I fucking kept my promise. But she never saw the
selfie Sweeny and I took at the club. I learned later I sent it one
minute and forty-seven seconds too late.

Tears rush my eyes. My throat feels like it's being crushed.

"I'm the last person she spoke to," I choke out. "*Me!* I had a
chance to help, and I didn't. Maybe it's just as much my fault for
not stopping her. For not loving my sister enough to recognize
a suicide note when it slaps me in the face."

"Casey..." Luke reaches for me, but I back away.

I have to finish this. For his sake as much as mine.

"I blamed myself for a long time too, but now I know that
blaming only helps if it has the power to change us. To make us
better." I find Luke again, begging him to hear this part.

"Elena's death made us better, Luke. And now we have a
chance to make it matter. To make *her* matter."

"She matters, Case," he says quietly, lifting his gaze to mine.
A muscle moves in his jaw. "So much."

Relief like I've never felt floods through me. I didn't even
know how badly I needed to hear him say that until this
moment.

"I know she does. I know."

I grip Luke's arm and complete the circle with a look to
Callie. Her watery eyes speak for her. I pray mine do too.

The silence that settles in is completely different this time.
It's soft and warm and sad. It's the healing that can transform a
hollow void into serene peace.

"I'm going to make some tea," Callie says, climbing to her feet.

"Tea sounds great," Luke says on an exhale.

Our universe has officially shifted.

CHAPTER 25

I didn't think I was a fan of tea. But when tea leads to flirting, which leads to being tackled by Callie for an impromptu make-out session, which leads to the two of us in the guestroom stripping each other, my opinion on the beverage changes dramatically.

She's breathtaking naked. I find every inch of her beautiful and fascinating. But beyond her attractive exterior is her gorgeous interior that shines out in everything she does. She's just as authentic and open with her feelings and desires as she is about everything else. I love how she can be so sweet and innocent one moment, then demanding and aggressive the next.

Right now she has me on my back, her hands flattened against my chest, pressing me into the mattress. Her expression is all playful temptress as she leans in for another devastating kiss.

Her tongue sweeps over mine, and I tangle my fingers in her hair to drag her in. I've never tasted anything so sweet, felt anything as sublime as the rhythmic syncopation of our bodies.

Rush after rush moves through me, and we roll until I'm on top, driving the beat I'm reading in her reactions.

Her gasps form the perfect melody, the shifting tension in her body a flawless harmony.

And when she finally lets go, I match her every breath, desperate to take it all in.

I don't know what I did to deserve this, but I will never take a single moment for granted. I've seen too much living lost to waste any more.

We remain still for several seconds, locked together amidst the soundtrack of our labored breathing. Her shy smile when she relaxes into the sheets warms every inch of me. She reaches up to frame my face and pulls me in for another deep, slow kiss. When I lean back, stunning hazel stars blink up at me, lighting up this entire damn planet.

"Want to know a secret?" she whispers, pink lips tipping into a sweet smile.

"As long as it's not about tea."

Her soft laugh is everything. She runs her thumb down my cheek and grazes the corner of my mouth.

"Not about tea. About you. Well, sort of... I've always had a thing for the drummer. Whenever we'd see a live band, I'd always call dibs on the drummer."

"Really," I draw out. "Interesting."

"Yep," she replies with a smug look.

"I see. So I'm not your first drummer?"

Her teeth sink into her lip as she scrunches one eye in thought. "Um..."

I snort a laugh and shake my head. She giggles as she pulls me in for another kiss.

This one ends with me dropping to the bed beside her. I hold up my hand between us and she links hers with mine. She drags our knotted fingers to her lips and kisses my knuckles.

"Okay. Well, I have a secret too," I say.

She shoots me a suspicious look. "I'm not your first poet?"

I laugh and brush a lock of hair from her eyes before settling to my back again.

"That's not what I was going to say. What I was *going* to say, is that I've had a crush on you since the moment I saw you in that diner."

She gasps, turning on me. "So you *were* flirting with me that day!"

"So hard," I laugh out. "Not that I thought I had a shot with Luke there, but you know. A guy can dream."

Her hand tightens around mine. "Well, then I have another secret. I was flirting with you too. I thought you were..." Her voice trails off, and I shift to face her.

My smile slips out at the pink on her cheeks.

"You thought I was what?" I press.

"Um... Hot? And sweet. And funny. And kind of perfect, to be honest."

Warmth floods through me as she casts another shy glance.

"Well, now you know I'm not," I tease, but she doesn't smile.

"No. Now I know I'm pretty much the luckiest woman on this planet."

Damn.

My heart bursts with love and hope as I pull her into me and press a kiss to her hair.

I close my eyes and breathe in the moment, pretty sure "luck" has nothing to do with it.

WAKING up beside Callie feels like a reward for something. I don't know what because there's no way I've done anything that would deserve such a gift. After a short cuddle and joint shower, I take off in search of sustenance worthy of an undercover princess.

There's only one thing I can think of.

My sunny mood shifts as soon as I step into Jemma's.

A somber pall falls over me when my gaze drifts to "the table." Since learning why Luke's stare kept flickering to the spot beside us the day we had breakfast, I've rewritten that entire encounter in a whole new light.

Fifteen months ago, Elena was here. At that table.

"Are you ready to be seated or still waiting for someone?"

I startle out of my trance and turn to face the host from the previous visits. Her expression brightens into excitement when she recognizes me.

"Oh, hi! Good to see you again. Do you need a table?"

A shiver runs through me at the loaded question.

"No, I'm just here to pick up an order. For Casey?"

"Absolutely! Let me check on that for you."

"Thanks."

She peeks back several times on her way to the kitchen, but my attention returns to the table. A younger couple occupies it now. They're enjoying an animated conversation while they eat, with no awareness of the tragedy embedded in the lacquered wood beneath them.

Or maybe it's the other way around.

The man reaches across the table and takes the woman's hand. She rests a smile on him and my chest goes tight. It's a new story for that table. One of many it will host over the course of its life.

There is nothing good about what happened to Elena, but that doesn't mean something good can't come out of it.

And maybe that's the point. Maybe the best way to show how much we love my sister is to magnify her legacy and carry her light with us. Transform it into a beacon that reflects the person she was, not how her story ended.

Instead of hiding the haunted chairs in a dark corner, we can fill them with fresh hope and new beginnings.

A sad smile forms as I watch the young couple write their own story, never knowing how it connects to ours.

"Here you go," Ailee says as she returns with two full bags and a drink carrier. She places them in a box on the counter between us. "You going to be okay carrying all of this?"

"I'll be fine. Thank you. Here."

I hand her a couple hundred dollars, and her eyes go wide. "Oh, sir, it's only seventy-three—"

"Keep it. Actually, wait. Can you do me a favor?"

She nods, eyes wide with shock.

I glance behind me, and seeing there's no one in line, lean close. "Can you run the checks for everyone in the restaurant?"

"Wha…"

I pull out my credit card. "Here. I can wait."

"Oh… Um… You… I guess we can do that."

I return a patient smile. "Great. Be sure to add a thirty percent tip to all the checks. Also, don't tell them who paid for it, okay?"

"What?" Her gaze darts to me. "Are you sure?"

"Very."

She shoots a baffled look at me but turns to the register.

While she rings up the checks entered into the system, I study the young couple again. It needs to be anonymous because this isn't about me. It's bigger than that. It's about changing the world one small act of kindness at a time.

Transforming tragedy into hope.

After paying the enormous bill, I balance the box in my arms, and leave Jemma's with a brand new legacy.

CHAPTER 26

*A*ccording to Eli's text, the trailer is supposed to arrive around three.

I nod in the direction of Mara's scowl on the way in, then stop and approach her at the desk when a thought rolls in.

"Need help with that?" she asks, eyeing my box of breakfast.

"No thanks, but I could use your help with something else."

She raises a brow with an expression bordering on impatience, and the idea cements in my head.

How do you turn enemies into friends? Make them co-conspirators.

I adopt the most clandestine spy-movie vibe I can muster and lean close. "It's kind of confidential. Is there somewhere we could talk?"

As hoped, her impatient look quickly becomes intrigued.

"Of course, Mr. Barrett. We can go to my office."

She has an office?

I manage a straight face as my newly recruited undercover agent adopts a somber, stealthy gait while leading me down an adjoining corridor to a locked "Employees Only" door.

After sneaking through, we weave through a maze of cubicles and offices, drawing plenty of curious looks. I can't tell if it's because drummer Casey Barrett of Night Shifts Black is invading their space or if it's because he's holding a giant box that says "Tildale Farms Tomatoes."

When we reach a dark office on the left, she unlocks the door and motions inside. She even checks for witnesses. For the record, there are plenty because... giant room of cubicles.

"How can I help you, Mr. Barrett?" she asks, once we're safely out of view.

Her tone has softened significantly since my first encounter with her the day I showed up to visit Luke.

"Well, as you may know, Night Shifts Black has been on a short let's say... 'writing hiatus.'"

She nods gravely, forehead creased to tell me she does know and is super concerned about it.

"This is top secret, okay?"

"Of course! Our guests' privacy is our highest priority."

"I know it is. I trust you."

She beams, and I pivot toward her as much as my tomato box will allow.

"The good news is, we finally have new material we're working on."

Her eyes go wide.

"The bad news is, we have a trailer with our gear coming today and nowhere to rehearse. The studio can't take us until Friday, and we have lots of work to do before then. I was hoping..."

My voice fades to leave room for her to save the day.

She clasps her hands with a thoughtful look. "Let me think... Our banquet rooms are all booked, but you wouldn't have much privacy there anyway. Oh! Would you be willing to use a space in the service portion of the hotel?"

"The service portion sounds private. Is it?"

"Extremely!"

"And it's big enough to host a rock band and their equipment?"

"Absolutely! I can have my team start clearing it right away. When will you need it?"

"Around three this afternoon. Is there a back loading dock our trailer can sneak into?"

"Of course! I will arrange that as well. In fact, here." She plucks a business card from a holder and hands it to me. "My cell is on there if you think of anything else you need."

"Perfect." I shift the weight of the box to take the card and stuff it in my pocket.

"It's my pleasure, Mr. Barrett. We're honored you've chosen our establishment to work on your music."

Well, Luke did.

"We appreciate your help. And please, call me Casey."

A smile peeks through her stern façade. "Whatever you prefer... *Casey.*"

She looks a second away from patting me on the cheek like I'm her favorite nephew.

Might've swung the pendulum a tad too far.

"Great, well, if you don't mind, I should get this food to my hungry bandmates."

"Of course! And your secret is safe with me."

Successfully converted, Mara leads me out of the office, locks the door, and marches us back through the maze of cubicles with all the confidence of a woman on a mission.

If music doesn't work out for me, it's good to know espionage might be an option.

* * *

MY SURPRISE BREAKFAST and update about the rehearsal space has everyone's anticipation and mood up, but the rest of the day drags from there.

By the time Mara calls Luke's suite to inform us the secret room is ready, I feel like a kid whose birthday party just got postponed by two hours due to rain. Callie thinks it's hilarious, but she'd feel the same if she heard the song brewing in my head. They haven't even experienced a fraction of what "Greetings from the Inside" will be when it's transformed from vision to reality. If she was impressed by what she heard after a few hours of production on a laptop, wait until she hears what four elite musicians do with it.

"Not bad," Sweeny says with an approving look as we scan the cleared storage room. I don't know what they keep in here, but it must be massive.

"We could get some nets and play a pickup game when we're finished," Eli jokes.

Mara's forehead scrunches in the first hint of concern since she introduced us to the space.

"He's not serious," I assure her.

At least I don't think so? Hard to tell with him.

His noncommittal shrug does nothing to clarify the situation.

Her severe stare brightens when she turns to Luke. "Let us know what you need, if there's anything else we can get for you."

Luke passes another evaluating scan over the space, and my heart does a small hiccup at how seamlessly he's slipped back into the role of band leader.

"This is great, Mara. Probably just a small table and some chairs, I guess. Maybe a few bottles of water?"

She returns an emphatic nod. "Absolutely, Mr. Craven. I'll take care of that right away."

But she makes no move to take care of that. In fact, she seems stuck in awe as she absorbs the sight of Luke and friends in *her* storage room.

He has that effect on most people. Good thing he's also a pro at mitigating his unintentional star power.

"Thanks, Mara. We appreciate it," he says with subtle encouragement toward the exit.

Her smile as she leaves makes it clear he could ask for a helicopter to the moon and she wouldn't rest until she could hand him the keys.

"I think she's starting to warm up to me," Callie says with a smirk once we're alone. Guess they have a history as well. "At the very least, accepting the fact that I will continue to exist."

Luke chuckles in that easy manner he has with Callie. "You're too hard on her. Do you have any idea how many people she has to thwart on a daily basis?"

Fair. Pretty sure every person in this room except Luke was one of those people.

"Fine. Good point," Callie sighs out. "Okay, well, I guess I'll go wait for your chairs and water while you work."

I barely contain a grunt of frustration as she turns to leave. How can she *still* not get it?

"Not a chance," I snap, taking her arm. She turns on me in surprise, and I cringe at the unintentional bite in my tone. I force a more patient approach. "You're not our road manager, Callie. It's not going to be like that, got it? We pay people to get us water and chairs. Not you."

She winces, and I feel like an ass, but I don't know how else to say it.

"I know, I just..."

I slide my hand down her arm to squeeze her fingers before letting go. "You like to take care of people, and I love you for it, but we need you here, okay? This is as much your song as ours."

ALY STILES

Her wide eyes lock on me, and the words echo through my head.

I love you for it.

Shit. Is that why she's stunned?

But when her gaze crosses to Luke, I breathe a sigh of relief. As usual, she's just in shock we want her in our world. I'm going to have to buy a damn billboard to get the message across.

"He's got a point," Luke says. "Besides, our security team needs to stay with us. Things could get dicey."

Her soft laugh flows over me like a warm breeze. "Okay, okay. But I'm going to be the best darn bootleg-recording-thwarter you've ever seen."

Bootleg-recording-thwarter? I shake my head with a grin.

Holding out my hand, I give her the sternest negotiator expression I can generate. "Deal. But only if you promise to work on more songs while you're waiting to thwart."

She takes my hand, her gaze locking on mine with a glint of mischief. "Deal. But only if you promise to make-out with me on your breaks."

I almost choke as the guys burst out laughing. A lifetime wouldn't be enough to sort out the surprises in this woman.

"I knew there was no way you could handle her," Sweeny snorts, slapping me on the shoulder. "Called that."

He did. He's also an ass. Good thing for him he's one of the best guitarists I know.

* * *

ELI AND SWEENY leave the hotel on a mission "to make new friends" while the rest of us wait for the trailer to arrive.

Callie wants to "freshen up" back in the suite, which leaves Luke and me alone in the empty concrete storage space.

The previous echo of activity that burst with excitement and life suddenly feels cavernous.

306

We study the floor and walls in silence, neither of us sure about what comes next.

"Kind of feels like we're back in the basement, huh?" he says finally.

A weak smile flickers on his lips, triggering one in me. "Yeah. Guess we've gone full circle. All we need is your aunt's stack of holiday decorations and expired canned goods. Do you think she'll show up with popsicles and fruit punch?"

I wince at my slip, but he doesn't withdraw into a shell like I expect at the reference to his aunt. He almost seems amused. I'm positive this topic would have sent him fleeing to his room just a few weeks ago.

"She definitely won't," he says dryly. "I doubt I'll ever hear from her again. I'm officially an orphan."

"You already were an orphan. This makes you a... double orphan?"

He smirks at the floor and shakes his head. "Maybe."

His gaze takes that glassy far-off look he gets when he loses himself in his head. I know that place well. Not only the recesses of my own mental abyss, but his. We've shared more history than blood brothers. Probably more pain and heartache too.

With his hands shoved in the pockets of his sweatpants and dark hair hanging in his eyes, it's easy to see remnants of the seventeen-year-old boy who'd been my rock and my hero since the moment we met. No one messed with me at school after Luke came into the picture. Almost overnight, I transformed from bullied band nerd to enigmatic sidekick. Even my father backed off to some extent when Luke was around.

His hypnotic aura that captivates the masses isn't new. It's not the result of celebrity, but what led to it. People naturally fear him and want to be around him at the same time. He's larger-than-life. The kind of person who never quite fits in the moment because he's too much for this world.

He was a quiet supernova, and for most of my life, my star orbited his. When I lost him, I lost more than a good friend. I lost my point of reference. A year later, I still hadn't found my way.

"You may be an orphan, but you have a family," I say, breaking the long silence.

His eyes dart to mine, and I shrug. "A big one. More than that."

With a deep breath, I turn to him. We can't dance around the truth anymore.

"I don't think you understand the colossal void you left in my life when you disappeared," I say as old frustration returns. "I know your lying brain has been telling you we'd be better off without you, but I'm telling you that's bullshit. This past year has been hell, and not just because of the external crap I had to deal with. Trying to do life with a huge chunk of your heart and soul missing? That's the real pain. That's the part that was breaking me."

He winces, but I can't stop. I won't. He needs to hear this as much as I need to say it.

"So call it selfish, but I'm not letting you give up again. I'm not doing this without you anymore, and I'm sure as hell not letting your brain take you away from me."

I search his face, silently begging him to listen. "You're not a hurricane, Luke. You're my rock—my fucking *anchor*—and I'll do whatever it takes to bring you back."

His eyes scan mine, before he directs a pensive frown at the floor again.

He may not like hearing any of that, but I'm not messing around this time. Therapy, medication, whatever he needs to get out of this abyss—we're going to find it. Because he's too important to give up. He's barely begun touching the lives he's here to impact.

After a long, painful silence, his voice cracks the tension in the air.

"Do you truly believe people can change?" he asks quietly.

Haunted blue-green eyes lift to mine. Searching. Pleading.

Sparks of love and hope surge through my chest.

"Yes. One hundred percent," I say with a firm nod. "Not only *can* we. We have to, Luke. We fucking *have to.*"

CHAPTER 27

"Where's the road crew when you need one?" Sweeny mumbles as we stare into the wall of black crates and cases packed into the trailer. It's almost four, but the late arrival of our gear doesn't matter nearly as much as getting it into that room and unpacked.

"When did you become such a diva?" I shoot back.

He grunts and reaches for the first crate, while Eli jumps in to help him. The two guys who drove the pickup grab another one, and I extract an amp from the world's most expensive 3-D puzzle.

"What can I carry?" Callie asks, eyeing the remaining equipment.

"It's fine. We'll get it," I say, then wince at her laser scowl.

Right. Zero chance she'll sit this out.

"The round one there," I correct. "Just be careful because it's heavier than…"

Yeah, she's already halfway up the ramp.

I shift the weight of the amp to follow her, but stop when I realize Luke hasn't moved. He's still staring into the trailer with a blank look.

"You okay, dude?" I call to him.

He flinches and casts a quick glance in my direction. "What? Yeah."

He used to be a much better liar.

I move beside him and suck in a breath.

His pedal board case.

The gray box still has the faded Landry's Bar logo we jokingly applied on one of our tours. I don't even remember which one. The sticker was a weird velvet material in the shape of the bar's obnoxious "L" logo. Eli slapped it on Luke's case so he'd know which was his and we never took it off.

"They must have loaded it last," he says in an absent tone.

Because it wasn't with the rest of our equipment.

I swallow the lump in my throat. "Yeah."

After a long silence, he inhales deeply and grips the handle. "Let's hope all the pedals still work."

"If they don't, we'll get it sorted out by Friday."

A flash of fear erupts in his eyes before he blinks it away.

"Right. Yeah, good." He clears his throat and starts up the ramp toward the bay door.

I want to offer a word of encouragement, but what is there to say? Of course he's terrified to get back into the studio. So am I. Pretending otherwise is just a waste of brain cells.

Callie prevents further commentary when she skips back to the open dock door for her next load.

"Hey, rockstar," she jokes, nudging Luke's arm with her shoulder when he passes.

The cloud dissolves from his face as he shakes his head with a smile. He continues toward the storage room while Callie moves toward me.

"You didn't get very far with that," she observes, scanning the amp in my arms.

"Yeah, I got lost. Which way is the building again?"

She snorts and runs a hand over my bicep. "Not gonna lie, I don't hate watching you carry heavy stuff."

"Why, Callie Roland, are you flirting with me?"

"Maybe," she replies in a coy tone. "What are you gonna do about it?"

Intrigued, I scan for witnesses, but my gaze snags on my cymbals case. Definitely getting those next. My entire kit is calling to me from the depths of the trailer.

A smack on the arm makes me jump.

Callie is staring at me in bewildered amusement when I focus back on her. "Are you seriously ogling your equipment instead of me right now?!"

"What? No! I mean..."

I shrug with an apologetic grin, and she smacks me again.

I didn't think there was anything more fun than igniting a crowd with your music, but pushing this woman's buttons is quickly making a play for the top slot.

She leaves nothing to chance this time when she tugs my head down for a quick kiss. Sweeny's amp is becoming incredibly inconvenient.

"I can't wait to see you play," she says softly as we separate.

"I can't wait for you to see me play," I return with a teasing smile.

Eye roll—*and* thank you.

* * *

ALL JOKING ASIDE, I can't unpack my kit fast enough once we're unloaded.

I could do this in my sleep—and arguably *have* a time or two —but pulling my instruments from their cases and assembling them into my own little percussion kingdom feels fresh and new. Part of it is the novel environment, but mostly it's Luke's presence. Watching him adjust his pedal board and guitar strap is pure cinema for my soul that thought it would never see this image again.

He's in conversation with Callie while he works. I can't hear their dialogue over the wail of guitar tuning and effects testing, but he's probably answering her endless questions. She's fascinated by anything that's important to other people.

I leave them to it and quickly get wrapped up in my own universe. Once I have the toms and cymbals in place, I pull out a set of sticks, drop to the seat, and test out the spacing of the hi-hats, snare, and kick.

"So this is it. You in your native habitat," Callie says, drawing my attention.

I straighten from adjusting the kick pedal and shoot a grin at her.

"Be prepared to be amazed," I boast, pointing my sticks at her.

"I already am," she says with a measure of excitement.

A rush moves through me at her heated look, triggering a strange need to show off. Maybe it's the drummer equivalent of a peacock, but I use the next few seconds to throw everything I have into a test run of the kit.

I pretend not to notice Callie's awed expression a few feet away, but my heart feels every ounce of it. All the record execs in the world have nothing on the opinions of this one person.

Out of the corner of my eye, I see Luke shaking his head with a knowing smile. He's fully aware I'm showing off, but whatever. Like he's never given a little extra to impress a girl. I happen to remember a time when he made us repeat the same four bars of a chorus for over ten minutes while waiting for my sister to "accidentally walk in on our practice session." All because he knew how good his voice sounded on that line.

She did eventually wander in. And yes, she was looking at him the way Callie is looking at me now. Probably the way I'm looking at her as she retreats to the other side of the room with her laptop. I smile to myself when she drags a chair in front of the door to block it. She's taking her guard duty very seriously, not that I expected anything less.

"So you ready to do this, or what?" Eli calls when the warmups die down. "Sweeny and I listened to the track a bunch last night. I think we're ready to go."

I look to Luke, who shrugs. "We're ready," he says. "Let's run through the intro and get a quick sound check."

That's all I need to hear.

Sticks in the air, I tap out the count.

One. Two. Three. Four.

We're back, baby!

* * *

AFTER WE GET OUR LEVELS, the first real pass is *rough,* but that's to be expected. We don't even make it through half the intro before I cut the beat.

"Seriously? Already?" Sweeny grunts as he dampens the strings of his guitar and fires a look at me.

Luke smirks at the familiar scene.

"We need to swap the riffs," I say, ignoring their reactions.

"Huh?" Sweeny says.

"The bridge and intro riffs. Swap them."

Sweeny shoots a glance at Luke, who shrugs. "I kind of hear it. Just try it," he says.

I relax a little at Luke's support and settle back on my seat.

"From the top. And Eli, don't come in until the second line of the intro."

"You want just the guitar?" Eli asks in surprise. "He's only playing a lead line. Won't that be a little thin?"

"Yep. It will be a good transition out of the piano opening. Then we'll add a sweep into the full groove." They exchange a look, and I narrow my eyes. "Just trust me, okay? I'll show you in production."

Eli and Sweeny shuffle back to their positions in the musician equivalent of throwing up your hands.

I count us in again, Sweeny starts his riff, and Eli, Luke, and I join in on the second line.

When all three snap a grin in my direction, I know we're back in sync. When Luke shuts us down after the first verse to say we need to add a full stop going into the chorus, I know we're officially in business.

As the session wears on, though, traces of panic whisper beneath the initial excitement. They grow with every start and stop, every adjustment that's turning this song into something special.

My gaze keeps finding Luke. The way he commands the room, the band, the song. He's a force, a fucking gift to artistry. And the more comfortable I get with the familiar silhouette in front of me, the more a cold trickle of dread pollutes the moment.

I need this. Our music needs this. We can't go back to the way it was.

I can't touch the magic only to have it ripped away again.

Luke twists a smile back at me as he slays the second chorus. I knew he would. This song was made for his raspy vocal that currently has all of us in a chokehold. He furrows his brows at what he must see on my face, and I paint a brighter expression.

The transition into the bridge saves me when he's pulled back to his rhythm guitar to support Sweeny's lick.

I was right about that too. Switching the intro and bridge was the correct call, and the way the band locks in during the instrumental tells me they agree. It feels so good to be riding this high again. To be creating and forming something beautiful out of the ashes of pain.

But I can't shake that disturbing undercurrent. A warning echo worms through my brain, and by the time we break for the food Callie ordered, I'm struggling to project the same excited energy the other guys have.

"Sounding great, dude," Sweeny says, clapping my shoulder as I rise and stretch my aching body. "Good call on the riff. Well, on all of it, I guess."

I return a stiff smile and run the hem of my shirt over my forehead in a pretend attempt to wipe off sweat. Really, I just don't know how to hide the strange burning in my chest.

"I think you should unleash for the outro," I say. He tilts his head, and I nod toward his guitar on the stand. "Don't play the same riff at the end. Just let loose and see what happens."

His expression brightens at the green light. "You got it, boss."

While Sweeny takes off for the restrooms, Luke and Eli chat about basslines by Eli's amp.

I use the break to find Callie at the other side of the room. I try to muster more fake excitement for her sake, but I'm too depleted. I can't hide from her anyway. I never could. It's one of the many things I love about her.

"Thanks, Callie," I say, inspecting the sandwiches and snacks as a last ditch effort to distract her from my sudden shadows. "You didn't have to do this."

"Just don't yell at me," she jokes. I try to reward her with a smile but must fail when she softens into encouragement mode.

"You guys sound amazing," she says, confirming my fears. She knows I'm struggling.

"Yeah?"

317

My fingers press into the wheat roll I'm holding. I don't even realize how hard I'm squeezing until the contents ooze out.

I drop the sandwich onto a plate.

"What is it? What's wrong?" Callie asks, shifting close.

I could lie. Maybe I should.

Sweeny is back from the bathroom and joins Luke and Eli. They're now debating a variation on the progression for the final chorus. I love seeing them joking around and swapping ideas like old times. It also hurts like hell.

Yeah, I could lie, but I'm not sure what that would accomplish.

I drop the plate on the cart and motion for her to follow me from the room. Once we're in the hall, I turn to her, but no words come out. I don't even know how to explain what I'm feeling. I should be flying high. I *was* flying high. Parts of me still are.

But there's this other part...

"Casey, what's wrong? Are you not happy with the song?"

She draws my attention back to her, and I breathe through a swell of mangled emotions.

"No, it's not that. I mean, the song is going well, great actually, it's just..."

That first show without Luke.
The interviews without Luke.
The radio appearances without Luke.
The long nights, empty hotel rooms, quiet tour buses, never ending questions I can't answer for myself let alone everyone else.
The pressure, the pain, the lonely trudge through what could have been...

Callie startles me back to the present with a squeeze on my arm.

My gaze collides with hers. "This is killing me, Callie."

The words come out weak and shattered, like the state of my heart.

Her expression mirrors the rest of me that's just as confused about that perplexing confession.

"What is? What do you mean?"

I motion toward the door, the ghosts on the other side.

"This. Having Luke back. What if it's not for real? What if this is it?" Once the words start they won't stop. "I don't think I can handle losing him again. I don't want to do this without him anymore. I *can't*."

It's all pouring out. Pain, fear, history she'll never understand, even though she wants to.

She shifts forward to pull me in. Her arms wrap around my back, and I hold her close. The pressure on my chest eases the second my heartbeat finds hers.

"Do you think it's not?" she murmurs.

"I don't know," I whisper against her hair. My lips stay there as I try to gather my thoughts. "He seems sincere, like he's happy to be back, but what if... I don't know. What if we wake up tomorrow and learn this was it, all we're getting?"

My eyes slip closed. A knot forms in my chest.

I don't know if I'd survive that. I don't know if I could sit behind my kit and stare into the vacuum again.

This afternoon is all I've been fighting for since he disappeared. And now that it's here, I realize it's not enough. I don't want a hologram of my best friend. I want the real thing.

"You need to tell him this," she says, leaning back. Her gaze locks on mine with silent warning. "He needs to know how important he is."

My gaze drifts back to the door. On the other side is a fantasy come true, along with a potential nightmare. *That's* how important he is. The critical power of this monumental phase shift.

"He just needs to come back," I say quietly.

God, please *bring him back.*

* * *

No one else seems to be affected by my hidden panic as the night wears on.

Caught in the familiar tide of creation, hours pass quickly before we even realize it.

Callie stays engrossed in her laptop, while we refine the song.

Luke's song.

The deeper we get into the process, the more it becomes his. Callie and I wrote it, but it always belonged to him.

By the time we wrap for the day, the future fate of this track is sealed. If Luke doesn't claim "Greetings from the Inside," no one will. It can't possibly be led by anyone else.

I'm mentally, physically, and emotionally exhausted when Eli and Sweeny announce they want to go out. Their plan doesn't surprise me, and neither does Luke's decision to pass and Callie's decision to stay home with us.

The ride up the elevator to the fourth floor is quiet but not strained. Aiden isn't on duty and the night attendant is understandably more reserved in his interactions with guests.

Callie's silence is different than ours, though. She keeps casting weighted looks at us, like she wants to say something, but doesn't know how.

When we reach our floor, I decide to give her an opening.

"Saw you working. Looked intense," I say as we move down the hall.

She returns a shy smile. "Yeah, I had some stuff I had to get out."

"Can I see it?"

"Once we get inside."

Luke leads us into the suite, looking as drained as I feel.

"You guys sounded great. Unbelievable, actually," Callie says, while I close and lock the door.

"You think?" Luke replies.

"Absolutely. As a rabid fangirl, totally impressed."

Luke's laugh is thin, but doesn't sound forced. "Well, good. Thanks for guarding the door."

"Any time."

"So what's this new piece?" I cut in before we small-talk our way out of the real conversation.

Callie offers a tight smile as she pulls out her laptop and places it on the island. Luke and I slide onto the stools and wait.

A heaviness settles over Callie's face as she scans the screen. Her gaze lifts to us, and I can tell she's wrestling with something.

"Watching you guys together, how incredible you were, and yet, thinking that it was almost lost... I was... I don't know. So full of love and fear and regret at the same time." She blinks back emotion, and I resist the urge to go to her. This is her moment, her message.

"Do you two even know how amazing you are?" she continues in an urgent tone. "I mean, not just individually, but together. I had no idea. It was breathtaking and so sad at the same time."

Her words smash into me. Everything I felt over the course of that rehearsal comes racing back. But it's more than fear this time. Callie's confession breathes validation into the moment as well.

And hope.

I don't have words for the complex feelings twisting inside me. Luke seems lost in thought as well.

"I wrote this for both of you," she says, inhaling deeply. "It's called 'Laughing Stock.'"

She spins the laptop toward us, and we lean forward in unison.

There's a tension in the room. A saturated mix of anticipation and fear as we confront her words. Those tiny poetic scalpels that always seem to cut to the heart of feelings we've barely acknowledged.

> "It's not funny how far you've strayed, I'll say it
>   one time
> I can tell by your smile you know I'm right,
> still you hide behind the lie.
> It's not funny how far you've strayed, I'll say it this
>   time.
> I can tell by your eyes you know what I mean,
> still you find a reason to fight, but you'll never cry.
>
> How can you believe it's easier to be alone than
>   feel loved?
> You fear the embrace of a friend, yet welcome
>   your enemies' hands as they beat down.
> You listen for proof that no one understands you,
>   but we do
> And it's killing me.
>
> It's not funny to see how well you ignore the signs
> By the pain in your eyes I can see you're fading.
> Still you try, you're losing the fight.
>
> You're no better for falling apart
> Being alone won't make you stronger
> You'll fall harder the more space you put
>   between us
> But I'll catch you, oh I'll catch you.

How can you believe it's easier to feel alone than
    feel loved?
You fear the embrace of a friend, yet welcome
    your enemies' hands as they beat down.
You listen for proof that no one understands you,
    but I do
And it's killing me. It's killing me!

It's not funny how far you've strayed, just listen
    this one time
Look in my eyes and see how I love you."

I can't breathe for several seconds. My gaze scans the words over and over, but I'm not reading them. I don't have to. I felt them. Every syllable. Every gouge carving out the core of what I feel, what I've *felt*, but never found the words to explain it. Or had the courage to express them even if I had.

But she does.

This force who burst into our lives and exploded the barriers protecting the shadows that kept us apart.

Luke is deathly quiet. He's staring at the screen like I am, but he's not reading either. My pulse races as I wait to see what he does with this. Everything in me knows he's going to run. He'll scurry back to his room and hide from the uncomfortable truth until he's able to rebuild the fortress around his pain.

I'm going to lose him again.

I see it in the way his fingers claw at his knee.

The way his gaze shifts in absent torment.

He's going to run.

He'll leave me alone with these devastating words and a shattered heart and a fucking abscess in my soul that will—

"Is it true?" His tormented gaze locks on me, and small explosions detonate inside me at the surprise connection.

I inhale a sharp breath. I wasn't ready for him to stay. I don't know what to do with the question I've been waiting for since Elena's death.

Is it true?

I can't speak. Tears burn behind my eyes.

Is it true?

It doesn't even matter what truth he's referring to. The answer is yes. It's true. It's all fucking true. Every last painful word and thought. Feeling and memory that I can't shake no matter how hard I fight.

I want to say it, but the only words for this are already on that screen. Nothing I say will be more true than that.

He shifts in his stool, and my heart cracks apart.

He's going to run, and this time, there's no way he'll come back.

A moment like this is too important to undo.

He slides off the stool. I brace for the sting.

But instead of moving left toward escape, he covers the short distance between us. Instead of pushing me away, he pulls me into a tight embrace.

Time stops. Air, space... all of it frozen as I lean into him, holding on with everything I have.

Tears drip down my cheeks, and I let them fall. They stain his shirt, like his bleed into mine.

It's brutal and beautiful. Two shattered souls silently repairing themselves.

Two tortured pasts coming together to form a healing bond that only shared pain can forge.

His grip tightens, and I drag in a ragged breath. For several long seconds we stay like that. When he finally releases me, we wipe our eyes in a silent agreement to protect this moment.

I'm shocked again when he turns to Callie instead of retreating to his room.

"Can we use these, Callie?" he asks.

She seems just as surprised. "What do you mean?"

"I…" He shoots me a brief look filled with complex thoughts. "For the EP. We still need two to three more songs."

I flinch. "Wait. Seriously? You're in?"

I can barely get the words out. My heart is pounding.

Luke's pleading gaze locks on mine. "If you'll have me back."

Callie yelps and circles the island to launch at him. He chuckles as he catches her.

On instinct, I complete the shocking encounter with a three-person hug that should feel weird, but doesn't. We've waited too long, suffered too much to take anything away from this exquisite connection.

"Of course you can use it!" Joy leaks out of her as she pulls back to meet his gaze. "But only if you use 'Perfect Day' too."

Luke winces. A shadow passes over his face. "Really? I don't know. I didn't write that for anyone else."

"Neither did I," Callie returns.

No. Nothing that's happened over these last few weeks was meant for anyone outside of this room. None of it was about anything other than deep personal journeys—but the best, most authentic art usually is.

"Dude, she's right," I say, excitement mounting. "Think about the journey those three songs would represent. After everything we've been through, that's some epic comeback shit right there."

"You just need to add a good breakup song," Callie jokes.

A ray of humor pokes through the somber pall. Maybe the Jana drama will have a purpose after all.

"I think I can handle that one," I say with a laugh.

"Oh really?" Callie returns with a mock scowl.

"Not for you, silly! The angry ex who hit me."

She snorts a laugh. "You could call it 'Bella Amberosi.'"

"Hey, maybe. I have some ideas," I reply with a smirk.

My humor fades when my gaze settles on Luke again. He's still deep in thought, but there's a softness to him I haven't seen in a very long time. I'm not sure I ever have.

He wanted to know if people can change? He's living proof.

I told Callie at that first breakfast we knew two completely different people. At the time, I meant it as a point of concern and critique. Now, I see it as the opposite.

I knew the man our world tried to break. She met the trapped soul fighting to break free.

"Really, man, you have no idea…" I force out. "I mean…"

God, I don't even know what I mean. I mean everything. I mean things that can't be put into words.

Only music.

Luke claps my shoulder and pulls me in again.

"I know, brother. I do," he says quietly.

CHAPTER 28

The door knocks the wind out of me as I'm shoved into it.

Or maybe it's the perfect lips attacking mine.

Callie clutches my hair, dragging me to her with a passion I haven't experienced before. Her desperation triggers every hot impulse in my body. Her lust is a drug.

"I've been wanting to do this all day," she gasps through a series of kisses. "It was torture watching you."

A grin leaks onto my lips as she continues to grind me into the door.

Her hips scrape mine, over and over. Seeking. Imploring. Demanding.

I'm on fire.

Still kissing her, I back her toward the guest room bed, and she pulls me down on top of her.

She grips the back of my t-shirt and yanks it over my head.

We separate just enough for her to remove hers.

Skin-on-skin, we fall back into perfect rhythm. Our bodies fit together as harmoniously as our souls.

"Guess this means… you liked watching me in action?" I rasp out in labored breaths.

She moans and tightens her grip on my hair. I kiss down her neck, sampling the most intoxicating blend of citrus and spice. Her heels lock behind my thighs, forcing us together in all the right places.

Fuck, she's gonna kill me.

"Callie…" I groan in sweet torture.

"What? I told you I had a thing for drummers."

* * *

I WAKE with a feeling of dread.

Callie is still sleeping soundly beside me, so I know it's not an external threat causing the disturbance.

I scan the darkness, half-expecting to see a ghost hovering in the corner, but the guest room is empty.

Sinking back to the pillow, I draw in deep breaths to calm my racing pulse. Yesterday was a hard, emotional day. Of course my subconscious is taking it out on me now.

My phone says it's well after four, which means it's been a few hours since Callie and I fell asleep in each other's arms after the most amazing sex.

I close my eyes to return to sleep, but the cold sensation won't go away. It's too close to another memory. I can almost smell the pungent burn of decaying earth. Feel the icy drops of rain pelting my skin.

Unable to relax, I carefully climb out of bed, open the door, and slip into the hall.

I've just started toward the kitchen to get a drink when I hear noise coming from Luke's end of the suite. Weird. He must not be able to sleep either.

Changing course, I approach his room and freeze at the sound of a guitar.

His voice drifts softly through the closed door. I cover the distance and lean against it to listen.

I don't recognize the melody, so this must be a new one. The lyrics are muffled at first, but the pain in the chord progression tells its own story.

When his voice grows more confident, my eyes sink closed as his gut-wrenching words claw through the door.

"Can't you see I did it for you?
While you cried, I tried to blow up your life
Why? Because you're mine and when you forget
I have no regrets

Can't you see I did it for you?
I'm fearless when I wreck with finesse
While I leave you to guess what I'll break next
I have no regrets

Can't you see I did it for you?
You belong in the dark, apart from the life you
    built
Still thinking you can outrun what's done

I won, so have fun with the latest collage of
    sabotage.
Maybe now you'll respect you're a fucking mess.
I have no regrets"

Luke's gaze shoots to me when I push into the room.

His eyes glisten in the dim lamp light. When he blinks, a tear slides down his cheek.

We say nothing. He knows I heard him. I know he wishes I hadn't.

After a long silence, he returns his attention to the guitar and picks at the strings, not unlike I do when there's nothing else to hold onto in the present.

I enter his room and close the door. He doesn't look up when I join him on the end of the bed and sit quietly while he plays absent progressions.

Another tear slips down his cheek. And another. But I don't speak. This moment isn't about words. He has plenty of those.

I'm not sure how long we sit like that. Him playing, me staring at the dresser in front of us so I don't have to confront our reflections in the mirror.

"We sing it so we don't have to carry it," he says faintly over the endless guitar loop.

My gaze darts to him, and he meets it briefly before focusing back on his strings.

"The pain, the hate, the anger, the grief... We transform it into music to take away its power to harm and turn it into a tool to heal."

I swallow hard at his quiet explanation. His voice contains none of the hostility I expect, just quiet observation as if he needs me to understand.

"I gave up on music because I didn't think I deserved to heal," he continues in a broken voice. "I had to keep the poison locked inside and let it slowly kill me. It was working, and if I played, if I let it out... I couldn't. I just *couldn't*."

He shakes his head and drops his hand from the strings.

The silence is loud without the drone of the guitar. Maybe that's his point.

"I couldn't play, Case," he whispers. "I didn't deserve the transformation after what I did."

I wince, angry and heartbroken at the same time.

"Elena wouldn't have wanted that," I reply. My eyes drift to the mirror where I find his locked on me. "Your music was the only thing she still believed in at the end."

He flinches, but his gaze stays glued on mine. He doesn't hide from it anymore.

I swallow a thick lump in my throat. It's time for another truth. Maybe if I'd told him in the beginning, we wouldn't have gotten to this point. But I couldn't, and now I see why. I wanted to punish him too. Deep down, despite what I told my conscience, I blamed him. Just like everyone else did. And when he left, I turned the blame on myself.

"The day before..." I stumble on the words and force in a deep breath.

Luke's fingers clench around the neck of his guitar.

Say it. You have to tell him.

"The day before what happened, she texted me. I'd sent her the rough mix of 'Catastrophe.'"

I sense his strong reaction. His shock. He knows where I'm going with this.

I scrub rogue tears from my eyes.

"I didn't know at the time," I continue in a strangled tone. "I didn't make the connection because I didn't see it until you told us she wanted to reconcile that night."

I blink back to him, my heart a tangled mass in my chest. "It was the song, Luke. Your music. That's what sent her back to you that night. She heard 'Catastrophe' and remembered how much she loved you."

Tears flow down his cheeks as he gazes at me in stunned silence. My own vision blurs, but I can't move. I don't know what to do with that truth any more now than I did then. I didn't even know it was a truth until this moment.

He rubs at his eyes, his chest rising and falling in uneven breaths.

"Casey? Do you..." His words crumble around us.

I blink more tears down my cheeks as I wait.

After a long silence he clears his throat and tries again. "Do you think she hears us?" He turns to me with earnest grief and hope. "Wherever she is, do you think I can still play for her somehow?"

I have no idea. I don't know how I could. But some questions are more about the answer than the question.

"Yeah, man," I say in a hoarse tone. "You can definitely play for her."

I don't know if my sister will ever hear her song, but we'll damn well make sure the rest of the world does.

Luke's relieved smile breaks through the thick shadows around him. For a brief moment, light returns to his eyes. He focuses back on his guitar, and I slowly push up from the bed.

But before I can take a step, his guitar goes silent. I twist back to find his gaze on me again.

"I want to come back, Case," he whispers. "I want to play for her again. I want to rewrite the ending of this story the way she'd want it."

More emotion burns behind my eyes. I force a nod.

"I want that too."

A thought passes over him as he searches my face. "I... Um..." He briefly looks away before finding my eyes again. "I'm glad you and Callie found each other. Truly. But do you think... Can you convince her to stay? I think I need her if I'm going to do this. I need both of you."

I swallow the lump in my throat and blink back the threatening pressure. My heart is bursting, my brain spinning.

"I get it, man. I do," I manage in a choked voice. "And yeah, I think we can convince her to stick around."

Relief floods his eyes. He draws in a heavy inhale. "Thanks," he breathes out. "Thank you."

He drops his focus back to the guitar. His fingers return to absent strumming.

Whatever impulse told me to sit with him earlier is now urging me to give him time alone.

With a quick nod, I return to my room, feeling the opposite of how I left it a half hour ago.

Callie stirs when I climb back into the sheets beside her.

"Everything okay?" she mumbles in a sleepy tone.

"Yeah," I say with a smile. "I'm pretty sure it is."

CHAPTER 29

$\mathcal{W}$e spend all of Thursday perfecting the song so our studio session can go as smoothly as possible. There will be enough mental and emotional hurdles to overcome without adding musical ones.

By the end of the day, we feel really good about the mechanics of the song. The rest? I don't know.

As we pack up our gear and reload it into the trailer, my nerves grow with each passing minute. Luke's silence tells me he's anxious as well. Eli and Sweeny don't seem to notice, but Callie does.

She asks multiple times that evening if we're okay.

I do my best to reassure her, but I'm not sure how effective it is. She's always going to be concerned, and rightfully so. I just don't know how to explain that this trepidation is different. It's no longer fear that something won't happen. It's fear over what will happen when it does.

We'll definitely be going to that studio tomorrow. What's waiting for us when we do, I have no idea.

I never tell Callie about my pre-sunrise interaction with

Luke. Most of that moment was just for us, just as I'm sure they've had their own private encounters.

I'm already awake by the time my alarm goes off Friday morning. After a quick shower, we grab a coffee at the hotel café and meet Sweeny and Eli in the lobby. A hired car is waiting for us at the valet stand. Our equipment should already be at the studio.

"You ready?" I ask Callie, forcing brightness once we're underway.

I can tell she's excited, and I don't want to take anything away from that.

"Me? Are *you* ready?" she returns.

Her easy smile draws one from me.

"Hard to believe this is happening," I admit.

Eli and Sweeny acknowledge me, but Luke seems lost in thought as he gazes out the window. His startled response when Callie squeezes his hand confirms my theory.

I pull her close, and the tension in my body melts away at the feel of her warmth against me.

We ride the rest of the way like that, and by the time the driver double parks in front of the studio, excitement is breaking through the fear.

It's been a long time since I've been in a studio with these guys. Conflicting memories of our last session tempers some of the anticipation.

We enter the building to find Julian already waiting for us. After a quick greeting, he turns to Luke with an air of reverence.

"Luke, good to see you, man," he says with a warm smile.

His sincerity sends a wave of relief through me. Luke's gaze flickers to Julian's before he returns an apologetic nod.

"Good to be back." His tone reflects his regret about the last time we were here.

He and Julian got in a huge fight over some technical glitch I don't even remember. Words were exchanged, threats made.

It's why "Catastrophe" is still just a jumble of unfinished tracks instead of a chart-topping single.

Julian knows what happened later that night after their argument. And if I know human nature, like the rest of us, he probably errantly blames himself to some extent.

Tragedy casts a huge debris field.

I introduce Callie before things go down the wrong path and derail the day.

Pleasantries complete, Julian leads us to the control room, and the good news continues when we learn we'll be working with Jon because Michel is "overseas." I can't help but wonder if this change was less about Michel's travel plans and more about keeping the engineer involved in the blowup out of today's session.

We only worked with Jon once that I can remember, but he did a solid job. I'll take solid over volatile any day.

Callie's expression of wide-eyed wonder goes a long way in soothing any lingering tension. Even Luke seems amused by her fascination with everything from the artist lounge, to the diffusers, to the pristine wood of the tracking room. To be fair Jackson Street is an elite studio, so it's a dream even for jaded artists. We did most of our recording here prior to the "Catastrophe" catastrophe. After that we did *no* recording, so I suppose it's fitting we mount our comeback in the place we broke apart.

"Why are there other rooms?" Callie asks as she peers through the window of the control room into the tracking room.

"Well, that's the main tracking room there, and then those are iso booths," I explain.

"Iso booths?" she asks.

I love how hungry she is to understand my world. I will never get tired of sharing it with her.

"Yeah, so people like Sweeny can lock themselves in with their cabs and blow their eardrums out without killing anyone," I joke.

"I heard that!" Sweeny calls.

"Am I wrong?" I fire back.

"And what are those little walls? They look portable," Callie asks.

"Those are baffles. They're on wheels and help absorb the sound," Jon explains. "Hey, guys. Good to see you again."

After we exchange greetings and meet Jon's assistant for the day, I give him a quick rundown of the plan. Luke and I already decided the two of us would do a keys and vocal reference track, so we head into the tracking room to set up.

Callie wants to watch from the control room with Jon, and her excitement over the process amplifies my own. I still can't get a read on Luke, though.

"You good, dude?" I ask as I do some test runs of the keyboard to get a feel for it.

Luke adjusts the mic to a comfortable level.

"Fine. It's just the scratch, right?"

"That's not what I meant," I return in a wry tone.

He shoots a smile back at me, but it doesn't reach his eyes.

The assistant engineer's attention rests on us from a few feet away, so I give up and pull on my headphones. It's not like we're going to have a serious discussion with an entire studio listening in on our conversation.

Literally.

"How's it going?" Jon says through the talkback mic.

We give him the thumbs up to confirm we're ready.

After a quick soundcheck and adjustments, I turn off my left brain and let my right take over.

The click track jumps to life in our ears, and I launch into a piano version of the song.

Luke's nerves are evident in the first take of his vocal, unsettling me as well. He ends late on the verses and comes in too early on the choruses, making the turns feel compacted. The musical vibe of this song is all about tense anticipation, so that won't work.

"Thoughts?" Jon asks after we listen back.

Luke shuffles at the mic, so I know he's thinking what I am.

"Can we run it again? The turns need work," I shout loud enough for Jon to hear me through Luke's mic.

"Of course. It sounded a little rushed. I'm loving the track overall, though."

"Thanks," Luke says with a weak smile.

His gaze brushes mine, and I wince at the apology there. It hurts like hell.

If only he knew what it means to me that he's even here.

"You got this, man," my voice says. My eyes have a much deeper message, and he inhales a shuddered breath.

I pretend to make some adjustments on my keyboard to give him time to center himself.

He's so fucking brave. I can't imagine what's going through his head right now, especially after our conversation the other night.

His gaze keeps skimming the room like he's searching for something.

My heart clenches when I realize what. *Who.*

I pull in a steadying breath of my own.

"You ready?" I ask quietly.

He closes his eyes. With a deep exhale, he nods.

"Yeah. Let's do it."

This time, he fucking slays it.

* * *

CALLIE JUMPS up from the couch when we return to the control room. Her bright smile diffuses the heaviness in my chest as much as the foam walls diffuse the sound.

While the assistant engineer sets up my kit in the tracking room, I have a few minutes to enjoy the moment with my girl-friend. Not gonna lie, my nerves are winding up at the thought of her finally seeing me do this for real. Everything up until now were literal practice runs.

This is where the artist in me comes out, and the pressure squeezing my ribs is making it hard to breathe.

Because it's not just about the music. My perfectionist brain puts enough strain on myself when it comes to producing my art, but this is different. This is monumental. Destiny changing.

This is my story and Luke's reuniting in an epic collision.

My journey with Callie finding its footing in a lasting part-nership.

These next few moments represent all the most important aspects of my life converging into one room. One drum kit that suddenly seems woefully insufficient.

My pulse pounds when Jon sends me back to the tracking room to record. I stare at the kit for several long seconds, stuck between the past and the present.

Even after forcing myself to the seat, I'm feeling lost. I've sat in this position thousands of times, and yet, it feels completely out of sync now. Nothing is the right height when I test out the kit. Everything sounds off.

I know they're all watching, judging, waiting with expecta-tion. My limbs tingle with anxiety.

Jon calls for mic checks on all the drums, and the fog in my head only gets worse.

The kick is too boxy. The snare too tight. The stick clicks on the hi-hats are too sharp, and the toms... Nothing is right about the toms.

Jon assures me everything sounds great. I want to believe him. I have no clue how I'm going to do that.

Sticks in hand, I wipe my arm over my forehead to clear the sweat.

I drag in a deep breath, resisting the urge to demand another full sound check. This is already going to be a long day.

With a deep breath, I signal Jon to start the track. The click thunders in my ears. My previous piano recording chimes the intro, and I command my brain and body to engage.

But as soon as Luke's voice explodes in my ears, the vise around my ribs constricts with a jolt. My rhythm stumbles for a beat. I miss a hit on the snare. My kick beat is slightly off.

God, it's all wrong. I've prayed for this moment for so long and now *I'm* the one blowing it.

By the time the song comes to an end, my heart is in my stomach. My throat is tight with restricted emotion and I blink back a threatening burn. I can't imagine what the others are thinking. I was so excited for Callie to see me play, and all I feel is humiliation that *this* mess was what we got. I don't even need to hear it back to know it was a disaster.

It's been too long. I'm too nervous, too rusty. I should have worked out more of the components to cement them into memory instead of trusting myself to ride the moment like I used to do.

Shaking, I lift the hem of my tee to scrub at my face and give myself a chance to recover. Really, it's my eyes I'm clearing as I drag the fabric over them. Luke is watching. Callie, Jon, and who knows who else. They can't see me fall apart.

Get it together. You built this ship. Steered it. Now you're going to sink it too?

"Can we run that again?" I say to Jon after composing myself.

"Yeah, no problem. Sounded like a decent first take out here, but we can run it again."

Decent first take. He's being generous.

"Thanks," I mumble.

I settle back into my seat. With a few measured breaths, I flex my hands around the sticks and twirl them a few times to center myself.

Breathe. Just do what you do.

My gaze crosses to the window of the control room and catches on Callie, then Luke. Both look the opposite of what I expect—not disappointment or confusion, but quiet anticipation.

Like they believe I'm as strong and brave as they are.

Maybe I have it wrong. Maybe I need to trust myself *more,* not less.

Tick, tock, tock, tock.

The click fills my ears.

Piano intro.

I take a deep breath.

And let myself go.

* * *

"THAT WAS GOOD, man. Great take. What'd you think?" Jon says when I enter the control room.

Callie's grin feels amazing and lifts my already heightened spirits.

The second take was much better. Not perfect, but enough to believe in myself again.

"I don't know," I reply. "I'm still not sure about the bridge. Can we hear it?"

Jon plays it back, and I brace myself.

As the song goes on, I begin to relax. Up until the bridge, it's not bad. In fact, it's better than not bad. It's pretty freaking perfect, until I hit a weak fill into Sweeny's lick.

I don't even wait for Jon's instructions as I head toward the tracking room.

"Yeah, we need to run the bridge again. I don't like the build," I explain, pulling open the door.

"You need a bigger fill, Case," Luke adds.

"Yeah. I also came in too early on the chorus."

His small smile at the familiar exchange hits me in the chest.

"Okay. Let's take it from the turn after chorus two," Jon says, and I settle back into my tiny kingdom.

This time when I twirl the sticks, it's because I fucking own them.

CHAPTER 30

"We're heading over to Oak & Ash," Sweeny says when we break for lunch.

I'm about to tell him Callie and I will join, until I see her dazed expression. She didn't even hear him. She's still trying to wrap her brain around what she's already absorbed. The last thing she needs is another hour of shop talk over steak.

"Actually, I've been dying for a turkey club from Tiffanie's," I say instead. "We'll catch up with you after lunch."

"Oh! Is that the place with those bagels?"

I return a noncommittal shrug, silently willing him to forget bagels and stick with a juicy filet. By the time we reach the sidewalk, he's jumped into Luke and Eli's debate about guitar pick gauges and forgotten all about us.

I take Callie's hand and lead her in the other direction to one of my favorite delis. We get a few glances along the way, but no one approaches. I can fly under the radar better than Luke. People *think* they recognize me, but they're not confident enough about who or why to approach. Not like what Luke gets. I still can't believe he managed to hide in that diner as long as he did.

It's a gorgeous day, so after getting our orders, we find a bench under a tree instead of heading back into the studio.

Not that I'll be able to eat with my stomach in knots.

While Callie unwraps her sandwich, I study the entrance to the studio across the street. It's been a long morning within its walls, and the real challenge is yet to come.

Luke has been acting like everything's fine, but his assurances that he's ready are my biggest clue he's not.

He's terrified, and I doubt he'll be eating much of whatever he orders either.

I feel Callie's gaze and shoot her a quick smile. Although part of me wants to talk about my concerns, I can't bring myself to burden her. Besides, I don't know how to explain the strange mix of excitement and dread churning in my stomach.

"What do you think so far?" I ask instead.

"Pretty amazing. I'm tired, though."

I huff a dry laugh. We've barely begun. "It's a long day for sure. We still have at least another six or seven hours."

Her eyes go wide. "Really? You're finished with your part, though, right?"

I stifle another snort. My role won't be finished until this song is mastered and sent off for release, but I don't have the energy to get into all of that.

"No, I'll help with the synth work after we get the guitars down," I hedge.

That's what she's really asking anyway.

Her brows knit as she chews. "I don't understand, though. If you're playing drums, who plays the synths and keys at the shows?"

Great question. We've been using tracks for that since Luke's departure. We're already paying a guitarist to replace him and didn't want to deal with a contract keys player also. If Luke comes back full-time, though...

I suppress the thought. One miracle at a time.

"We'll usually get someone to play a lot of it live, but we run some in tracks too," I say. "You just can't get everything you want live."

We tried doing "Where You Are" without the synth for an acoustic radio set one time and almost stopped halfway through because it was so bad. For months afterward, we laughed about the host's forced enthusiasm for our mess.

"Oh! What an interesting twist on an NSB classic," he'd said.

We still jokingly throw around the term "interesting" whenever we don't like something.

"And I thought music was just a few guys strumming guitars," Callie mumbles.

"Yeah, maybe fifty years ago," I say with amusement. Wait until she finds out what goes into the production and engineering.

"I can't wait to see you play live."

Her sweet words make me wince. It's a strange reaction to an innocuous statement. Especially since I've been excited for the same thing.

But now, reality is crashing in.

I haven't been letting myself think about what's next. One step at a time. And in my head, we had months to figure it out. After today, though, everything changes. Luke's return to the studio means attention and expectations. Spotlights, appearances, and endless questions. There's no way the Label doesn't try to capitalize on what's happening in that recording studio. Luke's comeback will be a bigger deal than his fall.

Shit, I need to call TJ and make sure he fully understands Luke's fragile state. We have to be very careful about what comes next. Do what we can to protect him and soften the blow.

I curl a smile to soothe the pressure in my chest.

"It might be sooner than you think," I say.

Callie frowns, looking how I feel. "I thought you didn't have to tour for a few more months."

"We don't, but we're still going to play some shows before then. With Luke's return, the Label is going to want to explode us back into the spotlight. I'm sure we'll do some high profile stuff to build up for the tour."

"And you think I'll be able to go?"

I almost laugh. "You better go."

She might be the only person who could coax Luke onto a stage right now.

"Well, I want to be there, of course, but I don't know," she says as she picks at the bagel in her lap. "I don't want to get in your way. I mean, with Luke just getting back into it, I don't want to mess with the band's chemistry or anything."

I stare at her. I don't even know how to respond to that. "Seriously? Is that really what you think?"

Her gaze brushes mine and darts away.

It's almost absurd enough to piss me off. How exactly does she think we're going to move forward without the person responsible for the fact that we're even moving? Luke will need all the support he can get, and it starts with this woman.

She has to understand that, so yeah, if it means stretching the truth a little, fine. Luke told me to convince her to stay. It's a broad license I intend to use freely.

"Look, maybe now isn't the best time to talk about this, but Luke and I had a long conversation last night after you went to bed. He's serious about coming back, but he wants you to come with us."

Her stunned gaze proves how much we needed to have this discussion. I thought she was finally starting to understand her value, but maybe I was wrong.

"He needs you, Callie," I continue. "You're his rock, his

support, at least for now. He doesn't believe he would have gotten here without you, so he's not ready to let go."

"Wait, what? Are you serious? He said that?"

Maybe he didn't explicitly say it, but that's what he meant. It's what he'd say if he were sitting here right now.

"It's true. Anyone who's seen the two of you together can see how important you are to him."

She shakes her head in slow movements as she studies the sidewalk. "Wow... and you think the guys will be okay with that? The Label?"

"Are you kidding?" I laugh out. "To have Luke Craven back on the bus? They'd let him bring an entire psychiatric team if he said that's what it'd take. One girl from Shelteron, PA is nothing."

She shifts to face me again, and I hold my breath, trying to read her as she scours my face. But all I'm getting is the typical concern.

"What about you? What do *you* think?" she asks. "I mean, I know this whole thing is strange. Luke and I have a very complicated relationship, but you know I'm crazy about you."

Hang on. That's what this is about? Concerns over jealousy?

Maybe a few weeks ago it would have been a passing thought, but seems completely ridiculous now.

"Hey, look, this whole thing is totally screwed up," I say with a wry smile. "I know that, but I also think I understand it. I really do. What you and Luke have is very different than what you and I have, and I think the two can coexist."

I *know* it can.

It has to.

* * *

LUKE IS QUIETER than before when we return from lunch. The others don't seem to notice, but I catch the stern look on his face while he tracks the rhythm guitars. To anyone else, it would look like concentration, but the guy can do this shit in his sleep.

He's concentrating alright, but not on what he's playing. It's the vocal booth beside him that's haunting his brain.

Mine too.

My fears are confirmed when he doesn't even wait to listen back after his final take on guitar. He mumbles something about trusting us to choose the comps and takes off "to piss."

While the others turn their attention to setup for Sweeny, I follow Luke. I'm glad I did when I see him take a hard right instead of left toward the bathrooms.

He hangs another right, and my stomach sinks.

There's only one thing back there.

As if on cue, I hear the crash of the fire door to the stairwell.

Picking up my pace, I round the corner and spot his silhouette through the window.

Luke jumps when I push through the reinforced steel to join him. He fires a brief look at me, and I secure us inside the makeshift vault.

Resting one hand on the railing, he runs the other over his face.

He's angled too far for me to see his expression, but I don't have to. I feel it in the air. The self-doubt, the pain. The fear.

"I don't think I can do this, Case," he says quietly without moving.

His hard stare remains locked on something I can't see. His knuckles turn white around the safety railing.

Forcing in a shaky breath, I shift nervously on my feet. The stale air in this tomb has become almost unbreathable.

"Do you remember the day we met?" I ask, breaking the long silence.

He turns a confused look on me, and I meet his gaze.

"Of course. I'd been sitting by myself at lunch for a week when you invited me to join you."

I shake my head. "No. That was the first time we spoke. We *met* two days before when you told Riker McNalley to fuck off and stop being an asshole when he grabbed my backpack and took off with it."

He tilts his head, squinting at me. "I don't remember you, just that girl with the curly hair."

I shrug. "Well, I was there. You took the backpack from Riker and asked Lacey Rourke if she knew who it belonged to. She said yes and you gave it to her to return to the person." I swallow hard. "And she did. She returned it to me where I was still watching by my locker after Riker attacked me."

His eyes fill with shock. "*What?* That was *you?*"

I avert my gaze to watch my shoe scrape at the concrete landing. "I never told you because I was embarrassed, and then just kind of forgot about it," I continue. "Once we started sitting together at lunch, that became the beginning of our friendship. But looking back, it wasn't that. It was the backpack."

He squints at me, his surprise becoming confusion again.

"Okay? So what's your point?" he asks.

"Why did you do that?" I search his face.

"Do what?"

"Confront Riker. You were the new kid. He would have been your ticket to the popular crowd. You had to know that after your first hour in that school. Why did you sacrifice yourself to rescue some anonymous stranger?"

His gaze falters before he recovers with a shrug. "I don't know. The guy seemed like a dick. I hate bullies."

I nod. "Right. Because you're brave and compassionate. You'd already been through hell and back by that point, but that didn't stop you from a random act of kindness."

I take an earnest step toward him. "That's who you are, Luke. Not many people would have made that choice in that situation for a friend, let alone a complete stranger who would probably never know what you did for them."

ALY STILES

He flinches, his mouth set in a firm line.

Maybe he's starting to understand. I know I am. Not sure why it took so damn long for us to see it.

"You've made a lot of mistakes in your life," I continue. "Some were really bad ones, but your mistakes aren't who you are. What you do with them? That's what defines you. And there's only one other person I know who would have made the instinctive decision you did in the hallway that day."

I motion toward the door, my throat closing on the words. "You and Callie aren't as different as you think. You believe she's an angel for confronting a stranger's demons. Well, your instinct was to do the same thing."

When I glance back at Luke, his stunned eyes glisten in the dim fluorescent light.

He blinks at me, and I strengthen my stance.

"So don't tell me you don't know if you can do this," I say, looking him in the eye. "You've already *done* it."

* * *

I PUT on a brave front for the next hour of recording, but inside, there's nothing but turmoil. We haven't seen Luke since I tracked him down in the stairwell. Hell, he could still be there for all I know. No one else is concerned by his absence—it's not his time yet. They'd just assume he's relaxing and hanging out while he waits.

Only I know the truth. Only I'm carrying the weight of the risk that this whole thing could go to shit at any second. If Luke refuses to sing the vocal, this song will not happen. Full stop.

After dropping the truth bomb, I didn't stay to see the result. I know him well enough to know he needed to be alone to process it. Now all I can do is wait with a pounding heart to find out what impact my words had.

"You okay?" Callie asks, slipping her arms around me.

All the instruments are tracked. The only thing left are vocals. Luke didn't respond to the text that he was up, and Sweeny took off to find him while the rest of us wait in the control room.

I'm trying not to panic.

"Fine, why?"

"Fine?" She returns a skeptical look.

"Just weird to be back here, you know?"

That response goes over better.

"It's understandable. Luke is probably nervous too."

Understatement.

I almost confess the truth about his "nerves," but disclosing that now feels like a violation. If Luke comes back, he wouldn't want anyone to know how close he came to running again. If he doesn't, the timeline of that story shouldn't begin like this.

Jon and his assistant are in the vocal booth, making sure everything's perfect. Eli is sprawled out on the couch, scrolling through his phone. The fact that he's here proves even our clueless bass player gets the significance of what's about to happen.

I bite the inside of my cheek, fighting to remain calm.

Callie leans into me, and I pull her close, partly for comfort, but mostly so she doesn't see my anxious gaze continually darting toward the door.

What if Sweeny can't find him?

I know for a fact, if he decided not to go through with it, Luke isn't here anymore. He would have run back to the suite to avoid the pain of the fallout.

Shuffling at the door draws our attention, and I inhale sharply as it opens.

Sweeny moves inside.

Alone.

Disappointment chokes my lungs. More than that—Frustration. Anger. Betrayal.

I release Callie, ready to storm back to the hotel on foot, when another body blocks the door.

I stop cold as Luke's gaze collides with mine.

The corner of his mouth turns up in a small smile. "Sorry I'm late. Had to finish my warmups."

CHAPTER 31

"You got this, dude," I say, holding out my fist to Luke.

He bumps it with a weak smile and returns to adjusting his headphones.

I back out of the vocal booth and close the door.

It feels wrong leaving him alone in there, yet right at the same time. I can't explain it, but maybe it's fitting he takes this huge step on his own.

The poetry of what's happening settles in my chest as I return to the control room. An actual poet like Callie must be feeling it too.

I know she is when I come up beside her. She's squirming with barely filtered excitement as I pull her back to my front. She tips an excited smile up at me, and I plant a kiss on her cheek before letting her go.

She turns back to the window, and I shove my trembling hands into my pockets.

Once Luke and Jon are happy with the levels, Jon cues up the track.

The energy settling over the room is electric.

"Can we do a full take?" Luke asks from the distant vocal booth. "We can punch in later, but I'd like to go all the way through from intro to outro first."

I hear the tension in his voice, the part he's not saying. It's been too long since he did this. He wants to do a full take to make sure he even *can.*

A twinge moves through my chest and I want to jump through the walls to stand by his side. As if sensing my concern, Callie squeezes my forearm.

I force in a steadying breath.

The click counts in. My faint piano intro pings through the room, joined by a short percussion sample. Sweeny's lead guitar cuts in next and... bam.

Grins spread around the room when the guitars, bass, and drums explode into the room in a ghostly tribute to former glory. I sense the excitement. The appreciation.

All that's missing to claim it back is an iconic voice.

No one moves as we approach the verse. I doubt anyone even breathes.

This is it. The moment that will make or break everything.

I close my eyes.

Callie's fingertips dig into my arm again.

Come on, Luke. You can do this. Please do this!

A human breath coasts over the music, a gift from the booth. Then...

"Mirror mirror, what do you see..."

Air releases from my lungs.

"When you are looking back at me..."

Tears rush my eyes.
I blink them away.

"Mirror mirror, what are you thinking... I see those staring eyes."

Callie swats at her cheeks in my periphery. I can't breathe, and when I reach for her hand, all bets are off. She squeezes back, shredding all that's left of my walls.

"Mirror mirror, what are you saying, it's always something I believe.
Mirror mirror, you're a liar, so why do you own me?"

My heart hammers against my ribs. My skin buzzes with anticipation as the drum fill supports Luke's raspy hold of the note and...

"Hello! Hello! Greetings from the inside."

Callie chokes on a sob when Luke's voice explodes around us.

"Hello! Hello! Framed in all your lies."

Blazing through us and over us, his strong, haunting vocal fills every crevice with the story he never thought he'd be able to tell. The air is saturated with it.
The agony. The beauty.
A month ago, he was ready to say goodbye. He'd given up, imprisoned in his mirror's deadly, distorted reflection. He'd lost the battle after it stole everything from him.

A month ago, he was ready for his story to end, but one woman said no.

In a moment of exquisite compassion, a stranger stood in the way. Fought, bled, and won to claim him back and share his pain. To turn a tragic goodbye into...

"Hello! Hello! How you love to see me cry. Always so..."

Do I believe in miracles?

"That's it, isn't it?" Callie whispers. "That's what was in your head."

She twists back a look of awe, and my throat closes around my response.

I see it in her eyes, her smile. She gets it. She finally hears her words the way they're meant to be heard. The way only the three of us coming together with our own unique stories could stitch them into messy perfection and make them shine.

"That was it," I say softly.

I shake my head, still in disbelief at what just happened. What's still to come.

And most of all, the woman in my arms.

So yeah, I believe in miracles.

I'm holding one. Hearing one. Living one.

"You did this, Callie," I whisper, pulling her close. "Don't ever tell me you're no one."

CHAPTER 32

*A*fter we wrap, Eli and Sweeny talk us into going to a club to celebrate the monumental day. It doesn't take long to see more evidence of how much has changed.

The lights, the crowds, the glamor... it's all lost its appeal now that we've found something richer. There's nothing wrong with any of it, but it no longer feels like a necessary release or offers a high like it used to.

Hanging out and being treated like royalty for a few hours is fun, but nothing more.

Entering suite 403 with my best friend and girlfriend feels like more of a reward than anything else that happened tonight.

Once we're settled on the couch, Callie slides the remote off the coffee table, then hesitates.

"You okay?" she asks Luke.

Concerned, I lean past her to check his expression, but relax at his soft smile.

"You know, a year ago I wouldn't have been able to do what we did tonight without getting wasted and making a dick of myself," he says in a reflective tone. "Six months ago I wouldn't have been able to even make it through those doors at all. And then tonight..."

He casts a brief glance at me before resting his gaze on her. "I think I'm a different person now."

Warmth blossoms inside me. Hope.

He is. But so is Callie. So am I.

"We all are, man," I say.

"We are," Callie agrees. "You don't have to be a ghost anymore."

Luke returns a weak smile and settles back against the cushion. I'm not sure what he's thinking, but for the first time in a long time, I'm not afraid of it.

"So what do you guys want to watch?" Callie asks, brightening the mood.

"Anything is fine with me," Luke says.

"There's still another season of *Dead Head*," I suggest just to watch her eyes do what they're doing now.

"You promised I'd get to choose the next show!" she argues.

"So why did you ask what we wanted to watch?" I counter.

"I..." She stops and angles toward the TV in an adorable pout.

Luke smirks as I release a triumphant grin. But we've only just begun.

"Not that it matters," I direct at Luke in a conversational tone. "She'll be asleep fifteen seconds in no matter what we choose."

"Hey!" she cries, smacking my chest.

I laugh and pull her into me.

She pretend struggles for barely a second before relaxing against me with a sigh.

Still wrapped in my arms, she returns her focus to the screen to scroll through the menus. I rest my lips on her hair, and my gaze collides with Luke's.

His knowing grin sinks deep into my soul.

He motions toward Callie with his eyes. *"Told you so,"* he mouths.

I return his smile. There's no point arguing.

He did.

And when I glance down at Callie, I almost burst out laughing.

Luke's smile grows when he notices what I just did—Callie, out cold in my arms.

I tip a grin at him.

"Told you so," I mouth back.

* * *

"Casey!"

The panicked cry jolts me awake. We stayed up late watching some Hollywood action flick starring Andis Carver. Callie picked it after her two minute nap she insisted didn't happen.

We eventually all fell asleep on the couch, but now she's running toward me with a terrified look on her face.

"What? What's wrong?" I ask in a groggy voice.

"It's Luke! He's gone!"

"What do you mean he's gone?"

"I don't know. He's not here! I was worried about him and went to check on him and he's not in his room, not in the office!"

"Okay, calm down. Maybe he just left to get breakfast or something." But nothing in my voice sounds like it believes that.

I slip my arms around her, trying to calm myself and think at the same time. There must be an explanation.

"Oh, god, Casey. What if he was saying goodbye last night?" she whispers.

I go rigid, and her arms cinch around me.

No. Not possible. No way.

"No he wasn't. He's fine. He has to be fine."

Fuck!

"I'm going to call the front desk and see if they can give me any information. Callie, it's going to be fine. I'm sure there's an explanation."

Do I believe that? I have to.

I circle the couch to get to the room phone. My hands are shaking as I dial the front desk. Logic is telling me we're overreacting. There are a thousand reasons why Luke wouldn't be here. But history is telling me something else, and in the human psyche, history usually beats logic.

"Front desk, how may I help you?" a deep voice says.

"Hi, this is Casey Barrett from room 403. We're trying to get in touch with Luke and are wondering if he mentioned where he was headed this morning on his way out."

"Good morning, Mr. Barrett. I just started my shift, but I can ask the staff who were in the lobby this morning. Do you mind holding?"

"Sure, yeah, I can wait."

Callie's intense gaze is locked on me, pleading for an update.

"They're going to ask the lobby employees if any of them saw or spoke to him," I say.

Her teeth sink into her lip. My knee bounces against the edge of the couch.

"Mr. Barrett? Are you still there?"

I stiffen back to attention. "Yeah, I'm here."

"Excellent. I Just spoke to Reggie who's been at the door since six. No one could have left without him noticing. He said Luke left the building about an hour ago... carrying an old chair."

"Wait, what? Really. Did he say where he was going or what he was doing?"

"No, he didn't. Reggie made a joke about the chair, but Luke just smiled and kept walking."

"Okay. Thanks."

"Would you like me to check with anyone else? I can keep looking into it."

"Um, no, that's okay. Thanks for your help."

"It's my pleasure."

I hang up, feeling numb. What the hell is going on?

I turn to Callie, more confused than before.

"What is it?" she asks in a strained voice

I clear my throat, not sure where to begin. "They said they saw him leave about an hour ago carrying an old chair. He didn't talk to anyone."

She freezes, then bolts down the hall. I run after her and stop when I find her staring in horror. Scanning the room from over her shoulder, my blood goes cold when I spot the empty corner.

"It's gone," she whispers.

Her chest moves in a sharp inhale. Then another. And another. Soon, the empty room echoes with her tears.

"Callie…" I say softly. My own voice is raw and weak.

She twists around and falls into my arms.

I wrap her tight, for my own sake as much as hers.

My world feels like it's rocking out of control. I'm still not sure what's going on, let alone what to do next. Callie must have theories to react the way she is, but she's too upset to share them at the moment.

We need to calm down. Regroup. Come up with—

A loud clatter fires down the hall.

Callie shoots up straight, and our gazes lock for a split second before we take off in the direction of the noise.

Luke stares at us in bewilderment when we launch ourselves at him. I don't even notice the stuff he's holding until he almost drops it.

"What's this?" he asks through a soft laugh.

I don't know how to answer that. I just know that nothing seems as important as holding onto these two people right now.

"You were gone," Callie murmurs. "We were so scared."

Luke attempts to extricate himself from the ambush, but Callie isn't allowing it. His baffled expression turns amused. "I went to get breakfast," he explains, waving the takeout bag at us.

His smile fades as he scans our faces. "Wow, you guys were really scared."

"The chair was gone," Callie says, still clinging to him. "The lobby employees said you left with it."

She finally frees him, and he deposits the food on the counter.

"Yeah. I returned it," he replies in a casual tone.

We go still.

"You returned it?" Callie repeats.

I'm just as confused.

He nods with a shrug like *we're* the ones not making sense. "To Jemma's. I shouldn't have stolen it in the first place."

"But..."

"I don't need it anymore, Callie. It's not who I am, like you said."

With a muffled yelp, she launches herself at him again. Her tears wet his shirt as he hugs her back, crossing an exasperated look to me.

If he's expecting an ally, he can suck it.

"Dammit, Luke," I mumble. "Can you leave us a freaking note next time?"

His grin almost makes me forgive him for scaring the shit out of us.

If there's French toast in that bag, maybe I will.

* * *

"Want to hear the master? I just got it back from Julian."

Luke glances up from his guitar, his eyes igniting with excitement.

"Sure. Of course. How'd it come out?"

I shrug. "Don't know. Just came in. I thought we should listen together."

His expression fills with warmth, but he doesn't say anything as he nods.

I drop to the bed beside him with my laptop and hand him a pair of studio headphones. I insert my custom in-ears, also plugged into the splitter jutting from the computer.

I already have the .wav file saved on my desktop.

Once he has the headphones on, I start the track. Crisp piano explodes in our ears. Percussion, guitars, and finally…

Luke's voice.

An army couldn't tear my gaze away from his face when his shiver-inducing vocal breaks through.

His eyes widen a fraction. His lips hang open just slightly before tipping up in a smile.

His gaze cuts to mine, and the smile slides into a grin.

My joy slips out in return.

He blinks a few times, then settles an absent stare on the floor to truly listen.

I do the same.

At the turn after the first chorus, he motions for me to stop.

I press the space bar and pull out my left earpiece.

"The guitars sound muddy in the turn. The rhythm is drowning out the lead," he says.

"Agreed. What about your vocal? A little more reverb?"

"Yeah. It's also sounding too compressed."

"You think? I kind of liked it."

He shrugs with his "we can argue about it later" look, then does the finger twirl telling me to continue playing.

As I shove my earpiece back in and press the space bar, another smile forms deep in my gut. It spreads quickly, surging into my chest, up my neck, and onto my lips.

Luke doesn't notice as he listens intently to a song he's created, like he's done thousands of times over the years.

Except he hasn't.

Not like this.

Callie once told me Luke and I are both brilliant, but together we're untouchable.

She was wrong.

No matter how good it was, our music would have always been missing something. And when Luke grins during the final chorus, I know he hears it too.

We finally found it.

The missing piece.

The anchor *and* the dreamer who crashed into our lives and changed countless destinies with her stubborn light.

Her name is Callie Roland. She's a poet. You've never heard of her.

But you fucking will.

* * *

For updates and announcements, subscribe to Aly's newsletter.

Experience the original song "Greetings from the Inside," along with the rest of Aly's music, wherever you stream music.
Spotify
Apple Music
Amazon Music

MORE FROM ALY

From angsty and dark to snort-laugh funny, Aly writes romance from her soul to yours.

THE SAVE ME SERIES
RISING WEST (available on audiobook)
FALLING NORTH
BREAKING SOUTH
CRASHING EAST
GUARDING SHADOWS
CHASING RIPTIDES

THE WRECK ME SERIES
ASHTON MORGAN: Apartment 17B
CAMDEN WALKER: Apartment 8C
TRISTAN & ISABEL: Apartment 11F

THE HOLD ME SERIES
Available on audiobook.
NIGHT SHIFTS BLACK
TRACING HOLLAND

VIPER
LIMELIGHT
AN NSB WEDDING
THE DRUMMER

SMARTYPANTS ROMANCE ROM-COMS
STREET SMART
PLAY SMART
LOOK SMART
STAGE SMART

STANDALONE CONTEMPORARY
YOUNG LOVE

PARANORMAL/SUSPENSE
UNDERTOW
GIFTED (Gifted, Vol 1)
CURSED (Gifted, Vol 2)
SÖREN (Gifted, Vol 3)
HAUNTED MELODY
TRAITOR

ANOTHER NOTE FROM ALY

Depression is a serious illness that can go unrecognized by the victim and surrounding loved ones.

If you, or anyone you know, have plans to harm yourself, or you just need someone to talk to, help is available. Dial 988 for the Suicide and Crisis Lifeline, which is a 24-hour, toll-free hotline available to anyone in suicidal crisis or emotional distress.

Please know you are not alone, you are important, and you are loved.

Sincerely,
Aly

STAY IN TOUCH

Thank you for taking this journey with me. I would love to hear from you! For updates, reveals, and more subscribe to my newsletter and join my fun, laidback reader group on Facebook: Aly's Breakfast Club.

You can also follow Aly's original music wherever you stream music:
Spotify
Apple Music
Amazon Music

Find Aly here:
Amazon
Facebook Reader Group (Aly's Breakfast Club)
Newsletter
BookBub
TikTok
Goodreads
Website
Instagram

YouTube
Pinterest
Spotify
Apple Music
Facebook (Author Aly Stiles)

Mail:
Aly Stiles
PO Box 577
Trexlertown, PA 18087-0577

www.ingramcontent.com/pod-product-compliance
Lightning Source LLC
Chambersburg PA
CBHW070838260626
47170CB00007B/2419